MW01601913

THE CERULEAN STAR

LIBERTY

The Cerulean Star Chronicles
(Book One)

A Novel By

Sharon Cramer

Written by Sharon Cramer

Copy edited by D.L. Torrent and Barbara Kindness

Content edited by Bonnie Lea Elliott

Publishers Note:This is a work of fiction. All names, characters, places, and events are the work of the author's imagination. Any resemblance to real persons, places, events, or laws of physics is entirely coincidental.

Author's NoteIt is my supreme desire that you would enjoy this happy piece of fiction. I believe there is something of Liberty in all of us, human and otherwise.

For Daryl—This one is for you.

For Cole, Shad, Chase, Vonnie, and Debra.
You give me all the reason to see amazement in the stars.

A special thank you to Dan Bowkley—"The Truck Guy"
For helping me keep *that* scene real.

A special thank you to Tina. My friend forever.

THE CERULEAN STAR

LIBERTY

They came because they had to.
They will leave…if you let them.

PROLOGUE

Δ

CERULEAN |Suh-Roo-Lee-n'| *adjective, noun*
Definition in this case: Blue beyond all imagination.

Equivalent Earth Date: 2011

The ship is small, not intended for deep space travel, really. It's more of a weekend vacation craft if you think about it, which is something the small crew tries not to do very often. In earth terms, it is not quite as long as a football field.

It is called the *Cerulean Star*. Such a beautiful word, *cerulean*, and it slides off your tongue in a pleasant way. Chances are you've said cerulean several times by now, just for the fun of it.

But the *Cerulean Star* was named this not just because it is blue. It *is* blue, and when it reaches deep space, it becomes an exquisite, vivid blue, as blue as dusk on Plasteen Seven. That was a lovely little planet they'd passed on their way through the Keeva System not so long ago.

Plasteen Seven was one of nine planets that circled a Yellow Dwarf star, but the only one worth stopping at because it was the only planet that had surface water. This was important because the small crew breathes exactly twenty-four percent oxygen. You and I breathe twenty-one percent, just in case you've forgotten.

So the crew needed to resupply water at intervals. Then, after the water was subjected to electrolysis and the explosive hydrogen jettisoned, they would have enough of the precious gas—one of several critical dependencies they have—and it would last for another few months.

They hadn't stayed long, though, on Plasteen Seven.

Like every other planet they'd stopped on…so far, there was no sentient life to speak of and no reason to linger beyond the water harvest. Not that there wasn't life on any of the planets they had visited; there was, but it'd always been either dangerously aggressive or sub-evolved to the point of being mostly squishy. Neither appealed to the young crew very much.

Back to the *Cerulean Star*. She (people always call ships *she*, though I'm not sure why) is a magnificent ship, sleek and finely built. The three couples who designed and created her were scientists and dear friends, all of them gifted in many ways. Grago was married to Cyla. Quite the smartest of the six, he was also the primary intellect behind the creation of the *Cerulean Star*, making sure everything was perfect. And it was, or so they thought. No expense and, more critically, no creativity was spared when the six crafted their masterpiece, and Grago was very proud of his contribution.

One more thing about Grago; he wasn't on the beautiful little ship…but his son *was*.

Back again to the *Cerulean Star*. It is called *Cerulean* not just because it glows the most brilliant deep blue, but also because it is rare, very rare. Truthfully, the *Star* was such a fine vessel and so very unique that it received the Queen's Medal of Distinction for being unmatched—a truly remarkable ship. One reason for this is the *Star* has a skeleton made of Vasteen, and that is very significant, but more about that later.

There are few spacecraft as fine as the *Cerulean Star* and none of the sub-cruising size that this ship is. This made it one of a kind, practically unrivaled and, as you've already been told, very rare, like a type O-class blue star. Everyone knows that Class O stars are extremely hot and extraordinarily luminous, being blue in color, so blue that they are almost violet. Everyone also knows there are only one in three million main sequence stars that are Class O stars.

The *Cerulean Star* was, therefore, the perfect name for the perfect ship.

However, on that fateful day when the *Star* disappeared, Grago and Cyla didn't mourn its loss at all—not one bit. What they grieved, instead, was the loss of their son.

Now, there are three aboard the *Star*. Well, technically four, if you count the chakrat. The small creature bounded behind the three children when they boarded the *Star* that distant afternoon two years ago. Cleo is a round puff of fur that changes color with her moods. Mostly she is orange. That's her *agitated* color. And, she has glossy, black eyes that seem to hide in the fluff of her face, blunt claws, and a long tail that slithers like a rat's. Annoy her beyond what she is willing to endure, and she will smack you on the ankles with that tail, though she'll pretend that she didn't mean to.

Sartek had ordered the animal to stay and was summarily dismissed by the hairy little beast. Scampering up the loading ramp, claws click-clacking on the deck panels, she ran past Sartek's ankles to hide under the captain's chair. Panting, she grinned at her own cleverness, beady eyes sparkling in joyful defiance.

"It's all right," Blalok, the youngest alien, said. "We're not going to be gone so long. She can come."

Cleo was Blalok's pet and his one true weakness. Truthfully, he loved her, and would have sacrificed video games for eternity for her, if he had to, though he imagined no possible scenario where that would ever happen....

So the chakrat made four aboard the sturdy little ship—three kids and one moderately misbehaved pet.

Sartek was the eldest by eight months. He was also the son Grago and Cyla lost that terrible afternoon. He would be the equivalent of eleven earth years old when the accident happened, and he was the tallest of the three Bettuan children. That was their home planet—Bettua.

They were nowhere near Bettua now. In fact, they were much farther than any Bettuan had ever gone and even farther than any Bettuan had ever *dreamed* they might go.

Perhaps, that's not entirely accurate on two counts. First, it might be supposed that a Bettuan, like you and I, can dream they are very far away. Nevertheless, the truth was, they were now unfathomably far away with no idea of how to get home.

Sartek suffered grave responsibility for this. He believed they were lost because of him, and this was his last thought every night as he struggled to fall asleep, although he never said so outright. That just wouldn't serve any purpose. Instead, along with his guilt-ridden sense of responsibility, he wore a demeanor of defiant willfulness.

On good days, when he wasn't smothered with remorse for the accident, Sartek had extremely good instincts regarding pressing matters. He was a natural leader, which is good because he and his friends were entirely occupied of their own defenses now.

Oh…and the second count, which we will discover some time later, would give them grief in great numbers.

But for now, let us continue with the crew of the *Cerulean Star*.

Isara was the second eldest, also eleven earth years and nearly as tall as Sartek, but thinner. She was so willowy that she might appear frail, but this wasn't true. Isara was a swimmer.

Now, of course, all Bettuan swim, but Isara was unusually strong for a female and lightning quick. She was also an only child, and this contributed strongly to her will to live, although this had yet to be tested.

Her parents nearly lost Isara when she was born and were told they would never spawn another. They'd thanked all six of Bettuan's moons for their chortling bundle of happiness and loved her more than anything in all the worlds, although Isara felt they fawned too much.

That dreadfully close call—that horrible event which nearly happened at Isara's birth—*did* happen eleven years later…they lost her.

Bettua is a water planet. You have probably figured this out by now. Just over ninety-six percent is covered with water, and many of their cities are built upon the seas. Their oceans are vast and deep, and some of them are very treacherous, but the Bettuan respect this and live in harmony with their planet, accepting loss when it comes.

To give you an idea of the size of their oceans, you first need to know that Bettua is approximately the same size as the planet Earth. However, while Earth is covered with roughly seventy-two percent water, a portion of our water is in frozen ice caps, lakes, rivers, and streams. Bettua's water is nearly all oceans.

And so, it's only natural that Isara is a swimmer. Swimming is considered a mandatory skill, and most Bettuans swim by the time they're one year old. It's convenient that they have evolved with a hemoglobin cell that carries eight molecules of oxygen on the surface, very similar to the oxygen carrying red blood cell of the Earth's whale. As a result, they can stay under water for long amounts of time. A rare, gifted few can stay under for over an hour. Isara would be one of those, one day, though she doesn't know this.

Blalok is the third and smallest of the three castaways. He is also the smartest—alarmingly smart, and sometimes, most of the time, annoyingly smart. He is also exceedingly literal. If you tell him to jump off a bridge, he'll challenge such a stupid notion. There are obviously no bridges, none of significance, anyway, aboard the *Star*.

We all know, and are occasionally maddened, by someone like Blalok…if we're lucky. When he was only five years old, he wrote what was considered a collegiate-level physics paper that defied some of Bettua's oldest and most entrenched laws of empirical physical behavior. This set him apart from most other kids in a way he would never recover. But this all sounds somewhat complicated, so we'll talk no further about it. Suffice it to say, the academic system didn't really know what to do with Blalok. So, he sat alone—a child amongst scientists and mathematicians at the university level—wondering how to most efficiently beat the next level of his favorite computer game. Blalok was also eleven when *it* happened or, as he would probably tell you, "Nearly twelve." He is also a nerd.

Some days, it was next to impossible to pull Blalok away from his computers, and on that extraordinary day when they were thrust into the deepest of deep spaces, Isara and Sartek cajoled him for five minutes to persuade him to venture out for the afternoon, to join them aboard the *Star*. Sometimes, as Sartek put it, "Nerd stuck to him like stink on…." Well, you get the picture.

Blalok was forty-seven levels into *Quest for Dominion*, his most recent and, at the moment, favorite interactive role-playing game, that fateful day. He was wearing the hover-suit and helmet that created the virtual world he quested in when his friends intruded upon him. His virtual character, by the way, was very tall, very handsome, and curiously seemed to gather many virtual, female admirers.

Neither Isara nor Sartek played *Quest for Dominion*. His passion for the game, and his character, were secrets that Blalok generally kept from them. He loved his character dearly and held the very rare and highly coveted level of supreme eminence. His friends weren't aware that Blalok was a *Quest for Dominion* legend and possessed the virtual medals to prove it.

When Sartek and Isara stepped into Blalok's room, unannounced, he was hovering in the middle of his room, swinging his rather skinny arms around himself, in dead air. In his virtual world, however, he wielded a mighty sword and shield, and did it brilliantly.

"C'mon," Sartek said. "Let's go hang out in the *black beyond*."

He thumped on Blalok's helmet with his knuckles, which was incredibly annoying. That's what they called space, the "black beyond."

The black beyond was where the three would escape to play games, shoot the moons, and turn off the auto-gravity, laughing about the effects of weightlessness.

Their parents didn't like them to do this. "It's unhealthy," the three had been told, but then again, the kids already figured out that many of life's "unhealthy" things were the most fun.

This particular afternoon, Sartek and Isara wouldn't take no for an answer, and Sartek poked Blalok in the ribs, one side, then the other.

"Quit!" Blalok appealed, too distracted by his game to object more eloquently. He blindly tried to slap Sartek's hands away and missed each time. Finally resigning himself to his fate, he powered the game down and floated softly to his bedroom floor.

Pulling the gaming helmet off, he tossed it more carelessly than usual onto his bed. "You're *really* obnoxious, you know!"

"C'mon," Isara coaxed. "Let's go lie on the *Star*'s sun deck and eat darja and crackers." She held the bag of green treats up, trying to coax Blalok away from his virtual afternoon. This would be no easy task, but Isara knew darja and crackers were his favorite. "Mom made 'em." She smiled sweetly, swinging the baggie to and fro.

Isara wasn't just willowy, she was stunning—an exquisite natural beauty that seemed expressed not just in her appearance but in the way she moved. It was as though she carried herself in an effortless dance, and life was her perfect partner.

That wasn't what caught Blalok's attention now; it was the darja and crackers. Isara was one of his two very best friends, but she'd annoyed him often enough to be well beyond appearing attractive to him in *that* way.

"You know you want to," she crooned sweetly, holding the bag out to him.

Glancing sideways through slitted eyes, Blalok took a seat at his computer console as though he might busy himself with something else. He wasn't ready to concede defeat just yet. "Will we be back in time for Luna Physica?"

"That's a dumb show, and yeah, we'll be back in time." Sartek headed for the door.

Blalok shoved himself away from his computer and slapped his knees before jumping out of his chair. "Then count me in!" He snatched the darja and crackers from Isara's hand as he stalked past them. Isara cast a knowing smile at Sartek, and they followed their younger friend.

They never would make it back for Luna Physica; they would never make it back at all, and Blalok was the least sorry about this. The accident offered up to him the stuff of dreams, and though he missed his family as much as anyone might, he had few regrets.

To Blalok, he didn't see that wretched day as an extremely unfortunate accident. He believed he was meant to be out here, in the blackest of all beyonds. The terrible event was, to him, destiny.

Tonight, the three slept as the *Cerulean Star* cruised. The reassuring hum of the engines was always there, a gentle murmur in the background.

When they'd first been lost, this was the sound that eased their fears, lulling them to sleep during sad and lonely moments. When all they had was each other and the awful unknown, the *Star* whispered to them, a constant reminder of home. Nearly two years later, they were so accustomed to the constant drone they didn't even hear it anymore and, all the while, the *Star* kept a constant, vigilant watch over them.

While they slept, the ship's sensors maintained a steady gravity similar to Bettua's, a climate with the temperature at a cool eighty-two degrees, and a suitably mixed oxygen ratio.

The sensors also analyzed space current, deflecting small space debris like micro-meteoroids and space sand, and an intricate shield system protected the hull from erosion. The concept was brilliant, really—a living shell that regenerated itself from helium, the second most abundant element in the universe.

The *Star* literally regrew her hull from space, which was a good thing. This meant that if they could find the basic necessities of Bettuan life, they might survive. That was *if* they could stay a step ahead of the Rayze, the second concern mentioned a bit earlier, but more on that later.

The *Cerulean Star* also had a complex autopilot and alarm system, which allowed the ship to avoid impact with larger, more dangerous objects. At a moment's notice, the crew would be alerted to any impending collision. There was virtually no risk they might strike something as big as a planet or large meteor. The ship very cleverly plotted their travels using a learning space map, so to speak. Sensing ahead of them the layout of a system, the computer mapped the stellar bodies in advance as they went.

The only risk, rare though it was? A vessel might come out of Time-Time travel to collide with them. This was incredibly unlikely, but then again, the terrible accident had been just as unlikely, and it'd happened before anyone could do anything about it.

All the same, the alarm system would alert them of any imminent strike, and it had never gone off. Nevertheless, Blalok insisted the three of them test it daily to make sure everything remained fully functional. He felt responsible for allowing them to disable the alarm system on that dreadful day. That had contributed greatly to the accident.

It was unfortunate, but they were all, in some way, guilty of conspiracy to commit stupidity.

In middle space—this is what they called the space between stars—there was, for the most part, a whole lot of nothing. They didn't travel at what used to be called *Light Time*. "That would just be stupid," Blalok explained. Light Time was one hundred times the speed of light, archaic, and incredibly slow. It was also considered supremely impractical because once you reached above one hundred times the speed of light, more accurately at about one hundred twenty-three times the speed of light, a spaceship risked evaporating, along with everything in it. Well, it wasn't exactly evaporating.

It was more like stretching. Your ship got stretched, and so did you until you became a thousand little pieces, and those pieces each became a thousand little pieces until you were just a lovely micro-string of mostly greenish cells, strewn along in space. It was the same thing that would happen to you if you made the unfortunate mistake of getting sucked into a Black Hole.

Therefore, it was unreasonable to star jump in Light Time anymore. This was how Blalok explained Time-Time travel to his two friends.

It was Blalok's great-great grandfather who'd discovered Time-Time, spearheading the invention of "Time-Trotting," as a layperson called it, which was most everyone, including Sartek and Isara. Blalok tried to get them to use the proper terminology—*Geodesic Occasium Infinitum*—but landed no success. He was, after all, a nerd.

The concept of *Time Trotting* was brilliant, the notion that time wasn't constant, that the sequence of time was irregular, and so it could be manipulated. Blalok's great-great grandfather had hypothesized the idea of back-to-back wormholes, which are only elaborate time tunnels anyway. In short, this would allow you to literally "trot" to the nearest star in an afternoon. *That* is a remarkable thing.

Time trotting allowed a ship like the *Cerulean Star* to cover vast distances between stars in its home galaxy by setting time, not speed of light.

This changed so many things in such a dramatic way! Bettua became linked to its sister stars, and the Galaxy they lived in evolved. Art, science, and commerce flourished, that was, after the wars finally ceased. That had been a long, terrible episode in Bettuan evolution, and is a story best saved for another chapter.

That fateful afternoon when the three Bettuan children left to play, they'd not anticipated the dark matter thread that would suck them from their beloved Ambrik Galaxy to the greatest of black beyonds. On that dreadful day, there'd been a shift in the fabric of the galaxy they called home. This happened, mmm…approximately never, but it *did* happen that day.

A shift, even microscopically small, can do wonderful and frightful things to a galaxy. Imagine dropping a pea into the middle of the ocean. It creates the tiniest ripple, but that ripple matches the frequency of the ripple next to it and they mesh. Then it happens again, and again. Eventually, after this tiny ripple has grown and matched the frequency of enough other waves, it becomes monstrous and crashes against the cliffs of a shore somewhere, creating a breathtaking display of magnificence…or horror.

There was no reasonable explanation why it happened in the first place— who dropped the pea—but it lent itself to the belief that the essence of divinity was real. Perhaps the all-knowing simply stuck a finger in and stirred the proverbial pot.

Anyway, whatever the cause, it happened. Furthermore, when it did, it created a galactic tsunami that rolled violently across the Ambrik galaxy…and Bettua. All ships were immediately ported, all except one, and I think you know which one that was.

The children never knew the tsunami was coming; their communication console and all the alerts were foolishly disabled. The *Star* was veiled, thanks to the very clever child named Blalok and some creatively brilliant programming. To them, and everyone else in their galaxy, they were completely invisible.

They were *not* supposed to take the *Star* out that long ago afternoon, or any other afternoon for that matter. In fact, Sartek was supposed to be cleaning his room, and Isara skipped deep-diving lessons to cavort with her two best friends.

Blalok wasn't innocent either. He'd bypassed the security settings and helped them shortcut several critical dock monitors to ease the vessel from her star bay. He'd even left a halo-image in their wake so it appeared the ship was in dock when it really wasn't—a brilliant piece of programming.

It would be several hours before the grown-ups figured this out. Then the frantic, futile search for the missing children would begin.

Sartek said the plan was to be back long before anyone was home and none the wiser. Any other day it would have worked magnificently. Truthfully, previously it had!

But today would be their final undoing. They'd done the equivalent of running with a giant pair of galactic scissors, and their blunder would backfire terribly upon them!

The three very clever kids never heard the interstellar alert that resounded across their galaxy. None of them were aware, and none of their parents assumed the three would be so impulsive as to take the *Star* out without permission.

Second intergalactic newsflash of the day; they *were* that impulsive, and as we already know, it wasn't the first time they'd done it!

So the grand escape went off without a hitch. Consequently, they were cosmically screwed….

Veiled and with the communication and alert devices on standby, the three were able to sneak away. But, they hadn't noticed the *Star*'s alarm system going haywire because they'd muted it, overriding all of their critical sensors.

Sartek and Isara complained that the sensors disturbed their music. Likewise, none of them noticed the emergency flashing lights because they'd set them on strobe anyway. That was a spectacular effect along with their blaring music. There was a very popular band that the three, well, Sartek and Isara anyway, particularly liked. Blalok found the music annoyingly repetitive, but he was outnumbered, so the tunes were blasting loudly overhead as the tsunami sucked the *Star* violently into the initial backwash.

The tiny vessel careened onto its side, groaned terribly, and shuddered to the point that they thought the ship would implode. Blalok clutched at the console to remain seated, his hands rifling over the engineering controls as he tried to alter the stress moments the best he could. Ultimately, everything became too violent for them to maintain their balance, and they were all thrown from their chairs.

The *Star* emitted a horrendous, metallic wail, not unlike the leviathans that called to each other from Bettua's ocean depths, as its fabrication was tested beyond anything its creators ever dreamed it would endure. Spinning and tumbling, the sad little ship was tossed as though caught beneath one of the monsoon waves that sometimes pummeled Bettua's land masses. Then, the dark-matter thread reached its inky tendrils out, ensnared the ship, and dragged it into oblivion.

Even though only a few seconds passed, to the children the chaos seemed as though it went on forever.

Should the *Cerulean Star*'s computer interpreted an eminent life-threatening situation, it would initiate an emergency suspension protocol. And this is exactly what happened the instant everything became so violent that Blalok and the others were thrown from their chairs.

The computer captured each of the children with a protective shield bubble and floated them safely around the bridge. All they could do now was watch, terrified and helpless.

The navigation override took over emergency operations, reading and reacting to the hull threatening forces that pummeled the ship. By the time it trembled to a stop and the engines groaned into a standby idle, the three aboard were utterly disoriented, and Blalok had puked in his bubble.

When the suspension shields finally vaporized, setting them each gently back onto the bridge, they gazed in disbelief at what lay before them. The sudden silence was more deafening than all the noise from just seconds before. They could only watch, helpless as the black-matter thread that had captured them retreated, snaking away before disappearing altogether.

Sartek stepped from the captain's chair where he'd been dropped from emergency suspension and joined his two friends on the deck, helping Isara from her knees. Blalok stepped gingerly around the vomit and darja that had fallen to the floor when the suspension lifted. They stood together, silent, motionless, and terrified, in front of the massive screen that wrapped around the small bridge of the ship. Across the screen was spread a very strange black beyond. *Nothing* was familiar.

If one could imagine a piece of sand rolling around on a happy beach on one side of a world, and then if they would imagine taking this tiny speck of sand and flinging it impossibly far, all the way to the other side of the world onto a very different beach, that is essentially what happened to the children aboard the *Cerulean Star*. They were that speck of sand, thrown very, very far away. No Bettuan had ever traveled so far.

The children just stared. Standing frozen on the bridge, they hadn't the slightest idea of what this spiral galaxy, coiling with its elegant and milky helix before them, had in store for them.

This is their story....

CHAPTER ONE

Δ

Kansas City, Kansas: July 2010

The clear, crisp morning shone like a gem as nine-year-old Liberty crawled into the back of his parents' Toyota Camry. He struggled with the clips but eventually buckled himself into the kiddy booster seat, resigning himself to the humiliating fact that he still needed one. It would be no use fighting with his parents about it; they were quite firm about the safety rules. No matter. Secretly, he appreciated that at least the seat provided him with enough elevation to have a view out the windows.

Summer was at a glorious start, although Liberty considered this insignificant. He went to school year round, and this was fine with him. On this particular day, he was heading to a chess tournament in the city and was very excited about it. There were no ridiculous age restrictions at the tournament like there were on Jeopardy, which was an incredibly simple game show anyway. Today, he would play chess against adults—brilliant minds—and would be challenged...he hoped.

In his lap lay Liberty's favorite chess set safely stored in its faux-leather case. He knew he wouldn't be allowed to use it for the tournament—it wasn't permitted to use *personal* sets—but there was just something about the simply elegant ebony and bone pieces, passed down from his grandfather, that was like traveling with an old friend.

He ran his finger idly back and forth along the case while his parents argued softly about whether he should go to Harvard or Cambridge. Liberty would graduate high school in just less than two years and happily ignored their banter—he wanted to go to MIT—and was lost in one of his favorite mind games. He was fabricating palindromes in his head, a driving game that he'd invented. The challenge was to come up with words or phrases that were the same spelled frontward or backward, for example, kayak, only he'd upped the stakes. His phrases had to have the same number of letters as each street sign they approached, and he had to accomplish it before they passed the sign. The rules were if he failed to contrive one, he lost immediately.

Liberty was thirty-two palindromes into his game, having just come up with "evil olive" to the sign that read "slow ahead" when the black pickup with the lift-kit ran the red light and T-boned their car.

When the boy woke up thirteen days later, he was the only patient in the pediatric intensive care unit at Kansas City Memorial. Liberty looked around at the blank, silent faces, all staring regretfully down at him. That was when he discovered something new about himself. For the first time ever…he was alone.

Two Years Later: August 2012

Roxy's Foster home

Erie, Kansas

Thirteen-year-old Alex pulled her feet out of the water and tugged at the fishing string, secured with a slipknot to her pinky toe. Her overalls were wet up to the knees because she'd not bothered to roll them up. Now she was bent over, intent upon untying the string.

"What are you doing?" Liberty asked.

"I'm bored. Gonna let him go," Alex mumbled.

She fiddled with the string. It was long, about eight feet, and on the other end of it was a little catfish, nicely tethered through its mouth, around its pectoral fins, and up in front of its tiny dorsal. This clever arrangement made a nifty harness that allowed the very sturdy fish to swim about, tugging on Alex's pinky toe while she sat on the bank, feet dangling in the water, fishing for more catfish quasi-victims.

Given enough time, Alex would have two or three trussed up and doing loops, all tied to its own respective toe. The good news was that, in the end, she spared them all, releasing them to their bottomless lives, happy to swim another day. Alex always released the fish and only used bread dough balls—never live bait. Furthermore, she whaled on anyone who teased her about it.

Liberty studied her as she did this, the way she chewed on her lip when she was thoughtful…or distracted. He wondered which it was today.

David, the third of this trio, offered his opinion on the subject.

"Bored is stupid. Say that at home and we get chores, you know."

Alex didn't look up from her task.

"It's not home, and you know it. We don't have a home…*yet.*"

Liberty watched David reach up to brush his dark hair out of his eyes and shrug Alex's reply away. The two were the first to arrive at the foster home almost three years ago. David was twelve and still convinced that his father would return for him "soon." He appeared to ignore the fact that his dad had been sentenced to thirty years without parole. It was an incredibly painful subject, and he seldom spoke of his father anymore.

Fumbling through his pocket for his Albuterol, for his breathing was not right again this morning, Liberty found his inhaler. Shaking it five times—he always shook it five times—he took a short puff and contemplated his two best friends. He considered Alex to be the kindest and toughest girl he'd ever known. At that particular moment, she was casting a *Mind your own business* look Liberty's way.

Alex had a peculiar habit, rather a philosophy, about living things. He'd seen her discover a struggling caterpillar on the sidewalk and gently lift the creature in cupped hands to place it somewhere safe in the bushes to recover. Another time, she'd sprinted much too closely into traffic to snatch a box turtle from its kamikaze trip across a busy avenue. David had become fairly unhinged about the whole affair, and she had told him that if a turtle shouldn't be saved, none of them should.

Liberty was also fairly sure that Alex was the only girl in Erie, perhaps in the whole world, who'd ever wrangled a catfish. That's where they lived, Erie, Kansas, population just over one thousand, also known as Beantown, USA, and it was easy to imagine why. The kids joked about it, calling it "Fart-Town" whenever the opportunity offered itself.

Magoo, or just plain Goo as they called him, lay beside Alex. His back legs extended straight back behind him in a remarkably flexible way, and his nose rested perfectly balanced on his front paws. Goo was a short hair Daschund mix, and he went everywhere with the kids.

At night at *"The Home"*, the dog tunneled beneath the blankets to sleep curled up next to Liberty, his designated human.

Now, the wiener dog's eyes followed the fishing scene without too much excitement. He would perhaps have been much more interested if there were treats involved, but today was just catch and release, and Alex appeared unwilling to part with any of her *Wonder Bread* dough balls.

David had laughed at her once, regarding the bread. "It's a *wonder* you can eat it and live!" His dark brown eyes danced with amusement at his joke.

Goo could eat it; Goo could eat anything and be just fine.

Once, right after last Christmas, he'd gotten into a package of Andes Mints that Hog bought for Roxy.

Roxy ran the foster home, and Hog was her current boyfriend. They were a matched pair, and she was insanely upset when she discovered her precious candy had been confiscated and eaten by the little dog. "Never mind Goo was doing her fat ass a favor," Alex had mumbled.

Roxy was convinced that Goo would die from it, and refused to bring him to the vet, threatening to get rid of the "...mongrel. He deserves what he gets!" she snapped, all puffed up with indignation. Roxy was cruel to the core.

Where chocolate is supposed to be very bad for a dog, Goo not only meticulously unwrapped all the mints, he'd neatly eaten, without incident, every last one of them, leaving only a littering of silvery, green wrappers behind. Goo was a gastric phenomenon.

On another occasion, when Liberty was making BLTs, he dropped a whole, ripe tomato onto the kitchen floor. Before he could stoop to pick it up, *schloop*—it was gone. All that remained was Goo, tail wagging and a happy grin on his face.

Now, the dog appeared to be considering a nap more reasonable fare than a possible dough ball from a thirteen-year-old girl with fish tied to her toes.

Alex lifted the little fish gently from the water and flipped out her real Swiss Army Knife. It'd been the last thing her brother had given her, she'd once explained, and now she used the smallest blade to gently cut the harness free, careful to hold the catfish in what she called "the claw" so it wouldn't spine her with one of its painfully sharp fins.

Taking time to admire the sleek, inky glossiness of the fish before holding it gently in the water, she began fake-swimming it back and forth until it experienced that *ah-ha* phenomenon, recognized its freedom, and darted to safety. Swiping the catfish slime on her pants leg, she carefully wiped the knife blade off with the hem of her T-shirt before returning her prized possession to the long pocket by her knee.

She took the string she'd salvaged from her pinky toe and coiled it up neatly before stuffing it into the bib of her overalls to save for next time— another day of fish wrangling.

Alex, whose real name was Alexandra Elizabeth Stutton, had no misconceptions about her fate the way David seemed to.

Two things: she *hated* her name, and so everybody just called her Alex, and second, she knew there was *no one* who would someday return for her or David, or Liberty, for that matter.

For now, she summed everything up saying they were *in it together, until death do Roxy part.* She'd then crossed her chest dramatically and spat on the ground.

Liberty was so named because his parents decided he needed a name signifying freedom and independence—a liberator from mediocrity, an intellectual leader. They'd been Berkeley graduates and, when his mother became pregnant, they picked a good, strong name because they thought of their unborn son in just this way. He would be smart, and strong, and he would go to the very best schools and colleges. Liberty would be a great thinker, a fighter for equal rights. Most importantly, he would change the world in ways that would benefit the good of humanity.

This had been their dream for their very gifted son. And this is what they told Liberty. They had been right on track, too, well on their way with these magnificent plans, embracing mother earth as they both worked full time to save enough money to make their dreams for their son come true. But that was before they died, of course.

The car crash took both of them in an instant and left nine-year-old Liberty in the back seat of the mangled car, unconscious and strapped into his kiddy booster chair because, of course, he had yet to satisfy the weight limit to use a regular seatbelt or sit in a front seat.

When he at last emerged from the rehab institute with a single, black chess piece in his pocket, his parents' small fortune had been depleted to pay for his convalescence. And it would appear that nine-year-old boys, no matter how brilliant, were not easily adopted. Liberty landed in foster care, with Alex and David.

So the three of them were all fostered at *The Home*. Alex and David are twelve. Liberty is eleven, and he has lived there for not quite two years.

It was summer in Kansas, and today they were playing in one of the rare, forested areas of the state. Alex and David were barefoot. David was shirtless, as he was on most days, and brown as the Indians' children who'd lived on the Kansas prairie long before it was ever called Kansas.

Liberty thought the state was drab compared to the exotic places he read about—fantastic locations he knew existed elsewhere in the world. He especially didn't like the hot weather. The long, dusty summers made his asthma act up and his diabetes harder to control.

He, unlike Alex and David, was not barefoot because he couldn't risk a foot injury. Infections were particularly nasty for Liberty and a constant struggle, but he managed his diabetes as best he could. The state delivered his insulin and syringes, but rarely did he make his doctor appointments.

Even so, he'd spent many hours poring through everything he could find about diabetes, mostly on the school's library computers. Now, he could contribute fairly significantly to the field of diabetes research, but instead, he spent his quiet moments secretly absorbing anything and everything his mind could access, and his not so quiet moments were spent with the two he had come to know as family. Well, three, if you counted Goo.

August was hot and sultry, and the forest they were playing in was originally planted in the nineteen thirties as a windbreak to stop some of the terrible dust storms that Kansas was famous for. Erie was best known for dust, corn, beans, and…at least one very below average foster home.

Nevertheless, the little forest offered a bit of shady respite at times and was where the children could most often be found. There was scarcely a square inch they had not, over the long summer days, explored.

The Home, as they called it, was an old farmhouse and sat one and a half miles from the outskirts of Erie. It fostered eight kids: three under the age of five, two older teenagers who were more often absent than home, and the three who played on the banks of the muddy catfish pond today.

Alex and David were sent to *The Home* within six months of each other. Liberty came along four months later. Hard circumstances and loneliness were the catalysts that brought them together, but it was their extraordinary personalities that soon bonded the three.

Each of them had suffered grave periods of disappointment and despair, and there were times early on when they huddled around whichever one of them was the most vulnerable.

It was frightening to be the object of Roxy's wrath, but together the three would whisper words of encouragement to allay fears and tears. This was usually accomplished beneath a blanket tent, and as time went by, this refuge hid fantastic moments of smiles, giggles, and games.

In short order, the three of them were fairly inseparable, and today, evidently, they needed to go looking for a corn snake.

"You know I want one," Alex insisted. "They make the best pets."

"She's right. Corn snakes are the most docile and easy to care for of all the midwestern snakes. They live a lot longer in captivity than in the wild, actually," Liberty said, tipping his chin back so he could look up at David.

He had an endearing habit of ending his sentences with the word *actually*, which amused David greatly.

"So what, and don't call me 'actually'." David poked fun at his friend.

Alex seemed less than entertained. "Hey, I'm looking for a snake. You coming?"

"You know they won't let you keep it," David cautioned.

"*They* don't need to know as long as you keep your fat trap shut," she snapped, "and quit being so negative already." She started off, evidently prepared to leave both the boys behind.

This puzzled Liberty a small bit. Alex could be strong-willed, even downright opinionated, and it wasn't uncommon for her to occasionally lock horns with David. For her to be so randomly short with him, however, was unusual.

He glanced over at David, who only shrugged. "She can pay thirty-nine bucks for one at the Pet Palace, or she could catch one," Liberty confided to David as they trailed behind her. Goo glared, evidently put off that he must rouse himself enough to follow.

"Yeah, and where's she gonna come up with forty bucks?"

"Well, it's doubtful we're gonna catch one out here," Liberty said. "They're very timid in the wild, you know."

"Hurry up!" Alex hollered, looking back over her shoulder as she made her way deeper into the woods.

Poking around, they tried to find the elusive, lovely, orange and gold-banded constrictor, stirring up the leafy beds at the base of the trees with their walking sticks. It was an ideal snake, as far as snake pets go; Liberty was right about that. And behind their foster house was a corncrib that would be perfect to shelter one in, complete with plenty of mice for it to nibble on.

Time passed, and an unusual silence fell over the three. Something was up, and neither of the boys appeared prepared to confront the issue. They'd wandered deeper into the woods than they normally did, and just when Liberty was about to suggest they go back, something happened.

Alex was the first to top a tiny wooded hill that looked down into a secluded draw below. Liberty, dragging behind, heard her mutter, "Happy *Birthday*," as she halted in her tracks, eyes wide with amazement.

By then, David caught up with her and pulled up so abruptly that Liberty ran smack into him. He wriggled between the pair until he saw what *they* saw— a brilliant blue glow, mostly hidden by the trees.

"What is it?" David asked.

"I don't know. Wanna find out?" Alex took a step toward it.

What they witnessed next was unlike any blue they had ever seen, and surrounded with a silvery aura. And there was something else about it. Even as far away as the strange object was, it hummed, almost too quiet to hear—a sensation more like something they felt between their ears. There was also a peculiar static in the air, like a pleasant, electric breeze, brisk and almost cold.

"What is it?" David repeated, squinting, his dark features very serious. He held both arms out as though he would keep his friends from approaching something that could be dangerous. He did this sometimes, tried to step into the role of leader.

Liberty had long ago realized that, along with his leadership role, David sometimes seemed to bear the weight of the world on his shoulders. When he was like this, it was usually best to leave him alone for a bit.

There wasn't anything David could've done to persuade his father not to print the money. That's what Liberty told him. He had conceded this with a nod, but never said anything more on it. The counterfeiting scandal had rocked David's life and landed his father in prison for a very long time. The currency had been so perfect, the best the government had ever seen, and because it'd been sold overseas to be used in questionable activities, a stiff treason charge was added to his offenses.

Treason was hard to assign to an American citizen, but once it was, sunshine became a rare commodity for those unfortunate souls. Odds were David would never see his father outside of prison again. He could never acknowledge this outright, probably never would.

Liberty thought he was sad more often than he let on.

David was also naturally athletic—gifted, really. But while he should have been doing junior league sports, making his way toward a college athletic scholarship, he instead escaped with his orphaned friends into the eastern Kansas woods.

And, because of this, he seemed happier than he'd ever been. One cool afternoon, on Halloween, as they sat smearing fireplace ash on their faces so they could pass the requirements to trick or treat, David told Alex and Liberty that they were his very best friends, *ever*. Liberty thought that was one of the most sincere things he'd ever heard anyone say.

Alex pinched David on his bare ribs and shoved her best friend's arm aside. "It's aliens, stupid. Move it."

"Ow! Why do you hafta' be such a—?"

"Wait!" Liberty broke in.

They halted immediately. Alex and David almost always listened when Liberty said something urgently.

It was an accepted fact that he was beyond brilliant, and he could go on and on about the most boring things.

When he did this, his eyes would light up with an excitement his friends didn't always share. He also wore his father's old, spare glasses—gold, wire-framed that were the exact prescription Liberty needed. They were big and round and made his eyes seem even larger than they really were.

However, when Liberty spoke so earnestly, Alex and David had come to recognize that it was important for them to listen up. Most times, when they ignored him in such situations, things went poorly.

He gestured down the hill, his face a study in dead seriousness. "There's the distinct possibility that we've encountered a vessel from another planet."

Alex stared at him as though he'd sprouted a third eye. "Yeah, Einstein. I just said that."

"And we have no way of knowing if it is safe," he added lamely.

"*You*...wait, let me get this straight...*you* think that's an alien ship?" David hiked his thumb at it. "Seriously?"

"Well, if it is," Alex said, "we discovered it!"

David shifted his bare feet in the dried leaf bed of the forest floor. "Do you think we should tell someone first?"

"No!" Alex pushed abruptly past them to sneak a closer peak at the object that glimmered so enchantingly down the way.

"Alex, wait! You don't know if it's safe!" Liberty whispered too loud. "What if there's *radiation*?"

"Well, then maybe I'll grow another head and be as smart as you," she whispered loudly back and continued to crab-crawl down the hill.

"You coming?"

The boys dragged behind, and before long they were bunched together, peering from behind a thick shock of bushes at the elegant shape, about fifty yards away, floating absolutely still in the tiny meadow.

The ship hovered only about three feet above the ground, and the buffalo grass swayed gently beneath it.

It didn't sound any louder, even this close, but the electric buzz they'd felt before was much more pronounced. Liberty's skin tingled, like he had goose bumps all over, and everything seemed so suddenly surreal, as though he'd done this before.

"Hey, look at Bert!" David exclaimed.

"Bert" was what they called him, seldom using his formal name.

Liberty's hair was so blond as to be nearly white and was "fine as fish hair," Alex had been known to joke. There was also quite a lot of it, and the way it was trimmed in a perfect, ridiculous bowl-cut only made his glasses seem even bigger than they really were.

"What?" Liberty's eyes shot wide. "Retinal hemorrhage? Petechiae? Am I...*glowing*?"

David snorted, and Alex giggled. Liberty's hair was standing completely on edge, sticking straight out all over. It had a fairly startling effect and made him look like a fuzzy, white, human Chia pet. Alex ran her hand across the top, trying to make it lie down again. No good. It snapped straight back up.

"Stop it! We have more important issues at hand here than my hair!" This was true, but even so, he couldn't resist reaching up and rubbing his own hand across it. He tried several times to smooth it down as they turned their attention back to the craft, and then accepted that, for now, he would strongly resemble a fully blossomed dandelion.

Goo seemed happy to keep his distance from the strange object that perhaps made his doggie ears tingle a bit too much. He nosed around the base of the shrubs before plopping down to give his legs a break. It'd been a long day; the kids had gone much farther than they usually did, and evidently this was all the enthusiasm Goo could muster.

"What should we do?" Alex stared, eyes wide and fixed on the strange object. "Should we try to make *contact*?"

"I'm guessing that isn't necessary," Liberty replied straight up. "If they have the technology to be here, which should be next to impossible anyway, then they already know we're sitting here behind these shrubs."

"What?" David stood up. "We snuck down this hill and are sitting behind these bushes like a bunch of idiots, and they know we're here?"

"Yes, and it's your own fault. You didn't ask me." He shrugged.

That was evidently all Alex needed to hear. Before the boys could stop her, she stepped out of the bushes and marched directly beneath the vessel.

Reaching up—an ant beneath an elephant—she waved.

David leapt forward. "Alex, stop! We don't know if it's—"

Before he could finish, it was gone!

In an instant, it vanished. There was no powering up, no swoosh as it left orbit, no fire or vapor trail. It was just all of a sudden not there.

Alex blinked hard twice.

"What the…?"

She took one staggering step toward the spot where only an instant before the ship had been.

"*Fuck!*"

Liberty stepped cautiously from behind the shrubs and offered, not unkindly, "See? Told you they knew we were here."

"Shut up!" Alex snapped as she scanned the treeline, a hand over her eyes to shield the sun. It was unusual for Alex to be this suddenly profane, and sure as shit, Liberty shut up.

The energy they'd experienced before lingered for a second or two longer, and then that too was gone. As the warm, humid summer afternoon wrapped once more around them, they just stood there, next to a fat, sleepy wiener dog in a small Kansas woods. For a long instant, nobody said anything.

David reached a hand out, gently resting it on Alex's shoulder. "Sorry, Al. I know you really wanted to get closer. Maybe…" He dropped his gaze.

She said nothing, only blinked back tears.

"But you gotta admit," Liberty chimed in, "it was neater than a corn snake!" He could think of nothing more to say.

She turned away.

"Alex, you okay? I mean, we all saw it, but you seem, I don't know…sad about it."

"It's my birthday," she said flatly.

David exclaimed, "What? Already? How come you didn't tell us? That's great! I mean…I…" He paused.

Birthdays at *The Home* weren't celebrated. After food and cigarettes, there was little money left for "fluff n' puff" Roxy had made very clear.

Liberty tried to rescue the situation. "You know, maybe the aliens knew that too! Maybe they, uh…knew it was your birthday and came to wish you a happy birthday!"

It was such a sweet thing to say and so incredibly illogical. Alex smiled weakly. "You know, for as smart as you are, you really are stupid."

Liberty grinned. "Yeah, I know."

"And what a show!" David said. "Especially with Bert's hair doing that thing! By the way, gratz on being a teenager. You know you're the first one."

This brought a soft grin to Alex's lips.

"C'mon, Goo!" Liberty called.

The little dog's head popped up, and he scrambled to his feet. Ears flopping up and down, Goo hustled to take up his position behind his human.

The rest of the way home, they walked in silence. Liberty thought very hard about the sighting of the strange object in the meadow. He suspected that David and Alex would struggle with what they'd seen today. He, on the other hand, would not. He knew without a doubt what the blue orb had been.

That night, when everyone else had long gone to bed, he watched the late news to see if there were any mentions of a UFO sighting. Nothing. Evidently it *was* Alex's birthday surprise and their secret. Scrambling to his feet, he went to the front door and peered for a long while out the screen at the star-splashed sky.

"Where are you?" he murmured.

The warm night breeze gave him no answers.

CHAPTER TWO

Δ

Aboard the *Cerulean Star*, the three Bettuan were gathered on the bridge. Open and sweeping, it was oval shaped, and the entire front third of it arced with a floor-to-ceiling screen that could display a view from any angle or direction they wished. At this moment, the screen revealed the three Earthlings standing on the edge of the small meadow below.

"What happened?" Sartek demanded as the *Star* lifted gently, gaining altitude until it hovered some six hundred meters overhead.

Blalok powered the engines down to the equivalent of a low idle. The *Cerulean Star* was again veiled and, for all practical purposes, invisible to any instrument that might pick up radiation, heat, or an alteration in energy fields. Now, nothing on Earth could sense the presence of the alien ship.

Sartek leaned on the navigation panel, frantically interfering with Blalok's interpretation of data. Running his hands back and forth over the gel-like bubbles that were the controls, he checked and rechecked the readings, wanting to make absolutely certain the ship was veiled and safe.

The computer was silent, evidently content with the momentary stasis. Below them, the three small Earthlings seemed confused and fragile as they milled about, communicating amongst themselves.

"It was Cleo," Isara confessed, holding the chakrat tightly in her arms. Cleo dropped her head onto her claws in shame, an obvious effort to appear pathetic.

"She jumped up on the console from the navigation chair and must have switched off our veil. You know she likes to sit there. It was an accident, really it was," Isara said.

The chakrat whipped her tail around, panting nervously as though it sensed it was in grave trouble. Isara looked mortified enough for the two of them while Cleo wriggled, trying to free herself enough to get to the security of her master's arms. As unpredictable as the little creature was, the amusement was never-ending that Blalok was her Bettuan of choice.

"That's not okay!" Sartek continued pacing back and forth, checking the monitors one last time to make sure they hadn't been discovered.

The screens were all neutral again; all detection devices were silent. It appeared that the fleeting error had gone unnoticed, except by the three small creatures below.

"She's not supposed to be on the bridge. It's just not safe!" Sartek raised his voice again.

"Calm down. Everything's all right! I've gone over our readings three times now." Blalok shoved Sartek's hand aside, rechecking his monitors. "Nobody saw, except those three and that weird little…whatever it is with them. There is no chatter on their media networks regarding the event. Besides, even if we were seen on a larger scale, there is next to nothing that can be done as long as we remain veiled. Their technology is much too primitive for them to detect us now. We are safe."

"It's still not acceptable! If we're discovered, no one knows what could happen to us. It could risk everything!" Sartek swept his hand in front of him, gesturing toward the black beyond. "We might never make it home!"

Blalok's eyes fell, and Isara appeared stricken at his words. She approached Sartek, reaching to set the chakrat on the floor beside her.

"Sartek," she paused and said softly, "it's been a year and a half. We don't know what happened; we don't even know where we are." She had a look of sad regret on her face as though she was sorry for the vigilant belief that Sartek maintained—that someone might find them and bring them home, back to Bettua. "We need to make the best of things, Sartek. We're…lost."

"It doesn't matter!" He threw a hand up toward the screen. "They could be looking for us right now! We have to maintain ourselves here, in this galaxy, until they find us!"

Blalok and Isara stared at him. Isara reached up and rested one pale green hand on his shoulder. "It's not your fault."

"I didn't say everything was my fault! I know it's not …it's just that…"

He swallowed thickly and glared at the big forward screen as though it was a new enemy. The image of the three retreating aliens, with their small, fat, four-legged creature loomed large. "I just want to make sure we're all right, you know, till something happens."

"We *are* all right," Blalok insisted. "We're safe! The *Star* is doing fine"

Sartek sighed wearily, closing his dark green eyes as he hung his head. Gathering himself, he stood tall. "Thanks. You're right. I guess there's no harm." He paused. "We are okay, aren't we?"

They nodded enthusiastically, and Isara added, "Better than okay. We're best friends." She held out her hand, inviting the group handclasp. They gripped hands firmly until the energy pulse that bound them to one another sparked gently, then let go.

"But Cleo has to be kenneled from now on! Whenever we're in orbit at least, especially when we're harvesting," Sartek insisted.

When he said, "Harvesting," he meant when they were harvesting water of course.

"Sure thing—that's a good idea," Blalok replied.

This wouldn't be such a bad thing for Cleo, in all truthfulness. Kenneling on the *Cerulean Star* simply meant that there was a force-field track that the chakrat was limited to. She would still be free to wander the ship, only out from under foot and trouble.

For a moment, the three watched in silence as the creatures below disappeared, snaking their way back into the woods.

The Earthlings seemed hesitant. As they moved away, the small creature, that appeared to have attached itself to them, panted along behind. Finally, they were gone, swallowed up by the canopy.

"What do we know about them?" Isara glanced over at Blalok.

"There are roughly seven billion of them."

He studied the species-specific analyzer as he reported. "They inhabit all land masses on this planet, but have not developed the seas. As a matter of fact, they exclusively exploit them."

The *Cerulean Star* rose and swept silently into a gently arcing orbit while the three of them looked down on the darkening horizon of the planet called Earth. They were momentarily mesmerized by the elegant blue, white, and green swirls that marked the land, sea, and weather masses of the extraordinary planet.

Coming from Bettua, the three aliens considered Earth morosely devoid of water, strangely solid with its enormous land areas, but oddly inviting even so. Sartek thought it was strangely beautiful, like a great fishing lure, ready to draw them in…and trap them.

Before now, for over a year and a half, they'd spent long days on desolate, hostile planets to harvest water. In all their travels, they'd seen only three planets that were remotely safe enough for them to approach. When they'd come across these, the small crew had always been hesitant to move on, afraid of what may or may not await them in the vast unknown.

This tiny planet, on the other hand, seemed inviting, with its seas and its rich, temperate climate. As it spun serenely on its axis, stars twinkled beyond the horizon, and a single white moon rose over the Pacific.

They all stared, dangerously captivated.

"We should stay for a while," Isara murmured quietly.

Blalok ignored her comment and continued with his narrative. "They have eight biomes, all fairly similar, all with an oxygen content of twenty-point ninety-five percent, compatible, as we already know."

When he said that Earth was compatible, he meant the three of them could breathe the atmosphere easily and indefinitely. Being 'swimmers,' they could survive in atmospheric conditions down to seventeen percent before feeling ill-affected.

"However, despite the relatively scarce ocean cover, the inhabitants do little to sustain it. It is very devalued."

"And these particular creatures?" Sartek asked.

"It is my assumption that the three that discovered us are juveniles," he replied without hesitation.

"*What?*" Sartek and Isara said in perfect unison.

"What?" Isara repeated urgently.

"Juveniles—spawnlings. They're…" Blalok answered nonchalantly, "kids…like us."

This information had the effect of slapping his friends in the face with a wet towel. They stared, dumbfounded.

"It makes sense, if you think about it," he added. "Why would adults from this world waste time exploring an already surveyed woods?" He said this as though it should be so very obvious.

"You're so annoying sometimes," Sartek replied.

"Good." Blalok seemed mildly satisfied with this remark.

That night, or rather the time they'd set aside for night, they each went to their quarters, crawled into their respective sleep chambers, switched on their bio-regulation modules, and floated into stasis.

Stasis was rejuvenating. They were free to move as they slept.

It wasn't antigravity—it was uniform gravity. Stasis was pressure, equal from all sides and angles. It pulsated against them, stimulating circulation from all surface areas, resembling very much an aquatic environment. The effect was healthy and soothing, and as they drifted off, each pondered deeply the events of the day.

Isara, however, contemplated the event more heavily than the boys. She couldn't seem to brush the image of the three Earthling life forms from her mind and rolled restlessly in stasis. Finally, she abandoned rest and got up. Fabricating a cup of tea, she settled in front of her personal console.

"E-I," she addressed the computer.

* * *

E-I was what they called the very intricate computer system that was the brain, heart, and soul of the *Cerulean Star*. E-I stood for Electronic Intelligence, but there was much more to it than just that. The computer had instinct and intuition, but most importantly, it could *feel,* not in a physical way but in an emotional one.

However, E-I would only offer opinion on casual matters if asked. It would not blindly interject unless a situation was considered emergent. This technology was designed so that Bettuan instinct would always have the final say in most situations. They believed this would create a more natural evolution of the vital spirit of them while allowing E-I to evolve as it should.

The plant plasma circuitry within the computer was fabricated from the very difficult to harvest sea-moss which grew in the blackened cold at the depths of one of Bettua's deepest seas. Pretty much nothing grew at those depths. There was no light, and all the monsters that ventured there, great and small, possessed elaborate self-illumination systems. So did the moss.

The Bettuan were surprised at how lush the fields were that grew in such deep water, on the ebony cliffs and chasms below them, when they first discovered the delicate, inky green moss that flittered with flashes of luminescence. At first they'd harvested only a sampling of it, carefully planting it in the shallower, much safer depths around some of their cities.

It quickly succumbed to the sunlight, and the Bettuan, recognizing their mistake, eventually planted the delicate moss in cliff side ocean caves. In the cool, dark water of these caves, the moss survived and even flourished. It took some adjustment at first, but after some careful cultivation, the schlange moss grew happily in the darkened farms. Velvety smooth, its microscopic fronds glittered with light when the delicate plant was most happy. The caves were a perfect placement for it as the Bettuan could now harvest it safely and avoid negotiating some of the monsters of their deep oceans.

There is, however, a very critical component to this plant. The moss wasn't simply content in its new environment in the cave farms, it *thought* about things. Schlange moss was the first plant life ever identified to possess sentient thought, and though its feelings were very fundamental—*I'm afraid, I'm too hot, I have fear*—it wasn't just a simple reflex, for the plant also exhibited sorrow when a harvest was first taken. The remainder of the small field languished, mourning the loss of its own.

Some time passed before the Bettuan were able to identify this phenomenon. When the Bettuan were ultimately able to communicate to the fields, they informed the moss that the harvest was alive and well and that it would be sheltered impeccably, allowing it to flourish in a new home. With this news, and because its nature was very trusting, the schlange moss snapped right back to life, its bioluminescent patterns flitting bright and vibrant once again.

On the *Cerulean Star*, when cells of the moss were fabricated into the incredibly refined circuitry of E-I, it did two remarkably unexpected things. The most amazing was that it allowed logical thought to be enhanced with emotion. This gave E-I intuition, something very precious for a computer. Just as critical, it also allowed for spontaneous regeneration of the computer's components themselves. Like the hull of the *Star*, the elaborate circuitry of E-I experienced a continuous rebirth. It would essentially never age. Incorporation of the moss also allowed E-I to think beyond the hard science and math that it was programmed for.

The computer developed instincts and conscience, and all of E-I's circuitry was encased in perfect tiny tubes of water that were filtered and recirculated to give happy life to the precious moss within. And the moss maintained the structure of these tubes! Quite remarkable, and none other than Blalok really appreciated the brilliance of it for what it was.

* * *

"E-I," Isara commanded, "Replay *Cerulean Star* date three-three-oh-nine, fourteen forty-two."

"Affirmative." The computer confirmed in a pleasant, androgynous tone.

The screen illuminated slowly so as not to shock her eyes.

The soft, swirling blue morphed gently until the three dimensional image of the little forest was apparent as though it sat right on her desk.

"Good evening, Isara," E-I offered. "You are awake at an unusually late hour. Is everything all right?"

"Zoom," she requested, ignoring the computer's query.

The screen gradually pulled into the image of earlier today, closer and closer, wrapping the forest in a queer way as though up and around her.

"May I inquire as to what concerns you might have at this hour?" E-I probed.

Isara ignored E-I again, peering instead at the three Earthlings and their pet, all sneaking stealthily down the hillside. They looked silly as they slipped and slid, stopping at intervals to communicate with each other.

E-I zoomed in even more, and Isara's eyes widened when she noticed the Earthlings enjoying the effects of vapidation, especially upon the smallest one's hair. The two taller Earthlings appeared to be highly amused by the way it stuck out all over like a white halo.

Isara had seen the vapidation effect often enough before, on Cleo even. It'd long since lost its entertainment factor, although she had to admit it *was* fairly ridiculous on the one with the shockingly white hair. What captivated her the most, however, was that the three creatures seemed somehow amused by it. *Amusement? That is a Bettuan emotion! Humor!* She was more than a bit uncomfortable with this and shifted in her chair as she replayed the scene one more time to make certain. Yes, there was no doubt; the creatures found vapidation to be funny.

Next, she observed how the thinnest of the three, the one who appeared decidedly female, was also the most forward of them, shoving her comrades aside to venture all alone as she stepped into the open meadow. This was a bold move by any species' standards.

"Zoom again," Isara said quickly, "and freeze."

The screen came to rest, crystal clear and vivid, upon the female's face.

Isara was mesmerized. She studied her, the light brown hair so soft and fine. The delicate tresses appeared dry, wavy, and sun-streaked, hastily pulled back into a device of sorts, but that hadn't stopped considerable strands from escaping and floating about the creature's face. Bettuan also had hair, but it was all charcoal grey, slick, and coarse, like ropes of wet clay. And, it grew very slowly—only a fraction of an inch per year.

The Bettuan never cut theirs, and the hair of the very eldest Bettuan, who approached nearly three hundred years old, would sometime darken to an inky black, streaked with ash, hanging almost to their waists.

She peered at the frozen image again, at the hazel brown of the alien's eyes, so round and fringed with fur. There was a smattering of spots across her nose and cheeks, and the skin—it was such an unusual color, like the belly of a fish. She studied the wideness of the face, the too large mouth and small eyes. Isara rubbed her chin thoughtfully, like she did when she read about something wonderful or unfamiliar. Then she focused on the Earthling's expression.

"Play...slowly," she commanded and watched as the female raised her hand in a gesture that could only seem friendly. Her mouth widened into something the Bettuan would have classified as a smile, an expression of utter anticipation, of...hope? Then the expression disappeared in a stricken flash as the female took one halting step toward beneath where the *Cerulean Star* had been.

The Earthling couldn't know that the *Star* was now hovering and veiled just a short ways above. She just stood there with a thin hand hanging in the air, a look of absolute disappointment on her face.

The Earthling slowly lowered her hand, obviously forlorn, shoulders sagging. The two others appeared to...comfort her? The tallest of the three even put his arm around her shoulders.

Isara studied the frozen screen for a few moments longer. It was obvious that the female Earthling felt an unexpected disappointment, affected with some emotion that Isara wasn't entirely sure of. Had it been the sudden disappearance of the *Cerulean Star*?

"Off, E-I."

"Isara, do you need to talk about something?" the sophisticated network queried gently.

"Goodnight, E-I," she answered simply.

"Goodnight, Isara," the computer replied warmly and flickered off, the lifelike image of the small woods vanishing from her room.

Isara was too lost in thought to be engaged by the mainframe's concern. She crawled back into bed, leaving her tea, cold and undrunk, on the console counter.

CHAPTER THREE

Δ

Alex was up at what David called the "butt-crack of dawn." She hadn't slept very much, had flipped and flopped in the bunk overhead, entangling herself hopelessly in her sheets as she played over and over in her mind the events of yesterday. Ordinarily, she would've been all over her friends to get up with her to get a jump on the summer day. That didn't happen this morning; this morning was different.

She waited until the first sliver of dawn separated the earth from the sky before she slid out of the top bunk and into her overalls. Tiptoeing across the floor, she snuck from the room, leaving David and Liberty behind. This she had done before, approximately never.

A quick trip to the bathroom, and then she finger scrubbed her teeth with just a swipe of toothpaste. Some days, there just wasn't time for the toothbrush, but she couldn't tolerate morning mouth ever since Bert compared it to the bottom of the long abandoned chicken house. Finger scrubbing, however, was reserved for emergencies only.

Taking the stairs from the attic to the second floor, she skipped the two that squeaked by lifting herself over them, using the handrail like on the monkey bar walk at the elementary school. It'd been her experience that the two stairs were approximately right above Roxy's head.

It wouldn't be good to wake Roxy or Hog. A visceral hatred stirred in

Alex's belly as the brief subconscious thought of those two wretched human beings surfaced, and just as subconsciously, she repressed it.

Hopping as silently as she could, she then took the second flight of stairs down to the kitchen. As soon as her bare feet landed on the cool linoleum, Alex pulled her thick, wavy hair recklessly back in a worn rubber band and scaled the backdoor steps two at a time, spitting what was left of the toothpaste onto the dirt that served as a lawn at *The Home*.

She bounded, still barefoot, for the edge of the cornfield and the barely lit woods beyond. The path between the stalks was well worn from their trips to the forest, and as she ran, the dirt was velvety soft beneath her feet.

Ever since she'd seen the glowing blue ellipse floating in the secluded little meadow, Alex hadn't been the same. Something happened to her, something that compelled her to leave her friends behind and run alone back to the woods. The remarkable event on her thirteenth birthday somehow changed everything for her in a very sober way.

Much of Alex's life had been like drifting—flotsam in a stagnant eddy. She and her brother James had been fostered ever since her mother was found negligent, for the fifth time, by the district court of Kansas. Alex was three; James was ten. Life soon became a string of foster homes for them.

When she turned nine, Alex and James were split apart. They told her she could see him sometimes. They lied. She never saw James again, not until he showed up last year to let her know he was joining the Army.

He'd hugged her, told her he loved her, gave her his real Swiss-army pocketknife, and jumped into the back seat of an old Cadillac convertible with three other guys. Then, he disappeared, waving over his head as the car screamed away down the dusty drive.

Alex had been in *The Home* for barely a month when this happened. When James left, so did something else. She withdrew, becoming lonely and isolated. Defiant and angry, she truly believed she needed no one in her life.

The result was a motionless existence; time became flat—a mere continuation of lifeless minutes. There was no purpose and no one to need her either. She smiled less often and spent much more time alone.

Then, something extraordinary happened. The eddy broke and the river started to run again, in the form of another injured soul.

The first of the three to be placed in *The Home*, and having spent time in and out of many homes before, Alex immediately developed an unbending lack of compassion for anyone who might feel sorry for themselves.

At the time, the other children at *The Home* were either much younger or older than Alex was, and so she found herself isolated in the middle. She often told herself being alone suited her just fine.

When David showed up five months later, so quiet and withdrawn, Alex was unwilling to extend her friendship to him in even the smallest capacity.

She considered him weak and unworthy.

Sure, life has its knocks, but people have risen above worse; get over it! She snorted her derision outwardly, but the sad nine-year-old only looked away, hiding something behind his forlorn expression. It seemed he couldn't be baited; he wouldn't engage her either. This only confused and frustrated Alex.

David never talked about the big *why* he was there, never hurling scorn back into the face of circumstance the way she did. They were the same age, staring at each other across the card table that served as the kitchen table, and they were miles apart.

That was until one frosty winter day, when Alex took the last of the Fruit Loops for breakfast. She sat smugly, wrapped up in her favorite hand-me-down bathrobe with her legs crisscrossed on the chair. She'd overfilled her bowl, perhaps a little bit selfishly, but the box was close to empty and she'd gone ahead and done it anyway.

David looked her square in the eye and asked one word, "Share?"

Alex shot back, "Why should I?"

"Because if you don't…who will?" David answered without hesitation. He just stared at her, holding out his empty bowl.

Finally, reluctantly, she shook the short half of her bowl into David's, then watched, dumbfounded, as the quiet, brooding boy poured milk onto it and slipped the bowl under the table. Alex lifted up the plastic red-checked tablecloth with her finger and peered beneath.

Underneath the table, the stray wiener dog—the one that'd showed up cold and hungry on the doorstep a few days before—wagged its tail gratefully. They'd been warned not to feed this mongrel, but evidently David decided otherwise and was willing to risk all hell breaking loose.

The gesture immediately broke Alex down. This singular deed shattered her heart in a perfect way, and the shell cracked and fell away.

Alex attached herself to David, and before long, they were inseparable. It brought life back into the little girl who had no one and gave the sad, dark-haired boy the fire to fight another day. From that morning on, they had each other.

Liberty came to *The Home* three months after the car crash. He was mute, shell-shocked, and fresh from the children's psychiatric rehabilitation ward after his parents' trust fund ran dry. There would be no incredible schools, no elite tutors, no perfect dynamics to stimulate the savant child. Liberty was curled up in his foster bed, thin, silent, and so pale as to be almost translucent.

His knees were tucked up all the way under his chin, and the sheet was pulled up over his head.

"Leave him alone," Roxy warned them. "He don't talk much; got his head cracked. And has some disease and will probably die anyways."

"He's on his way out," Alex decided as they peeked through the crack in the attic door.

That's where they slept, the three of them, in the attic.

"He's disappearing," she explained worriedly to David. "We have to do something."

David nodded, and so the two of them did the most extraordinary thing. It was sheer brilliance. They went for Goo.

When Alex lifted the foot of the invisible boy's blanket and shoved the wiener dog underneath, Goo tunneled up to Liberty's chest, rooting his doggie nose underneath an armpit to stick his muzzle close to his face. Magically, and for the first time since he'd arrived, Liberty spoke in whispers to the Daschund mutt, cuddled with him under the sheet.

"He can talk!" David exclaimed excitedly after they'd backed from the room.

They didn't know Liberty had never in his life been face licked by a happy dog. Pets were not allowed where he'd grown up—it was too unsanitary and, besides, he had "allergies."

A few mornings later, the silent, frail child, with the ridiculous amount of white hair and a bald spot the size of a fist on one side of his head, came to the breakfast table. He sat opposite David and Alex, eyes so pale blue as to be almost white as well. Goo sat at his feet.

Pulling from his pocket an inhaler, the odd boy shook it first before drawing in a puff, holding his breath for a few seconds until his face turned a brilliant red.

"That's for the full benefit of the medication," he explained in a squeaky voice as he slowly exhaled, even though no one had asked.

The other two just stared, breakfast spoons held in suspended animation as they watched for the first time Liberty's strange morning ritual.

"Hello," he greeted them as he pocketed his inhaler, eyes enormous behind his wire-rimmed glasses.

"Hey," they replied in unison and watched him intently.

The very small, strange boy poured a bowl of Dollar Daze cereal into a bowl and ate it dry. "Cuz, I'm lactose intolerant," he explained, again without being asked.

"That's some seriously crazy hair," was all Alex remarked.

The boy shrugged, and all three went back to their breakfasts.

In this fashion, Liberty became the third musketeer to join the group.

When he did speak, Alex and David were shocked and delighted at what came out of his mouth. Furthermore, once he started talking, he never stopped. He was brilliant, a genius really. Nobody else in the world knew it but Alex and David, and no one cared.

In very short time, the three were accomplices for life—inseparable. Every day for them, no matter how mundane, was an adventure. "There's no such thing as *just another day*," was one of Liberty's favorite sayings, and in the unlikely atmosphere of *The Home*, a family of three—four if you counted Goo—was born. In the midst of marginal food, questionable hygiene, and even worse structure, they flourished in a remarkable way.

From then on, they were never very far apart.

* * *

That is why it was so unusual when this August morning Alex sprinted back to the woods alone. It was very unlike her. Yes, sometimes she still liked to pretend she didn't need anyone, but she never ventured out into the day without David and Bert anymore, until today.

Goo, who generally had more energy in the early morning than at any other time of the day, bounded from Liberty's bed and trotted after her, toenails clicking on the linoleum kitchen floor. He seemed thrilled that somebody wanted to be up as early as he liked to be, and he had all the splendid anticipation he could muster on his sweet doggie face.

Goo, his wide, muttly grin indicating he thought there might be delicious snacks to eat and wonderful things to smell, stood with one paw in the air. Minimally, there was no disputing how ecstatic he was that Alex might want his company! It could only be better if Liberty were up, too. Still, the little dog couldn't resist an adventure, and so after her he went.

Alex told Goo to stay.

Goo hesitated and sat with all the appeal a wiener dog could muster in his sad doggy eyes, and she caved.

"Here Goo, come on boy," she finally encouraged him, slapping her thighs gently.

The daschund bolted toward her and loped happily behind, ears lifting and falling much more effortlessly than his short legs did, and followed her into the woods.

* * *

When Liberty awoke, he lay in bed, staring at the bottom of the top bunk mattress. Sleep still had a marginal hold of him, but he was faintly aware something was different. That's where Alex slept, on the top bunk. He had to allow this because he was too short to jump up there, and the ladder was lost two yard sales ago.

David and Alex laughed outright as Liberty tried again and again to leap onto the top bunk. It was no good. He could hook one bowed leg up onto the mattress but would struggle, grunt, and flail, ultimately falling to the floor with another thud. Finally resigning himself to his failure, he took the bottom bunk. He would've given anything for such a splendid vantage point, having been up there once before when David gave him a boost.

Alex rubbed it in a bit, vaulting and hiking herself on top with one easy, cool movement. Liberty, in a rare instant of frustration, called her a stupid imbecile then tried to correct his own double meaning. She laughed so hard she drooled by accident, and it nearly landed on Liberty. Then they all laughed until their sides hurt.

The lower bunk turned out okay after all. He got to kick Alex in the butt when she was obnoxious, and because it was so much effort to jump down and pound on him, she seldom retaliated more than verbally, which, by the way, she was generally very good at.

This morning, however, he didn't see the familiar droop that was Alex's body on the thin mattress overhead and thought to himself for a groggy few seconds that she must have slid off the top bunk very quietly, because it always woke him when she hopped down. He wondered why for about half a second, then remembered the spaceship.

Liberty had no trouble deciding this was what they'd seen yesterday. After all, Sherlock Holmes, a personal favorite of his, said it so elegantly to Watson at least once, "…when you have eliminated the impossible, whatever remains, however improbable, must be the truth?" Even *Star Trek*'s famous first officer, Spock, had re-quoted that gem on occasion.

"Damn," Liberty muttered aloud to himself. That was about the extent of his use of profanity, and rare enough as it were. He believed strongly that profanity was used, "when you're too stupid to engage in intelligent repartee." David dumbly agreed, then admitted to secretly looking up "repartee" in the dictionary later. Alex had, in a good-natured way, told him with aplomb to…well, it just didn't bear repeating.

Perhaps, she didn't always have a way with words, and she routinely swore only mildly, but one couldn't argue her timing, and the F-bomb was dropped perfectly, setting them all off in hysterics.

Liberty shot out of bed the instant he realized where Alex had gone and poked David twice in the chest before running to the bathroom.

By the time he got back, David was sitting up on the side of his bed. "What's up?" He glanced around the room, rubbing the sleep from his eyes.

"Get up," Liberty said flatly. "She's gone."

There was no need to elaborate any more than that, and they both bailed into the same clothes they'd worn the day before, only today David pulled on his sneakers.

They ran for the kitchen and paused only long enough to grab a few essential provisions—Oat-ee-O's, dried oatmeal packets, and a bag of Homeland Cheese Puffs. None of it was expensive, none of it was nutritious, but it was foster food at its best.

They drank deeply from the kitchen spigot before filling their dime-store canteens. There was no juice at *The Home*, and milk was forbidden except on cereal. David poked a hole in the Cheese Puffs bag, squished the air out so it would fit, and stuffed it down into Liberty's backpack while his friend drew up his morning insulin.

"You'll make em' go stale" Liberty tapped the air to the top of the syringe to clear it.

"Well, then I guess we'll just have to eat *all* the evidence, won't we?" David grinned. They would for sure be in trouble for that.

Liberty grinned back, just a bit nervous for breaking the rules. If Roxy or Hog caught them, there would be hell to pay. He admired how David was able to play the rebel so effortlessly.

Pulling up his *Come to the Nerd side—We have pi* T-shirt, Liberty jabbed himself in the stomach with his morning injection. He'd found the shirt at a yard sale and tried to impress his friends with the "score of the century" when the lady sold it to him for a quarter.

"You need me to stick your ear?" David asked.

The boys were up well before anyone else in the house and talked in whispers. Liberty usually checked his blood sugar first thing in the morning, and ears were much less painful to stick than fingertips, especially over time.

"No, it's okay. I feel all right. I'll eat something in a little while, and it'll be fine." Liberty was a type I juvenile diabetic, had been since the age of three. Sometimes David stuck his ear in the morning for his blood sugar check. It was the kind thing to do. Alex tried once but nearly fainted.

Finally, David stuffed the zip-locked baggies of Oat-ee-O's and the dried oatmeal packets on top of the squished Cheese Puffs and hiked the backpack onto Liberty's thin shoulders, studying the pack to make sure it rode well.

Liberty shoved his glasses farther up on his nose with one finger and nodded that everything was fine. "We need to hurry. If the ship comes back…"

David hoisted the canteens of water, crisscrossing them over his own shoulders.

Glancing sideways at him, Liberty knew why he did this. The canteens were heavier than his own backpack full of dried foods, so David took the heavier load. Liberty was, intellectually speaking, unmatched pound for pound. Physically, however, Alex said that he couldn't fight his way out of a wet paper bag, and she wasn't very far off with that observation.

Truthfully, Liberty would never need to fight, not as long as David and Alex were with him. They would take on the worst the world could offer before they would allow him to get picked on, not that he didn't have to take his share of knocks from them. But they would level the playing field with the devil himself if their friend was ever threatened.

When they were satisfied they could make it to nightfall without starving, David checked in.

"Ready?"

Liberty gave him a thumbs up. "Yes, captain! Make it so!"

"Huh?" The *Star Trek* reference was completely lost on David.

"Never mind; let's go!"

The boys leapt from the back porch and sprinted for the woods. A half hour passed, and neither of them talked very much, which was unusual for Liberty.

He sensed an urgency about the day, as though something significant was going to happen. More than likely, Alex would be in the middle of it. And if she were…they would be too.

Alex was fast as quicksilver. Liberty knew this, so she obviously had a good jump on them. He also knew David was faster than Alex, barely. When the two of them raced, David would try to make it look easy but later admit to Liberty how hard he really had to work to beat her.

One more thing Liberty knew—he could scarcely run. Chronically weakened by his asthma and with the dry, dusty Kansas summer, it was nearly impossible for him to run very far.

This morning he tried, but David had to rate himself for his friend to keep up. It made Liberty feel bad that they had to slow their pace. "Go ahead, Dave. I'll catch up."

"No worries. What's she gonna do? Get beamed up or something? You know they'd have about two minutes of her and send her right back down." He shot a look back over his shoulder and grinned.

Liberty knew David's instinct would have been to go wide open until he was breathless, lungs burning and raw, to catch up with Alex and make sure she was okay. Nevertheless, his friend wouldn't leave him behind, and so the two boys jogged-walked, slowly, through the woods, allowing the gap that Alex had on them to widen as the morning went on. David was quieter now, and Liberty knew he was worried.

"Do you think she's okay?" David asked as the woods got deeper and they were forced to slow down to a walk.

"Why wouldn't she be?" he panted. "It's not like the aliens are going to come back for her. That would just be plain stupid since we've seen them and all." He tried to sound nonchalant as he added, "It wouldn't be the best choice on their part."

Truthfully, Liberty recognized the folly of thinking that Earth was all there was to the universe and intelligent life. He'd tried to talk to David and Alex about such things as the "God Particle" and "black matter," but they'd abandoned his lecture for a replay of *Christmas Vacation* on TV. He sincerely believed aliens *could* come and, perhaps, had come in the past. He was also not entirely convinced humanity would necessarily be kind to them when they did show up, given how easily humans tended to disrespect other earthbound species.

They carried along in silence again. Liberty was ready for a break, sweating and tired, and just about to complain about the backpack when they topped another wooded hill, the same hill that would drop them down into the hidden meadow.

"Are we there? I didn't realize we came so far yesterday."

"Yeah, just about."

Now they slowed even more and started to call Alex by name. Their voices echoed loudly down the valley, and the forest birds hushed in response. As they neared the bottom of the hill and closed in on the little meadow, they heard a screeching reply.

"Shut up you idiots! You're gonna disturb the peace already!"

Liberty smiled at Alex belting out her greeting loud enough for the whole world to hear. When they finally reached her, she was sitting cross-legged on a patch of dirt and absently chewing on a twig.

"How'd you know I'd be here?" she squinted at them when they came into view.

"Where else would you be? This was the spot where we quit looking for that corn snake you wanted." Liberty grinned, pretending like he didn't know why she'd really come back to this spot. "Figured we'd just start up where we left off."

She ignored him, glancing back at the meadow.

David plopped down next to her and wordlessly passed her a canteen.

She would be thirsty by now, and sure enough, Alex drank deeply before swiping her lips with the back of her hand and handing the canteen back.

Liberty wrestled out of his backpack, taking a seat on her other side. Pulling out the instant oatmeal packets, he handed one apple cinnamon to each of them. "Breakfast of champions," he said and tossed two handfuls of cheese puffs to Goo.

They ate silently, licking their fingers before dipping them back into the packets each time. Chewing until the dried oatmeal flakes became softer and easier to swallow, they savored the simple fare. They knew from experience that if they ate slowly enough, the oatmeal would swell nicely in their bellies, giving them a good, full feeling.

"So what are you two doing here?" Alex crinkled her empty packet before stuffing it into the front pocket of David's button down shirt, squinting into the sun as she peered up at him. The early light made the freckles on her nose stand out even more, and a few strands of hair escaped her rubber band, sticking in sweaty tendrils to her neck.

"Waiting," was all David said as he pulled the crumpled packet from his pocket and threw it at her head.

"Mmm-hmmfff," Liberty agreed, still chewing.

Then, they sat for a spell doing just that…waiting.

Nearly an hour later passed, and Goo snored, leaning heavily against Liberty's leg. David reclined on a grassy clump of dirt, his ball cap pulled down over his eyes.

"Look!" Alex suddenly exclaimed, loud enough to make them all jump.

David shot into a sitting position, and Liberty scrutinized a full circle around himself.

Goo opened one eye then shut it again. Evidently he was used to sudden, ridiculous outbursts from Alex.

Suddenly, Liberty's hair stuck out again, just a bit. Alex reached up to plaster it down with both hands, but back up it floated the second she let go. Silence settled over all three of them. This time, it wasn't funny at all. They sat stock-still, as though afraid to move

Liberty trembled a bit as the strange electric sensation from the day before returned. The familiar chilly breeze swept across them, and it gave all three goose bumps even though the day was already turning hot. Yet, there was no ship, no blue beacon or sleek orb descending upon them.

By then, Goo was bothered as well and leapt up, darting to the middle of the meadow where he proceeded to bark overhead at absolutely nothing.

Reaching out to David and Liberty, Alex clasped them by the hand with a hard grip that almost hurt Liberty.

They couldn't see it…but they knew the ship was back.

CHAPTER FOUR

Δ

Isara had wakened Blalok, hounding him mercilessly until he ultimately gave in and followed her to the bridge. She sunk into a levi-chair, cradling a fresh cup of tea with both hands. Pulling her legs up under herself, she blew the steam from the top of the mug. "Put *Star* into the atmosphere, where we were yesterday. I want to see the meadow."

"Quit bossing me. I haven't even had breakfast yet, and I know what you're thinking." He plopped into his own chair. "And don't you think we should tell Sartek?"

"It's reasonable; we still need to harvest. Might as well be the same spot."

"Might as well *not*," he replied wryly, maneuvering the ship out of orbit all the same and swinging it from the west, over North America. "You know what happened yesterday only complicated things, and now you're asking me to do something that could mess things up even worse."

He scowled at her. "And you're bossy in the morning, by the way."

Isara ignored him, taking a sip of her tea and peering instead at the forward screen. The graceful arc of nighttime receded in front of them as they soared from the Pacific Ocean east over the continent. It was midmorning in Kansas.

The *Star* swooped lower into the stratosphere of the beautiful planet, dropping to a cruising rate to match its rotation.

Isara played with the forward monitor controls for a bit, passing her fingers smoothly over them. The screen zoomed in and brought into view not just the continent but also the select region and few specific square miles of the small meadow.

Blalok glanced around to make certain Cleo wasn't nearby this time. The chakrat grinned, stomping her tiny, clawed feet in happy anticipation when she met her master's glance. She was sitting safely in her invisible kennel track.

"Good girl..." Blalok praised her then added under his breath, "Better than *Isara*."

Just then, Sartek walked onto the bridge. "We're not going back there!" he said with finality and took his seat in the captain's chair.

"Yes, we are," Isara countered immediately.

"No, we're not! It's too dangerous; there's no reason."

Blalok remained neutrally silent.

"Listen to me." Isara hopped up. "We have all the reason in the world to go back. If something happens, if we lose the *Star*, we need something else, someone else." She gestured toward the meadow, swinging her arm wide.

"We won't lose the *Star*!" Sartek argued. "It's not going to happen!"

"You don't know that! And if something does happens, what then, Sartek? What do we do then?" She stood with her hands on her hips. It made her look much older than her thirteen years.

Blalok started to open his mouth.

"And you shut up." She pointed, glaring at him.

He closed his mouth, watching the two thoughtfully. It made him edgy when Isara got like this. It usually meant she was going to be irrational, and he would lose the good fight. Logic would fly out the window, and a stronger force—one he couldn't explain or dispute—would be victorious.

"She's right," he stated flatly.

"I said..." Isara stopped, mouth open. "I am?" she asked cautiously.

Blalok spun around in his chair. "Yes...you are, even if you *are* obnoxious. And there is no denying that you are." He turned his attention directly to Sartek. "We don't know what this galaxy holds in store for us; we *can't* know. If something happens—and it is statistically only a matter of time before something does—we have no backup plan. It is unwise to be without one. Therefore...Isara is correct. We should go back."

"Our backup plan is that we get rescued! We continue to harvest until they find us!" Sartek jumped up, pacing, his dark locks swinging smoothly each time he spun about.

Blalok stepped out of his chair, walked over to Sartek, and looked earnestly up at him. Taking him by both arms, he stopped him, holding on as he spoke very seriously.

"Sartek, they will not find us. We can harvest forever…but they will *not*."

"Don't say that!" Sartek cried.

Blalok knew no one had ever said it out loud before but held firm.

"*No*, Sartek! It won't happen!"

"Blalok—" Isara began gently.

"No, Isara!" He shot her a glance over his shoulder. "It's true, and we all need to realize and accept this. They will not find us." He let go of Sartek and moved away, up several of the bridge steps so that he was more eye-to-eye with his friends.

They stared dumbly at him, obviously not sure what to say.

Blalok took a deep breath. "The technology to recreate the black plasma in the exact configuration that we were swept into does not exist. It would be like recreating the movement of an ocean, wave for wave, swell for swell, molecule for molecule, exactly as it had occurred at any specific moment."

His words were not meant to be unkind, but the terrible realization of what he was saying seemed to paralyze Isara and Sartek. Blalok glanced away, to the screen and the lifelike image of the little meadow. "Neither we nor those we left behind can re-create what happened to us. It would be like controlling the universe, atom per atom. That power doesn't exist. We are not Gods."

He focused on his friends again.

"We are lost, and there is no way back." His words fell flat and cruel, even though he didn't mean for them to be so.

Isara and Sartek had held onto a glimmer of hope, the smallest belief that something could be done to bring them home. Blalok, however, had all along believed, without a doubt, that there wasn't anything that could be done. In this way, he'd been the strongest of the three and just now decided they needed to hear the truth as well.

He stood very straight, shoulders back, as he swept an arm toward the screen. "The worlds we seek are our salvation now. This is our hope, our new destiny, like it or not." These were startling words, coming from a child so young.

Isara and Sartek stared at the awful truth.

Stepping down the steps, Blalok approached them, gazing kindly from one shocked expression to the other before settling on Sartek.

"It makes perfect sense to stack the odds in our favor. We could use a few allies. I'm sorry it is so unpleasant, but you needed to hear it." With that, he returned to his computer console to monitor the *Star*.

"Now, if you will excuse me, I have work to do."

Pained silence settled upon them as the awful reality of Blalok's analysis sunk in. No one could say what was worse: the awful truth that he'd just unleashed or the sobering way he'd laid it out.

Either way, it was like a bomb had gone off. Isara rested a trembling hand gently on Sartek's arm, her eyes tearing up. "Blalok's not always right." That in itself was seldom true, and they both knew that. "I still believe that—"

"*Don't.* Just…don't…" He shook his head violently, hands clenched, and turned away.

She blinked back tears, hands to her mouth.

It was just then that Blalok exclaimed, "Hey, look!"

Plastered across the main screen was the meadow they'd been harvesting in the day before, and on the edge of it rooted the small creature that followed the three Earthling children yesterday.

"It's a pet," Blalok said matter-of-factly.

Isara glared briefly at him. "Really…"

She moved closer to the 3-D screen as though she might step into it, as if that would help her see better. A mere instant later, the female Earthling came into view. The visual seemed as though she stood right below the bridge of the ship.

No one said anything. They were paralyzed as though if they moved she would disappear. The Earthling walked tentatively into the quiet meadow. She looked up…right *at* them.

The gesture was unnerving, and Sartek took an involuntary step back. "You don't think it can see us, do you? Like, I don't know, some sorta power or something?"

"You're stupid," was all Blalok offered.

Suddenly, and for no reason, the Earthling lifted a hand, waved gently, and then glanced around until she settled on a patch of clear ground. Flopping down onto the dirt, she crossed her legs as though intending to be there a while. She looked at the eastern sky and, without knowing it, right at the *Cerulean Star*, which hovered veiled, approximately twenty-three miles.

The small, four-legged animal continued to root around close by.

"What's it doing?" Sartek asked.

"It's digging around for something," Blalok answered.

"No, not the pet—the Earthling."

"*She*," Isara corrected. "It's a she."

"How do you know that?" Sartek asked.

"I concur," Blalok said, "That one appears decidedly female."

They watched the human girl, bringing the screen in close enough to observe the expressions on her face. She just sat scratching in the dirt with a stick, chin resting in her other hand as she chewed on a long blade of grass. All the while she gazed up at the sky. The animal, finally having identified all the nearby smells to its apparent satisfaction, came over and plopped down next to her, its back against her thigh, stubby legs sticking straight outward.

Sartek frowned. "That's just weird."

"I know, it's so *fat*," Blalok agreed.

"No, the way she's just waiting."

"Okay. So what now?" Isara asked.

"I don't know." Blalok continued to consider the scene below. "But I think we should communicate somehow. It would make sense to first study them, get a sense of their level of intelligence, their motivation for peace or war."

"They're kids, you said. I don't know many kids who wage war," Sartek remarked.

"Bettuan, maybe, but how many alien kids have you met? And obviously you've never read *The Kingdom of the Lost Ones*. In it, a troop of kids organize and—"

"She's not here for war," Isara said. "She's here because she knows we're here too." She moved to the navigation console and manipulated the controls until the *Star* started a slow and arcing descent over Missouri, toward the tiny corner of Kansas, sweeping ever closer to where the Earthling sat.

"Look, there!" Blalok pointed at the screen again.

The male Earthlings emerged from the woods, the taller, dark-haired one alongside the frail one with the skinny legs and white hair. They sat down, either side of the female, and appeared to share food and water with her.

"I think they're friends, like us," Sartek observed.

"Yes, and they look like they're waiting for something." Isara noted as the three Earthlings casually pondered the sky above them.

A half hour lapsed, and still the humans seemed unwilling to leave their spots. They were doing pretty much nothing. Occasionally they would gaze toward the sky, especially the female, and sometimes would lie back and shield their eyes with their hands.

The small creature with them would every so often rise and nose about the periphery a bit but always returned to the side of the white-haired one.

"Let's move in closer," Isara suggested.

Surprisingly, Sartek nodded his agreement. Blalok eased the *Star* even closer, slowly dipping into the meadow. As the ship neared, the smallest Earthling's fine, white hair started to stand on end. This time, the three below didn't appear nearly so taken with amusement.

Their fat, little pet roused and loped fiercely to the middle of the clearing. It looked up at absolutely nothing and started to bark, running in frenzied circles, apparently not willing to allow the sensations of the day before to visit them again. The Earthlings stood up at once and stepped closer to the clearing, though not leaving the safety of the tree line.

"What now?" Sartek asked.

"I'm going down," Isara announced and summoned a shift suit.

E-I complied, and within minutes, she was slickly outfitted in the suit.

"You can't!" Sartek insisted as she slipped it on. "You don't know what they'll do. They could be dangerous!"

She paused. "Yes, they could be. Or, they could be friendly. I choose to believe they will be friendly." She finished securing the suit, grabbed two translator rings, and moved toward the shape shifter.

"Wait, I'm going with you," Sartek said.

"No, you need to stay." Isara held a hand up at him. "If it does go poorly, Blalok will need you. The *Star* will need you."

It was true. There were certain traveling procedures that required at least two of them onboard. The *Cerulean Star* wasn't designed to be a solo-operated vessel, although it could be.

"She's right...again," Blalok added straight up.

"Will you *stop* saying that?" Sartek shot back, then refocused on Isara. "Then I'll go."

"Nope. It has to be me."

Sartek grabbed her by the arm gently. "How does that work? Explain that to me."

"I dreamed about her, Sartek. You know it has to be me."

This was a very meaningful thing for Isara to disclose. Her grandmother had been a "dreamer." Most Bettuan did not dream at all. There were a rare few, however, who did, and those dreams were significant, almost like prophecies. The trait frequently skipped a generation. Isara's mother did not dream, but Isara did.

Sartek and Blalok realized the gravity of what Isara shared. Sartek folded his arms across his chest, rubbed his eyes with his thumb and index finger, and shook his head. "Okay, you go. But the signal will be both hands up if you get into trouble. Three minutes and I bring you back, no exceptions." Then he added, "I wish we had a weapon."

The *Star* did have weapons but was never built as a tactical vessel. Most of the offensive mechanisms were *defensive* mechanisms, and fortunately, of these the vessel had many. In space, an assailant would have their work cut out for them trying to overrun the ship. Dry-docked, however, the *Star* was vulnerable. Even worse, off the *Star* the Bettuan children were woefully unprotected.

"I'm going with the intention of establishing communication," Isara scoffed. "A weapon would seem to defeat that purpose, don't you think?"

"I'll suck you back in a heartbeat if you get into a fix," Blalok assured her. "Trust me. Years of playing *Frigate Brigade* will not go to waste!"

Isara smiled weakly at that. There was no doubt that Blalok was as good as his word. "Just keep an eye out." She snugged the catch at the throat of her suit and gathered up two translation rings before stepping into the shift module.

She and Sartek exchanged nervous glances.

"I'll be okay; *we'll* be okay. This is the right thing to do," Isara murmured. Then, she was enveloped in a swirling sheet of light.

Seconds later, she was gone.

CHAPTER FIVE

Δ

The vapidation increased to an intensity even greater than yesterday. The musical electricity seemed to bathe them all over, and even David's thick, black hair stood on end. Goo was going nuts, barking and running in crazy loops in the middle of the meadow.

The three never saw the vessel as the *Star* never did unveil. What they saw, instead, was a small, upright form that slowly appeared as an oily shadow above the grass, down farther in the meadow.

David blinked hard like his eyes were playing tricks on him. Alex stood frozen, her mouth hanging clean open. Liberty clutched her arm like a vise without even realizing.

The oily form slipped and shimmered, eventually solidifying into a silvery glow, then settled gently onto the ground, flashing brilliantly as it took its final shape.

Goo quit barking and sprinted to a safe position behind Liberty's leg.

What they saw left them speechless. Well, mostly speechless as Liberty mumbled, "I'll be a monkey's uncle."

"Shh!" Alex scolded as the alien walked carefully through the meadow toward them. "It's our first impression. Be polite!"

The creature moved with an otherworldly elegance, parting the grass gently with its hands as it approached. Finally, it stopped directly in front of them. It made no attempt to advance or retreat; just stood there.

David then took what Alex said to heart and blurted, "Hi. He's not really a monkey; he's a Huh-*yooo*-man."

"Oh, for Christ's...David, shut up!" Alex hissed and turned swiftly back to the creature before doing a half curtsey, half bow.

"Way to impress them." David rolled his eyes. "'Cuz *that's* a real human custom they're likely to see a lot."

Alex ignored him, addressing the creature instead.

"Hi there. We're...humans."

"Slick," David quipped.

The alien tilted its head to the side in a peculiar way, as though to hear them better. It was hard to read the expression on its face. Liberty had never seen anything like it before. *No one* had ever seen anything like it before.

With the midday sun filtering down through the forest leaves, the alien's features were very obvious. Its ears were close to the sides of the creature's head, streamlined against the skin, which was the palest lime green—smooth as the pretty little catfish Alex spared the day before. Large, dark eyes—a glistening turquoise—flashed at them. There were no lashes, but a paler green lid blinked only rarely because a second, clear eyelid covered the eye as well. The pupils were shaped like cat's eyes and narrowed very effectively in the bright light of the meadow.

Its nose was longish and flat, the mouth finely shaped, small and delicate, and it had very thin lips. Hair hung down, charcoal gray in heavy, slick strands, each almost as thick as a pencil. It glistened iridescent and was blunt, all the same length at the shoulders, and appeared wet. And the strands swayed all together in a weird way when the alien moved.

The creature was tall, almost as tall as David, lithe and much leaner, but gave the appearance of subtle strength. "It's...beautiful," Alex murmured.

The alien appeared comfortable standing on terra firma and reached a hand gracefully up to touch a small device in its ear. Then it spoke, murmuring something in a voice that was music-like and unintelligible. It spoke as though to itself.

In its other hand, it held a looped, round device, delicate and wire-like, with no obvious opening. The alien also wore one of these loop devices around its neck. Shining a deep, rich orange, the ring swirled and ran in rivulets, like living copper, as it lay smooth against the green skin and delicate bone structure of the alien's neck.

The creature spoke again, in that song-like voice, looking slowly back and forth between the three before settling its stare firmly on Alex. Then it did a remarkable thing. It took a step forward and held the device out to her.

"No!" David took a step toward Alex.

The alien glanced at him briefly, its brilliant eyes flashing, before returning its attention to its chosen human.

Alex started to tremble as she reached out to take the device from the pale hand of the alien. Liberty noticed, as the alien released the ring, the fine, almost transparent webbing between its fingers—five of them, just like them.

Holding the ring loosely in one hand, Alex said, "I-I don't know…" She didn't know how to unlatch the device.

The alien gestured with both hands for her to pull firmly, anywhere on the ring.

Alex did just that, and the ring separated.

"Alex, what are you doing?" David exclaimed as she started to slide the device up and around her neck. "You don't know what that thing is!" He reached out to stop her, but it was too late. The device was looped around her neck before anything could be done. The ring appeared to move of its own accord and sealed itself with no obvious evidence of a catch. David let go of her arm and stepped back but focused on the alien.

"Please…don't hurt her."

The ring hung down like a fine choker necklace, cool and smooth beneath the collar of her *This is what awesome looks like* T-shirt. Instantly, Alex's body went rigid. If she could speak, she would have told them that her head felt lighter, as though weightless upon her shoulders. Her eyes flew wide, and her mouth fell open into a silent *"Oh"*. She remained like this, hands clenched at her sides.

* * *

"Don't worry; it's only temporary, while you adjust," the creature spoke clearly and softly with that same singsong voice.

It spoke the truth; the effect diminished almost immediately.

"You understand me." Alex reached up to run her fingers along the smooth loop around her neck.

"Now I do. It's a universal translator. I couldn't be certain it would work for you, so I'm pleased that it did."

Alex asked, "Can they?"

"No. Only you can. I chose to give the translator to you."

"Oh, I see." Then Alex's face brightened. "I'm Alex. This is David, and this is Bert." She indicated her friends in turn.

"And that's Goo. Well, Magoo, really, but we just call him Goo."

The alien took all of this in with a slow blink of its eyes before replying, "I am Isara. I am from Bettua."

"Isara," Alex murmured the name out loud. She couldn't take her eyes off of the visitor, and finally, in pure Alex style, she cut straight to the matter at hand. "Why'd you come back?"

The alien appeared to give this question very thoughtful consideration, pausing before she replied. "I don't know, exactly." There was another long pause before she said, "I think we were meant to meet." She gestured with an outstretched hand, sweeping toward Liberty and David as well.

"Destiny!" Alex announced and grinned widely. "Yes!"

"Hmmm, Blalok would call it that." The creature shrugged. "Or a logical decision."

"Blalok?" Alex looked Isara up and down, their height nearly similar. "Are you a kid? Is he a kid?"

Isara's head tipped delicately to one side, and she paused as though to compose an explanation. "We are...juveniles."

"What do you mean, juveniles? Cuz we're kids." She motioned to David and Liberty.

The two boys remained rooted where they stood, thoroughly mesmerized by the interchange between Alex and the alien. They were only able to understand half the conversation and had to conjecture what the alien's replies were.

"Where's all the grown-ups?" Alex looked up as though she might see them any second.

Isara seemed a small bit uncomfortable and never did reply, for as she opened her mouth to answer, she slipped away into the silvery shimmer of a few minutes before and disappeared.

"Wait!" Alex grasped at the empty space. "Wait! Come back!" she called again, her hand outstretched as though she might pull the alien out of thin air.

The static in the air slowly diminished until the three humans felt alone once more.

* * *

Goo remained crouched beneath a nearby bush, nose on his paws, as though that would be the most prudent spot to wait this silliness out.

He didn't seem at all pleased by the recent return of the strange sensations that likely played havoc with his sensitive doggy ears.

"What happened?" Liberty and David asked Alex, both at once.

"They're aliens—kids!" she blurted out.

"And I think that one's a girl, but maybe she got in trouble and the grown-ups sucked her back!" Alex talked so fast it was hard to keep up with her.

"Whoa! Whoa, slow down!" David held both hands up.

"Kids," Liberty asked, "like us?"

"Yeah! Like us!" Alex exclaimed, hardly able to control her excitement. "At least I think they're kids. She, Isara, called herself a juvenile."

"Her name is Isara?" Liberty was completely awestruck.

"Yeah, I asked her where the grown-ups were, and that seemed to set her on edge." Alex flipped her hands, palms up. "That's when she disappeared."

"Is that how you talked to her?" He pointed at the ring still hanging around Alex's neck.

"Yeah. When I slipped it on, I could understand her just fine." Alex pulled the ring from her neck. It took a bit of tension, but ultimately the invisible fastener unhinged, and it came loose in her hands. She ran her fingers over the soft, smooth object before handing it to Liberty.

Bert turned the ring over in his hands. It was warm and sleek—smooth like velvet but also hard and shiny like gold, only he doubted it was. The color was almost transparent, a rich amber, like honey, and the device appeared to give off light of its own accord.

"I wonder why she left?" he murmured, looking back to the spot where Isara had vanished.

* * *

On board the *Star*, a similar conversation was taking place as Sartek and Blalok watched the smallest human fumble with the translator ring.

What the human with the white hair didn't know was that the metal wasn't only uncommon, it was *very* uncommon. The metal was mined from Bitta, sister planet to Bettua. There is little else on Bitta; it's virtually a big rock of solid ore and had become exclusively a mining planet. The ore is called Vasteen, and besides being very light, like titanium, it's nearly fourteen times as strong. Vasteen is also the primary component of the *Star* beneath the Helium outer shell, and the Rayze would kill for it, in a heartbeat.

Millions had succumbed to the vicious efforts of the Rayze to control mining of Bitta.

"They're juveniles, just like us!" Isara announced excitedly.

"No, they're *not* like us," Sartek stabbed at the screen. "They're aliens."

"Technically, you are incorrect," Blalok interrupted. "That statement can only be accurately made for their perception of us. We are the intruders; we've intruded upon their galaxy, and home."

Sartek paused. In the nearly two years they'd been lost, he'd never thought of himself as an outsider—as not belonging. He more considered himself an unlikely visitor bent on finding his way home. Until now, the rest of the universe was the uninvited one, and he was the victim.

"Huh…" he muttered thoughtfully. "That's true enough, I guess."

Sartek was the most headstrong of the three. His stubborn streak sometimes created obstacles but more often lent itself to uncommon tenacity, and Isara and Blalok naturally looked to him for leadership. The three were, most of the time, perfect together. They probably never thought of it this way, but Blalok, with his exceptional and sometimes tiresome intellect, Isara with her uncanny intuition, and Sartek with his leadership made for a perfect star-hopping team. And their unbending friendship had helped hold them together through the devastating past couple of years. This is what gave them good direction now.

"Okay, so they're like us, sort of. What next?" Sartek asked.

"I think we should go back down, two of us maybe, and spend a little more time with them," Isara suggested. "It just makes good sense to develop this first contact."

"Count me out," Blalok stated with finality. "Don't get me wrong. I agree; one of us needs to establish further contact. Just…not me. I'm best qualified to mind the ship."

"Fair enough," Isara agreed. Then, to Sartek, "So, back down we go?"

"Yes." He glanced at Blalok. "But keep the *Star* over the meadow. We'll walk to the tree line. If something happens, get out of here as fast as you can. Agreed?"

"I will monitor you closely the entire time," Blalok promised. "And try not to do anything stupid."

Sartek glared at him, slipped into the shift suit, and stepped toward the shift module with Isara.

Seconds later, two images shimmered into shape in the center of the clearing.

If Isara appeared tall and thin, Sartek was her counter image—taller and athletic. As it would turn out, he and David would stand exactly eye-to-eye, well, on most things anyway.

The two aliens glanced about, shielding their eyes from the bright sun before noticing the humans lingering on the fringe of the trees. They walked toward them.

* * *

The visitors carried two more rings. David and Liberty exchanged nervous glances. Alex had already taken her ring back from Liberty and hastily slipped the device on when she saw the aliens rematerialize.

The Bettuan walked straight up to them and immediately held the additional rings out to Liberty and David. Liberty took a collar from Isara and bobbed his head dumbly, a big grin on his face. He was astounded by the reality of standing before an alien lifeform and was entirely captivated by her. Try as he may, however, he was unable to read the female's reaction. She seemed reserved, perhaps, but he wasn't sure.

He slipped the collar on, pulling it apart as he'd seen Alex do, and instantly experienced the same effect that she had earlier, only he staggered as a result of it.

Alex reached out and grabbed him by the elbow.

"You okay?" she asked softly.

"Yeah, just lost my footing there for a sec." Liberty wasn't what most would consider coordinated. Physical tasks were always just that, tasks, and phys-ed at school was no education at all, only a ridiculous exercise in brutality. That didn't matter anymore, though. David and Alex would always be there to bolster him up.

Even so, Isara's eyes narrowed. "Are you sure you're all right, *Liberty*?"

That was, he thought, the most beautiful word he'd ever heard spoken. The alien murmured his name in such an eloquent way that his heart felt suddenly very full. All he was able to do was nod dumbly.

Meanwhile, David accepted a collar from Sartek, staring long and defiantly at the male alien's face. He was larger than the female, his eyes a darker and more brilliant emerald green. The strands of his hair were thicker, and there was an obvious, serrated ridge that ran from his forehead, up and over the crest of his head—something the female did not have.

Sartek met David's gaze clearly and fearlessly, holding onto the ring a few seconds longer than was perhaps necessary before releasing it to the human. This was a good moment, a strong moment, and David nodded with a glimmer of a smile when Sartek finally let go. Without breaking eye contact, he lifted the ring up toward Sartek's face as though to say, "I'm doing this because I want to, not because you want me to."

"Why do you hafta' be so stubborn all the time?" Alex elbowed David.

This might have amused David, except that just then, as he slipped the ring onto his neck, he immediately became too rigid and disoriented to reply. He also appeared to be trying hard not to piss his pants, his body assuming the universal "I gotta pee" cross-legged semi-squat as the translator equilibrated to his system. Finally, he managed to right himself.

"Son of a…"

Now something astonishing happened. As the temporary sensation of adjustment to the collars passed, the children, worlds apart, came together in an unlikely and wondrous instant.

Alex was the first to speak. She gazed calmly between the two visitors before asking straight up, "There aren't any grown-ups, are there. Up on your ship, I mean."

Sartek seemed surprised, and Isara glanced nervously at him before taking the initiative to answer, "No, there are not." Silence filled the awkward space left by her response.

Liberty considered what Isara said very carefully, recognizing that the five of them had something in common—something sadly and wondrously in common. The visitors had *chosen* them; there was a design to their meeting. This brought to mind Alex's birthday and—.

"Yesterday was my birthday," she offered abruptly, as though reading his mind.

Isara and Sartek appeared to contemplate the significance of this.

"Hi, I'm Liberty." He shook his head toward Alex. "She's thirteen now. David is too, almost. I'm still eleven." He was suddenly just a small bit embarrassed that he'd shared that.

"We are thirteen," Isara replied immediately. She seemed mildly confused about the importance of establishing their ages but then dismissed it as though deciding this might simply be a tradition.

Sartek remained noticeably quiet; so did David.

Isara added, "There are three of us. Our ship, the *Cerulean Star*, is here."

She gestured, sweeping softly with one hand behind her.

"Where?" Liberty was suddenly very curious.

"It's farther down in the meadow, about fifteen meters up. It's veiled." She explained this as though it should be obvious.

"Sweet! A cloaking device!" Liberty stepped happily into full-fledged nerd mode.

The two aliens nearly smiled.

"You're not here because you want to be, are you?" David asked, very seriously.

All fell silent, and the awkwardness lingered.

Sartek spoke for the first time. "No, we're not." His voice was also very musical, but not singsong like Isara's. It was more like the echo of wind in a canyon.

Isara regarded him sharply before answering for Sartek. "We were in a…" She hesitated. "An accident—an *event* of sorts. It's placed us in your galaxy." She glanced at Sartek, who nodded gently. "We don't know how to get home." She scuffed the toe of her boot in the dry grass—a very human gesture.

David, Liberty, and Alex said nothing. There was little likelihood that Isara and Sartek realized how completely their new companions *did* understand their dilemma.

"I was in an accident too," Liberty said, "so were they…kinda." He motioned with a hooked thumb toward his friends. "We can't get back either."

Whether David and Alex comprehended what Liberty was trying to say was uncertain, but it was a pivotal statement and seemed to genuinely surprise the Bettuan. Isara and Sartek glanced at each other again.

Liberty thought all of them, all at once, shared an expression of relief. Yes, that was exactly it! And nothing in his life ever felt so right to him as this moment did, with the five of them standing on the edge of this meadow, speaking their first words of acquaintance. This was no accident. This was destiny!

The feeling lingered in a perfect way, warm and safe, and Liberty was convinced it must be so for the rest of them as well. And of this, he was fairly spot on.

Just like that, a human-Bettuan connection was born. This was perhaps the most extraordinary event to happen on Earth, *ever*.

It was also very short-lived.

* * *

The stealth modified *AH-64 Apache helicopters* swooped swiftly over the trees and down into the meadow like a swarm of angry bees. Their blades chopped the air like woofing dogs, and there were so many, so fast, that within seconds they dotted the sky above and around where the *Cerulean Star* remained veiled. Without the knowledge that the ship hovered just ahead, impact was imminent.

The episode of the afternoon before, when Cleo inadvertently unveiled the *Star*, had not gone unnoticed as the children first believed. On the contrary, it had been intercepted by the military as an energy blip that wasn't identified as familiar on any count.

As a matter of fact, it was critically unfamiliar—not remotely identifiable as covert military chatter from a non-ally, and neither had any meteor of significant size been charted entering the atmosphere. Nor had there been any seismic activity to explain the energy disturbance that was intercepted by the government space-watch agency the day before.

The brief unveiling of the *Cerulean Star* was noticed by several very great powers, though none of the kids were aware of this.

Meanwhile, aboard the *Star*, Blalok was completely engrossed as he intently followed the engagement below. He recorded the vital first-contact between Sartek, Isara, and the Earthlings believing this initial acquaintance could carry significant historical import. Consequently, he wanted to capture the meeting accurately, even though, truthfully, he was most intrigued with the smallest one—the one with the strange hair.

As a matter of record, Blalok could hear the translated conversation from below, and was so utterly engaged that it simply hadn't occurred to him the *Star* might be suddenly approached and vulnerable from an alternate direction. This was very unlike Blalok, but he was, after all, only twelve years old and susceptible to a rare lapse. And this lapse, at this particular moment, was his rarest, best, worst one ever.

The aft sensors picked up the swarm of helicopters, but the *Star* hadn't interpreted this as a problem until the mass of them approached at such a rapid rate, directly toward the ship.

When planet-side, and in space for that matter, there are many such objects—insects and birds for example—that approach the shields of the *Star* almost continuously.

These creatures are ordinarily gently diverted, and little harm is hardly ever done to them, other than mild surprise.

However, as the helicopters drew so swiftly near and their mass was calculated and interpreted by the *Star*'s sensors as non-organic and significant in size, it was quickly determined that their velocity created a much different probable outcome for them than a mere flock of birds. Consequently, the *Star*'s computer decided the impact would be perilous, not for the ship, but for the approaching objects.

As E-I made this determination in less than a nano-second, he informed Blalok of the impending collision just about as fast.

Taken entirely by surprise, Blalok berated himself for his recklessness.

"Spawn of a mud-sucking leech!"

Jumping into action, he demanded, "Analysis, *now!*"

"Impact imminent," E-I advised without hesitation.

Blalok knew immediately what E-I meant. There were two possible scenarios for the helicopters. He could do nothing, and if the flying objects hit the shields with such force, they would be instantly reduced to particulate matter, just as a meteor might.

Maneuvering away from the swarm was also very complicated, for the airspace directly above had been so immediately cut off by the helicopters that liftoff would most certainly result in shield absorption of one, if not several, of them.

Even if the *Star* attempted a slow ascent, the peripheral shields would immobilize the nearest helicopters as they were manipulated to the edge of the shield margins. This would undeniably result in terminal trauma to the much smaller, more fragile vessels, and the creatures within, as their flying mechanisms would become critically disabled. Then they would be left to the cruel effect of the planet's gravity, plummeting to the Earth and their certain doom.

Lastly, escaping lower and across the meadow was also out of the question, for the air was thickly dotted at various levels with the mob of flying hellicraft, and ground vehicles were rapidly moving in.

With complete calm and insight, Blalok reacted as any Bettuan should but few would be so straightaway capable of. He refused to endanger the less sophisticated Earthlings, even without knowing whether or not they were hostile. This was called "principal fiat" on Bettua. *Harm no other.*

This very young Bettuan was a scientist first, and despite his tender years, would never compromise his scientific integrity. Blalok realized he, Isara, and Sartek were the visitors on this developing planet. Consequently, Earth deserved to evolve without meddling and interference from the outside, even if that meant the ultimate sacrifice of their ship.

It was a very clear and defined moment for him as he made an insanely critical decision. Blalok…unveiled the *Star.*

This was very bad for them but also very good for the humans. The closest Apache helicopter, which was just about to collide with the *Cerulean Star*'s aft force field, veered abruptly away.

Instead of being absorbed and disintegrated into a billion tiny bits that would fall harmlessly away from the ship, the helicopter shuddered, shaking horribly in the effects of a distal margin of the *Star*'s energy field.

The Apache's massive blades buffeted wildly up and down, and the little vessel careened back and forth. After a terrifying span of what seemed like forever, the craft finally righted itself and backed away.

All the hellicraft stopped right where they were, as though suspended like so many black origami cranes. They hovered motionless for only a second before moving to quickly surround the *Star.* Almost instantly, suspension cables were being dragged over and around the alien ship.

"*Great,*" Blalok muttered to himself as chaos ensued.

He ran his hands like lightening over the main control console and shut the *Star* down completely.

The elegant blue ship flashed briefly, brilliantly, and lost all of its exquisite detail at once. What had been the stunning, jaw-dropping shape of a drop of water about to fall from a leaf disappeared, instantly replaced with an amorphous orb. Gone were the luminescent stripes that radiated and ran the length of it, like on the belly of a great whale. The *Star* was strangely transformed as it sank into drone mode. It was then, for all practical purposes, hibernating.

Losing all form, the ship became a floating, glowing Mentos Mint, with no obvious front or back and, most critically, no access point. But, that meant another thing—people or aliens could no longer be shifted.

* * *

Below, standing on the edge of the meadow in the tree line, Isara and Sartek watched helplessly the sudden paralyzing turn of events. Sartek gasped, an expression of horror on his face.

Isara let go a stricken sob.

Naturally, they both turned to run back to their ship.

It was Liberty who first recognized the horrible disaster of it all. He knew what the swarm of helicopters meant and what a terrible turn of events this was for Isara and Sartek. Shamefully, should they be captured, the Bettuan would never see their beautiful ship, or the light of day…again. That was a nasty pill to swallow—the *truth*.

Liberty was an accomplished, self-taught student of military and government conspiracy theories, and he pulled on his greatest resource and instinct to step in just now. Leaping into the edge of the clearing, he lunged forward, grabbing Sartek by the arm.

"No!" he yelled sharply enough to make Isara and Sartek hesitate. He was surprised at how strong the alien male's arm felt in his hand, but held on tight.

"No, don't! Sartek, *don't* go out there."

"Get off me!" Sartek, eyes flashing wide and terrified, yanked his arm free. "You betrayed us!"

"Please don't go out there. They'll *kill* you!" Alex pleaded with him.

The alien staggered to a stop as though not fully comprehending what the humans were saying. Just then, at this critical and awful moment, it was David who did something both reckless and brilliant.

Quite suddenly, he sprinted away, faster than he'd ever run in his life—as fast as his legs would carry him. Straight out into the meadow David ran, directly beneath the white blob that was now the hibernating alien ship.

Liberty, Alex, Isara, and Sartek stared, slack-jawed, as they watched David wave his arms violently at the sickening invasion of Apache helicopters that were, by now, entirely swarming the glowing, white disc.

"Hey! Hey, you up there! I'm an alien! I'm an alien!" He screamed at the top of his lungs and bolted for the far side of the meadow, drawing attention away from the other four.

"He's insane!" Alex choked out and started to stumble after him.

"He's awesome," Liberty shot back, grabbing her arm before she could follow David. Liberty recognized the brilliance of his sacrifice, and David was, in that instant, a bonafide hero to him. He would have given anything to be that brave, at least once in his life.

"Now come on, before it's all for nothing!"

Liberty dragged Alex back with him.

What David did was a bold and foolish move. It also had the desired affect in a superb way.

All military attention was instantly focused on not only the spaceship but also the dark-haired creature zigzagging toward the opposite woods. Every Apache helicopter redirected its nose toward the new target. After all, he *could* be an alien.

Now, at last recognizing David's strategy, Alex grabbed Isara by the hand and yanked her roughly back into the deeper cover of the woods. "C'mon! This way, hurry!" She gestured frantically for them all to follow.

Goo was already gone, paving the way. *I love you, but not that much.*

Liberty, running after him, cautioned, "Stay under cover! We've got to get out of here, before they bring out heat-seekers!"

"But, the *Star*!" Sartek cried.

"You can't!" Liberty said urgently. "You don't look human. If they see you, they'll shoot you; or they'll capture you. Either way, you'll never stand a chance!"

"They would kill us? How do you know this?" Isara eyes were wide with terror at the dawning realization of this wretched side of human nature.

"He's brilliant," Alex shot quickly. "If he says something's true, chances are it is."

The Apaches were so nearby Liberty could feel the thump-thump of the rotors in his chest. He'd never been that close to a powered up military helicopter, and thought it an awful, unnatural sound as though they would be overcome and shredded to bits at any moment.

He threaded his way through the forest. "C'mon. We have a safe place. We can hide out and figure out what to do next."

"But your friend?" Sartek wondered.

"Yeah. That seriously blows, but David'll be okay. Don't worry. At least, he *does* look human. Chances are they won't shoot him." Really, Liberty wasn't at all sure this was the case.

When Alex shot him a look, he added, "They'll hold him, but then they'll have to release him. He'll find his way to us; I'll make sure of that." To Alex, he whispered, "That was really brave of him, by the way."

She nodded, but her expression said she wasn't entirely convinced.

In truth, Liberty realized that he might never see David again, but now wasn't the time to think about this. There were more pressing matters at hand; they could still hear the buffeting of the helicopters' blades.

They snuck away as fast as they could.

Alex was quieter than usual, and as the helicopter sounds became more muted, Liberty frowned. He knew it was her nature to be more critical of David, perhaps as a means of keeping herself from admitting how much she truly cared. Liberty knew she loved them both, only with David she was…different.

Alex was obviously struggling to control a total freak out. Liberty had seen this happen only a few times before but had been so impressed by it that he had come to know the symptoms. And, the present situation was the perfect storm. After all, it was Alex who'd negotiated the re-connect with two aliens, and because of this David was suddenly and perilously gone. She'd come to the meadow today specifically for this—well, maybe not *this*, but there was no way she couldn't feel some responsibility for whatever happened now.

Yep, Liberty figured that would be just about enough to put Alex over the edge. Only now wasn't the time to deal with that either.

The best thing to do was run…*fast*.

"Hurry, Al," Liberty panted, short of breath "You're faster than me, take them with you and go. I'll catch up." Even Goo struggled to keep up, running his doggie heart out.

"No! Bert, I—"

"You have to! You gotta get 'em to the cave, else we're all screwed!" Liberty needed to concentrate on them, yet all he could think about was David sprinting like an Olympian across the meadow. It made him smile to think his friend just might give the soldiers a decent run for their money. Nobody at school came even close to catching David in P.E. if he got the ball. It was a done deal as far as anyone was concerned.

"I'm not leaving you!" Alex bolted ahead, still in the lead but refusing to desert him.

By the grace of mother luck—Liberty always said that it was better to be lucky than good—they *weren't* discovered, and they snaked their way urgently through the sweltering, mid-day woods.

Alex and Isara ran very fast, Alex clutching Isara's hand at intervals as they went. When Liberty started to fall behind, Sartek snagged him and charged along after the girls, literally dragging the much smaller human boy through the dense little forest.

"You're really strong," Liberty said, breathlessly, as the alien male yanked him along at breakneck speed.

Sartek said nothing as their feet pounded the dry forest floor. In truth, Sartek's wordless efforts at making sure Liberty kept up reminded him painfully of David. *This was something David would do.*

Tripping, falling down, scrambling back up, and launching onward, their flight seemed as though it went on forever. At any time they could be discovered and caught, the helicopters would swoop overhead to spotlight them, just like in the movies. This was an awful feeling, like when Liberty couldn't run up the unlit stairs fast enough as he imagined Jack the Ripper on his heels, only this time the stairs never ended.

They ran harder than they'd ever run before, Alex leading the way. Even Isara could barely keep up with her at times. Sartek held strong onto Bert's hand, almost crushing it as he dragged him along. Liberty's heart raced, partly from the run but mostly from the fear of being caught. He tried hard not to think about the ship and the friend he'd left behind.

And just when he thought he could endure no more, thought he would fall and they'd have to leave him, they miraculously reached the cave.

CHAPTER SIX

Δ

When David sprinted across the field, his intent had been to attract enough attention away from his friends to have the Apaches come for him instead. He knew Liberty would recognize his strategy immediately. Then he thought Alex would realize it only an instant later, because, well, she would worry about *him* first. This made him feel oddly happy for just a second.

Long gone into the forest, the others could not know David's final fate. Their flight didn't allow them to see what happened next.

As David ran, the *Cerulean Star* slipped from hibernation mode just briefly enough to engulf the sprinting boy in a shift beam. There was the *Star* in all her glory, magnificent in its true form. Then, in mid-stride, David shimmered and disappeared, right in front of the *U.S. Government Navy Seals Squad Twelve*.

David was still running like a hell-bat on fire when he was snapped up by the shift beam and deposited onto the bridge of the *Star* in an upright pool of something akin to shimmering Jell-O.

When his form solidified, he lurched forward, nearly face-planting. He flailed about, arms pin-wheeling before catching his balance. Staggering a last step, he stood with his feet wide, hands straight out to his sides to steady himself.

"*Whoa...*" He exhaled deeply.

The sensation was incredible. Later, he would compare it to the almost asleep feeling, when his body was oddly detached and his muscles would jerk in bed like he was an idiot. If you could imagine it happening while trying to float in ginger ale, you might understand what *shifting* felt like.

For now, he gazed about slowly, eyes as big as, well, flying saucers.

The bridge of the *Cerulean Star* was like nothing he'd ever seen or imagined, and certainly not like any sci-fi movie he'd ever watched.

As he looked cautiously about, his very first thought was that he wished Bert were there to see it with him. This was, without a doubt, the coolest thing he'd ever seen, and he'd just had his first look at an *alien* only minutes before!

Everything was varying shades of green or blue and seemed to have a biotic life to it. The console surfaces glowed gently and the toggles were not sharp and black at all. They had the appearance of being soft, as though they would move in a pleasing way if you touched them, like a soft cooked egg. They were exclusively round or oblong in shape, and shimmered a luminescent white. The chairs, if you could call them that, were smooth and vaporous, and they floated.

Demanding immediate attention was the enormous forward screen. It appeared wet, like a fish tank only without the glass, and wrapped half way around the bridge. The images displayed on it were not two-dimensional; they were three, presenting a vivid depth as though David was looking right out of a window. It made the scene raining down on them seem even more terrible.

David slowly righted himself and dropped his hands to his sides. He was still recovering from the weird, bathing in seltzer sensation of space shifting when he noticed someone sitting in one of the chairs.

He squinted. This was obviously another alien, only…different.

The two just gazed at each other without saying anything.

"H'lo," David offered awkwardly as he tried to plaster a friendly expression on his face.

This alien resembled the other two; there was no doubt it was the same species, but he—David decided immediately it was male—was much smaller than the others.

The alien's eyes, however, were larger. And this one, despite his slighter stature, had a more calculated look about him. Ridges crested from over the top of his head and down the back of his neck, barely separating the smooth black ropes of hair. There had been ridges on the other male Bettuan, the one below—Sartek he'd called himself—but they were not as evident on this one. Like the others, this alien's skin was pale, lime green, and smooth.

The alien just stared at him then swung around in his chair, his back again to David. He said something unintelligible, as though to somebody else, and a translation ring materialized out of nowhere on the counter.

The alien reached over, slipped the device around his neck, and turned back to David with a demeanor that could only be described as nonchalant.

On the screen behind him swarmed pandemonium as the angry Apache helicopters jockeyed for strategic positions. The network of cables that now draped the *Star* were horribly visible, like fine, black slices across the screen. All the while, the alien seemed fairly unaffected by it.

"I'm sorry; you were saying?" the smallest alien asked almost politely.

David's hand went up to his own translation ring, still around his neck. "Hey," was all he said, his eyes darting back and forth between the alien and the screen.

The alien hesitated then followed his visitor's lead. "*Heeey,*" he said, dragging the word out in a weird way. After another awkward moment, he added, "Well, now that we have that out of the way…."

The comment came across as flippant, although David wasn't sure that was really the intention. He countered, "Well, so not all aliens are tall then."

It didn't really have the desired effect on this particular alien. It was a lost stab at gentle sarcasm, and fell "…flat as a pancake under Roxy's ass," Alex had said once. David couldn't know that this alien was literal—exceedingly literal.

The Bettuan simply blinked, expression unchanged. "I am one point three meters tall. The average height of my species at age twelve, *my* age, is one point five three nine meters tall."

David just stared at him.

"Yes. I'm shorter than most. Is that pertinent to your data?"

"You remind me of someone."

"Excuse me?"

"Nothing, never mind." He indicated the screen. "We have a problem, Houston."

"Blalok," he corrected him, missing the joke entirely. "My name is Blalok—not Houston." He shot a brief look back over his shoulder at the screen. "But, you are correct. We do have a problem."

Blalok swung around to face the screen but peered sideways, studying his human visitor closely. "It was reasonable to bring you aboard. I was monitoring your conversation below, and I recognize that you are not an aggressor." He gestured toward the screen. "It remains to be seen regarding *them*, however."

David grinned. Blalok *did* remind him of Bert, if Bert suddenly had an attitude, but the urgency of the moment erased the smile on his face, and he stepped closer to the alien.

He tried to sound convincing. "Those aren't friends, Blalok. That's the military, and we're in serious trouble. I swear I didn't know this was going to happen."

"Hmmm, yes, I've determined that." He shot a glance at David. "What you did down there; it was very...logical."

David thought he was going to say "brave." In essence, he had.

"My name's David."

Blalok gave him what could only be a wry expression. "I've already gathered that from your introductions below." He brushed the opener aside, focusing instead on manipulating his controls. "We need to observe, gather data. Then we can formulate a plan."

He indicated the levi-chair next to him.

David, still not certain what to make of his unusual host, eased into the chair. His eyes shot open with surprise when it conformed to him, supporting him evenly from every angle. It moved like a second skin, supplying a temperature to match his own, and there were no apparent pressure points. "Nice!" he exclaimed. "Sweet ride!" He spun the chair in a complete three-sixty. "Wish I had one of these for gaming!"

Blalok demeanor was somewhat suspicious. "You are a gamer?"

"Yep, love it. I don't have a system or anything, but it's awesome. You've gotta meet Bert, though. He's the best, *owns* it, especially quests. I like first person shooters better though." David thought this may have amused the alien, but he wasn't sure.

Blalok nodded, barely. "The white haired one, I would have guessed that," he murmured, perhaps more to himself than to David. Then, as though having forgotten protocol entirely, he blurted, "I am pleased to make your acquaintance."

"Me too!" David exclaimed, shoving a hand out to shake.

Pausing, both hands still on the controls, Blalok only stared at David's outstretched hand. He shrugged and shoved one of his own smaller hands out toward the human, but neglected to grasp and shake, just left it hanging in the air for a half-second.

David kept his hand out. "No, don't leave me hangin'. You shake it. It means we're friends. You gotta do the deed."

Blalok seemed to think carefully about this, tipping his head back as he swiveled in his chair so that he might observe the human more closely. Finally, he lifted a hand and took David's, shaking it gingerly.

"Alright then, *friends*…I suppose."

The alien's hand was warm in his, which surprised David. From his appearance, he'd assumed his skin would be cool.

"Alex would crap!" He grinned.

"Pardon?"

"No, I mean, Alex would be so excited. She's the best. But…" He glanced at the screen. "I'm not sure she knows I'm aboard your ship."

Blalok didn't lend an opinion to this.

The screen, meanwhile, was very busy. The Apache helicopters had them virtually surrounded, and ground vehicles had swiftly enclosed the perimeter of the meadow. It was remarkable how efficiently the military could mobilize heavy artillery and ground forces. And all personnel appeared to have one goal—to organize a draping net of cables, evidently with the intent of securing the vessel.

This wouldn't be easy. The *Cerulean Star* was perhaps small by starship standards, but by *Earth* vessel standards, it was the size of a small cruise ship.

"They're trying to contain us," Blalok noted matter-of-factly and leaned back in his chair, lacing his fingers together as he rested them on the peculiarly smooth material of his shirt.

"Just fly away," David offered. "They can't contain this!" He gestured around himself with genuine awe.

"Negative," Blalok replied flatly. "If we lift off, we will almost certainly cause casualties."

"Yeah—*so*? In case you haven't noticed, they're not exactly friendly!"

To this, Blalok sat bolt upright. "Not acceptable! This was my fault. I…" He shifted uncomfortably in his chair. "Was neglecting to adequately monitor our periphery."

"First contact," David crossed his arms. "This was your first contact, wasn't it?"

"Yes, the first contact…yes it was, and I was distracted, caught by surprise. I admit it." He seemed embarrassed, and swung his feet slowly. "I've gotten us into this, and I will not harm your species getting us out."

David pursed his lips and looked overhead. "Yeah, I guess some poor soldier always bites it in situations like this—guy in the red shirt and all."

It was Blalok's confession that made David consider this, and he thought about Alex's brother when he said it. "Can't you just destroy the nets?"

"Not really, no. This ship, the *Cerulean Star*, is designed to avoid substance, not destroy it."

"What are you saying?"

"It means we're not an assault vessel. However, that doesn't make us necessarily vulnerable. If we remain passive, they can approximate us—put material close to and against us. They can even move us if they so choose, but they cannot actually make direct contact with the *Cerulean Star*."

When David just looked blankly at him, he tried again. "Our shields will hold. They cannot breach our hull."

"You mean if they launch a bomb or a rocket or something they can't hurt us?"

Blalok seemed surprised. "Well, *no*, not unless they placed the *Star* in an extremely confined environment. You don't have the weapons technology, but it would displace us…" the alien rolled his eyes, "quickly."

"Like how quickly?"

"They can blow us up, or, rather, try to. The *Star*'s hull would absorb the impact, but we would move somewhat, perhaps very fast."

"And we get scrambled inside, like *eggs*?" David was genuinely mortified by the possibility.

"No, uh-uh. It wouldn't be comfortable, but the *Star* would release gravity from any bio-organic object and shield our floating bodies until the impact passed. There is no scenario where the *Star* wouldn't do this, unless we approached something as powerful as, say, a star going supernova or…a galactic tsunami…which would just be stupid."

David just stared, entirely bewildered by the youngest alien.

* * *

For just a second, Blalok was reminded of the terrible event, two years before. They'd tumbled violently, but the most horrifying part had been the sickening groan the *Star* let out, as though it was in pain. Well, and then he'd vomited inside the emergency suspension bubble, which he also found extremely unpleasant.

His expression was vacant and far away, but then he refocused on his unexpected guest, the human called David. "It wouldn't be pleasant, but we would survive. But why, might I ask, would they 'bomb' us?"

He gestured at the screen, still alive with angry hornets.

David's eyes widened.

"Uhh, because they *can*?" He shook his head at his host as though to indicate everyone knows that.

"I see—primitive *hostiles*."

"Yeah, pretty much. It's how a lot of the grownups on this planet think."

Blalok nodded again.

David said, "But not all of them are like that; don't get me wrong. There's a ton of really awesome guys who'd be totally stoked about you, but they're not necessarily the ones that collect the bombs."

"Normal evolution of a species," Blalok shrugged. "But, if it makes you feel better, the peaceful ones usually prevail in the end."

"Good!" David spun another three-sixty in his levi-chair. "I like you, Blalok. You're all right. So, what's the plan, captain-K?"

For some reason, the human's cavalier approach annoyed the Bettuan a small bit. It also surprised him, all of a sudden, how much the human reminded him of Sartek, and a pang of worry nipped at his subconscious. "We observe." He remarked simply, indicating the forward screen. "And I am *not* a 'captain-K', not a captain at all."

"Oh, I get it, know thine enemy."

Blalok's eyes widened appreciably. "Yes, exactly. *Reciprocal victory. Partek Bassima*," he informed the human a bit smugly.

"*The Art of War*, Ancient Chinese dude," David corrected him.

A faint smiled revealed a mouth still half-full of Bettuan baby teeth.

David grinned widely back.

Then the two turned their levi-chairs together, toward the screen to watch and observe, and…to formulate a plan.

CHAPTER SEVEN

Δ

The *cave* wasn't exactly a cave. It was more of a small, cutaway rock formation, huge by Kansas standards but small nonetheless. Fortunately, the cave produced a tiny hidden cliff edge with a significant overhang. Tucked neatly into a rock hillside, it was at least fifteen feet up from the ground and entirely surrounded by trees. The scraggly brush that grew out of the steep wall of rock and dirt above the mouth of it effectively obscured the little cavern from practically every angle.

If someone didn't climb right up to it, they would never know it was there. And that's exactly how it'd first been found by the kids.

Alex, who was already prone to climbing high places, scrambled up the steep rock formation, trying to reach a branch overhead that hung fairly vertical. She'd explained that she was going to use it to monkey swing across to another branch dangling from an adjacent tree.

David and Liberty watched from below, holding their hands up to shield the overhead glare when she disappeared off the face of the cliff. Just poof! Right into thin air!

"You gotta see this!" She screamed, then peeked right out of nowhere as though the side of the cliff had grown a small girl's head. Waving enthusiastically, she motioned them up. That was how the cave was first discovered, and the reclusive getaway offered splendid hours of adventure to the children. It was a fugitive hideout, prehistoric man's first home, and the Bat-cave, all in one glorious afternoon. It provided the precious stuff of childhood that one remembered in the last moments of their life. It was, to them, perfect.

Sadly, they'd also used it on more than one occasion as a true hideout when the stress of living at *The Home* grew too much.

Once, Alex announced to Liberty and David that she was tired of "Mrs. Shitonus and her dickwit sidekick." She'd then waltzed into the living room and announced to Roxy and Hog that the three of them had an invitation to a kid's spend-the-night. Never mind that such a thing had never once happened for a kid at *The Home*, ever.

That first night, the three had camped in the cave. David even made a small fire on the edge, using his precious flint and steel. They toasted hotdogs and ate them without buns.

That was the first of many campouts in the cave. Roxy was never so prudent as to confirm something like a sleepover with other adults, and Hog couldn't possibly care less.

Now, with two aliens in tow, the cave would provide its most important shelter yet. It would hide the refugees perfectly. Even their bodies would be shielded from the overhead heat seeking, infrared radar scanners, equipped aboard the helicopters, which were scouring the area at that very moment.

The path up to the ledge was rocky and not well marked. Fortunately, Alex and Liberty had crawled up it often enough that there were natural handholds, created from exposed tree roots and rocks.

Isara and Sartek followed them easily. Scrambling as fast as they could, up, up they went, and after a short bit, the exhausted foursome crawled over the ledge and into the seclusion of the cave.

Sartek was kind enough to carry Goo up in David's backpack, the one he'd tossed to the ground just before his amazing sprint across the meadow, and Liberty explained how that was the generally accepted method for getting Goo usually up into the cave—via David. He was the only one strong enough to carry living, dead weight like Goo, and it was simply unacceptable that the dog would not go with them.

All of them were breathless when they finally crested the ledge. They clambered for the obscurity of the back of the cave and just sat, steadying their nerves.

Goo stood behind wherever Liberty was, keeping a watchful eye on the visitors, especially the one who'd dragged his human through the forest.

The cave was decently outfitted. The few natural large rocks and two threadbare, folding lawn chairs—great scores from the dump—made for plenty of seating. There were also a half-dozen old blankets and a fairly healthy pantry of snacks—cheese crackers, cocoa puffs, and even a jar of peanut butter.

However, even though it was midafternoon, none of them, perhaps with the exception of Goo, were very hungry.

Sartek glanced about, dark green eyes flashing in the subdued light of the overhang. Isara stared meekly out the entrance up into the canopy of leaves and branches. Both the aliens wore what could only be described as shell-shocked expressions.

Liberty motioned for Isara to come away from the edge. "Safer back here, for now, anyway."

Alex plopped onto the ground and dropped her head into her hands, her elbows resting on her knees. "Oh my God. What are they going to do to David?"

"Alex, he'll be okay," Bert knelt beside her. "As soon as we—"

"What will they do? Will they try to destroy it?" Isara's hands went to her face as she spun to face Alex. "What if they get Blalok and David?" Her fear was infective. "Will they *kill* them?"

At that question, Alex, stricken, jumped up. "No! I mean…" She looked at Liberty. "Bert? Will—"

"No!" Liberty answered immediately. "No, Isara, that *won't* happen. For one thing, if you have the technology to travel between stars, it's my guess that there's no way they'll easily penetrate the hull of your ship with our primitive weaponry. That just won't happen."

"How can we know you are speaking the truth? How can we trust you?" It was Sartek's turn to voice his concern, and he trembled, fists clenching and unclenching.

Isara was close to tears now. "This is all my fault! *I* did this." She looked at Sartek and shook her hands as though she could shake the haplessness of the situation away.

Alex reached a hand toward her but didn't touch her. "Isara, nothing's your fault. You were just trying to meet somebody friendly after getting lost and all. Any of us would've done the same. There's nothing wrong with that. It's *nobody's* fault," she hesitated, "…except maybe those assholes in the helicopters."

Liberty cringed at her bluntness. Alex was, as always, accurate and honest to the core. He added, "And even if your ship is captured, the government can't hurt it, not right off anyway. That's what we need to focus on first."

"What do you mean?" Isara's eyes shot even wider, making her look like some kind of exotic owl in the dim light of the back of the cave.

"He's right," Sartek added grimly. "If the Tsunami didn't destroy it, it's probably safe enough for now."

"Tsunami?" Liberty asked. "You guys were caught in a tsunami? Like dark matter? Of course! It makes total sense!"

"To you maybe," Alex rolled her eyes.

Sartek took a few minutes to explain in simple terms what had happened to them nearly two years before. He stuck to the grave facts, seemingly unwilling to go into painful detail.

Liberty was fascinated. "I totally get it! That could happen! The likelihood has to be next to impossible, and the odds astronomical, but—"

Alex coughed and shot him a sharp look. "Shut up with the science-fest, Bert." She hiked her head toward the Bettuan. "And this is all really educating, but the bigger question is will they take the ship somewhere? And what if they water board David, try to get him to talk or something?" Her growing concern was evident in her wavering voice.

"They won't waterboard David! You can't torture kids. It's not legal."

In reality, Liberty believed that they could and *would* torture kids, but was only saying this for Alex's benefit. He chose to keep this thought private for now.

"Where will they take them?" Alex pressed.

"Hutchinson," Liberty answered immediately.

"Where?" all three asked at once.

Liberty picked up a stick and started to scratch a rudimentary map in the dirt. Isara and Sartek leaned in, and Alex peered over his back, her elbow resting on his shoulder.

As Liberty scribbled, he explained, "Hutchinson, and it's not far from here. Top-secret underground military facility, kinda like a Kansas NORAD." He said this as if they should all know what NORAD was.

Sartek and Isara regarded each other blankly.

"Bert..." Alex did nothing to disguise her frustration.

"Oh, right, sorry. NORAD stands for North American Aerospace Defense Command. It's cut two thousand feet into the side of a mountain in Colorado.

Super top secret, run by the Army, Navy, Marine Corps, Air Force…you get the idea. It's super secret lockdown."

This information still appeared to mean nothing to the other three, and Liberty tried hard to put an explanation into words they might more easily understand. "Like I said, Hutchinson is kinda like NORAD. It's lock-down classified and a central hub to other strategic areas of government operations.

"It's not as technologically decked out as NORAD, but it's much less known, which they'll want. And it may lead to other underground facilities, like the one in Denver and, of course, NORAD in Colorado Springs."

"How do you know all this?" Sartek asked and then answered his own question. "Oh, I forgot; you're like Blalok."

"Blalok?" Alex asked.

"Yes, the third one of us, back on the ship," Isara motioned toward the sky, even though the ship was no longer there. "And he'll know what to do. We just have to find a way to connect with him."

"That's not the only reason the military will take the ship there." Liberty stabbed at the dirt map. "Hutchinson has the Kansas Cosmosphere and Space Center."

"So?" Alex asked simply.

"That facility is a cutting-edge aerospace science and history museum and one of only two museums entitled to restore used spacecraft, the other being the Smithsonian."

His voice was like a dead weight in the hollow of the cave.

"They will have the technology and intellect close at hand to evaluate your ship. But I'm worried about that cuz they'll have the knowledge to study it, and that's bad."

Liberty couldn't maintain eye contact just then and reached to pull Goo into his lap. He steeled himself before saying, "They'll take it apart and learn from it. That's when the military will step in and have the biggest say. For them, it's all about weapons. Unfortunately, that space center will just enable them to do it that much faster."

"That would change your planet," Isara spoke softly, her voice echoing against the damp stone walls.

This moved Liberty greatly, that in such a terribly vulnerable moment, the alien was concerned most about his planet—*his* home. "Yeah it would, and not in a good way. It would be too much too fast. Most likely it'll catalyze a final world war. It would be infinitely catastrophic."

"The one with the most toys in the end wins?" Alex asked.

Liberty nodded gravely.

"And we all lose." She spat on the ground.

"There is no way this can happen!" Sartek leapt up and spun around, his back to them. His hands clutched his head. "We can't let this happen!"

"It won't, Sartek. I'm not going to let it happen," Liberty stated flatly with perfect resolve.

He shoved Goo from his lap and scrambled up. "I may be just a kid, but I do know a thing or two about strategy."

Sartek faced him again as Liberty tapped his temple with his index finger. "And I may be well below the poverty line, but I'm not without resources. Most critically, it's not everyone who has a straight link with the aliens who own the ship."

He held his hand out to his new friend.

This prompted a small look of confusion and relief on Sartek's face.

Liberty gestured, his hand still out. "Please trust me Sartek, Isara. I'll do anything I can to stop this. Anything…"

Sartek hesitated, then took the human's smaller hand into his own, grasping it firmly, and shook.

"How do we get to this Hutchinson base?" Isara asked.

"It's not gonna be like wandering into the ball," Alex interjected. "It's probably locked down tighter than a hooker with a…" She trailed off when Liberty shot her an admonishing look.

"What she means is we have some work ahead of us; this isn't going to be easy. But before we can do anything, we need to make sure Hutchinson is really where they're taking your ship. Then, once we know, we need to contact Blalok—formulate a plan."

They all agreed that a plan was in order and settled down to putting together a primary strategy. Hutchinson wasn't far away, but the kids had no ready form of transportation. Furthermore, Liberty suspected there would be a major lockdown on whichever route the military chose to drag the *Star*.

Matters were further complicated by the fact that they needed to get back to *The Home*, at least for tonight. Liberty needed insulin, and it wouldn't do to alert anyone of their absence just yet, even if those *anyones* were as dumb as Roxy and Hog. Once they were discovered missing and word got out they would be on a ticking clock. That would stack the odds against them. As brilliant as Liberty might be, he knew they lacked the resources that adults possessed, and the small advantage of time was precious to them.

Alex and Liberty hastily explained the circumstances of *The Home* to the aliens, and by three o'clock in the afternoon, they were all hiking directly northwest, out of the woods, and toward the small heart of Erie. They needed to catch a bus for the little town of Pittsburgh, Kansas.

"Why Pittsburgh? Why're we going there?" Alex squinted skeptically.

"'Cuz Pittsburgh has a train, and we need to jump a train, and...you can help us do it." Liberty shot her a knowing expression before explaining further. "The KCS railway will follow highway forty-seven, right up to Hutchinson. We'll be able to scout for unusual road activity along the way. It's our best shot of locating your ship."

"But won't we be noticed?" Isara wondered. "I mean, we're not exactly going to fit in."

By now they weren't far from the edge of Erie and were swiftly running out of significant cover as the tiny forest dwindled from around them.

"Yeah, we need to disguise you two up a bit," Alex suggested. "A quick trip to the Bargain Barn, and nobody on buses will notice or care. Plus, there won't be anybody on the train to worry about. We'll pick a freighter and jump a boxcar."

She grinned big. "It's practically foolproof!"

Isara and Sartek regarded each other as though not at all convinced of the reliability of the plan, but they had no better ideas and couldn't dispute their new friends' enthusiasm.

"Don't worry," Alex said. She had great intuition sometimes and was likely picking up on Isara's reservations. "Bert and I won't be long. I promise. Just hang with Goo and we'll be back quicker'n Jack Flash."

Isara could not know the reference but agreed anyway. "I know. I trust you, Alex." Her eyes, however, still carried an expression of vague uncertainty.

Liberty thought how difficult it must be, to be so far away from their home planet, just them and their ship—which now lay within the clutches of the greatest superpower on Earth. He also recognized the unlikely odds that his new friends would ever discover a way home. It was remarkable that they'd even survived the Tsunami and managed to stumble through the universe alone and unscathed for two long years.

These thoughts were not productive, but as they filtered in seconds through his awareness, Liberty found himself thinking of Alex and David. It suddenly occurred to him how much the three aliens were like them.

His heart swelled with the emotion. Just then, he did something extraordinary; he reached out and rested his hand on each of the aliens' shoulders.

"I promise. We'll come back…and everything's gonna be okay. We'll get you back to your ship." When he lifted his hands, a strange current jolted through his body, hardly perceptible, but definitely electrical. It surprised him. "Did…did you feel that?"

Isara shook her head, and Sartek just stared blankly at him.

Alex nudged Liberty. "C'mon, homeboy. Let's get going. We don't have much time." Then, motioning to Isara that she needed to hold onto Goo's collar, Alex scrambled up from under the bridge and ran as fast as her secondhand Reeboks could take her into town, dragging Liberty behind her.

The aliens sat beneath a bridge on the outskirts of the town, behind a dense thatch of shrubs. Shoulders rubbing, they waited for the humans' return.

* * *

Along the way into town, Liberty staggered. "Stop. Not so fast." He dropped to a walk. "Sorry, Al. I'm too tired." His wheezing was fairly significant. He'd run too much today.

Used to be, Alex would tease him mercilessly about this, but over time she'd come to realize that Liberty had an undying longing to keep up. He only asked her and David to slow down when he absolutely could not hold on. She broke her pace immediately, and they walked for a while. Liberty fumbled for his inhaler.

"I *knew* they were coming back," Alex said as she avoided stepping on any of the cracks in the weed-ridden sidewalk. With each hop, her elbows came flying up in the air, like a chick emerging from its shell.

"I have no doubt of that." He smiled. Liberty thought she very much resembled a scrawny bird—a stubborn, sometimes obnoxious little bird, flapping her way along, so supremely sure of herself.

Becoming quite serious, she stopped hopping and just walked. "No, really, Bert. I *did*."

He was quiet, allowing her the dignity of his consideration. "I know, Alex. You're like that. You have amazing instinct. I wish I did."

Her eyes flew open. "You? Seriously, you're like the smartest person that ever lived!"

"I also have no doubt of that." He grinned smugly.

"Too bad you're such a dork, though." She laughed, clasping her hands together in glee. "Bert, we have *alien* friends!"

This rocked him on his heels, the gravity of her comment and the utter commitment to it. It was wonderful, and he laughed outright. "Yeah, we do, don't we!" Then he broke into a jog again, forcing himself along. "And we gotta save them!"

Alex took his hand, and they ran together the rest of the way.

In just a short while, they stood in front of the Bargain Barn, Erie's number one second-hand thrift store.

"You ready for this?" Liberty rubbed his palms invitingly together.

"Hey, you're the one who has to keep it cool, okay? Just don't freak out or anything."

"When have I ever freaked out?" He stiffened, genuinely indignant.

"Like anytime I make you do something you don't wanna?" She punched him gently on the shoulder. "Like right now, probably."

"Yeah, well, but that's only because it's almost always dangerous, or stupid."

She grabbed him by the arm and pushed him through the doorway. "Alright, Mr. Pacino. It's show time. Put on your game face cuz we got some serious ass to kick." Her glib encouragement only served to make him more nervous than he already was.

Liberty drew attention wherever they went, mostly because his appearance was so uncommon. His hair, thick glasses, intellectual demeanor, and ragamuffin hand-me-downs all served to create the very definition of odd. It was normal that he would glean the most attention in the place, and so the plan was tailored that direction.

Going immediately to the back of the store, he pretended to thumb through some mildly worn action figures, including one practically mint model of the Green Lantern that he would sincerely have liked to have. He glanced nervously around, then *accidentally* pulled down the highest shelf in the toy department. Plush toys rained down on him, and he lay beneath a segment of the shelving, Dino the Dinosaur's butt right in his face.

"My arm!" he cried, only modestly trying to kick out from underneath the pile. This promptly diverted all personnel to his immediate area. The diversion was perfect. Alex made away with several pairs of jeans, long sleeve shirts, ball caps, two pairs of sunglasses, and a couple of high collared coats.

The store manager came running to the back of the store, and when he eventually sorted out the melee and determined that the boy wasn't, in fact, mortally injured, he demanded, "Where do you live, son?"

"Foster home—the one out on Old Goat Road." Liberty grinned stupidly, making sure the man was not only convinced that he was a hard luck case, but that he wasn't very clever either.

The manager kicked the white-haired waif out of the store. "And stay out!"

Liberty, winded by the time he cleared the door, pulled another few breaths on his inhaler. He couldn't see how his lips were faintly blue.

"You okay?" Alex was ecstatic with her spoils and slipped on a pair of sunglasses, the pink ones with the white polka dots.

Ignoring the question, Liberty only motioned in the direction they needed to go. Hurrying back, they found their friends just where they'd left them. Isara let go of Goo's collar, and the dog, overjoyed to see his master, gave the alien a look of sincere disapproval as he leapt about Liberty's feet.

Alex pulled their Bargain Barn score from David's backpack. As she did, his baseball cards, triple wrapped in rubber bands, accidentally tumbled from the side pocket of the pack and came apart as they hit the ground.

Liberty scrambled to snatch them up from the dirt. No kid saved baseball cards anymore—no kid except David. None of them were even very good ones. Even so, Liberty made sure they were dusted off before he carefully re-banded them and placed them in the other side pocket of the backpack—the one held more securely closed with a safety pin.

It gave him a pang in his belly to think about his lost friend. He swallowed thickly and glanced over at Alex to see if she'd noticed. She met his gaze, her eyes profoundly sad.

"Don't worry; we're gonna get him back," he promised in a low voice.

Alex nodded dumbly but said nothing.

The aliens changed from their clothing into the Bargain Barn outfits. Their Bettuan attire had fit them perfectly—sleek and shimmering, molding to their movements as though it was a second skin. These otherworld outfits now lay folded up in the shrubbery with a healthy armful of grass and dirt pulled over them.

"Not so bad," Liberty observed as Isara struggled to shove as much of her sleek hair as possible under a Kansas City Chiefs ball cap. Oddly enough, he thought the aliens seemed to fit in fairly well, if you didn't look too closely.

Minutes later, two relatively normal and two somewhat odd children were sitting on the back seat of the county bus to Pittsburgh. The fare was a buck twenty-five each, but the driver allowed them on at two for the price of one.

"Ay-rabs?" A fat woman with twin girls on her lap jerked her chin toward Isara and Sartek, an expression of genuine apprehension plastered on her face. She directed her question at Alex as she pulled the girls closer, the twins practically disappearing beneath her bosom.

Isara and Sartek sat with heads down, the collars of their jackets pulled up around their faces, sunglasses obscuring their exotic eyes.

Goo, as though unhappy with the comment, lifted the edge of one lip, showing the tip of a single tooth before turning around on Liberty's lap to give the woman his ass end.

"Chinese," Alex replied without missing a beat, "and they got photosensitivity. Way to make fun of them, *lady*."

She crossed her arms smugly across her chest. Liberty was amazed at how fast Alex could create a complete fabrication of the situation.

The woman seemed indignant, and nothing more was said about the strange, *Chinese* pair, traveling with two American kids and dressed like it was a bright and sunny December day.

By three-thirty that afternoon, they were off the bus and on the outskirts of Pittsburgh. The bus driver shook his head, a confused look smattered across his face, but did as the children requested and let them off on a deserted stretch of road.

Nearly an hour later, the kids stood under a tall railroad bridge that spanned a narrow draw. The tracks ran directly overhead from where the kids crouched, and trains roared past every so often, causing a film of dust—sparkling in the sunlight as it fell—to shake from the old timbers and settle over them.

Liberty coughed. Alex shot him a concerned look.

"It's okay; I'm okay." He choked, then coughed brutally, longer this time.

"You sure you're alright?" Sartek reached out to steady him as the human eased to the ground.

"Nope; he doesn't breathe well, specially in dusty places," Alex explained. "And all that running today? That doesn't agree with him either."

They watched the ritual again as Liberty pulled out his inhaler, his face turning a purplish red as he pulled two puffs and held his breath.

"I'll be okay," he wheezed. "Just give me a second."

When he at last seemed all right, Sartek motioned overhead. "How are we going to get on one?"

Liberty described the process of a railway switch. "Eventually, one will stop; they have to. The KCS is only a two-rail system through here, and every now and then one train leaving Pittsburgh has to yield to another oncoming train, one heading south."

"Just follow my lead," Alex coached them.

As though on cue, a train approached and screeched horribly overhead, groaning its massive metal objection before grinding to a halt.

"Careful now, but we gotta go quick. They don't take kindly to train jumping. They'll arrest us or throw us right off." Alex swung her arms for emphasis. "So the plan is get on, ride it until we see something, and then get back off, fast. Got it?"

"Agreed." Isara said. "And they couldn't have gotten very far, could they?" She meant the military and the *Star*.

"I don't think so," Sartek shook his head. "In hibernation mode, *Star* will be very heavy in this gravity and pretty hard to tow."

"Hurry up! We only have so long!" Alex scampered up the hillside, sneaking a short ways, bent over and hiding behind brush as she went.

They all followed her lead and within seconds were alongside the train. Alex held her index finger to her lips as she tiptoed down the track. They copied her, remaining silent as they sneaked. It seemed to Liberty to take forever, but it really wasn't very long before they discovered a partially open car. This was a very fortunate event as these were rare. Most railroad companies disapproved of train jumping to the extent that open cars were practically nonexistent. However, on the KCS, there were still some older cars that were coupled open for return trips.

The kids were very lucky indeed; this particular train had arced around a long bend as it slowed, and the three locomotive engines that drew it were well out of sight. The last thing the engineer would expect was some runaway kids stowing away in an empty freight car, especially on a stretch of track as remote as this one was. Small town ghetto jumpers were almost unheard of anymore.

So, amazingly, it all went off without a hitch.

Alex and Sartek hiked Liberty up into the car first. That was a cinch because he was so light, and they tossed him in like a small sack of potatoes. Rolling out of the way, he spun around just in time to catch a flying dog when Sartek tossed Goo up. Then Liberty lay on his belly to help pull Isara up. That left only two on the ground.

Liberty had a growing appreciation for how strong the alien was.

Sartek nodded at Alex and held his hands out, fingers laced together to make a foothold for her to step into. As she grasped him on both shoulders, he heaved, tossing her effortlessly into the car. Eyes flashing, a grin stretched across Alex's face as she landed easily on her feet and spun about.

The train groaned, the heavy metal couplings slamming like monster dominoes as the cars connected. It shuddered ominously as it started to move.

Alex waved for Sartek to hurry, and the alien took three running steps, grasped a grab-iron, and leapt, vaulting onto his stomach onto the open door edge of the car. With the other three pulling him, he shinnied inside. It was the first time Liberty had ever seen the alien grin openly as Sartek scrambled to his feet.

Rubbing his belly, the alien exclaimed, "That was great!"

"Stay away from the door," Alex cautioned. "We don't want to be seen."

They each inched away from the door and took up individual stations to wait and watch. The floor of the car was grimy and smelled of petroleum fuel. Isara found a relatively clean spot, swept it with her hand, and motioned for Alex to join her. The girls sat back to back, out of a direct line of vision so they wouldn't be easily seen. Liberty could scarcely take his eyes off them. Alex had no female friends, none that he'd ever heard of, and to see her so willingly attach herself to Isara was, to him, something remarkable.

Needing a lookout from the opposite side as well, Liberty took up a post at the other door. He struggled with the catch before eventually getting it unlocked, but it took Sartek shoving his shoulder against it to break it open. As the door slid a few feet, the rusty moan of the runner was drowned out by the louder groan of the train picking up speed.

"So...have you always been a train jumper?" Sartek asked Alex from across the way.

She continued to look away and avoided eye contact with Liberty as well. He watched her pull her pant leg down far enough to cover a scar. The truth was Alex had been a runaway at times, and her favorite mode of travel had been trains. That landed her into a bit of trouble with the state, and had she not been so young, she would've spent some time in juvenile detention for it. Her child protective services file even had her flagged as a train jumper.

That, of course, was before she'd been placed at *The Home*. Once, David decided they should all jump a train for fun. That was when Alex told them it wasn't as safe or fun as he thought it might be. They'd eventually begged the story out of her, but she wasn't proud of it, swearing them to secrecy with the younger kids in *The Home*. Alex had a scar, three-fourths the length of her left shin, from when she'd once fallen from a train car.

I guess we all have our secrets, Liberty heard Sartek start to say, but the alien hadn't opened his mouth at all.

"What?" Liberty asked him suddenly. "What did you say?"

Sartek hesitated. "I only asked about her jumping the trains—"

"No," Liberty interrupted, "about the secrets?"

Sartek frowned. "I didn't say anything about secrets. I don't know…what you're talking about."

Liberty didn't press the issue, and they rode the train in silence for nearly half an hour before finally spying what they were looking for.

Across the valley stretched a caravan of military vehicles, towing a very large, draped object. From the looks of the cargo, it could have been a small battle ship. In actuality, it *was* a ship of sorts, for concealed beneath it was the *Cerulean Star*.

Helicopters buzzed around the caravan, and there was even a tank escort. No civilian vehicles were seen anywhere; the entire highway was completely shut down. The kids crowded the doorway to catch a glimpse of the convoy as it ground painfully along.

Liberty thought the whole procession looked about as tedious as trying to pull a spoon through cold honey, and was glad for their struggle. "That's it!" he exclaimed. "Old highway forty-seven! Next stop, Hutchinson Air Base. We're right on target!"

The kids waited until the train slowed at another double rail exchange, then hopped off into the cover of a small stand of dusty, dry saplings. Fifteen minutes later, they jumped another car heading to Pittsburgh.

Much later, they caught a city bus back to Erie.

CHAPTER EIGHT

Δ

"What are they doing?" David asked.

"They're obviously taking us somewhere, I assume to contain the ship." Blalok spun his chair to more directly face his new guest. "Do you know of any facility around here, military, government, place they might bring a ship of this size?"

"No, not really. Bert would know. Sorry." Suddenly, David wished Liberty was there.

"Where do you live? Additionally, what communication devices do you possess?"

David gave him the address of *The Home*. "We don't have any communication devices, just an old *Sega* system and a CD player, but they're really old. I'm not even sure they work."

Blalok frowned. "What about your university? Does it have a computer system, preferably with a linked network?"

David shook his head. "Nope, school's out for the summer." Then his eyes lit up. "But there's free computer with Internet at the school library! When school is in session, anyway."

"Excellent! Do you have access to it?"

"I don't. Never saw much use for it," David admitted. "It doesn't allow games."

At that, Blalok rolled his eyes.

"But Bert does!" the human added quickly. "He's a member of some sort of geek science club, I think, and a chess club. And he has an e-mail or something."

"Good. We need to figure that out."

"How? Why?"

"Because your friends, and mine, have returned to your home for the night. It is only logical. Tomorrow morning, when day breaks, the school library is where your friend, Bert, will be. That is, if he is as clever as you believe him to be."

"You're right! That's exactly what Bert would do! And he's the cleverest you'll ever meet, way smarter than anyone you've ever known," he added, just a bit defensively.

With a look of skepticism, Blalok started to reply, but just then, E-I said, "If I allow the Terrans to briefly access my mainframe, I would be able to gain access to theirs."

"What was that?" David exclaimed, looking up and around.

"That's E-I—Electronic Intelligence. He is the central intelligence of the *Star*."

"He? The computer's a *he*?" David chuckled out loud.

Blalok's eyes narrowed. "*It* has chosen for *itself* a male voice. His format of analysis is gender neutral, however."

David just stared blankly at Blalok.

"My organic circuitry allows me not just deductive capability," E-I spoke again from the cosmosphere around David's head, "but in words that you might better understand, conscious thought and intuition."

"That's freaky!"

"I have feelings," E-I continued in a flat tone.

"What? You're *human*?" Then he answered himself, "Well I guess not human, but…"

Blalok rolled his eyes again, but it was E-I that answered, "Yes. I am human, and Bettuan, and schlange. If you wish to cross reference my entity with any other species, please feel free to do so."

"That's so cool!" David laughed outright. "A computer that thinks it's a *he*, and thinks for itself, and—"

"Don't be ignorant," E-I said abruptly.

That set David right back on his heels.

"I-I?" he stammered to apologize.

E-I stopped him. "Let's just assume that I respect your capabilities, and that you will respect mine."

David's mouth fell open.

Blalok snickered and whispered with his hand up to the side of his lips. "He gets kind of touchy when you call him an *it*."

Looking around—David wasn't sure which direction he should face—he tried to identify a speaker system.

"Okay, E-I...sir," he grimaced, "then how do we let them hook into your mainframe?"

"I will send a signal. It will be limited and primitive in format and contain no data which might compromise my framework or allow your species' evolution to advance unnaturally."

"So keep the secrets secret?" David was catching onto the plan more and more.

"Yes," E-I confirmed, sounding much more amiable than before. "David, with your assistance, I will be able to determine your friend's computer login information and—"

"Bert..." David interrupted. "His name is Bert; it's short for Liberty. Get it? Li—*Bert*—eee."

"Very good," E-I paused. "I need to know where Bert went to university, the name of any organizations that he is a part of, and anything else that might connect him to a central network."

"You mean like school? Just regular public, like the rest of us. I'm guessing he had a lot more connections before the accident." David stared at the floor, his forehead crinkled in thought.

"Accident?" Blalok's eyes widened.

David waved him to silence. Finally, his face lit up. "Erie junior chess club! He's a member of the Erie junior chess club. I think it's through the high school, even though he's only fifth grade." He smiled at Blalok. "He's the president; smartest kid that ever played that game, for sure. He's got all kinda ribbons, keeps them in a shoebox."

"What is this game, chess?" Blalok was suddenly very curious.

"It's a thinking man's game," David replied in a tone that suggested it would be over Blalok's head. "You might like it, might not even *lose* too bad if you ever played him."

"Is this game obtainable?" Blalok was instantly intrigued.

"E-I, can we acquire this?" he asked.

"In all likelihood, yes," E-I said. "However, that is unimportant at the moment. I have located Isara and Sartek."

"What?" David was drawn back to the here and now. "How? Where?"

The screen on the bridge was an eerie, milky white, but E-I described how the two Bettuan, along with two humans, were paralleling their current path of travel, about a mile north of them.

"I have the capability of tracking the translation rings, because they contain Vasteen," the computer explained. "It provides a marker that is otherwise not present on your planet."

"It's the train!" David exclaimed. "Alex must have jumped a train!" It thrilled him that Alex would have the nerve to do this, and gave him a happy feeling in his chest followed with a pang of worry.

"Is that safe?" Blalok asked.

"Well, it depends, but this wouldn't be the first time she's done it. She's like a master, and has the scars to prove it."

Blalok eyes widened somewhat.

E-I continued, "I would say that they have taken the initiative to determine our destination. Very clever, and they've just reversed their trajectory, we must assume to backtrack to familiar territory."

"Bert musta' figured out where they're taking us. Now they're heading back to *The Home*," David reasoned.

"Then it becomes even more critically important that we establish contact with him," Blalok noted, "so we can coordinate our plan."

The thought of having purpose and direction thrilled David. "You're right. Let's do this! But how?"

"What is Bert's full name?" E-I first wished to know. "Also, do you know what his login identifiers would be?"

"You mean e-mail? No, but his name is Liberty Lennox." Then he mused more to himself, "I don't even know his middle name."

This cast his spirits down somewhat, that he didn't know this small detail about one of his two very best friends, but then he brightened. "But he loves puzzles! Mind twisters—and scrabble, only no one will play him cuz he's a brainiac and all. He really likes *Sherlock Holmes*, too. That's his favorite. And *Professor Pyg*. You know, the *Batman* villain."

Blalok seemed mildly amused. "No, I *don't*. But I can well imagine…"

* * *

The *Star* was being towed, or more accurately, painstakingly dragged at approximately twenty-miles an hour along remote Highway Forty-Seven, from Erie toward Hutchinson, Kansas.

The ship was at this point completely draped with braided industrial Kevlar and tethered with two hundred cables, altogether strong enough to suspend the Golden Gate Bridge.

The cables were attached to M-1 Abrams main battle tanks, thirteen of them, which ground along in a long, dramatic V down the highway. There was no way the *Star* was lifting off now, not with an excess of a million pounds of Government Issue metal attached to it.

Ahead and behind the *Star*, Apache helicopters and military Humvee's cleared a path, securing air and ground space and effectively keeping civilians well beyond discoverability. It was a stealth procedure if ever there was one.

E-I soon had access to the information they needed. The download of virtually all of Earth's information and intelligence was complete and the ship re-veiled in less than ten-seconds. All anyone saw beneath the drapes was the beautiful, incandescent blue outline of the ship before it morphed back into the hazy white form of hibernation.

"I have information," E-I stated simply.

"Report," Blalok requested.

They both sounded very efficient, David thought.

"You are correct, David. Bert is a member of a Junior League Chess Club. He is also the president of the Erie Municipal Science Club. More significantly, however, he is a member of *Mensa,* and on occasion, plays chess with their membership. He does this virtually and also quite successfully."

"Mensa?" David was confused, but E-I continued without explanation.

"He lists as his personal information a family of only two. Alexandra Elizabeth Stutton—sister, and David Carmine Mattoretti—brother.

"What?" David was clearly flabbergasted.

E-I continued, "He is also a poorly controlled asthmatic and brittle diabetic, received orthopedic corrective surgery on both legs at the age of one, and suffered a critical motor vehicle accident at the age of nine, which resulted in an emergent craniotomy. Both parents are deceased, and he has no other living relatives besides Alexandra and David."

David was no longer impressed. He was stunned clean out of his mind and suddenly realized that there was a lot about Bert he didn't know. So that's why his hair was so much shorter on one side when he and Alex first discovered him curled up under the sheet at *The Home*. He'd undergone surgery…on his skull!

Pinching his chin, David frowned. Bert was playing chess with a bunch of smart people from some secret group. He'd never heard of Mensa but could well imagine who they were, and he *imagined* very correctly.

All this time, Bert never mentioned any of this to him or Alex.

"Liberty is…" E-I appeared to consider his wording carefully, "…advanced. He has received e-mail correspondence from Mensa with an offer to remove him from Kansas State Foster Care, to step up his collegiate education, but he has refused on several occasions."

"I don't understand," David's brow creased in dismay. "Why would they want Bert? You mean, he didn't…You're saying he could have *left* us?"

"Liberty's actual correspondence states his unwillingness to be separated from his family," E-I stated flatly.

"His *family*?"

David realized Bert was still at *The Home* because he'd refused to leave him and Alex. He swallowed thickly. E-I had just launched a killer curveball, and it'd smacked David right between the ears.

With scarcely a moment's hesitation, E-I announced, "I have his email and his passcode."

"You cracked his e-mail? *And* his passcode?" David was wondering now if there was no limit to the capability of the Electronic-Intelligence.

"No, I reasonably deduced. Liberty has had no reason to encrypt it, yet."

If it was possible to double-take dead air space, David just did. "Uh…what is it?"

"His e-mail is simply Pygmalion six, six, six at hotmail dot com, passcode, Moriarty sixty-two," E-I said. When David and Blalok stared blankly at each other, he explained further, "*Professor Pyg* was characterized after the play *Pygmalion* and first released as a *Batman* villain in the comic issue number 666. *Moriarty* was the archenemy who killed *Sherlock Holmes*, at the age of sixty-two. It took only five hundred twenty-six possible combinations to discover it. Quite simple, really."

David's mouth hung open. Blalok smiled outright for the first time since meeting the human, and slapped him on the shoulder. "I look forward to making Bert's acquaintance and, perhaps, playing some chess with him. But, for now, let us see if we can get in touch with him, hmmm?"

He turned to compose a message to the human named Liberty.

"E-I?" David asked.

"Yes?"

"What is his middle name? Bert's, do you know?"

The computer answered simply, "He does not have one. Neither, by the way, does his favorite theoretical physicist."

"What?"

"*Who*. Not what," the computer corrected. "*Albert Einstein*. Liberty's favorite theoretical physicist likewise does not possess a middle name."

All of this was just a bit too much for David to absorb all at once. He sat down heavily next to Blalok, their elbows brushing. Immediately, an electric jolt ran from David's elbow up to his shoulder, snapping to a halt on his right earlobe.

"Sheesh, Blalok! What was *that*?" David shook his arm and reached up to rub his ear.

Blalok, absorbed with his task, murmured, "I didn't feel anything."

"Yeah, well, you need some cling-free or something, cuz you got a whole lotta' static goin' on."

The Bettuan appeared to ignore this as well.

Then, David inched closer and, together, the two composed a message. Before long, they sent it to an ordinary hotmail account, attention to one very extraordinary boy.

CHAPTER NINE

Δ

It was quite dark when the kids crept through the sparse stand of pine trees into the backyard of *The Home*.

"Wait here," Liberty said. "I'll go in and make sure the coast is clear. Then you guys crawl up the back way and come in through the bathroom window. I'll unlock it and give you the sign."

Alex waited with Sartek and Isara, crouched behind the corn bin.

Just then, as Liberty stood up, he saw a lovely little corn snake slither out of the bin and off into the tall grass. Not really given to superstition, he still couldn't help smiling at the good omen.

Swallowing thickly—it always made him nervous when he returned to *The Home*—he tried to walk casually as he up to the back of the house. So far so good. He didn't see any movement from Roxy's second-floor bedroom.

Climbing the back porch steps with a bedraggled dog on his heels, Liberty pulled open the door only after he glanced through the screen to spy around the kitchen.

No one was there.

He stepped inside and quietly shut the door.

A T.V. glowed in an otherwise dark living room, and Liberty could see three small heads circled around it. The kids sat cross-legged on the nappy, old, carpeted living room floor, watching reruns of *SpongeBob Squarepants*. It was a *SpongeBob* marathon day, and he'd known it would be playing as soon as the younger ones were up. And, evidently, it'd been on all day.

He thought briefly how ridiculous it was that there was cable television at *The Home*. Never mind that some of the kids could use better school supplies or a math tutor, something Liberty filled in as on occasion.

Julian, the five-year-old, gazed up with happy, bleary eyes and ran for Liberty. All the young ones at *The Home* loved him dearly as he was always very patient with them, even when Alex and David were not.

"Heya, Bert! Wanna watch? We got *Spongebob* on!"

"That's so awesome! But maybe later, little buddy. Howza-bout some *popcorn* though?" He made it sound so much better than it really was.

"Yeah! Yeah!" Julian squealed and ran back to share the good news with his comrades.

After searching for a bit, there was no popcorn to be found in the pantry, but he did find Roxy's Twinkie stash and a rare, unopened bag of potato chips. He snuck three of the Twinkies and opened the bag of chips, emptying a few good handfuls into three empty margarine tubs, then delivered the treasures to the red-eyed batch in front of the T.V.

Roxy and her live-in boyfriend, Dallas, who went by Hog, were in their mid fifties and conspicuously absent. This made Liberty nervous. It wasn't their designated *bar time* anymore, so they would almost certainly be home. Roxy and Hog were always off the street by ten, before the "po-po" were out patrolling for DUI's. They'd both been stung with these on several occasions and were told *The Home* would be closed if Roxy got one more.

Liberty went to the fridge and grabbed two vials of insulin—one short acting, the other long—and made for the stairs only to run smack into Roxy. Goo slunk past her, head down, and rifled up the stairs with a "you're on your own" look over his shoulder.

She peered beyond him, out the closed screen door as though she knew David and Alex must be close behind. Going to the fridge, she pulled it open and grabbed two cans of PBR beer.

Turning her bulk back to face him, she wiped the sweaty cans onto her too tight, pink stretch pants. Liberty backed up as she scanned him up and down with her squinty, pig eyes and harrumphed, "What are you kids up to?"

"Just playing cards." He held up the vials. "I forgot to take my insulin."

"You kids are sure quiet up there. We ain't heard nothing from you all evening. You get something to eat?"

Liberty knew that Roxy was required to make sure he had three square meals a day to prevent her from losing fostership. Evidently she and Hog had been gone most of the day if she was unaware that the three kids hadn't been home at all. Liberty picked up on this and ran with it.

"We caught fish at the lake and cooked them. Thank you, though," he said politely.

Roxy harrumphed again, then her eyes narrowed even more, which was next to impossible anyway. "What's that on your neck?"

Liberty had forgotten about the translation ring; it was so comfortable that he was totally unaware he even still wore it.

"Oh, yeah. Alex found them. Some old chokers at a yard sale, traded her pocketknife for them. It's kind of like a club thing." He tried to shrug it away, but a wave of cold sweat broke out under his T-shirt, across his shoulders.

The likelihood of Roxy realizing that Alex would never, under any circumstances—even the threat of death—part willingly with her Swiss army knife was sketchy. Even so, it was a long, suffering moment before the big woman dismissed the explanation and, huffing and puffing, climbed the stairs back to the second floor. She and Hog had cable T.V. in their bedroom as well, and once the door was shut, it wouldn't open again until there was a bathroom run.

"Well, don't you kids be starting no fires in the woods," she groused without looking back. "It's awful dry for that, an if you get in trouble, they'll kick you right outa' here, and we won't stop 'em."

This threat seemed incredibly illogical to Liberty. Roxy's survival, and Hog's for that matter, depended on keeping *The Home* full. He suddenly and irrationally considered lighting a fire in the woods, when everything was said and done, just to make good on her stupid threat.

Shaking his head, he waited at the foot of the stairs until her bedroom door clicked shut. Then, creeping more quietly than he believed he ever had before, he made his way to the second floor bathroom. Closing the bathroom door first, he unlocked the window and flipped the lights on and off, giving the signal the coast was clear.

Out from behind the corn-crib, the other three stood up as though they'd simply popped out of the ground. Across the dry lawn and up the outside back stairs they snuck, crawling carefully across the flat porch roof before hopping through the open bathroom window.

Liberty held his index finger up to his lips as they filed one at a time into the bathroom. Out into the hall and up the narrow flight of stairs to the attic they crept.

Closing the door carefully, Alex made sure the catch was secure. They weren't supposed to lock their door; it was *against the rules*, and she had no difficulty locking it just out of spite.

For a few seconds, they stood motionless and just listened, Alex with her ear against the door.

Finally, they went to work, quietly making a blanket fort out of the bunk beds and their bedding. That way, if anyone peeked in on them, which was fairly unlikely, the aliens would be hidden.

They all stood back, admiring their efforts. Even though Isara and Sartek were from another planet, it seemed that bed linen forts were a universal skill amongst kids of all species.

"It's perfect!" Isara held the red plaid flannel sheet aside invitingly.

Liberty moved the only table lamp they had into the fort and scattered pillows so they could gather together on the floor. The other three crawled in after him, and they sat in a circle, whispering about their plans.

It was late, and they were all fairly starved. Alex, who was much stealthier than Liberty, snuck down to the kitchen and brought back a sleeve of saltines, a jar of peanut butter, and a spoon. Handing a single cracker to each of them, she used the back of the spoon to slather them in turn with peanut butter, then passed out more crackers to make sandwiches out of.

Sartek watched her seat the second cracker carefully onto the peanut butter and squish it together. Doing the same, he beamed as he bit into it.

"This is good!"

The real surprise came when Alex handed them each a Bob's Club root beer. Isara's eyes shot open, and she choked, holding her hand up to her face as soda shot non-elegantly out her elegant nose. They all laughed, stifling the noise in pillows.

Liberty hopped up. "Be right back. Gotta shoot up." He threw the sheet flap aside and disappeared from the blanket fort.

Isara and Sartek looked at Alex, confusion on their faces. "He's diabetic," she explained simply. "It seriously sucks; he has to take injections and all, but he never complains about it."

The alien pair silently nibbled their peanut butter crackers as they considered what Alex had disclosed about their new friend. It was minutes before Liberty rejoined them and wriggled between Isara and Alex.

Finally, not so hungry and back to serious business, Isara indicated the door. "Won't they worry about David, wonder where he is?" By *they*, she meant the adults at *The Home*.

"Not so much, no," Alex said flatly. "Long as they think he's here. After five o'clock, Coors is king."

Liberty flipped his hands palm up. "They'll hear us sneaking around up here and just assume it's David, Alex, and me. But Alex is right; they never do a head count. Your voices are different, though, so let's just whisper so they don't get suspicious."

Then Liberty drew an invisible diagram with his finger on the wooden attic floor as he spoke. "So, we have to assume that the ship will be secured underground, or in a large outdoor hangar. If I had to guess, I'd say they'll bring it underground. If that's the case, we'll need a diversion to get in—a big one."

"There's a problem," Sartek said.

"Yeah there *is*," Alex interjected. "We still don't know where they have David, or what they're doing to him."

"They don't have David," Liberty announced flatly. "At least not the way they would *like* to have him."

"Huh?" Alex lit up.

"How do you know that?" Sartek's set his can of root beer down and leaned forward earnestly.

"Cuz they would have contacted *The Home* by now. If they haven't contacted Roxy to let her know they have him, then they don't, *technically*." Liberty was acutely aware that the military wouldn't know a kid would probably have to be missing for at least a week before Roxy would even notice or bother to tell someone.

"So…" Isara paused.

He glanced the direction of the door. "And they haven't come looking for us, either, to get details. They would have come for us for sure." Snapping another cracker in two, he just played with it, brushing away the salt. Goo, sensing this one might be up for grabs, edged in closer, and the boy handed it to the dog

"And that's another reason we need to leave here soon as possible, on the off chance that I'm wrong and someone does come snooping around."

"Then what's happened to him?" Sartek's voice carried genuine concern.

"Blalok has him!" Isara exclaimed with sudden certainty.

"What?" Alex grabbed her by the arm, but then jerked her hand free as though she'd been shocked. "Jeez! Did you feel that? What was that?"

Isara ignored her questions. "It makes sense! Blalok must have shifted him."

"And chances are the military thought he was another alien that was able to get back on the ship just in time," Sartek added, finishing off the equation.

"I agree." Liberty said. "It makes total sense that Blalok would've done that, and very impressive that he was able to pull it off. And, after inspecting their footage, the military may have decided the aliens look a lot like humans."

"If we're going to get the ship back and free David, Blalok's going to need inside help—*human* help." Sartek tapped his temple gently with one knuckle.

Isara was obviously encouraged. "Well, then that's good! You know David; we know Blalok. We should be able to figure out what they each might be thinking!"

"Yes!" Alex blurted.

"For one," Sartek said, "Blalok wouldn't have engaged the forces, and he obviously didn't. That's how they captured the *Star* in the first place. He would never have allowed the humans to be hurt."

"Well, that's dumb," Alex shot.

He glanced her way and tried to further explain. "It's not our way, and Blalok's, well, stubborn. He wouldn't have risked it at any cost."

"So that explains why he didn't just whoosh outa' there when he had the chance?"

"Yes," Isara nodded. "But that doesn't mean we can't try to recover the *Star*—get them and freed. We just can't hurt anyone in the process."

"You know," Alex shrugged, "that's all fine and good, but in the long run, if you're gonna make it in the galaxy, you might need to reconsider your rules. Sooner or later, in my experience, you're going to come across someone who just needs thumped on."

Isara and Sartek both stared at Alex as though carefully considering the human's curious take on their age-old belief system.

"We need a diversion," Liberty pressed on. "We need to find a way inside, to release their hold on the ship."

"Sure," Alex agreed. "Why don't we just fly right in there like *Star Wars* and plant a bomb on the death star? Blow it all to crap."

Liberty grinned at her. "Exactly…"

CHAPTER TEN

Δ

Isara was the first to awaken. She was chilly in the early, cool seventy-three degrees of a Kansas August morning. Momentarily forgetting where she was, she instinctively reached to drag the blanket more snugly up over her shoulder.

Just as she started to doze off again, the blanket was swiftly yanked back off. Snapping more to her senses, it was about then that she felt the presence of something living and warm, curled up against her back.

She shot a look over her shoulder to discover Alex, still in her overalls from the day before, sleeping soundly with the blanket clutched in both hands, stuffed up under her chin. It was a charming image, and Isara couldn't help but smile.

She briefly studied the human's face in the morning light. How unusual— the elongated nose, wide-set eyes, and full mouth. And her coloring was so pale and golden, with faint little spots all across her nose.

It was just then that Isara remembered David and Blalok and sat up with a start. She gently shook Alex by the shoulder until she heard a soft moan.

"Shut up, Bert. Go away," Alex mumbled, then her eyes shot open. She stared, briefly confused by the alien sitting next to her, hogging her blanket.

"It's morning, Alex," Isara whispered. "We need to get up."

Sitting upright in a flash, Alex tossed the blanket aside and was down in the kitchen in another flash, digging through the pantry and collecting provisions.

* * *

While Alex foraged, Liberty shuffled his new friends out the bathroom window, across the porch, and down to the corncrib to wait for Alex.

It was cooler in the shade of the crib; dew clung yet to the grass, and Sartek wrapped his hoodie jacket around Isara's shoulders.

It seemed like forever, but at long last, Alex trotted down the back porch stairs with a bag of snacks—more dried oatmeal, more peanut butter, five day-old bananas, and a can of Vienna sausages along with another half rack of saltine crackers. There were also four more cans of Bob's Root Beer. After listing off the inventory, she said, "Eight cans gone in less than twelve hours. That'll be another reason to call out the military."

Liberty ordinarily would have worried about that as well, but today he didn't. He wasn't even sure, just then, if they were ever coming back. That is why what he did next was one of the hardest things ever.

Goo came bouncing down the back porch steps, smiling and full of anticipation of a day out with his human and his new, strange friends.

"Stay," Liberty commanded firmly, and it broke his heart. "*Stay…*Goo."

The dog hung his head and paused with one paw up. His expression was one of, "That can't be right? I always go with you." His eyes were larger than usual, and damp. That was always his first tactic, a stab at looking pathetic to see if Liberty would cave.

"Go on, boy. Go home. I'll be back soon."

The little dog turned to amble slowly back, pausing only once to look over his shoulder at the group in a last ditch effort to sway them.

"Go, Goo!" Liberty snapped at the dog, waving his arms.

The dog hustled, tail tucked forlornly, and took a dejected seat on the lowest step. Obviously unhappy with the turn of events, Goo watched his master leave with sad, bewildered eyes.

Liberty knew he would sit on the steps for a good, long while. Then, Goo would eventually crawl upstairs and claim the lower bunk bed. Snuggling down into his master's blanket, he would wait out the lazy day. It was always a difficult climb for the little dog—two flights up to the attic with his short legs, but that's where he'd wind up.

Later, as evening approached, Goo would be confused that Liberty hadn't returned. He'd probably spend most of his time curled up in the familiar smell of his human's bed to wait the confusion out.

Liberty wanted to go back inside. He wanted to wake up Sage or Julian and ask them to keep an eye on his dog for him, but he knew he could not.   It would just be too risky. But knowing the youngest ones would try to sneak Goo snacks, just like they'd seen him do, gave Liberty some small comfort.

It should hold the fat little hound for a bit, anyway.

Not sure when he'd ever see his dog again, he swallowed, blinking back. Unwilling to let his friends see his weakness, he looked away and took a deep breath to clear his emotions.

"C'mon Bert, let's get a move on," Alex said gently. "Goo'll be okay."

Liberty only nodded.

They started wordlessly for town. It was barely light as they wandered down fifth to Jefferson, toward the Erie K-8 elementary-middle school that used to be the old high school.

They stayed in the shadows, and when an occasional car passed, Isara and Sartek looked away, hiding their features beneath their hoodies. They'd confiscated them from David's wardrobe, and Isara also sported a pair of Alex's worn overalls. They were a bit short up the shins, and gave her a very charming, country appearance. Sartek's pair of faded jeans, also from David's drawer, fit perfectly, though he kept hiking them up. Isara glanced at them more than once.

After they were underway a while, Sartek asked, "Do you have any fish?"

"What? For breakfast? That's just gross." Alex wrinkled her nose.

Liberty offered, "Well, I guess it would make sense. They look like they come from a fairly fishy planet," then blushed, thinking to himself, *That was probably the dumbest thing I've ever said.*

Kneeling down behind a retaining wall on the corner of Fourth Avenue, he pulled off his backpack. It took a bit of rummaging around before he pulled a small tin can from the pack and opened up the Vienna sausages.

Alex peeled open the package of saltines and handed them to him, one at a time. He sandwiched one sausage between two crackers before handing it to Isara.

"Here, this is probably as close as we have to fish, but not half bad."

"If you close your eyes, you can imagine it's whatever you want it to be!" Alex beamed.

Isara looked unconvinced, but once she bit into the sandwich, her eyes flew open with delight.

"It's delicious!"

"Yep—scrumptious as mystery meat can get!" Liberty slapped another sausage between two more crackers and handed it to Sartek. Then he popped open a root beer and they shared it, passing it around.

Curiously, none of the children even thought for a second that the other species might carry something that might make them ill—a virus or bacteria from an alien species. It just wasn't a part of their makeup to consider such a thing. That would have been a decidedly adult fear.

In quick fashion, the raw edge of their hunger was smoothed, and they ventured on, soon finding themselves outside of the elementary school—with no way in.

"How will we get in?" Isara wondered.

"I don't know," Liberty thought hard. "That's not really my strong area. I've never broken in someplace before." They were standing under a small thicket of trees just outside of the boy's bathroom, looking up at an overhead, frosted window with a lever catch on it.

"Well, I guess we could break it, but that might draw some attention." Alex scanned the ground for a rock to throw. Nothing—the schoolyard had been cleared of all such implements long ago. She opted for a nearby beer bottle somebody had hucked at a garbage can and missed.

"We better do something, quick," Liberty worried. "We look plenty suspicious, four kids standing around outside a closed school like this."

Alex wound up for the throw.

"Wait, how does the catch work?" Sartek peered at the overhead window again.

"It's a handle lever; you just flip it ninety degrees," Liberty explained.

Sartek glanced at Isara and nodded. She stepped onto his knee, into his laced hands, and then onto his shoulders. He held firmly onto her legs as she leaned in close to the brick of the old building.

Mesmerized, Liberty watched as Isara first rested her cheek against the wall, then extended her arm with her palm resting softly against the glass where the lever was. She and Sartek closed their eyes. Seconds later, the catch trembled, then shifted. The window popped barely open.

"How'd you do that?" Alex clasped her hands together in excitement.

"You're telekinetic?" Liberty tipped his head sideways.

Sartek was lifting Isara up even farther, extending his arms completely so that she could pull the window farther open and shinny through. When he was satisfied she was in, he turned around. "I can move objects with my thoughts, but not big things so much. Mostly just small. Isara can too…sometimes, if I'm touching her."

"That is so cool! I would be moving stuff all the time!" Alex exclaimed. "Right into Roxy's face!"

Sartek shrugged. "It's considered an art of necessity on Bettua."

"Well, it couldn't have been more necessary than it is now." Liberty could hardly contain his excitement.

His new alien friend was telekinetic, or more accurately, psychokinetic! He'd read about psychokinetics, but never met one.

Just then, they heard a *tap, tap, tap* from a lower classroom window to the left, from around a corner. Hurrying to the window, they saw Isara inside, unlatching the window. "Hurry, in here; there's no alarms as far as I can tell."

The three climbed through the window and stood for a moment, their eyes adjusting to the relative darkness of the closed-up school. It had a dusty, dank smell to it and Sartek wrinkled his nose. "Lights?" he suggested.

Liberty shook his head. "Too risky." He motioned for them to follow him. "Come on, the computers are this way."

They made their way out into the hall and toward the main entrance until they came to a large double door with frosted glass that was etched with the word *LIBRARY*.

Liberty tested the handle and was relieved to find it unlocked. Opposite the circulation desk was a bank of cubbies that had some seriously outdated Dell PC's packed into them. They were archaic by all standards, but Liberty knew they would serve well enough. "All we need is Internet access and we're good to go."

He pressed the power button of one of the towers. It took a few seconds before the screen flickered to life, lit with universal-computer electric blue.

Before long, Liberty was logged onto his email account and saw a message from "David the Great." He gave a thumbs up over his shoulder at his friends before he clicked the file open and read…

Hi, Bert. It's David and Blalok. I guess by now you probably know who Blalok is, and E-I says you'll know to come to the school and check your e-mail. E-I is really smart. It's, I mean he's a computer. So is Blalok for that matter…kinda, but I'll bet you'd beat him at chess.

You don't know that.

Yes, he would.

Shut up! Once I learn? ...no, he wouldn't.

YOU shut up...stupid head.

It was about then that Liberty recognized the e-mail message must have been verbally composed and translated, complete with occasional interjection from the alien called Blalok.

He smiled and read on.

Anyway, we're in the ship, heading to some super secret place named Hutchinson. E-I said you'd know that. Not sure if that's the end stop, but we're thinking probably so. Bert, we have to get these guys their ship back and out of here. It's only right. They don't belong here; they won't make it, if you know what I mean, and I know you do

.

Tell him about the communication device.

I'm GETTING to it... Just hold the phone already! Bert, E-I says you need a laptop with Wi-Fi and a universal range extender, and guess what? He bought it for you! That's right, it's early Christmas for the BERTSTER! I'm not exactly sure how he did it, but it has something to do with a hedgehog fund...

Hedge fund.

Oh, right, hedge fund, that he stole somehow and put to your name. You got money, Bert! You're rich! Only you can't get to it.... You're too young; isn't that always how it is? But the laptop and range extender are waiting for you at the Chanute Walmart. And Bert, it's not exactly a laptop; it's some super sophisticated tablet with Wi-Fi and...free VuDu.

By now, Liberty's eyes were enormous. He certainly recognized the gravity of their overlying situation, but to have a device like that? It was almost too good to be true. He blinked and read on.

Once you get the tablet, head on to Hutchinson. There's a house there;

key's by the front doorstep, hidden inside a plastic rock, go figure. It's on 629 Crazy Horse Road, and once you're there, log on. Anything else, little dude?

My name's Blalok, and no, I think you have covered it.

Cool. Tell everyone, "Hi," and…miss you, Bert. C'ya soon, and we'll spring this baby. Over and out.

You don't need to say that.

You don't have much of a sense of adventure, do you?

That was the end of the transmission. Liberty swung around in his chair.

Alex had been reading over his shoulder.

"Let me encrypt this," he said, "then we need to get out of here, fast." He went directly back to the keyboard, and wrote…

Hi, David and Blalok. Yep, we figured out to come to the school and get online. Isara and Sartek are safe, although we risk them getting discovered at any time. I recommend we do a preemptive strike as soon as possible. I have an idea, but for now, we're going to go get the tablet, then get to Hutchinson. I'll visual contact you at that point.

I'm so glad you're okay, David; that was really amazing…what you did.

These guys have super powers, by the way. You'll have to hit Blalok up for a demo. For now, I'm encrypting this e-mail. The new email will be Qt83nfX9@gmail.com, and the passcode is ITk39g7j39. It will rotate.

We'll catch up with you guys soon, and be careful.

Until next time, Bert…over and out.

He encrypted his e-mail account and went online one more time.

"Hurry up, Bert." Alex fidgeted. "It's getting lighter."

"Just a sec. Gotta cover our tracks."

He shuffled through a few more sites, and after what seemed like an eternity, entered a virtual room called "DeadDungeon" and left a code-locked message for someone named Vole. Finally satisfied, he pushed away from the computer.

"What was that all about?" Sartek gestured toward the now blank screen.

"Vole's a hacker and runs a network from his basement. And, he's seriously antigovernment, has a pretty big chip on his shoulder."

"So he'll help us?" Isara seemed encouraged.

"Yep, if it comes down to it, I think he will. He's still kind of raw about doing a year in federal juvie for the Katipo virus.

"Katipo virus?" Isara wondered.

"Yeah. That one enrolled everyone in the Pentagon on a perpetual dating site. Guess a few divorces came of it. They were all pretty pissed and never could get rid of it, not until Vole killed it.

"They told him they'd only let him out of prison if he fixed it, and then only if he worked for them. He agreed, got out, cleaned up the virus then slipped away and disappeared."

They just stared at him, and he added, "Now he lives in a basement in Pittsburgh with a brand new identity, but they don't know that."

"And you do?" Sartek asked.

Liberty nodded. "They can't track him, and it's made them real nervous. But he's a friend of mine, and he'll clean the hard drive on this machine from his site. Then, he'll send it a virus and nobody around here will be able to fix it. The school will wind up junking it."

Liberty turned around in his chair.

"And like I said, when the time comes, he'll also be there, virtually, to help us out if we need him."

"How did you meet him?" Isara wondered.

"Chess...." He grinned. "Vole is fifteen, but has a twenty-one year old identity, so he gets around pretty good. He'll help us, especially when I give him the details. Don't worry; Vole can be trusted, especially if it gives him another chance for payback. He doesn't take on friends easily, but those he does, he's committed to."

Liberty grinned.

"And I think he's always wanted to hack the North American Aerospace Defense Command. Now's his big chance."

"Very cool," Sartek said, adopting the earth slang he'd read in Liberty's note. Isara raised a single eyebrow and gave him the Bettuan equivalent of a bemused look.

"Quit it. You're not being *cooool.*" He dragged the word out and did a weird thing with his hands, shifting them back and forth at his waistline.

It came across as so incredibly un-cool that the others laughed in unison.

Next, the kids found the kitchen and rifled through it for more food. Nothing but instant cocoa, but Alex grabbed a couple packets anyway and stuffed them into her back pockets.

"Seriously? Instant cocoa?" Liberty asked.

"I like it, and you know we never have it at *The Home*." Looking around, she spied an insinkerator at one of the utility sinks. "See! Ask and you shall receive stuff!"

Confiscating Dixie cups from a sink-side wall dispenser, she made hot chocolate for everyone. Sitting on the kitchen floor, well hidden and away from any windows, they might have been just four ordinary kids, kicking it on a late summer's day.

Alex was tipping a dry packet back so she could take cocoa hits from it, sticking her chocolaty tongue out at Liberty at intervals, only because he told her to *quit playing around*. At one point, she must have inhaled some because she let go a big cough and brown powder poofed out of her mouth.

The others tried hard to stifle laughter, and Liberty said, "You look like a dragon, a scary, dirt breathing dragon!"

After a quick snack of cocoa and oatmeal, they plundered through the drawers and cabinets for money. Nothing, so they went to the office. It was locked, but not for long.

Sartek leaned his dark head against the jamb and closed his eyes.

The lighting was poor, so Liberty noticed how, as Sartek concentrated, the ridge of scales that ran over the crest of his head came more to life with tiny flecks of light jumping from one spot to the next like a miniature laser show. It was mesmerizing, and he realized how much there was to learn about the Bettuan.

The deadbolt clicked open, and in short time they found the emergency cash stash. Soon, they'd confiscated barely enough change to get them to Hutchinson. Then, it was time to go back to the library and out the ground floor window.

Sartek leaned against the window and closed his eyes one last time, his hand resting on the pane directly over the catch. Almost immediately, the lever flipped ninety degrees and locked the window from the inside.

The four left the school, heading to the Jefferson Depot where they bought four tickets and boarded a mostly empty bus for Chanute, Kansas. Making their way to the back of the bus, Isara and Sartek slid down in their seats, their hoodies pulled down over much of their faces, sunglasses concealing their eyes.

The only other passengers on the bus were an elderly couple, and they'd chosen the front seats. The bus driver glanced back at them once or twice, but the kids were being very quiet, and so he put in one ear-bud, powered up his MP3 payer, and drove on, effectively ignoring them.

* * *

The bus ride would be a few hours long. Isara sat beside Alex, and after a while, they whispered questions to each other.

"Is Sartek your brother?" Alex wondered.

Isara seemed surprised. "*Brother*? No, he's my friend."

"Is he your boyfriend?"

"No!" Isara said a bit hasty, then looked around and slid farther down in her chair. "I mean, of course not."

"So you, and Sartek, and Blalok are best friends, like me, David, and Bert?"

"Yes, I guess so." She hesitated. "We were taking the *Star* out one day, to play, just for the afternoon. That's…" she stared at her feet, "…when it happened." Pulling off her sunglasses, she rubbed at her eyes with the heel of her hand.

"You guys don't know how to get back, do you?" Alex's question didn't really sound like a question.

"No, we don't, and Blalok doesn't think we can; he thinks we're lost for good," Isara confided, her gaze wandering out the window to the rows of empty cornfields beyond.

"Well, sometimes really smart people aren't always right. Once Bert was so sure we could start this old truck if we crossed these three wires. Couldn't ever get it to run, but the windshield wipers turned on great!" Alex gestured, hands open. "He still says it shoulda' worked. Funny thing is…I believe him. It *should* have.

"Maybe it's like that, and Blalok's wrong…in the right way. Maybe there isn't a way back, till you stumble across it and some giant, space windshield wiper slaps you home." Alex shrugged. "I think you should just keep looking."

Isara appeared to have no idea what Alex was talking about, but the way she said it sounded hopeful and kind, and she smiled softly back. "Perhaps, you're right."

"There might not be any way back," Alex added after a few minutes of silence, "but, at least, you have Sartek and Blalok. And now *I'm* your friend."

She looked up from picking at her fingernail to meet Isara's gaze.

Isara's turquoise eyes were very solemn as she focused on Alex. "You know what? You're right, and I'm very happy to have you as my friend."

"Yep, we're both lost and have best friends." She tossed a thumb toward Liberty, who was engaged in conversation with Sartek. "We can't go back either; there's nothing to go back to. Bert lost his folks in a wreck."

Isara immediately had a very hurt expression about her. At least her mother and father weren't dead, as far as she knew. "I'm so sorry. And where are your parents?"

"Hmm…" Alex thought sincerely about the question. "I don't know. I can't remember them, really, but I have a brother."

"A brother? And where is he?" Isara was very attentive now.

"Hell if I know. Afghanistan, I think. He must be alive though; nobody told me he *isn't*…yet. That's a law, you know. They have to tell you if someone dies in your family, in the army, I mean."

She kicked the empty seat in front of her.

"I haven't seen him for a long time, not since I was eight or nine. But I got a letter when he was deployed."

Alex gazed past Isara and out the window. Well, wherever James is and whatever he's doing, it probably isn't crazy as sitting next to an alien on a bus, headed to try to steal a from the government." Alex smiled—that rare, sweet smile that she didn't know David thought was one of the most beautiful things he'd ever seen—and tilted her head, her eyes partly closed.

"I'm glad we're in this together, Isara."

"Me, too. It makes it not so…lonely.

CHAPTER ELEVEN

Δ

On board the *Cerulean Star*, Blalok and David were adjusting to each other's company. After composing their e-mail and making sure the *Star* was secure, David became restless. Nothing was happening other than they were being dragged along at a moderately poor bicycle land-speed.

For a while, he'd wandered the ship, leaving Blalok to what appeared to be redundantly boring tasks, all involving his precious computer console. But he came upon mostly dead ends as he'd no idea of how to access the different floors or rooms of the ship.

The ship was, to David, very organic. Even the hum of the engines, so faint in the background, seemed living. It felt as though it almost breathed. He thought it not unlike living inside the belly of a whale—a very friendly whale, perhaps, with comfortable furniture and a good rug. Furthermore, it could protect him and fly him through an ocean of stars if asked to. The astonishment of all this was too much, and he could feel exhaustion creeping up on him.

"Come with me. We'll get something to eat, and I'll show you where you can sleep for a while." Blalok hopped up from his levi-chair.

For the first time, David was aware of just how hungry he was and how small this particular alien was.

"Wow, you remind me so much of Bert, it's weird."

"Weird creepy, or weird unbelievable?" Blalok crossed his arms and stood as tall as he could. Even so, he had to tip his head back to meet David's eyes.

"Weird cool. You're alright, Blalok, and when you meet Bert, you're gonna love him." David soft-punched him on the shoulder.

Blalok stared at his own shoulder, shook his head, and said more to himself, "And *I'm* the weird one." He regarded David through narrowed eyes. "So, what say we have some dinner?"

"Great idea. I'm so starved I could eat the butt outa' a skunk! Do you have cheeseburgers?"

Blalok hesitated. "No, I do not know what that is, but let's get E-I to address the situation."

"You sound like a little computer, you know that?" David grinned.

"Thank you," he replied smugly. "You do not…"

Blalok lead the way off the bridge. A short ways down a corridor, an emblem glowed softly, midway up the ceiling.

"Open," Blalok spoke to the emblem. An elevator simply appeared, the wall doing exactly as he'd commanded. It dissipated in a faint, sparkling pattern, creating the small housing that was to be their elevator.

"So that's why I couldn't get anywhere," David observed and was ignored.

Stepping inside, David saw no controls. It was lit, but not by any obvious lighting. For the first time, he realized that in the elevator, and on the bridge for that matter, there was light but no obvious fixtures. And it was natural, like daylight on a bright but cloudy day.

While on the elevator, Blalok instructed E-I to allow David's voice to carry *recognition presiding authority*. "That will allow you to access areas of the ship as you need to," he explained.

"Thanks. Shoot us to the moon!" he joked. The elevator decelerated anticlimactically and stopped. David glanced sheepishly around.

Blalok sighed audibly. "Belay that, uh…stupidity. Dining hall, please." The elevator whooshed them up and sideways to what appeared to be the combination kitchen/dining room.

Stepping off the elevator and into the room, David was once again amazed at the otherworld technology. As on the bridge, everything was in shades of blue, white, and green.

There was no obvious cooking surface, refrigerator, or pantry—only a table, chairs, and some very artistic ornamentation. Water flowed, sometimes from the floor to the ceiling. It swirled and swept, softly and pleasingly in ways water might not ordinarily go.

There were plants—unusual plants—some smooth and slick, some lacy and frond like, others submerged entirely under the water. It was, aesthetically, very appealing, as though someone had brought an underwater garden into the room.

"Nice!" David glanced around. "But, where do we fix something?"

Blalok shook his head, then motioned David over to a screen that shimmered in beautiful blue and green patterns. Blalok paused. "Skunk butt? Or cheeseburger?"

"Huh? Oh…cheeseburger."

Blalok summoned E-I, then analyzed from the earth obtained files everything there was to know about cheeseburgers. Then he ran his hands over a few smooth controls, until he seemed satisfied. Turning around, he motioned with one hand back over David's shoulder.

The human spun about just as a small window dissolved revealing a small cubicle and clear blue platter. Upon the platter sat a cheeseburger, the steam rising from it as though it'd just been barbecued.

The second he got a good whiff of it, Blalok's look of satisfaction turned to pure disgust. "Ugh! Are you really going to eat that?" He tilted his head away from the offending burger.

"How did you do that?" David was across the room in three long strides. "That's amazing!" It *was* amazing, and the aroma greeted the human in a splendid way.

Eyeing the platter, Blalok held it as far from himself as he could set the burger down on the table. "It's bio-organic synthesis," the alien explained. "The computer determines the exact sequence of protein, carbohydrates, fats, sugars, stuff like that, and fabricates it in that particular molecular order. It allows us a diversified diet with only a few essential building blocks."

"Seriously? It made this out of *nothing*? You could totally own the veggie market on Earth with this! No more dead cows n' chickens; you'd be a hero, and it'd make a million!"

"And what would I do with *a million*?" Blalok wondered, his eyes narrowing in a frown.

But there were more important matters at hand. Not realizing how hungry he was, David picked up the cheeseburger with both hands and started to bite into it, then paused, eyes twinkling as he held it out to Blalok. "Want some? It's *really* good."

Blalok shook his head, went to the fabricator, and minutes later, retrieved something that very much resembled a squid. And, it smelled, David imagined, exactly like a squid might smell.

"Seriously? You'd take that over this?"

"*Seriously?* Yes," was all Blalok replied.

David bit into the cheeseburger and crinkled his forehead. "Got any salt?" Passing his palm across the center of the table, Blalok summoned condiments.

Between them appeared a small caddy with various Bettuan spices. Most were very foreign to David, like something he'd seen in a cooking magazine once about a sushi restaurant, but amidst the seasonings was a delicate bowl half full with what appeared to be rough, granular salt. Evidently, this was a basic necessity they all had in common, and David wondered briefly if all species, from all planets, enjoyed salt.

Following Blalok's lead, he pinched the salt with two fingers and sprinkled it onto his own meal, and together, they dined. In between bites, David carried the conversation, asking Blalok about Bettua, Sartek, and Isara.

His companion replied in mostly short answers, then quite suddenly asked, "Is Liberty your best friend?"

David thought sincerely about the question, considering what E-I disclosed to him earlier—things about Bert he hadn't known. "Yeah, Bert is one of my best friends. Alex is the other. They're *both* my best friends."

Blalok said nothing, only chewed his food thoughtfully.

"Probably like Isara and Sartek are to you; that's my guess, anyway," David added

"But, Bert is different," Blalok said flatly.

"Different? Well, yeah, I guess so. He's really, really smart for one thing. So smart, it'll make your head spin."

Blalok stared blankly, and David waved it off. "But, we're all different, aren't we?" David continued in between bites. "Think about it. Bert's really different, but so are you. And you got stuck with me, but we're doing great." That was met with an alien scowl.

"C'mon. Really, who do you think you'd get on with better, me or Bert?"

"Bert," Blalok answered without hesitation, but then, "Or...perhaps I would get along well with you both."

David pretended to go squinty eyed and said suspiciously, "Blalok, are you trying to be my friend?" He held his hand out again, just as he'd done on the bridge.

Blalok took it, shaking enthusiastically. "Yes, I endeavor to be your friend, and just for the sake of it."

"I'm not sure what that means, but back atcha'." David grinned widely.

After a thoroughly enjoyable dinner, Blalok showed the human to his sleep quarters. They were simple but elegant, decorated similarly to the dining room, only there were a few objects that David thought must be art.

Across the room in the corner, there was a small grotto with what appeared to be a shower, only the water ran very slowly in a tubular, fine mist, again from the floor to the ceiling, where it just seemed to disappear. It was lit within—a lovely turquoise.

"Step in there to clean up," Blalok explained bluntly.

"Towels? Toilet paper? You know, the essentials?" David asked.

"You won't need a towel. The hydrolysis shower will wash you, then leave you dry. And don't worry, you should be able to breathe while you are in it."

He spun about.

"There are facilities in here."

Motioning to another wall, he passed his hand over yet another emblem. It vaporized, revealing a small cubicle with what appeared to be a cylindrical tube about the size of a chair.

"I don't get it. You guys go to the bathroom in there...on *that*?" David gestured toward the tube.

"When the time comes, just sit; you'll figure it out," Blalok said almost smugly then pointed to the sleep chamber on the opposite side of the room. "You can rest here. It is restorative. Sleep unclothed, or not, as you wish, and I will see you in six hours."

"Whoa! Whoa, wait. What are you saying? I lay on that thing naked?" He pointed to the sleep chamber. "Sorry, Blalok, I'm guessing that's really not gonna work out."

"*In*. You lie in it, not on it. And it is your preference, but clothing can chafe," Blalok warned.

"Chafe? You mean like a wedgie?" David shook his head, "I don't think so, little dude; just point me to a couch or something."

Blalok said a bit gruffly, jutting his chin out in defiance, "There are no couches aboard this ship; sleep in your chamber, or don't sleep."

David glanced nervously back and forth from Blalok to the empty. "Are you gonna, you know, go into one of these?"

"I do, every night."

David shifted his weight from one foot to the next. "All right...okay, but show me how to lock the door. If those marines bust in on us in the middle of the night, I don't want them seeing this, you know."

He swept both hands from his chest down past his groin and out.

Blalok cocked his head to one side. "I assure you, no one will not break in tonight. The *Star* is secure for approximately three point two days. Not until then will they be able to breach the hull."

"Excuse me, *what*? Are you saying that the shields are gonna fail?"

Suddenly much more serious, he took a step toward Blalok, not really meaning to appear aggressive. "And when were you going to tell me this?"

Blalok backed stepped back from him, his eyes wide. "I'm saying that we only have so much time before the hull deteriorates. The *Cerulean Star* requires space travel to regenerate. Its outer shell will not survive indefinitely in this atmosphere."

David towered over him. "We have three days? You're just now telling me we only have *three days*? Blalok, we need to get our shit together! And we need to do it fast!"

"I don't understand, 'to get your shit togeth—'?"

"We don't have time to fool around! We need a plan, and we need it now! In three days, we're gonna be in terminal lockdown!" David swung his arms over his head. "Do you understand what I'm *saying*? They're gonna stick me in a hole so deep I'll never see the light of day, and they're gonna stick a probe up your—they're gonna…" He trailed off, his mind racing.

Just then, something extraordinary happened.

The only other object in the room was a levi-chair. It sat opposite what appeared to be a computer panel and, it moved. The chair shifted, not very far, only a few feet, but definitely a shift. Then it spun around several times before thudding quite hard against the wall.

David jumped back. "Hey! Why'd you do that?"

Blalok only stared wordlessly at the chair.

"*You* did do that, right?" David pointed.

"No, I don't think so."

"You don't think so? What does that mean, like maybe you did?"

"No, I can pretty much guarantee that I did not." Blalok crossed his arms over his chest in finality.

"Then what? Who?" David's eyes narrowed as he stepped closer to Blalok.

"Some Bettuan are telekinetic, and also mildly telepathic. In addition, some females can be minimally avataristic."

"What does that mean? What are you saying? I don't understand the words coming out of your mouth!" David caught himself just then as he remembered Bert mentioned something about superpowers.

Blalok took a slow breath before explaining to David that Bettuan could move small objects in fine ways. "Like the clasp of a necklace, or the shift of a lever. It's fairly common, but only a few Bettuan have ever been able to move objects larger than, say, a dinner plate. Sartek is the best at it, of the three of us." Then he added wryly, "And he's not really that good."

The alien gave David a moment to process this before he continued.

"And some of us can plant and interpret ideas on a subconscious level, but mostly just instinctual suggestions. Only a rare few Bettuan can formulate actual thoughts. I work very hard to *not* do this and to prevent others from doing it to me. I find it annoying and distracting."

"That's just crazy! And avatarbism? That other thing you said, what's that?"

"Avatar*ism*—the ability to take electrical energy and channel it into an inanimate object. As I said, only the females of our species have exhibited this, and Isara doesn't appear to have that capability, not yet anyway. She is, however, a healer. In reality, avatarism is quite rare."

Blalok seemed completely satisfied with his explanations and gazed blankly at David.

"And you?"

Blalok stood motionless, his lips not moving, but David heard him speak, in his head, very clearly. "Telepathic, yes. But, as I said, I prefer not to engage or be engaged with it."

David was stunned. He also had the feeling that his mind had been subtly probed as well, and he wasn't at all amused. "I thought you said it was rare to be able to plant real thoughts."

"It is."

The gravity of what Blalok was telling him started to sink in. "You're one freaky little guy, Blalok, but that doesn't explain the chair."

"I did not move the chair. And since I can guarantee that you and I are the only ones present, it appears that you did."

This gave David serious pause. "That's insane! I...I can't move stuff, haven't even ever tried."

"But you were agitated when it happened."

"I've been agitated before when things happen, but furniture never flew anywhere! It's just not right!"

"However, you have never been agitated around a Bettuan," Blalok hypothesized.

David stopped himself. "What are you saying, that *you* did this to me? Gave me this...*power*?" He was oversimplifying the notion a great deal.

Blalok blinked slowly. "I am simply suggesting that given our limited evidence, and as improbable as it seems, it is the distinct probability."

"Sweet mother..." David began but trailed off.

"I would suggest we revisit this in the morning. I am tired, and I would assume you are as well. Yes, we need a plan, but we've been awake for nearly twenty-seven point two hours. We need rest. E-I will take care of the ship while we sleep."

David was silent. He stared at the levi-chair, now apparently content to remain unmoving on the other side of the room.

"David, I know we don't know each other well, and this is very foreign to you," Blalok spoke solemnly and sincerely. "But I am not just cerebral. I have good instincts, and I know you are sincerely concerned for our ship and your friends. Please don't panic. We have made the correct choices so far.

"We will communicate with them this afternoon, after they secure their computer device. It is the logical thing to do, and E-I will help. Then, as they say on Bettua, we must let fate direct the seas. It becomes beyond our control."

David didn't say anything for a moment. He simply regarded the odd little alien closely.

Blalok blinked and tilted his head back. The inky strands of his hair swung, smooth and sleek, before settling into place again, and the small, pointed peaks on his crown sparkled in tiny, lightening flashes.

"David, we'll be okay," he said.

The human shook his head. "I hope you're right. I...hope you're right."

They said goodnight, and David was left alone with an intimidating sleep chamber and his own questionable tenacity. He eventually compromised, stripped down to only his boxer shorts, and stepped, one foot and then another, into the tube. The chair incident still had him somewhat rattled.

"This is stupid," he muttered, "like I'm gonna' sleep naked on a floor."

As he stepped into the chamber tube and began to sit, his feet slipped from beneath him, and he went instantly buoyant. The light within the tube dimmed as his body first bobbed and then stabilized.

Almost immediately, David was overcome with the sensation of a gentle, even pressure over every square inch of his body. It was warm, and soothing, and somehow hypnotizing. It even seemed to go into his ears and nose, but not unpleasantly. And, the effect was rather moist, in a lovely way, against his eyes and mouth when they were open.

The weight of their situation—the horrible odds that David now clearly recognized—crashed heavy against him just then.

This particular boy carried great burdens, regarding and disregarding his current situation. Instantly aware of just how exhausted he was, he closed his eyes, allowing the sensation of *stasis* to wash over him even more as the lighting dimmed to nearly dark.

Within moments, the cares of the day faded, and all that was left was the gentle hum of the *Star*'s engines. It was the most relaxing thing he'd ever experienced, and suddenly he felt like crying and wasn't at all sure why.

In another instant, the human boy was sleeping and, except for some very mild chafing in places he would prefer not to speak of…it was perfect.

CHAPTER TWELVE

Δ

Nearly two hours later, the kids stepped off a bus in Chanute, Kansas. Liberty squinted into the late morning sun. The air was dry in his throat, and he noticed the brief, pained expression on Sartek's face as the alien swallowed thickly. He wondered if his new friend missed Bettua just now, with its vast oceans and hardly a scrap of dust.

During their bus ride, Sartek described, while observing the seemingly endless fields of corn that stretched flat and dry all the way to the horizon, how there was virtually no land spot on his home planet from which water wasn't visible.

As if reading his mind, Alex nudged Liberty, handing him a bottle of water and indicating that he should pass it to Sartek.

"Thank you." The alien drank deeply and passed the bottle to Isara.

"Sure," Alex said. "Now let's get Bert that thingy and get outa' here."

"This way." Liberty waved, moving toward the intersection of Twenty-Sixth and Santa Fe. "Looks like there's an RV lot outside with a park. I think you guys should wait there. Try not to be noticed; I shouldn't be too long."

"Wal-Mart nomads?" Alex piped in cheerfully. "We'll blend right in...."

Liberty appreciated her optimism, and the three waited for him on the periphery of the small park, maintaining a good distance from anybody who might see them. Truthfully, the only other people in the area were a handful of vagrants, most of whom were enjoying a midmorning siesta on the benches.

Once inside, Liberty went straight to the service department to retrieve a two hundred dollar gift card and the tablet bundle that had been overnighted from Amazon. Curiously, all he had to show them to claim it was his tattered library card. He was never without it. It was one of the few things Liberty possessed that identified who he was, and it did so in a most perfect way.

David knew this and now, evidently...so did E-I. The ship's intelligence had configured the Wal-Mart transaction perfectly. Clearly the boy didn't have a driver's license, and so the items were only be handed over with proof of the library card.

Liberty fished his card from his front pants pocket and handed it to the woman behind the counter, barely able to contain his excitement. It was certainly highly unusual for a transaction to have these criteria, and she turned the ragged card over in her hands several times, a skeptical frown on her face.

"It's me," he assured her.

For an instant, Liberty feared she would to toss the card into the trash, but then, after studying the little boy with the endearingly crazy hair, she double-checked her batch orders before kindly handing over the expensive items.

"Well, someone sure loves you! Don't they?"

She smiled widely as though the items were a gift coming straight from her. Liberty's hands visibly trembled as she passed him the smooth, plastic bag containing a possible link to an alien ship.

"You guys really are great with service." He grinned up at her as he took the bag. Then he made a quick sweep of the store, picking up toothbrushes, soap, bottled water, and a bag of trail mix. On his way out, he also grabbed a bag of fishburgers from the in-store McDonalds.

"Fishburgers? Really?" Alex wrinkled her nose as he passed them around.

"I was trying to think what they might like for lunch," Liberty defended himself, hitching his thumb toward Isara and Sartek, but by the grimaces on their faces, it was a bust.

They left the remains in the brush for the raccoons, gobbled up the French-fries and some of the trail mix, and left the park.

Within the hour, they were on a bus to Hutchinson. After a morning of success, their confidence was escalating, and Liberty anticipated free sailing to their next destination. They were perhaps a bit more cavalier than they should have been as, after just a few more stops, the bus was chock full.

Settled comfortably toward the back, it was only thirty minutes or so, just

as they were chatting in hopeful whispers, when they met their first close call
with discovery.

Three older males, in their late teens or early twenties, were sitting four
rows ahead of the kids. Evidently bored with the drive to Hutchinson, they were
laughing too loudly and pointing, targeting other passengers on the bus for their
own amusement. It was one of those situations where the louder the group
grew, the quieter, and smaller, everyone else became.

"What's that?" one of them, the obvious leader, asked of no one in
particular, pointing at Sartek. He spoke loud enough for everyone on the bus to
hear. The noise on the bus fell to a deafening silence as most everyone turned to
look.

Sartek slumped down in his seat, pulling his hoodie farther down over his
eyes.

Isara shifted sideways in her seat, valiantly pretending to look out the
window.

Realizing he needed to run damage control, but not at all sure how, Liberty
stuttered to offer an explanation, having no idea what he was going to say. And
it really wasn't an issue, because he was superbly interrupted. Alex was on her
feet in a flash and shoved Liberty's fluffy white head in an *I got this* gesture.

"Alex," Liberty warned under his voice, "just let it go."

It was too late. The young man pushed himself up out of his seat and into
the aisle as though to confront the thirteen-year-old girl. He towered easily over
Alex, but it was she who advanced, closing the distance.

"Why don't you mind your own business, halfwit?" she barked.

"Why don't you make me?" The stranger pointed at Isara and Sartek. "And
what are a couple freaks doin' on the bus anyways?" He stepped toward Alex,
but pulled up short when she stood her ground, fearlessly counter attacking.

"What? You gonna go all redneck racist? Be a bigot? All tough in front of
everyone here, when we have visitors from Russia? And *cancer* patients, no
less? Way to be a man! You treat your momma that way?"

Alex flung her hands upward toward his face.

Liberty was amazed, first that Alex was so instantly prepared to take on
someone so much bigger than she was, and second, that she'd chosen to
identify the visiting aliens as cancer stricken Russians. She never failed to
surprise him, and her approach certainly worked, setting the young man right
back on his heels.

"You know the problem with bullies?" Alex threw the question right out there. "Nobody kicked their ass when they first needed it!"

The stranger started to stammer something, now obviously uncertain how to proceed with the irate girl. Liberty still felt the strong need to intervene and stepped into the aisle. Curiously, he didn't need to....

Before he could say or do anything, two impossible things happened.

Up until now, most of the passengers had been occupied by their own laptops, tablets, and other various personal-electronic devices. A pair of older Amish women were chatting quietly, gnarled hands click-clacking with their knitting, and a handful of passengers reclined in whatever unlikely position granted them a nap, that is until the bully and Alex had wakened them.

As is human nature, almost simultaneously, everyone on the bus abandoned whatever they were doing to watch the fight. So, no one noticed when all the electronics devices—the ones that were activated—shut off at exactly the same time.

Alex was firing up for round two but stuttered when something very unusual distracted both her and her target. An MP3 player was wedged in the man's front jeans pocket. The ear buds suddenly disengaged from the unit, pulling themselves and the attaching wires free. Entirely loose and dangling in the clear, they flew up and around in the air, all of their own accord, swinging wildly in a circle. Then, they wrapped themselves quite alarmingly about the youth's neck and began to tighten.

All eyes were on him as he seemed to instantly forget about Alex, now very preoccupied with his own reasonably desperate situation. The wires tightened even more, the earbuds hovering like angry hornets and pecking at his face. He clawed at the device, easily breaking the delicate wires. It fell, lifeless and in broken segments, to the floor in front of him.

Everyone stared dumfounded at the youth with the faint, red strangulation marks around his neck. Everyone shared the same wide-eyed, slacked jawed expression on his or her face, everyone but Alex.

She was bent over, clutching her belly, and staggered backward. Flopping into her seat, she dropped her head between her knees and grabbed for the vomit bag from the pocket on the back of the seat in front of her. She held the bag open in front of her face and fanned herself with her other hand. No one really noticed, still engrossed with the youth and perhaps waiting to see what else might come strangely to life.

Incidentally, this wasn't the end of it. Before anyone had time to consider what had just occurred, something else quite unusual happened.

Words—like a thought—entered the minds of everyone on the bus, and they were painfully loud, as though being called from an intrinsic, mind-blowing megaphone.

They aren't aliens. They're normal—just like us.

Everyone, aliens included, cowered and looked about as though the words had come overhead from the world's best loudspeaker system. And the loudspeaker was *very* persuasive.

Liberty, however, pitched violently backward in his seat, his hands going immediately up to his head.

The young man, who'd only a minute before been practically choked to death by his own headphones, was suddenly visibly relaxed. "I can see they're just like us. Don't know what I was thinking a second ago. Sorry guys. No worries, kay?" He slid back down into his seat, gathered up and reseated his broken ear-buds into his ears—with the severed wires still dangling—and reclined his chair back, closing his eyes as though he might enjoy a nap.

Everybody else on the bus seemed likewise convinced that nothing at all was amiss and went back to their books, knitting, or enjoying the passing scenery. Furthermore, they appeared content to ignore their universally dead electronics.

By now, Bert's nausea and abdominal pain were abating. Alex leaned across the aisle. "You okay?"

"Yeah, I'm…it's just that…"

He didn't finish, only closed his eyes and cradled his head in his hands.

Sartek passed him what was left of his water and looked back and forth between the two. "Are you avataristic? Telepathic?"

"What? *No!*" Alex blurted. "I never even saw that movie." Then she seemed unsure of herself. "But something sure talked inside my head, and it didn't just talk to me, I believed what it said, like I was convinced."

"I know," Sartek nodded gravely. "It was definitely telepathic but also had a strong concealed suggestion."

"And the incident with the head wires? Perhaps…" Isara's let her voice trail off.

By then, Liberty, a worrisome ashen color, could take a sip of water. Alex poured a bit of her own water into her palm and flicked droplets onto his face, which only annoyed him until he waved her off.

"I'm okay," he protested, "but you're right, I was thinking exactly what everyone heard, only I was more *wishing* they believed it. I know that doesn't make any sense, but that's exactly how it happened, at least to me."

Isara and Sartek regarded one another for a long, serious moment.

"Has that ever happened before?" Alex asked in a low voice.

"No, never. I mean, yeah, sure I've wished for things. But never like it was broadcasted like that, and never like my head was gonna' explode afterwards."

Sinking farther down into his seat, Sartek spoke softly to the humans—covert explanations of the telepathic and subliminally suggestive powers that some Bettuan possessed.

"But mostly it's just fragments of thoughts, like a few pieces of a puzzle. It's seldom a complete sentence, and uncommon that someone can so strongly plant a suggestion, especially to more than one person at a time like you did." He paused. "Blalok can, but he's really different—the very rare exception."

"And for the most part, he refuses to do it and is pretty good at keeping others from doing it to him," Isara added.

"I wasn't controlling it, not really. I more wanted it to be heard, wanted them to believe it," Liberty quietly explained. "But what about that totally freak thing with the headphones?"

Alex shifted in her seat, all eyes suddenly on her.

"I don't know what happened." She admitted weakly.

They leaned in close as she whispered, "I didn't *mean* to do that. I wasn't even sure I did." She twister her finger in her hair like she sometimes did when she knew she was guilty of something. "I was just mad as crap—was thinking to myself that he should just shut up, that I'd like to wrap his headphones around his stupid neck."

She stared at her feet. "I didn't mean for it to happen, really I didn't. But, I thought it. For sure…I thought it."

Isara reached her arm around Alex's shoulders. "What you may have done is called Avatarism. It means you have taken energy from somewhere else and channeled it into an inanimate object, animating it."

"What? You're saying I brought those things to life?"

Alex gritted her teeth as Sartek filled in the missing details. "Alex, Bert, what the two of you just did are abilities some Bettuan possess, though not so profoundly. It makes sense that it may have something to do with you being in proximity to us."

Confusion clouded Alex's face.

Liberty stepped in. "Guys, we—and I mean humans when I say that—don't have the skills to do things like this. It's not normal."

"Well, I'm not sure about all that, but it sure made me feel sick for a few seconds." Alex stuffed the barf bag back into the seat back.

The four rode on in silence, a new gravity settling over all of them. Sartek and Isara slumped down in their seats, but that wasn't really necessary. It seemed everyone on the bus was quite convinced that the unusual passengers were just a couple more humans on their way to Hutchinson, Kansas.

Luckily, Liberty hadn't installed the battery pack or powered up the notebook before Alex's avatarism, so it was unaffected by the incident and had been spared the energy drain. It powered up just fine, and the remainder of the bus ride, he familiarized himself with the device, including Google Earth searching the address of the rental house.

It was late in the afternoon when they clambered off the bus, just under eight blocks from their new, temporary home. Fairly exhausted, they were dragging tails by the time they reached the house. Liberty was relieved to find the key in the fake rock, just where David said it would be. And to their delight, on the stoop of the little house also sat several boxes of groceries.

"Looks like E-I set us up with a delivery service." Liberty held up the order. Inside the boxes they found frozen chicken pot pies, pizzas, and smoked salmon. There were also cookies, a packet of frozen vegetables—which would likely be ignored—and several bottles of juices and sodas. Best of all, tucked into the cardboard cooler between several freezer packets, were four frozen pineapple banana smoothies. They dove into these like little raptors.

"This is awesome!" Alex, digging deeper into the box, held up frozen toaster pastries. "Thank you, E-I! I'm in love with you!"

"E-I's great. I don't know what we'd do without him." Isara beamed.

"Come on." Sartek hoisted the box easily onto one shoulder. "Let's get inside and get organized. We've got a lot to do."

Once they were all inside, Alex dead-bolted the door.

Inside the house was a balmy ninety-two degrees. Liberty slurped his smoothie, walked over to the thermostat, and set it to seventy-four. When the air-conditioner kicked on, Isara and Sartek jumped visibly at the sudden overhead drone.

"Air-conditioning," Alex explained, hoisting her drink above her head. "It's awesome. We don't have it at *The Home*."

Sartek went to the living room glass slider, which offered a dismal view out across the small back yard, an irrigation ditch, and a barren field beyond. On the far edge of the field, a tall chain-link fence topped with coiled barbed wire prohibited the average person from venturing any farther. Beyond that, vast acres of flat, barren expanse stretched into the very far distance to where heat waves distorted a cluster of dirt-colored buildings.

"The base?"

"Yep, that would be Hutchinson Naval Air Station." Liberty stood at Sartek's elbow and peered out. "It has a five-thousand foot runway with underground storage bays and covers nearly four thousand acres."

Pulling the hanging, vertical blinds shut, he moved away from the glass door, fingertips pressed together and head down as he walked a slow circle on the living-room carpet.

"They claim they converted it to a Vocational School, but you can't get into it as a civilian. Weird, huh?" Liberty went on to explain how in 1958, when the Russians launched the Sputnik satellite, the American response had been to dig several strategic facilities deep underground. One of these facilities, NORAD, became well known to the public. It had branches not only in Colorado but in Alaska and Canada as well, each of them enormous and incredibly fortified.

His excitement, and his voice, rose as he went on to describe the existence of several lesser-known "Special Access Program" facilities. According to Liberty, the functions of these varied widely, ranging from securing the U.S. Government in the event of a globally catastrophic incident (whose primary base was in West Virginia) to Area fifty-one in Nevada, which he remained convinced was the secret headquarters of UFO and paranormal activity, despite government denial. He also believed that a good portion of Hutchinson Air Force Base served a similar function.

"I'm still hungry," Alex slurped the last of her smoothie, interrupting him. "Let's clean up and eat. Then we can figure out what to do next."

"Yes, I could eat more," Sartek agreed, and so they each focused on settling in.

The rental house was furnished and had two full bathrooms. The girls quickly claimed one—the one with the tub.

Half an hour later, they were all washed up and sitting around the small dining room table, their youthful skin shining brightly with the grime scrubbed from it. The difference in skin color between the humans and aliens, Liberty thought, was more dramatic than he'd previously noticed.

Frozen pizzas were warming in the oven; they had a few minutes before dinner would be ready. Liberty pulled the notebook from his backpack, gathering the immediate attention of the others.

"It needs a name," Alex said flat out.

"A name?" Isara's wondered.

"Yeah, what we're doing. You know, a mission name. Or else it's not lucky."

"I don't understand?" Sartek shook his head.

"Let's call it *The Phoenix*," Bert offered suddenly.

"What's a phoenix?" Isara asked.

"Yeah." Alex didn't know either. "What's it mean?"

"It's a mythical bird. It dies terribly, catches fire, but is then reborn from its own ashes." Liberty's eyes widened as he described it, and he looked overhead as though he could envision the mythical bird. "It's graceful, brave, and immortal, and it rises again…against all odds."

Isara swallowed heavily. "I suppose it's a fitting name, given our situation."

"A fitting name and a good destiny," Liberty assured them. "I promise. We'll get the *Star* back, and it *will* fly again."

CHAPTER THIRTEEN

Δ

Liberty's theories regarding military and governmental secret operations, especially involving organizations like NORAD and Hutchinson, were spot on, even if most believed them to be conspiracy theories. And General Jacobs' secret assignments to special tasks, if known to the public, would certainly prove many of Liberty's beliefs to be true.

All six foot three inches of the general stood on an overhead scaffolding as the *Cerulean Star* was painstakingly pulled into the awaiting bay. They were almost exactly two miles underground—not straight down but strategically at an angle, following the natural slant of the subsurface geology.

Most people from Kansas were unaware that a great deal of the eastern part of the state, especially mid to Northeastern Kansas, was made up of nearly horizontal beds of limestone and shale, just beneath the topsoil. This lent itself perfectly to the development of underground tunnels and man-made caverns. Some of this relatively undisturbed millions of years of layered bedrock now supported a vast network of hidden facilities, and it was here that the *Star* was being taken.

Jacobs had a headache. Lately, he was increasingly preoccupied with the notion that aging was inevitable. This sat poorly with him. He saw himself as a warrior, and old age wasn't something a warrior was supposed to live to see.

This thought nipped at the edges of his subconscious as he scanned the cavernous room. He dug briefly through his fatigues vest pocket for the packets of Tylenol that were never far from his side but then abandoned his search, wondering instead if he had exceeded his allowed dose for the day. Just last week, he had been cautioned at his yearly physical about his overconsumption of them.

"Liver damage," the navy flight surgeon—a friend—had cautioned him. "And the bourbon on the rocks you're enjoying most evenings isn't going to help your liver either," he had been warned.

The general's brow was permanently creased from a long life of stressful, strategic operations, but in all truth, he'd never encountered anything like this before. He'd received ongoing reports about the strange find, updating him on the transport of the unidentified craft, but nothing could prepare him for what he now saw.

The battle tanks, tiny in comparison to the vessel, towed it almost halfway into the chamber before the cables were transferred to several giant winches anchored heavily to the wall at the opposite end of the cavern. They groaned with immense effort as the ship was strategically maneuvered into the center of the bay. Then the *Star* was swiftly secured with cables, from almost every angle, to a series of giant cleats, affixed roughly every ten feet apart.

Despite the enormous size of the underground chamber, the foreign object barely fit inside. When the Kevlar drape was slowly withdrawn from the ship, the milky-white, glowing ellipse illuminated the entire space in a very strange way. The *Cerulean Star* was breathtaking, even in its dormant form.

Like cobwebs in a vacant house, platforms sprang immediately into place up and around the *Star*. Scaffoldings climbed alongside, crawling up its sleek body, shaping a new, foreign exoskeleton that appeared terribly out of place.

"We believe there are extraterrestrials aboard, sir," announced Lieutenant Colonel Taylor, the general's assigned battle specialist. Inflated with self-importance, he walked his stocky frame briskly up to the general. "Possibly, a small platoon."

Taylor was young, in his mid-thirties, and had risen through the ranks with lightening speed. This was a result of his unbending, voracious tenacity and determination, but it was no secret the colonel ran short on compassion.

Jacobs stared at the *Star*, visibly overwhelmed by what he saw. "What makes you believe that?" He ran his fingers through his cropped, graying hair. The general was a man who took nothing for face value.

Taylor seemed surprised by the question, but gathered himself without hesitation. "Well, it's obvious that the vessel is not terrestrial, and given what we've seen, it is most likely a military ship—we believe."

"Who believes? And what have your seen?" General Jacobs' natural, inborn nature was one of suspicion, and he remained fairly unconvinced. Reaching into his pocket, he retrieved a flip-top bottle of antacids and poured the last one into his hand before tossing it into his mouth.

"And *how* are you so sure this isn't from Earth? And you better be specific, Mister..."

"Taylor—Lieutenant Colonel Taylor. And with all due respect, sir, we recognize none of this technology. We don't even know what it's made of."

The lieutenant peeled out of his uniform jacket, hanging it on the back of a chair. It was obvious he was fit as could be, the long sleeve shirt stretching too snug across his chest and biceps. For some reason, this rubbed Jacobs wrong today.

"You do not have my due respect unless it has been earned, which it hasn't. And isn't that what we've brought it here for in the first place? To figure it out?"

Patience was short for the general this afternoon. He was fifty-eight years old. His wife, Penny, was thirty-seven and not particularly happy with their recent reassignment to Kansas. Add to this the fact that he believed his daughter seemed to have lost her mind entirely, and he found himself more frequently at work, something he hadn't anticipated as he'd approached his sixties.

"When had it become so complicated to be a fifteen-year-old girl?" Jacobs asked his wife this morning, and she'd answered him with an accusation of insensitivity. He'd left for the base feeling it would be a welcome break from an already difficult day. But that wasn't proving to be the case after all.

"Yes, sir, but we've had scientists looking at it, even during the transport, and this ship isn't like anything we've ever seen before." Taylor was obviously thrilled with the thought of an alien military force within their grasp.

"When will we have the entire team here?" Jacobs asked.

The general referred to the international team of experts who were on standby for certain unforeseen "events" that might compromise humanity. It was top-secret, and should anyone receive the summons, they were to drop whatever they were doing and come immediately, no matter how far away they might be.

The list had never been activated...before now.

"At least half of them will be assembled by fifteen hundred, sir. They'll be ready for a briefing by fifteen thirty. I'm sure we'll know something by then."

The general turned away, much more intrigued with the vessel than with Taylor's prattling. It occurred to him how unusual it was that, once he laid eyes on the ship, he couldn't seem to drag his gaze from it.

He wondered if it had the same effect on others. This set him on edge—a weakness, perhaps. He was trained to pay close attention to weaknesses.

Forcing himself to look away, he pushed his left sleeve up and checked his watch. Squinting, he moved his wrist first near, then far, at last able to focus on the tiny roman numerals. He'd been too stubborn to bring his reading glasses to work yet, even though he could scarcely read without them anymore. *Another sign of weakness*, he thought to himself, and his mood darkened.

Taylor whipped out his cell phone. "It's fifteen twenty-two, sir."

This irked the general. He made a silent note to himself to get a watch with bigger numerals.

And why do a bunch of idiots believe a cell phone is so much better than a good watch? When an EM pulse blasts them, how are they gonna tell time THEN? Serves them right! Isn't it this dumbshit's generation that believes in the zombie apocalypse in the first place? Let Taylor try to figure it out when it's his turn to patrol for zombies!

Jacobs let go a silent groan. Fifteen twenty-two—just enough time to grab a bad cup of coffee before the meeting. He took one last look at the ship as it was being painstakingly unveiled of its Kevlar blanket. It was like watching a butterfly emerge from a cocoon. This made Jacobs terribly uneasy, but at the same time, on some level, it thrilled him. He turned on his heel. "I'll see you in the briefing room."

Minutes later, the general opened the door to the briefing room where fifteen men and women were assembled. Everyone at the table was talking all at once, a charged excitement fueling the multiple conversations. They fell nervously silent when Jacobs walked in. Even so, the air remained alive with an electric anticipation of this most extraordinary find.

The general paused, glancing briefly at each scientist in turn before clearing his throat and moving to the head of the table where he chose to remain standing.

Behind him, Taylor filed in and took a stance of attention—arms behind his back, feet apart—and remained like this at the opposite end of the table.

"Taylor, take a seat. This isn't an interrogation." Jacobs gestured toward the chair in the far corner, and the colonel begrudgingly obliged. The general continued. "First off, I need to know what we're up against. As of twelve thirty, the Commander-in-Chief has been notified. I anticipate we will have a briefing scheduled with him before too long."

The air was heavy with anticipation, but no one initially said anything.

Finally, a small man with silver hair, wearing a white lab jacket, eased up and out of his chair. "We've an alien ship, sir."

Taylor seemed smugly gratified, his chin jutting out.

Jacobs stared at the man as though he'd grown an arm out of his forehead. "*Really*. We have an alien ship. That's all you have for me?"

The slight fellow adjusted his absurd, green and red checked tie with no improvement. "That is to say, sir, we're strongly convinced it is not from our planet…sir."

"And what was your first clue?" The general reined himself in, realizing that perhaps he'd taken the sarcasm a bit too far.

The scientist, however, appeared to take the question literally. "The surface, sir. We've never seen anything like it." He became more animated. "We've been able to determine that the shell is composed of helium and something else. However, that something else is an element unknown, and how it bonds to helium is a mystery to us."

At this point, the scientist's eyes shone like sunshine off a raindrop. "It shouldn't do that, but it does! In a helical, honeycombed pattern that we've never seen before. And that's not all. We figured this out, not because we could take a sample of it—when we tried, it was impossible to harvest—but the surface appears to be decaying, for lack of a better word."

The general listened closely, remaining quiet for a good long while as he digested this information. He walked slowly back and forth at the head of the table. "Is there a chance North Korea could've pulled this…" he motioned toward where the ship hovered in the cavern beyond, "this whatever?"

He was met with blank stares all around.

"Negative, general," a woman spoke. She pushed up from her chair, all eyes focused on her. She waited for the murmuring buzz to subside. "That's not possible. This technology is beyond anything mankind can fabricate, friend or foe."

The woman was striking in a stark way, dark hair pulled severely back in a single ponytail, her charcoal grey suit in sharp contrast to the starched, white lab coat she wore, pockets stuffed with notepads, pens, calculator—the various tools of a scientist's life.

The general's eyes narrowed.

"What makes you so sure this technology is not owned by someone else, Miss....?"

"Bennett, sir." Her eyes were a vivid, electric blue, and though they seemed almost damp with fear, her voice indicated otherwise. "And to answer your question, allow me to say several things."

She extended her hands as though beginning a middle-grade lecture.

"First off, if this technology existed elsewhere on earth, it would have been next to impossible to hide. It emits an, uhmm…radiation, if you will." Bennett glanced at her colleagues as though to appeal to them for support.

"Kinda' like alpha radiation, but not only is the photon wave electric and magnetic, it's something else altogether." She shifted as though she was uncomfortable with her own lack of explanation. Lacing her fingers together, she held them up in front of her like a small tent and collapsed them together. "This wavelength is narrower than anything we've ever seen, and it appears to be unstable."

"What?" This got the general's attention straight up. "Like some kind of weapon?"

"No. No, not at all. At least I don't believe so. More like…" Bennett appeared almost too embarrassed to continue. "Like something faltering— failing. It defies what we know, but it *is* deteriorating randomly, and we can't be certain that it's stable."

"It's outside of our intelligence?"

"That is an oversimplification. It is outside of what we know about *physics*." She said this as though it should completely sum up the importance of the find.

She sighed. "This thing doesn't belong here, and…it's dying."

The entire team of scientists nodded in unison. Nobody said a word. In reality, there was a whole lot of nothing left to say, no further explanation of what rested so elegantly only a short one hundred and fifty meters from them.

"Why hasn't it resisted?" Jacobs pressed them. "Just up and flown away? Is it too damaged to fly?"

Mr. Geller, seated next to Bennett, struggled to rise from his chair, all five-feet-two inches of him. He was nearly as wide as he was tall, and his hair, what little he had, was smoothed in a singular wave back over his head like a duck's tail. Geller shifted his substantial weight back and forth, one foot to the other, as though he'd been much more comfortable sitting.

The general stared at him, wondering if the man was anxious or merely needed a trip to the latrine. Secretly, Jacobs judged the heavy man, simply for his obesity. It was one of his shortcomings, to assess a snap judgment of another human being like that, but Jacob's considered it a strength.

The scientist raised a pencil to ear level, mouth open, but nothing came out.

"Well?" Jacobs was impatient. "Is there a secret here we're going to keep, just for the hell of it?"

"We don't know…" Geller cleared his throat, "why it hasn't resisted.

"There's always the possibility that it isn't armed, but unless it suffered a disabling event, we've no good explanation why it didn't at least try to escape." He licked his lips and glanced nervously at Bennett. She gently indicated he should continue, and he said, "It was almost too passive in the way it presented itself. At least that's the conclusion most of us have come to." He gestured to the rest of the group.

Several scientists murmured their agreement before he found the courage to continue. "It was too easy to capture it, and…and its surface appeared fine, initially. It's only as time's gone by that the shell seems to have become increasingly unstable."

Geller appeared close to becoming unstable himself, so Bennett took the opportunity to rest a hand on his shoulder. The heavy man slipped back into his chair as she continued, "From the rate of decay, we estimate maybe four days tops before this thing loses whatever it is that surrounds it. What we *don't* know about this vessel is a lot. Rather than information, we're discovering just how much we can't seem to figure out, and in four days, good or bad, we're going to know a great deal more."

There were murmurs amongst the group as though they were all equally baffled and in agreement with this exceedingly over simplified explanation of the alien starship.

The general focused on Taylor. "You said you believe it to be a military vessel, and I still have no hard evidence other than your hunch, which frankly just irritates the shit out of me. But I'll be damned if I'm going to let some blob of who knows *what-the-fuk* land in my country and compromise national security."

Taylor stuttered something, but Jacobs waved him to silence before resting his hands on the edge of the conference table. "An unstable alien ship is not an option. Do I make myself clear?"

There was no response from the stricken group.

Jacobs added, "If we cannot stabilize it, and soon, I will bury it. Secure that vessel, gentlemen—and *ladies*, now! And clear this base of all non-essential personnel." He stabbed a finger at Taylor. "If we're sitting on some kind of a bomb, and it goes off in four days, I want to limit collateral damage as much as possible." Then, stabbing at the intercom on the conference room table, he demanded of no one, "And get me the president, *now!*"

A generically efficient voice came back through the intercom immediately. "Yes sir; he is scheduled for a visual conference in twenty-two minutes. We've implemented security level three. Please meet us in debriefing room-A, sir."

The general scrutinized his science team, his eyes narrowing. It frustrated him that he essentially knew a whole lot of absolutely nothing, and so he dismissed the group. At least his wife would be pleased to be out of Hutchinson. He'd already decided to get her and Sylvia back to D.C. tonight— back where they would be close to family and home and away from this train wreck.

Why can't aliens just stay in their own goddamn end of the universe?

CHAPTER FOURTEEN

Δ

The pizza wasn't quite ready, so while they waited, the kids crowded around Liberty's chair, peering over his shoulder as he hooked up the long-range extender and initiated the tablet. He gave them a weak smile, pressed connect, and in short time signaled the *Star* for the first time since they'd received the e-mail in the library.

Alex could hardly stand still. She kept grabbing Isara and Sartek, one then the other, by the arm, while letting go with outbursts like, "You think they're okay? You think they'll know we're trying to contact them?"

The aliens had no good answers, and Liberty hushed them. Almost instantly, he'd secured a session initiation protocol proxy on the tablet with a virtual private network. In essence, he'd devised his own platform so that, in the end, they had a secure video program.

Now he could privately conference with David, Blalok, and E-I, in video. They were going to "Super Secret Skype" an alien ship was how Liberty explained it. And he was meticulous with tasks such as these. Even so, when David's face appeared on the screen, he was immensely relieved.

Alex let out a squeal of delight. "Heya', Davey! How you doin'?"

She practically shoved Liberty off his chair to get a better look.

David appeared to be sitting. Adjusting his end of the transmission source, he pulled the screen down and another figure, nearly a head shorter, came briefly into view. Everything swung wildly for a few seconds before both figures stabilized at opposite diagonal corners of the screen.

"Hi guys! I'm okay, but we're seriously running out of time. This is Blalok," David said. "He's cool, and a super-nerd, but you'd annihilate him at chess, Bert. I know you would."

"Will you quit *saying* that? You are really annoying me, and I believe you are aware of that!" All they could see of the alien was from the nose up, but from the expression in his glowing eyes, Blalok's frustration was obvious.

David grinned and tilted the screen a bit more toward Blalok so that Alex and Liberty could further make his acquaintance.

The smallest alien immediately intrigued Liberty. His eyes, instead of the variable shade of green like Isara and Sartek's, were a brilliant lemon-yellow, and huge! Maybe it was because he was smaller than the others that they seemed so extraordinarily large for his head.

As though recognizing this, the little alien rolled his eyes, stating simply, "Your most irritating friend is correct. My name is Blalok, and since I am sure you already *knew* this, and now that we have now wasted a precious minute of our time, perhaps we can get to matters at hand."

In his lap sat a creature that could only be interpreted as a pet. It circled once, glowering, and disappeared, evidently content to be coiled in comfort on the knees of its irascible master.

There were grins all around from the group in the safe house, but Liberty was consumed with a strong sense of urgency and pressed on. "Hi guys; Blalok, nice to meet you. We made it here without too much problem, but like you said, it's only so long before they're onto us. So may I speak with E-I? I think I have an idea, but I'm gonna need his expertise."

Seconds later, the virtual voice, not at all similar to the standard, computer enhanced, robotic voice on earth's more advanced systems, could be heard. "Hello Bert. I'm pleased to make your acquaintance." It was almost…formal.

Liberty's imagination immediately conjured up an English butler, perhaps with ninja skills. He blurted, "E-I, I need plans, a facility layout. We need to know exactly where the *Star* is and all access points to it, no matter how minor they may appear. Electric, hydraulic—everything. If a bug can get through it, I need to know. Also, I need access codes and fail-safes."

"I understand completely," E-I said, then said nothing more.

The computer's short response prompted a mild look of surprise on Blalok's face.

Alex, Isara, and Sartek had so much to say—so many questions for their on-board friends—but Liberty hushed them again so he could concentrate. Within seconds, layers of classified schematic images flooded his screen. To his further amazement, he saw transcripts of incredibly confidential meetings, including correspondences between strategic members of the military *and* the president. His eyes were enormous as he scanned over a structural blueprint.

"E-I, I don't understand how you…" He trailed off as the documents continued to up-load, one after another.

"Simple, really," E-I replied. "Your government's computer security systems on Earth depend upon cryptographic technology that is a continually modified series of information clusters."

"Yeah, I know. That's why it's so hard to crack."

"Unless you have a friend," E-I added, sounding alarmingly human.

"I don't understand, who are you talking—?"

"The internet," E-I explained before he could finish, "with the help of someone with whom I believe you are acquainted. Vole."

Liberty's eyes widened even more.

"This individual is appreciably qualified, as none other on your planet are. With his help, I have coordinated the complex systems that represent your *Internet* into one arrangement. This arrangement, unlike any that have been intrinsic to it before now, has central authority—my authority."

"I-I don't understand," Isara said.

"It is sentient, and although I cannot override it from the *Cerulean Star*, Vole can." E-I seemed satisfied with this explanation.

"Uhmm…" Liberty was at a loss for words.

"It thinks," E-I said bluntly, meaning the central authority. "And yes, it is my friend. I have named it Aurora, although Vole wanted to name it Samuel-L. He would not explain why."

Sartek and Isara looked at each other. David was laughing from the corner of the notebook screen. It was Blalok who said what everyone was likely thinking. "E-I has his first friend." This was met with giggles from the girls, and Blalok added, his hand on the screen as though to prevent E-I from hearing. "It's going to be tough when we have to eventually *kill* it."

"I can hear you," E-I interjected.

"Can you get sequential updates, so we know what's going on from the military's point of view?" Liberty next needed to know.

"Not likely. They will certainly have specialists who are already aware of the compromise, and subsequent communication with Vole will put him at risk. Furthermore, continued breaches will only make us appear hostile. It may provoke them into an offensive. Contact at this point should be limited until absolutely necessary."

After more debate, about an hour later, the six children and E-I had a fundamental plan to go by. Liberty left the tablet turned on with a virtual alarm system loaded to trigger him awake in the event David or Blalok needed to urgently contact them.

The four in the house said goodnight to the two on-board. By then, the pizza was well overdone, so Alex broke it up and tossed the pieces into the back yard, "For the birds," and Liberty ordered delivery from some place called Big Bean Pies. In no time, they were sitting in a semicircle on the living room floor, diving into the fresh, steaming pizza.

"I've never had anchovies on a pizza." Alex mugged at Liberty's attempt to further accommodate their fish-eating friends.

"Me either. It's really not so bad, huh?" Liberty's voice carried much more enthusiasm than he really felt.

"It's terrible," Alex scoffed, tossing the slice back into the box before reaching for a plain pepperoni. "I didn't say I liked it, only that I've never had it before. It tastes like pond mud."

"More for me," Sartek said happily and snatched up the abandoned slice, shoving a bite into his mouth before chewing cheerily. It was fairly obvious that pizza with anchovies was a big hit with the Bettuan kids.

This evening unfolded very differently from the evening before. They sat comfortably and safely on the plush living room carpet while they shared dinner, openly telling stories about their respective homes, families, friends, and lives. The conversation was lighthearted, and laughter was abundant.

Alex and Liberty learned more details of the Bettuan kids' homes and the terrible disaster that cast them away. As the evening wore on, Liberty became more determined that his new friends should get to their ship and be free, back to the stars where they belonged.

Dinner was over, and the rest of the pizza was stored safely in the fridge "for breakfast." Alex got up to use the bathroom, and Liberty wandered into the kitchen to clean up.

Sartek crossed the living room and leaned casually against a sliding glass doorjamb, lifting the full-length louvered curtains aside with his index finger. Beyond the backyard and irrigation, the landscape was so flat that he could see the very distant conglomerate of sodium vapor lights that marked the edge of the complex. Somewhere underneath it all...was his ship.

Feeling a light hand on his arm, he turned to see Isara looking not at him, but past the fortified chain-link and barbwire fence at the distant lights.

"I'm afraid," she murmured.

"I trust them."

Sartek tossed his head back toward their friends. He tried to affect a smile.

"So do I." Her eyes were clear and damp.

"All of them are so kind, so...*Bettuan*."

Sartek glanced over her shoulder. Alex fiddled with a square contraption across the room, and it leapt to life with a flat, two-dimensional screen.

"We have to do our best," Sartek said to Isara in a low voice. "Alex and Bert have put themselves in great danger, and we can't fail them."

"What happens if we get...when we...?" She didn't finish her question. Only rested her head against Sartek's shoulder.

"I don't know. We'll just have to figure that out when the time comes."

The gravity of the mission ahead and the fatigue of a long day cast a serious quiet upon the aliens.

"Hey you guys!" Alex chirped happily from across the room now that the television was fired up. "You gotta see this!"

* * *

Alex exposed Isara and Sartek to their first ever episode of the Simpsons. It was doubtful the aliens understood all the jargon, but the wonderfully absurd humor of the cartoon connected with them perfectly. It was a welcome distraction, and they were reduced to ridiculous laughter more than once.

Sartek bellowed out loud—a wonderfully human sound—when Homer, in the land of chocolate, took a bite out of a passing dog.

They were halfway into a second episode when Liberty excused himself and disappeared into the kitchen. Sartek followed shortly, peeking from around the corner and flinched.

Liberty glanced up at him for only a second before redirecting his attention to the vial of insulin and syringe. Holding the barrel up to the light, he tapped it with his fingernail to get the last bubbles out.

"Diabetes," was all he said.

"I'm sorry," Sartek started to leave but lingered.

Pulling up his T-shirt up, Liberty held it out of the way between clenched teeth. He plunged the needle into the softer skin around his bellybutton, injecting himself as slickly as if it were an art form, and recapped the needle before tossing it into the brown paper bag that served as their garbage can.

"See? Nothing to it," he tried to reassure his new friend.

"What is it?" Sartek asked.

"That? Oh, needle and syringe. Let's me inject the medicine." He held up the vial of insulin and rubbed a hand over his abdomen, along the spot he'd just injected. A small drop of blood was left on his pinky finger.

Sartek's eyes widened, and he shook his head.

"No, diabetes—what is diabetes?"

"It's a disease." Liberty shrugged nonchalantly. "I don't have enough insulin in my body. Well, in my case, I don't seem to have *any*, so I have to replace it."

"Or what?" Sartek leaned back against the kitchen counter and crossed his arms.

It was such an unbelievably human gesture, and it reminded Liberty once more of David, so much so that he was compelled to answer the question honestly. "Uhmm, I get sick." When he saw the mounting look of concern on Sartek's face mount, he followed up, "It's okay. I'm not gonna run out of insulin any time soon. I'll be fine

This didn't appear to entirely satisfy Sartek. He shifted his weight and stared at his feet.

"It's not that big a deal." Liberty believed there were much more pressing issues at stake than the personal health problems of a single human. "There's a lot more to worry about than me and my stupid disease."

Sartek dropped his head, his rope-like hair covering his eyes. "I'm sorry I pried."

Liberty shrugged. "*Really*, I'm all right." He went to the fridge and pulled the freezer open. "It's no big deal. But, you know what is? Ice-cream…" He grinned broadly as he fished a quart of Double Chocolate Chunk out of the freezer and four spoons from the drawer.

That night…

…Liberty seized.

CHAPTER FIFTEEN

Δ

David wasn't sure how long he'd slept. He awakened simply because the light in his sleep chamber had slowly increased. Also, there was an odor to it now, not unpleasant but not familiar either. It subtly reminded him of when his father briefly moved them to Florida—the way those magnificent summer storms smelled when they came in from the gulf.

Bathroom duties, however, were not nearly so gratifying as the gentle wake-up call. After a near terrifying experience with the *evacuation chamber*, David staggered from it, spun around, and glared.

"Intuitively obvious, my *ass!*"

Still glowering, he grabbed his jeans off the floor, hesitated, and glanced at the Shower Chamber. Finally, he shrugged, dropped his jeans, and shed his boxer shorts before entering the tubular device Blalok said was a shower.

"Well," he muttered, "I'm seriously stinking like a teenager."

Part of David's desire to go into the wash chamber was simply genuine curiosity. His disposition was one of adventure, and it was on more than one occasion that he'd persuaded Alex and Liberty to press their luck at something they'd later wished they hadn't.

His confidence was fairly booming as he walked naked and into the tube. Turning slowly, he looked about himself. The chamber already had a curious effect of being underwater. A pleasing blue-green mist seemed to fill the air around him as though it sensed his presence, and it was very agreeable.

Okay, this is all right...so far..

Soft strains of music, not unlike earth's whales, echoed about him. He grinned complacently and spun slowly, palms up.

"I could get used to this."

But when David pushed a jelly-like knob on the wall, the only obvious *on* switch, nothing could prepare him for what happened next.

Panic was his first and immediate response as he was instantly engulfed in water. It wasn't even as though it flowed in, more that it was just suddenly there, all around him. His smile faded when the vortex gained speed and his feet left the solid feel of the floor. Now, he twirled inside the rapidly filling tube and slammed his hands against the sides.

Overcome with a near panic, he tried to make sense of his orientation and direction. It was impossible to swim up; the current maintained him centrally as it spun him slowly around, and it appeared it would maintain him there indefinitely. He kicked frantically, with his body arced and his head thrown back. He needed to find a release, and fast!

David held his breath for over one agonizing minute, even as his heart threatened to burst in his chest. Just when he was sure his only option left was to drown, he was surprised to find that he was thinking about Liberty and Alex. In his most dire moment of distress, and just before he thought he would pass out, there they were. If his eyes weren't already filled with the surrounding water, he might even have sensed his own tears.

It was then, when he could endure no more, that he gave in, doing as all drowning creatures will do. He let go and inhaled deeply of the water. To his wonder, and immense relief, he could breathe just fine! It was very strange, not entirely unlike breathing in an intense, cool sauna, but sure as could be, he could take in the clear, turquoise blue liquid that held him. It required some minor effort, like sucking through a large straw, but it wasn't painful. On the contrary, it was fresh and crisp, supporting him in a peculiar way.

And that wasn't all. The *shower* also rejuvenated him. It was like breathing in something that shot health into him, like he was coming even more to life!

After a few minutes, David was almost disappointed when the shower ended. There was no draining away or dripping off of him. It just seemed to disappear, instantly evaporating, inside and out. He didn't even need to cough or clear any passages for that matter.

The effect was exhilarating! Even his teeth and gums felt as if he'd just been to a dentist, and his breathing was clearer than it'd ever been. There he stood, naked and feeling cleaner than he'd ever felt in his life. Clean wasn't necessarily an urgent priority for David, but he grinned broadly, absolutely dumbfounded by the whole experience. When he stepped from the shower chamber, he noticed the clothes.

There across the back of a chair—the same chair that had launched itself across the room before he'd slept—was unfamiliar clothing. It resembled what the aliens wore.

David passed his hand across the material. It was smooth, sleek, and seemed to radiate an energy all its own. He left the clothing where it lay and climbed into the familiarity of his own blue jeans and T-shirt. *Maybe next time I'll just shower with my clothes on. How easy would that be?* he thought to himself as he strutted for the exit.

Motioning the door sensor, David managed to make his way to where they'd. He tried to order up bacon and waffles, but when something not entirely identifiable popped out of the device, he abandoned his efforts and went to find Blalok.

Locating the bridge proved not too difficult, and when he entered, he found the alien poring over some instrument readings. Walking directly over, David thumped him a good one with the heel of his hand, right on top of his head.

"Ow! Hey!" Blalok protested.

"That's for not telling me I wouldn't drown."

Blalok did carry a slightly satisfied expression on his face and accepted his punishment fair enough. "I *said* you could breathe in there," he muttered.

"You didn't make it hugely obvious how," David countered and sat down next to him, folding his arms across his chest.

Blalok glanced in his direction. "There were clothes for you."

"Looked like they might pinch."

"Mmm…"

David fidgeted as though unable to get comfortable for exactly sixty-three seconds before asking, "So, can we connect with Bert and Alex yet?"

"Yes, we can. But I'm awaiting the signal from your friend. We are dependent upon his initiating the proxy network."

"Yeah, I get that."

"You do?"

"No…so, what do you guys do for fun around here?" He gazed about the bridge, but before his host could say anything, a soft alarm sounded.

A small screen, about forty-five inches diagonal, elevated from apparently nothingness, right from the middle of the console. Moments later, there was Liberty—an impressive 3D image—contacting them from the safe house in Hutchinson.

David could not believe how relieved he was to see him again. And there, in the background of the screen, was Alex, bee-bopping in an out of view. This made him smile even more.

"Hey guys!" David half pushed Blalok off his levi-chair. Introductions were made, and before long, plans were in effect, much to the credit of Liberty and E-I. What seemed like only minutes was really just over an hour. It was now nighttime on Earth—time for those planet-side to sleep. But the two aboard ship had only recently awakened.

Blalok became immediately reabsorbed in his tasks, analyzing and reanalyzing, observing and studying. It went on like this for some time—Blalok working and David, well, just sitting. David picked at the hem of his T-shirt, spun around in his levi-chair, and at one point jogged back and forth along the bridge deck, shooting imaginary hoops. Blalok looked up on occasion, glaring.

Eventually, David settled restlessly back in the levi-chair. After the seventh heavy sigh, his smaller companion finally asked, "Would you like to play a game?"

"Game? Oh yeah! I call red…"

Blalok just stared at him then shook his head morosely. "You know, I really don't understand you."

"Just messin' with you." David slapped Blalok playfully on the knee. "So how's it work? We teaming?"

"No. We are not teaming. I'm not playing at all, just you." Blalok reached over, flipped a switch, slid a finger along a sleek, white bar, and up where the screen had previously been appeared a holo-helmet.

"No waaay…" David whispered, exhaling deeply.

"This is *Quest for Dominion*." Blalok said it with great reverence. "You must start as sub-level two-hundred."

"What does that mean, sub-level?"

"You are lowly, as lowly as pond scum."

"You have that on your planet, too?"

"Huh? Of course we—"

David snatched the helmet off the console. "How's it work?"

Blalok explained in modest detail how the game was played.

"Don't get killed, fit in, evolve."

"Piece of cake."

David grinned and stabbed an imaginary weapon at Blalok's head.

The alien closed his eyes as though to close off awareness of the human altogether. Then, with a sigh, he hopped up and directed David to one side of the bridge stage. "You'll play here. The world is interactive, but the program will keep you within a confined boundary."

"So... it's like being in a force-field."

"Exactly not."

"But—"

"Just put on the helmet. You'll figure it out."

The helmet slid on fairly easily, and David was surprised how good the fit was. "Ready?" he heard the muffled question from the alien—somewhere.

"Yeah. Fire this baby up!"

There was a soft hum as David found himself suspended in the world of Glom Guttahn. Even though, in reality, he floated scarcely two feet above the *Star*'s deck, his body settled into the virtual world of the game.

He felt his feet firmly plant on the grass of a sweeping field. It was impossible for David to separate his computer-generated surroundings from reality, and his heart quickened. The breeze on his skin was warm, and he looked at his hands. They were unfamiliar, thin and pale, but when he touched his face, it felt...right.

Glancing down, he saw that he wore tattered trousers of some sort of animal hide. They hung loosely on him, and his feet were bare and calloused. A shoulder strap held a leather pouch at his side. His torso was also bare, and he ran his hands up and down his chest and ribs.

"Okay. So I'm an Indian...sort of."

Shielding his eyes from the slanting red sun, David was able to make out a long row of leafy trees in the distance, black trunked with blue leaves. They were unusual and swayed back and forth with long tendrils. Beyond them, something stirred...

* * *

The *Cerulean Star* was equipped with many entertainment programs, and *Quest or Dominion* was Blalok's favorite. He grinned, hardly able to contain himself.

On the other side of the deck, about twenty feet away, David spun awkwardly in the air. His face wasn't visible through the helmet he wore; it was smooth and mirrored in its effect, so afforded no indication of what was going on, expression wise, with the human who wore it. David's body contortions, however, gave a greater idea of what the human experienced.

His head swung widely, this way and that, as though taking in a great deal of information all at once. His hands searched himself, evidently uncomfortable with the virtual body it was discovering.

"This is going to be good."

Blalok chuckled outright and tipped back in his chair to watch the show.

* * *

The peculiar movement, coming from the thick stand of trees, wasn't the only thing critically unusual about the new world, that is, if you didn't look too closely at the curly red grass beneath your feet. Rows of insects—armored, yellow shells about the size of a plum—marched purposefully in parallel lines toward some obscure goal in the distance.

David squinted beyond the trees. Three…no, four creatures lumbered from the edge of the forest directly toward him, covering the span alarmingly fast. Glancing behind himself, he became instantly aware of something from the corner of his eye. A long, blond braid ran down his back and fell over his shoulder, startling him somewhat as it did. For the briefest moment, he thought it was a spider, David's only primal object of terror. Even Alex had to get the spiders out of the attic while he cowered with Liberty.

Get a grip on yourself.

He ran his fingers up and down the tight weave of starkly blond hair. It felt just as he imagined it might. Then he yanked on it.

Ow, yeah, that's weird. That's gotta go.

He searched his belt and discovered a very small knife…or nail file, perhaps. Grabbing the braid, he sawed at it, finally abandoning his efforts and the pathetic knife. He tossed the braid behind him and the knife into the dirt, kicking it at the beetles. They scurried briefly, tiny wings fluttering, then reassumed their march.

David turned his attention to the four who were fast approaching. In no time at all, they were nearly upon him. He squinted. The men, not dissimilar to the Bettuan but obviously more primeval, rode the creatures he'd first spied lumbering from the forest. Massive, elephant-like beasts swung their curling tusks widely as their great heads bobbed. They had no trunks, however. Instead, long snouts snarled, lined neatly with row upon row of terrible teeth. These dripped green, and even from the distance David saw how it spotted the pretty red grass as they gnashed and hissed.

The creatures thundered along, and David was acutely aware of the trembling beneath his feet, just from the force of their sheer size.

He took an involuntary step backward as the four riders pulled up with a flourish directly in front of him.

"You there, *boy*...are you the messenger?" the leader asked bluntly.

The warrior's animal was quite the largest of the four and let forth a scream that forced David to cover his ears. He buckled to his knees. The strange man silenced the monster by smacking it on the head repeatedly with a long staff. The man threw one leg over the shoulder hump of the creature before sliding smoothly to the ground.

David was outright amazed. The warrior was like nothing he'd ever seen— tall, lithe, muscled beyond any second rate, action movie character, and armored magnificently. The stranger pulled his helmet off, and his face, David had to admit, was strikingly attractive. The stranger sported, besides the staff, a sword of sorts. He held one weapon in each hand, and both glowed brilliantly, especially closest to where the man gripped them.

"Huh?" was all David could manage.

"I say, are you or are you not the messenger, *boy*?" the stranger asked again, pausing a mere three feet from him.

This crawled beneath David's skin in an unpleasant way. He scowled. "Uh—no, I'm Dav—"

Too late.

With a sweeping gesture—one that appeared entirely too easy—the man swept him from his feet. David landed with a thud that knocked the non-virtual air from his lungs. With the onslaught, the bugs became quite animated and approached as though they might swarm him. Trying to spin away from his attacker, and the freakily horrifying swarm of yellow golf-ball bugs, David managed to thwart the second blow with the palm of his hand.

"*OUCH!* Son of a—"

In the next instant, the attacker roared and plunged his sword viciously into David's chest. With a gasp, the human boy cried out aloud, anticipating all the pain of having been run through.

There was, however, no pain. Instead, there was a blinding flash of light and a soft thud as the *Quest for Dominion* laid David, gasping, gently upon the bridge.

Game over…

* * *

"One hundred twenty-two," Blalok's voice registered flatly as the *Cerulean Star* materialized in a shower of sparkles around David.

"Huh? What?" the human groaned.

"That's how long you survived, one hundred twenty-two seconds." Blalok crossed his arms smugly. "You're a *noob*."

David rolled over heavily, pulled the helmet from his head, and glared at Blalok. His heart still raced, the adrenalin coursing through him because of the virtual death he'd just experienced. Sweat ran down his arms and legs, and he had to double check that there wasn't a bug running up his spine.

"It was crazy, like…so…*real*." He hopped to his feet and smiled brilliantly. "But for a first time, I owned it, right?"

Blalok was disinclined to admit that David had actually survived nearly four seconds longer than the first time he had played *Quest for Dominion*. "You're still sub-level two-hundred. You are the Ketzel scat on their boots."

"Oh." David didn't really need the Bettuan to explain further what that meant. "Advice?"

"All is not as it seems in this game. Perhaps look at it a different way."

"I get it; get into my character."

"Look in the pouch."

"Oh…okay." David swung the helmet back onto his head. "Round two. Fire this beeyatch up."

While the human was plunged back into *Quest for Dominion*, the alien turned to his monitors and began walking through some very complex calculations.

Nearly three hours later, David's real sweat dripped down his legs and onto the *Star*'s decking as he fought for survival in his virtual world. Close by, Blalok continued at his tasks, his brow furrowing in concentration. With a flip of his hand, he suddenly powered the human's game off and watched as David floated to solid footing.

"Hey, wait! Why'd you do that? I was just about to get running boots and..." David pulled up abruptly. "Blalok, what is it? What's wrong?"

Blalok didn't look up from his analysis but drew a heavy breath.

"We don't have as long as you thought...do we?"

Blalok shook his head. It seemed impossible for him to hide his disappointment. "No...we do not."

"We need to let them know."

"Yes, yes we do." Blalok swung around in his chair. "David, we need to talk." The Bettuan's eyes were unusually serious, and he wasn't his normal, smart-assed self.

"Whoa, slow up there, pal. Shouldn't we get to know each other a little better first?" David tried to joke as he laid the helmet on the console.

When Blalok offered no response, he worried they might be in more serious trouble than he thought. "Okay, how long?"

"The hull is deteriorating faster than it should. As far as I can tell, it is because there is greater partial pressure of carbon dioxide in the cavern they've placed us in."

"Yeah, it's cuz we drive too many SUV's."

This time, Blalok hesitated, a brief look of confusion clouding his face. "At this rate, they will have access to our inner hull in approximately twenty-six point eight hours."

David eased himself into the levi-chair beside the alien, pulling his T-shirt up to wipe the sweat off his face. Three days seemed so much more workable than twenty-seven hours.

"And what happens when they get access to the hull?" David was stricken by this news and felt sick even asking.

"In all likelihood, they will breach it." Blalok was very matter-of-fact.

"How can they breach it? What are you saying? This ship's gotta be stronger than anything we know! It flies through space!" David jumped up and began pacing the foredeck.

"It doesn't *fly*; it displaces time while simultaneously..." Blalok paused, evidently reconsidering the physics lesson he was about to give, then shook his head. "You're correct. The hull of the *Cerulean Star* is made of Vasteen. It is an ore that is forty-seven times stronger than Earth's strongest strength-to-weight material, but humans possess the technology to penetrate it."

"That can't happen. How?" David rested his hands on the console's edge but didn't give the alien a chance to answer. "Blalok, they'll be seriously pissed at me if they get in, but you—they'll..."

His voice trailed off. "I'm not gonna let that happen." He slashed at the air with his hand and gritted his teeth. "They're not getting hold of you; do you hear me? Damn if that's gonna happen…"

The smallest alien wore a look of surprise on his face. Perhaps David's rant reminded him a bit of someone else he knew, but David couldn't know how similar some of his own behaviors were to Sartek's.

"David, when your militia determines just how extraordinary Vasteen is, and it is only a matter of time before they do, they will stop at nothing to gain it. I can guarantee you that."

"I don't understand. Okay, so it's super strong, like Kryptonite or something, but so what?"

"It's not just strong, it possesses *other* qualities," Blalok explained with a sigh of resignation.

"Like what qualities," David's eyes narrowed in suspicion.

"Vasteen can emit a pulse if its electrons are aligned just so. A negligible amount, smaller than your fist, if harnessed properly, can generate a pulse strong enough to destroy something very large."

"Something really large. Like another spaceship?"

"Like a planet."

A wave of dizziness washed over David, and he visibly staggered, grasping the smooth green edge of the console to steady himself.

"That's…that's not possible. There's no way."

"I assure you, it is quite possible. There have been wars waged, with terrible losses, all in an effort to gain control of Bitta, the only planet that we know of with vasteen deposits."

"So you guys have a history of bad wars, too?"

"Wars between planets, solar systems, awful wars. Bettua controls Bitta, always has…but there was a time when we lost nearly everything."

Blalok went on to explain how the wars spanned nearly three centuries, how the Rayze united with another species, the Destrion, in a horrible effort to take control of the mining planet and its Vasteen.

"They almost destroyed our entire solar system." Blalok shook his head sadly. "Billions died, but the Rayze were relentless."

He pivoted from his console to face David more directly. "It was very bad, but in the end, Bettua, along with the United Alliance, retained control of Bitta."

He motioned around them. "After the wars, our cultures pledged themselves to peace at all costs, and to maintain that peace we've had to not only be stronger, but smarter. War is no longer an option. That is why we cannot damage your species," he folded his arms across his chest, "no matter what."

"You said this ship has vasteen on it. How is it allowed on a spaceship if it's that dangerous?"

"The *Cerulean Star* is an extraordinary ship, one of a kind, really."

Blalok puffed up with pride for an instant. "Our parents—mine and Sartek's and Isara's, designed it. It even won the Queen's rare medal of distinction."

"And..."

"And, if we encounter a do-not-survive scenario, E-I is programmed to trigger electromotive reduction of all vasteen and vasteen components. It would render the metal inert and useless."

"But?" David pressed further.

When Blalok could not hold his gaze, he said, "C'mon, Blalok. There's always a *but*."

"The *Star* would destroy itself within the defined set of circumstances...along with all life-forms in it."

David's expression fell. "It's a self-destruct sequence." He'd listened to everything Blalok told him with growing dread and imagined all the worst B-Grade space war and alien invasion movies he'd ever seen. "These Rayze—"

"Not an issue. They would've had to have been caught in the black plasma at exactly the same instant that we were. The likelihood of that is astronomical."

David rubbed his chin thoughtfully. Then said, "We gotta call Bert." He motioned to Blalok's computer. "Do it."

Blalok initiated the emergency contact transmission to awaken the four below. He was very seldom wrong, but on one issue he was...

...concerning the presence of the Rayze.

CHAPTER SIXTEEN

Δ

"Alex!" Isara shook her hard. "Alex, wake up!"

Alex was jarred awake and jumped to her knees, struggling to untangle herself from her blanket. Sartek was clutching Liberty, who was flailing on the carpet, arms clawing wildly in the air.

"Let him go!" Alex yelled. "Just let him go; hold him on his side, and watch his head!" Alex reached out for Liberty, snatching a pillow to shove under his head so it wouldn't thump on the floor.

Isara sat paralyzed, hands clutched to her mouth, her eyes enormous with the shock of it all.

The seizure lasted scarcely half a minute but, as always, seemed to Alex to go on forever.

Mercifully, Liberty finally lay motionless, eyes tightly shut, teeth clamped onto his tongue. His breathing stopped. His lips turned a dusky blue, and his eyes rolled vacantly back beneath his lids.

Alex held her breath. Just when it seemed her friend would never breathe again, he took a deep, ragged breath through the frothy, red clench of his teeth. He'd bit his tongue severely.

At long last, his rigor eased, and after what seemed like an eternity, he took another precious, gasping breath.

"What do we do?" Sartek continued to grip Liberty's wrists.

"Nothing. Just keep him on his side, let him get some air. He'll come around."

Alex sounded a whole lot more convincing than she felt.

"He's had a seizure. It's his diabetes."

"I don't understand." Isara knelt nearby, hugging a pillow and rocking.

Alex helped Sartek ease Liberty into a more comfortable position, propped up on some pillows. "Diabetes...it's a disease."

She was doing her best to remain calm and put forth a good front, but her voice was trembling. "He has to take shots. But sometimes it doesn't work right. If his sugar gets too low, he can have a seizure."

She tried to explain it the way Liberty had once explained it to her. Holding her hand in front of his mouth, to convince herself that he was indeed breathing, she added, "I've only seen him do it three times."

It was two in the morning, and the three of them sat patiently with Liberty, who remained unconscious but at least breathing more regularly. For a while, he just lay as though asleep. Then, he started to gaze about, wide-eyed and obviously confused by his surroundings.

Alex knew that once Liberty came to, it would be a few hours of confusion before his memory straightened out. That's what the seizure did. He'd even forget the most fundamental elements of his life for a while. She'd seen it before, when she and David sat with him, answering and re-answering his questions until he seemed sadly satisfied.

The first time, it'd terrified Alex, the not knowing if he would ever come back and be who he was before the seizure. But slowly, his memory always seemed to return. Liberty would recognize David and Alex and remember who he was and...whom he'd lost. Finally, he would drift off into a grief stricken sleep as all the bad events of his life came crashing down upon him as though for the first time.

It broke Alex's heart to see this. She knew that the horror of his parents' death would be the worst—as fresh as though it'd just happened today. This time, however, it could be even more difficult. He'd never met an alien before, and he certainly wouldn't remember meeting Isara and Sartek.

His eyes were wide with terror, and he clutched the blanket up under his chin. "Who are you? Where's mom?"

Alex knew it was best to stay calm and answer his questions simply, focusing on the fact that he'd had an insulin reaction. It was unpredictable what he would remember first, but oddly it was almost always Goo.

After that, he usually remembered Alex and David. The memory of the where and why of his placement in the foster home inevitably followed.

But Isara and Sartek were a brand new unknown, and explaining them to Bert would be…tricky. So it surprised all three of them when Liberty focused directly on them.

"You're not from here, but I know you, don't I?"

They all nodded in unison, and Sartek raised a pale hand to his own chest.

"I'm your friend, Bert. I know about your diabetes. We talked about it, earlier tonight."

"Where's Goo?" He looked suspiciously at the stranger, then regarded the other three in turn. Liberty seemed to relax a bit.

Alex assured him, "Goo's fine. He's at *The Home*. But you need some Coke."

She and David had, over time, developed the opinion that any juice took a distant second to the wondrous blood sugar rebound effects of Coca Cola.

"Just a sip, to make sure the sugar's on the up and up, then maybe a snack. I'll grab your glucometer."

Off to the kitchen she ran, returning with the soda and glucometer. She steeled herself to do what David so often did.

"I need to stick your ear." She held the lancet up.

With a blank look on his face, he agreed, "Okay," but then, in surprise, "Ow! You stuck my ear!"

"Sorry," she apologized as she struggled to touch the test strip to the dangling drop of blood on his ear.

"And now you must hurt him further?" Isara asked, appalled.

"I have to, we gotta know what his sugar is. He could go low again, or he might be high now." She added, seriously, "He could seize again."

His blood glucose registered sixty even. Not too low, but certainly not high. It could trend either direction, and lower was worse than higher in the short run.

She passed him the soda. "Here, try to take a sip."

"Wait," Sartek interjected, focusing solemnly on Isara.

"Sartek…*no*," Isara said, shaking her head. "I don't know if…" She scooted backward a bit.

"You don't know if you don't *try*."

"What? Guys, what are you talking about?" Alex asked urgently.

Liberty just gazed sleepily from one to the other, still obviously disoriented but willing enough to sit with the other three. He lifted his blanket up and peeked under. "Goo? Here boy."

"She's a dreamer and...a healer," Sartek explained. "So was her grandmother. It runs in families, skips generations."

"I'm *not* a healer. We don't know that!" Isara argued.

"A healer? What does that mean?" Alex, much more attentive now, asked hastily.

"It means I can affect the well-being of another...another Bettuan. But I'm certainly not advanced, and I can't be sure if it wouldn't harm a human."

"Try," Alex begged, suddenly desperate, "*Please*, you gotta try."

By now, the migraine was starting to hit Liberty. The waves of nausea would soon follow. The crushing headache would last about six hours and would be crippling for him.

He eased himself onto his side, pulling the blanket more over his shoulder as he pinched his eyes closed. He was evidently too preoccupied with the first onset of pain to care what the others were saying.

"I-I don't know," Isara faltered.

"Isara. He's your friend, our friend, and he's trying to help you. Please try," Alex begged.

"She's right," Sartek said. "He's doing everything he can to get the *Cerulean Star* back to us, even risking his own life." He reached out his hand, resting it on her knee. "Maybe you can help *him* like he's trying to help us."

Isara focused her gaze on Liberty, huddled miserably in the middle of the living room floor, occasionally looking for his lost dog. He seemed more fragile than usual, his white mop of hair sticking out every which way from beneath the edge of his blanket.

She edged closer. "Bert...Liberty? Can you hear me?"

He peeked from under the edge of the blanket, opened his eyes, and peered at her between slitted eyes. "I'm not at full capacity...whoever you are, but I can hear you okay."

She smiled. "Bert, my name is Isara. I'm from another planet, and I'm your friend."

Comically, Liberty's one eyebrow went up in an expression of, *Well, that's different, but if you say so.* "Go on."

"I'm going to touch you, try to make you feel a little better. Would that be okay?"

His expression remained blank. "You can't. I'm the boss of my body."

This confused Isara a bit, and she glanced at Alex for translation.

"Oh, don't worry. That's just something they teach us to say in school, you know, to keep the pervs away." She gestured for Isara to continue.

This time, Bert said nothing when Isara sidled even closer to her frail human friend and reached for him. Laying her hands on the top of Liberty's considerable head of hair, she pulled back and shot a look at Alex.

"It's so soft!"

"Yeah, he's a freak. Go on."

Isara laid her hands on his head once more and closed her eyes, dropping her chin to her chest.

"What's she do—"

"Shhh," Sartek whispered, motioning for her to be silent. "Let's backup some. This won't be easy for her." The two pushed away, giving Isara and Liberty plenty of room.

Liberty rolled onto his back, his eyes closed. Isara's hands practically disappeared in the white expanse that was Liberty's hair, and she swayed gently back and forth.

After waiting for what seemed like an eternity, Alex couldn't stand it anymore. She was just about to say something when Isara started to hum. It was soft, sweet, and so very tender—an ethereal, almost sad noise that seemed to fill the room in a heartbreaking whisper. It sounded not at all as though it came from the alien child, and Alex glanced overhead at one point.

Liberty just remained stock still, as though sleeping, hands crossed over his chest. It went on like this for some time until Isara eventually became silent. Her hands slipped from the boy's head to her lap, and her head lifted enough that she eyes met Sartek's. Suddenly, she toppled over onto the blanket pile, right next to Liberty.

"*Isara*," Sartek called out urgently.

She held one feeble hand up as though to stop him from advancing or speaking. Reaching out, she took Liberty's hand, blinked slowly, and closed her eyes.

Alex and Sartek sat close by, saying nothing, just watching the two as they lay there, both breathing shallow but steady.

"Here," Sartek pulled some blankets and two pillows toward Alex. "We're no use to them fatigued. Let's get some rest."

Exhausted, they curled up for a bit to catch some sleep. None of them heard the gentle alarm or noticed the light that flickered urgently on the notebook.

It was barely light when Isara touched Alex on the arm.

"Something's wrong…."

"What?" Alex asked urgently and scrambled to sitting, "How is he?"

Sartek pushed up groggily. "What's going on?"

"No, not Bert." Isara gestured toward the tablet.

Alex hopped up to silence the device before focusing her attention on Liberty first. As she straightened Liberty's blanket, Isara's brow creased in worry.

"Alex, what Liberty has, it isn't good."

Alex was getting the hang of reading the aliens' expressions, and it gave her a bad feeling in her stomach. "Well, no kidding, but there's nothing we can do about it. There isn't a cure."

"I think I might have helped him, but I can't be sure."

Just then, Liberty rolled over, stretched, and was startled by the proximity of his friends, all who sat lined up like cats on a fence, staring wide-eyed at him.

"What?"

Silence.

"*What?* Did I fart?" He swung the edge of the blanket to and fro as though to waft something truly lethal toward them, stopping only when the three remained altogether solemn. He shot up to sitting, immediately more serious. "Wait, what's wrong? Is it the *Star*?"

"Liberty, you had a reaction last night," Alex blurted.

"Not possible," Liberty shook his head. "I feel great. I'd have a headache for sure; you know it makes my brain swell for a while." He fingered his fat lower lip and aching tongue. "But…I did bite my lip, I guess."

"Alex is telling the truth," Sartek confirmed. "We saw it."

"But how? I don't remember forgetting, and remembering. That's always…"

"Isara helped you," Alex said. "She's a healer, Bert. She laid some healing on you."

Isara peered keenly at Alex as though perhaps that wasn't the best description. "Bert, the reaction was severe, but I think I was able to stabilize what was happening to you."

Alex gestured toward his glucometer. "You know your blood sugar's always high the morning after one of these."

"Yeah, it's the rebound glycogen that my liver lets go of with the seizure," Liberty tried to explain but was met with blank stares all around.

Sartek handed Liberty the glucometer, and Isara winced as he pricked his finger for a blood sample. The small machine beep-beeped, and Liberty stared at the device.

"What? What is it?" Alex asked urgently.

"Ninety five," he shared the reading, focusing his attention on Isara. "That's textbook perfect." His confusion was fairly complete.

* * *

Just then, Liberty noticed the blip-blip of the small light on the side of the notebook. Hastily disentangling himself from the blankets, he scrambled on hands and knees and snatched up the device, flipping open the folding cover. It came brilliantly to life, and he hit connect for the video link.

Blalok came instantly into view, and rolled his eyes. "We set up an emergency contact protocol for a reason, you know—emergency *contact*?"

"I know, I know." Liberty hastily waved Blalok's gentle sarcasm away. "We had an…an incident. Anyway, never mind. What's happening?"

"We have approximately twenty-five hours before the *Cerulean Star* is penetrable." Blalok wasted no time cutting straight to business.

"Twenty-five hours? But how?" Isara's voice cracked with worry.

"That's not enough time." Liberty, still somewhat flustered, rubbed between his eyebrows "Why are we…? Never mind, that's not important now."

David dropped into view next to Blalok, hip-checking him so he could share his chair. This seemed to distress the smallest alien somewhat.

"Is that necessary?"

Their exchange might have been amusing had the situation been less dire.

"We need a plan," David pressed on. "Blalok and E-I have some ideas, but it's game time."

"I think I know where to start," Liberty said suddenly. "It all came to me in my sleep. Listen to this…"

CHAPTER SEVENTEEN

Δ

Scarcely one hour later, two Bettuan and two Earthlings left through the rear door slider of their rental home. They crossed the dirt backyard, hopped across the dry irrigation ditch, and headed directly toward the perimeter fence of four thousand acres of restricted property. But they didn't cross over or under the fence, only looked west toward their goal.

"Somewhere under there is the *Star*." Sartek hung his hands on loops of the chain link in a decidedly human gesture. Resting his chin on his fingers, he gazed across the weed and pebble strewn landscape. All of it blew dry and dusty, the wind swirling in what Alex called "toilet-bowl" circles.

"Can we do this?" Isara's voice quivered with skepticism as she pulled her ball cap down, further concealing her lovely, almond shaped eyes.

Alex held a hand up in a hi-five gesture. "Yeah, we can. We just gotta stick to the plan." Isara, instead of slapping her hand, just took it and held on. Perhaps the electric current was still there, but Alex didn't react and said nothing.

Pulling a roughly scribbled shopping list out of his pocket, Liberty scanned over the two pages a last time. "Distraction is our enemy. We get in, and get out. Buddy system, kay?" He glanced at Alex. "Keep Isara low profile, but if something goes wrong—last ditch—you use that...thing that happened yesterday. Not getting the supplies isn't an option."

Alex and Isara nodded solemnly at each other.

"Let's get going and get this done." He ripped off one of the sheets and handed it to Alex. "There's an Ace Hardware on the corner of Seventh and Division. Take the city bus; meet us back here. We'll assemble stuff first, then head to the mine."

"You mean build bombs?" Sartek wondered grimly.

Liberty struggled with this question. He very much admired Mahatma Gandhi and ascribed to the activist's philosophy of nonviolence. He'd even read his comments regarding acts of violence in his paper, *The Cult of Bomb*, so it pained Liberty that he might be doing anything unethical. Yet, he knew they were seriously outmatched and outnumbered.

"It's not to hurt anyone. It's just to get in." His gaze wandered from Sartek to Isara. "I know that's important to you—not to harm anyone. Believe me, it's just as important to me."

Alex gazed out across the field again. "It's gonna be fine. We're not gonna kill anyone."

Liberty gestured to Sartek. "C'mon, we got some errands of our own. And don't forget to buy watches," he reminded Isara and Alex. "Two hours, okay?"

"Roger that." Alex threw a sloppy salute his direction.

"Roger this as well," Isara added with resolve.

The girls' responses prompted an immediate grin from Liberty. "See? You're totally getting this!"

Then Alex and Isara walked southeast, and Liberty and Sartek headed directly south.

* * *

In short order, the boys were at their destination, smack in the very center of town. Sartek gazed skeptically about at what appeared to be a remarkably remote location. Liberty bit his lip and pulled out his tablet to confirm the Craigslist address and cross coordinate it with the GPS that was thumb-nailed in the corner of the device's screen.

"Okay, I guess this looks like the place.".

"*This* is where we need to be? To find engines?" Sartek's skepticism was obvious as he considered the junked car lot on one side of the road and the stockyard on the other. "Are you sure about this?"

Liberty tilted his head to better see down the long, narrow dirt driveway.

Nearly three hundred feet back sat a small, rundown house with a mishmash of multi-colored add-ons jutting randomly from it. "Yep, this is it." He shrugged and stuffed the notebook back into his backpack before gesturing to the sign, tacked to a monstrous maple tree—the only one on the entire property.

It read, "Estate Sale—10:00 *NO EARLY BIRDS!*"

"It sounds like someone was a major collector here, and if we're lucky, they'll have the engines," Liberty tried to sound optimistic.

"Collector?"

"Yeah, you know. Someone who saves stuff. Whoever he was, it looks like he was seriously into rockets, at least from what the ad says. I'm guessing there's not very many rocket enthusiasts around here."

Sartek glanced around as though he might see one lurking in the overgrown grass.

"Rockets are really underappreciated cuz they can start fires." Liberty swept with his hands at the expanse of urban dryness. "You can see why that might be a risk, but once you get bit," he grinned at the Bettuan, "it's a bug you can't shake."

Liberty spoke with sincere respect. Though he'd never had the resources to be a serious rocketeer, he'd always loved the idea of it, and was excited for what he might find hidden in the recesses of the old estate sale.

He gestured to the maple tree. "You should probably hang out here, though. If it comes down to it, I'll give you a sign I need help. And…wish me luck."

"Luck to you, then." Sartek said soberly.

Liberty pulled the translation ring from around his neck and handed it to Sartek. "It might look suspicious," he said as an afterthought.

Sartek took the ring, briefly grasping Liberty's hand. He nodded gravely, his eyes serious and damp. Once more, he felt the strange, electric sensation that seemed to occur when he touched one of the Bettuan. This time, however, he was no longer alarmed and said nothing about it.

Releasing the human's hand, the Bettuan turned and crawled through the rusted barbwire fence. Wandering behind the tree, Sartek found a comfortable spot where he could sit and study an acutely odd creature that munched dried grass just beyond the fence. Quite suddenly, and with sound effects, the beast spewed something obscenely disgusting from its less desirable end, while it continued to eat.

Liberty glanced back just in time to see the look of repulsion on Sartek's face. The alien obviously couldn't take his eyes off the cow, and the heifer raised her head, focused directly on Sartek, and *mooed*. This set him completely on edge, and as though not sure whether the creature was dangerous or not, Sartek shifted to the other side of the tree, away from the cow and its vile expulsions.

Liberty grinned and headed again down the long, cracked driveway. Weeds pushed up everywhere, and as he walked dust swirled up around his legs in little tornadoes. The busted driveway ran about thirty feet up to the rancher style home, with its peeling pink paint. He paused as he neared the house.

Glancing about, he scanned what was an incredible amount of paraphernalia scattered over the driveway and weed-ridden lawn, most of it covered in a considerable layer of dust. He thought to himself that this could be one of those perpetual estate sales that never seemed to end, and the rocketry in the ad may just be a hook. Butterflies set into his belly.

There was a garage with a door that was mostly open and broken, hanging crooked compared to the frame. Just inside, an older, heavyset woman was price labeling some very fragile china. Seeing no indications yet of rockets or engines, Liberty plastered his happiest smile on his face and waved as he walked up to her.

She barely glanced up, did a double take, and stabbed with her marker toward the driveway, the wings of her fleshy upper arms flapping as she did. "You're an hour early! No Early Birds!"

Liberty halted, tried to give her his most forlorn, disappointed expression, and dug his toe into the dirt. "Okay, I understand."

The woman stopped what she was doing and wiped her hands on a well-worn kitchen apron before sweeping a stray lock of gray hair back into the bun at the back of her neck. "Was there some reason you're here pestering me so early, child?"

"I love rockets," he replied with a shrug. "My brothers do too, and they'll be here in an hour and take all the good ones." He gazed nostalgically back down the driveway as though he expected his imaginary brothers to swarm him at any moment. "It's always like that; they say I'm the runt, and that's true enough. So...I get the runt rockets."

He scuffed at the dirt again. "I guess that's how it goes." Liberty affected his most charming smile and showered false optimism upon his host. "But don't worry, I'll be back in an hour! I've saved up my chore money and just had a birthday. Maybe I can snag a good one before they get 'em all!"

Very little was required of Liberty to come across as utterly charming.

Even though it was an act, and he was about to bust apart at the seams, his natural disposition appeared as it always did. He was adorable, *period*.

The woman softened, rested her hands on her hips, and gave the boy a once-over before gesturing for him to follow her.

She sighed heavily, as though she'd just been coerced into giving up her first-born child. "That's quite the hairdo you have, son."

"It's hopeless," Liberty replied honestly. "The best have tried to tame it and failed."

She hesitated again, giving the child a longer look before a smile crept slowly across her lips. "C'mon." She motioned with her marker. "I think I can help you out."

"Awesome!" He tripped excitedly after her.

Walking down a narrow dimly lit hall, they passed a retro kitchen with fake mahogany paneling. Liberty followed her down a dark flight of rickety, wooden stairs, with only a marginally attached hand railing, into a clammy cellar.

The narrow, ground level windows on one side of the basement were caked with years of dust and grime and let in very little light. Liberty squinted to see around himself. The room had all the feeling of a bad, slasher movie, and his mouth was suddenly dry.

The woman fished for a shoelace that hung down from the ceiling and snagged it, triggering a bright overhead fluorescent panel. The small room lit up with obnoxiously glaring light. Coincidentally, an old radio kicked in, and Lenny Kravitz squeaked tinnily, commanding Liberty to *Fly Away*.

With the sudden brightness, the imaginary torture chamber disappeared and became oddly inviting. It was piled with the treasures of an old man's life—fishing poles, an abundance of tools, an odd collection of midwestern license plates on one wall. Liberty blinked as the woman motioned to a workbench that ran the entire length of the far side of the basement.

Scattered along the bench, several rocket bodies jutted out of a collection of boxes. Liberty could tell right away, by some of the fins that were exposed, that he was very close to what he'd come for. With true enthusiasm, he hurried over to the boxes.

"May I?" He paused.

She smiled for the second time since they'd met. "Sure, go ahead. My Earl was a collector. Earl's my husband, *was* my husband, anyway. I just haven't been able to put his little toys up for sale yet."

Pulling up an old, wooden kitchen chair, she sat heavily; Liberty wondered briefly whether or not the chair could possibly support her.

Snatching a dishtowel from her apron pocket, she wiped her eyes before cleaning her glasses with it.

"He was crazy about his little rockets, my Earl. I'm sure there's something there that'll catch your eye."

"Rocketry done well is a hobby of brilliance," Liberty acknowledged. "Your Earl must've been very special."

She murmured a sigh of appreciation.

Shuffling through the first box, Liberty was immediately in awe. Straight up, he saw *Viper III, NORAD,* and...his eyes flew wide, and he almost trembled as he gingerly lifted the *Stovi* rocket from the box, running his fingers along the sleek gold and black body with the elegant four-finned tail design.

"Whoa," he whispered more to himself than to her.

Liberty dug swiftly through the box and found a launch pad, controller, launch rods, and a roll of fuse. He turned to her, struggling to concentrate on the true purpose for his being there.

"This is amazing! Do you know if he had any engines?"

She gestured underneath the workbench to another collection of clear, plastic boxes. "I couldn't be sure, dear, but if there are, they'd probably be down there."

Pulling out the first box, he cracked the lid open. Beneath several E size engines, nestled in dry pack, Liberty discovered what he'd come for. He found a *G40 White Lightening,* several single use Motor *G80-13T HAZ*s, and no less than three *G80-7T Blue Thunder*s.

"No way. This is incredible! I was gonna get two rockets, but with these engines, I think I'd rather just get one rocket and stock up on these!" He held up one of the Blue Thunders.

It was just then that Liberty noticed a crate at the end of the bench. He gently laid the Blue Thunder down and stared in awe, realizing he'd just discovered the Holy Grail of rockets. He murmured, "That's an O-Level Engine, a BSD *Thor.*" The six-inch, smooth cylinder jutted out, nowhere close to fitting in the crate.

"If you say so," was all she said as she pushed up and off the chair.

"How could he have this?" Liberty pointed at the engine with reverent amazement in his voice. "It's a level three rocket engine."

"Yep, that's about right. Earl was real proud of his level three certification."

She indicated the beam overhead of the workbench where, sure enough, was stapled the certification. "I can probably make you a bargain for it." She reached for an empty box, stuffing several rockets and a wide assortment of engines into it.

"And the *Thor*?" Liberty was afraid to ask.

"If'n you want it, child, it's yours. I got no use for it, and it's taking up space down here. I've always worried my Earl would blow us up anyways. I'm glad to let it go." She peered at him, a knowing expression on her face. "I'm happy it's a boy like you winding up with 'em. I think my Earl would have liked you."

Liberty was stunned, and as for the space it was "taking up," he was fairly certain she had no pressing plans for the workshop that used to be Earl's man-cave. He pulled from his pocket sixty-four dollars. "I only have this." His hand trembled as he held the money out to her. "I don't think it's enough."

She reached out, plucking forty out of his hand. "We'll call it even."

Liberty was instantly aware that he'd just bought filet mignon for the price of a Big Mac, and he realized she knew it as well.

"Thank you so much. You have no idea what a kind thing you've just done."

"Oh, I think I might." She gave him a very knowing expression. "I've always believed that good things come around when you do what's right. My Earl was eighty-two. Did you know we were married for sixty-four years?" She didn't wait for Liberty to answer. "I think he'd want a child like you to have these, and I'm guessing I'll have a pretty good sale today as a result, karma and all. Maybe make enough to get that TV I've been wanting—the fancy one with the glasses."

Liberty had to concentrate to pull himself back to the real issue at hand. He shifted the biggest engines into several boxes and headed for the stairs with the first one. It took him two trips to get the rockets and engines out of the basement, but twenty minutes later, he was heading back down the long dirt driveway, towing his epic score in a radio flyer wagon he'd also bought for five bucks?

He wouldn't know it, but the woman wouldn't just have a good sale that day, she'd have a *great* one. She'd make just short of four grand, and with her newly acquired cash stash, not only would she get her garage door fixed, she'd buy the 3-D plasma TV she had her eye on, watch *The Avengers*, and fall in love with Robert Downey, Jr., all in one night.

As Liberty neared the tree, Sartek stood up from the long, dry grass. He handed the translation ring back to Bert and asked, "Get everything we need?"

"Oh, boy, did I ever."

Liberty motioned him over to the wagon as he knelt on the gravel shoulder of the road and flipped open the top of one of the boxes.

The two huddled together, and Liberty pulled out one of the engines, laying the flashy cardboard tube into Sartek's hands.

"Heavy," Sartek said.

"Yeah, rocket engines are like electronics. Generally, the heavier they are, the better they are." Liberty could hardly contain his excitement. He pointed to the biggest engine, jutting out of the wagon because it was too long to fit. "We even got a Thor. We have enough black powder in all of these to get the job done for sure." He closed the top of the cardboard box. "Let's just hope Isara and Alex got their stuff done too."

They rolled their winnings several lots away till they found a more secluded spot, then settled down to the task of dismantling the engines from the rocket mounts, breaking them down to raw ingredients. It broke Liberty's heart to do such a thing, but it must be done.

Lastly, Liberty stashed the remnants of the magnificent rockets into a drainage pipe at a deserted stop. "Thank you Earl," he murmured reverently. Sartek stood by with his head politely bowed. Then they covered the culvert end with dirt and brush.

Transferring the core of the engines to their backpacks, Sartek burdened most of the weight. The *Thor* engine alone looked like he was carrying a length of drainpipe.

As they head back to the rental, Liberty felt like he'd let Earl down, but only for a moment. He chirped to Sartek, "You know, if Earl knew his engines might help get some aliens launched back to space, I think he'd be pretty happy about it."

Sartek grinned. "I would think it's…a rocketeer's dream."

His heart lighter, Liberty shifted his own pack. "We gotta get to Radio Shack."

Within the hour they had five transmitters, five receivers, a collection of alligator clips, and a roll each of bonding wire and fine filament nichrome igniter wire.

"How does that all work?" Sartek asked.

"When we get back to the house, I'll assemble the explosives. We set them off with the transmitter, and "BOOM," it's foolproof."

"Seriously?"

"*No.*"

Liberty shook his head gravely and trucked on.

* * *

Before their trip to the Ace Hardware, Alex and Isara made a quick stop at a neighboring drug store. Only Alex went in, and after her purchases, they knelt behind it, next to a cardboard collection dumpster.

Alex, who'd never worn an ounce of makeup in her life, was appalled at the price she'd paid for the concealing foundation and loose powder. "I can see why girls shoplift this crap," she said as she spread the concealer onto Isara's cheeks and neck with a sponge. "Well, I mean...I *wouldn't*, but this stuff is expensive as gold!"

She dabbled a bit more before rocking back on her heels to assess her handiwork. "Wow, it's working! You look like you have the plague n' all, but at least you look more human."

Isara flashed a brilliant smile. "Thank you."

This was the first time Alex noticed that her friend's teeth were finely serrated.

"I'm really happy, Alex," Isara bubbled. "If I look more like you, all the better." Her eyes flashed with emotion, and suddenly she reached up to stop Alex from her task. "I understand that you, Liberty, and David maybe live in a...not great situation. But what you are doing to try to help us? It could land you in a great deal of trouble or get you hurt; I want you to know I'm aware of that."

"It wouldn't be the first time I got tagged by the long arm of the law." Alex shrugged and pulled Isara's sunglasses off so she could smear the foundation better on her nose. "Besides, summer was getting kinda boring before you guys came along."

Isara tried not to wiggle, looking up with excitement as the human gently spread the makeup under her eyes. As always, Alex was immediately awed by the strange effect of the alien's eyes, so large and unusual. Once, she'd seen a really fancy doll, and its glass eyes had so much depth to them. That same peculiar depth was also apparent on Isara's, although the blue-green of hers took up nearly the entire eye with very little white showing at all.

She handed Isara back her sunglasses.

"Anyway, you guys have really given this week a lot of potential."

The warm moment was short-lived. They capped the makeup and headed to the hardware store. Before long, the two stood across the street from the Lakeside Ace Hardware—unusual name for a store, as there was not a lake for miles.

"Kay, just lay low. I don't want anyone to notice you, but if I need you, I'll give you the sign. It if comes down to it, we do this. We can try to animate some garden tools or something to get what we need and make our escape."

Isara nodded, and Alex helped push her locks further up under her ball cap before they went in. With her dark sunglasses and a button down shirt with the collar flipped up, she was quite a bit less conspicuous than she'd been when she'd first materialized at the meadow in the woods. Keeping her hands stuffed into her overall pockets, she followed Alex through the front doors, her head down.

"Can I help you ladies?" the clerk asked kindly. This prompted another smile from Isara, that she'd been mistaken for a "human" lady.

"Plumbing." Alex, all business, shook her head and pointed. "Thanks, we got it."

The two girls wandered toward the back of the store and the plumbing section. Isara rummaged idly through a bargain bin and turned so that the salesman couldn't see her face but she could still see Alex from the corner of her eye.

Alex gave her a brief nod before approaching a man who was pulling toilet plungers out of a big box and lining them neatly along a shelf.

"Excuse me," Alex said politely. "Can you help me?" She plastered on her sweetest smile. If someone didn't know her very well, Alex could really pull off sweet. Her eyes were shining with all the promise of a summer morning, her hair was poorly contained in a ponytail, and her freckles splashed gloriously across her lovely, tanned face. She was every schoolboy's dream...until she opened her mouth.

The man was older, well over six feet, burly and broad, and he studied her with an expression akin to that of a kind uncle. "Sure, little lady. What can I get for you?"

Her smile transformed into a brilliant grin. "I need five pieces of metal pipe, thirteen inches long, three inches in diameter, threaded on both ends, and...with end caps." She laced her fingers together and swung them happily back and forth in front of her.

With a look of genuine surprise that turned immediately to suspicion, the salesman paused. "Uhmm, yeah, what you just described is something we don't really do." He noted with a tone of grave disappointment, "It sounds like you want something for making something that's up to no good."

As if to close the conversation, he went back to stocking the toilet plungers, then paused again.

"Your brother or someone put you up to this?"

He glanced up at her, a toilet plunger dangling from one hand, eyes narrowing to scan farther down the aisle to see if there were looming terrorists waiting for her.

Alex dropped her hands to her sides. "*What*? You just called me Ted Kazowski?" She affected a perfect demeanor of sweet outrage. "I'm a Girl Scout for God's—uh, for goodness sakes! And I need those pipes for our time capsules!"

She gave him no time to consider this new information.

"We're stuffing them with…stuff…from the earth's…uh, seasons, and you're gonna make me fail my final project? So I won't ever get my badge?" Her lower lip trembled, and she squeaked, "Or…my *scholarship*?"

She tried hard to think of David, to imagine that the ship had been ripped apart and he was being tortured, or worse, and genuine tears welled in her eyes.

Her performance was pitch perfect, and the salesman became instantly anxious, evidently past questioning why the child needed five lengths of pipe when there were only four seasons. He held his hands out as though he might stop the flow of tears, but it was too late; one ran down Alex's cheek, and she turned slowly and dramatically away, shoulders sagging heavily, before letting go a pathetic sob.

"Wait!" he said hastily. "Just wait a second."

He peered nervously around as though his supervisor might be watching and dropped his voice. "I can make your time capsules for you, but wouldn't you rather have PVC? It'd be a lot cheaper, and easier to cap, and you could get a lot bigger, fit a lot more stuff in 'em."

"But, it wouldn't last a thousand years," Alex sniffed without missing a beat. She'd not really thought all this through before coming into the store but was a master on the fly.

Sighing deeply, the salesman resigned himself to the task. "Come on." He motioned for Alex to follow him.

"That's so wonderful!" Alex feigned deep appreciation. "What's your name? I'd *love* to include you in my write-up as someone who was so awesome in helping me with my final project!"

"Dave," was all the man replied.

Alex froze, a look of supreme shock on her face.

Dave hesitated when her demeanor so swiftly changed. "You okay little miss? You look like you just seen a ghost."

"What did you say?"

"I said, 'Are you all right?'"

"No—no, before. Your *name*?"

"Dave; well, it's really David, but my friends just call me Big Dave."

The towering fellow patted the child gently on the shoulders as she heedlessly surrounded his girth with an enormous hug. At this point, it was obvious she'd totally baffled him on all fronts, and he offered only a simple,

"You're so welcome, little miss. Uh…" He patted her again.

Less than fifteen minutes later, Alex was at the checkout stand with the pipes, a half dozen small steel drill bits, a standard hammer, rock chisel, and four cheap, plastic wrist watches. She was genuinely distracted and scarcely murmured a "thanks" to the clerk before sprinting from the store, Isara following discretely behind.

When they were finally outside, Alex ducked around the corner of the building and squatted on her heels, leaning heavily against the brick of the wall. "Holy batshit, Robin!"

"What? What is it?" Isara knelt beside her. "Are you okay?"

"That guy in the store—guess what his name was?"

"I-I don't understand. I—"

"David! His name is *David*."

Isara made the connection immediately.

"Oh, wow. But I think it's a good sign," she said cheerily.

"I know!" Alex grabbed her by the shoulders. "I know it is! But I don't get sent signs. It just doesn't happen to me. Our plan, it's supposed to work! This is *supposed* to happen!" She slapped her hands together in excitement.

The two could hardly contain themselves as Alex fished through the bag for two of the wristwatches. She looked around as though she might see a clock somewhere.

"Wait here." She motioned for Isara to stay put and trotted back into the store. "Excuse me? Do you have the time?"

The younger man behind the counter who'd replaced the woman fished his cell phone from his pocket and activated it.

"Eleven thirty-two."

"Thanks!" Alex sprinted from the Ace Hardware for the second time and ran to the back of the building. "Set your watch to eleven thirty-two." She showed Isara how to pull out the tiny pin to set the time.

The alien peered closely at the caricature of the mouse with a bow in her hair, arms pointing with index fingers at the numbers. "It's cute." Then she shielded her eyes and squinted at the overhead sun.

"We better hurry, Alex. We're running out of time."

The two scampered toward the bus stop, Alex praying silently that Liberty and Sartek had been as successful as they were.

CHAPTER EIGHTEEN

Δ

"Let's cover this again," David was intensely serious about not screwing up. "I want to make sure we haven't missed anything."

They sat together at a table, a three-dimensional image of Kansas and the Ogallala aquifer spinning slowly in front of them. They were able to visualize, quite clearly, the geological structures of not only Hutchinson Air Base, but also a good part of the surrounding county and even states, if they reduced the image away. The aquifer, which became much deeper and dramatic as it approached Nebraska, was impressive. David never imagined such a feature existed, so vast, and hidden barely below the dry flat surface of Kansas.

Squinting, he studied the long, elegant finger that snaked beneath Hutchinson, silently giving life to a good part of the Midwest.

"I used to sit on the edge of our pond, fishing with Bert n' Alex; I'd wish we had some bigger piece of water, you know, like an ocean or something? All this time I did, only I didn't know it. It was right under my feet."

"It's good to have water close by," Blalok replied a bit whimsically. "It feeds the mind, I think, simply because it is so essential to life."

"I'd be fun to be able to swim a long ways, you know, and surf and stuff." David shot him a wry glance before returning his attention to the aquifer. "And the salt mine, where is that?"

"Enhance subterranean features." Blalok's voice rose slightly.

Within seconds, the landmass beneath the earthen crust came swirling into view, each with a distinct color that represented different densities.

The strata were easy to pick out—the long, folding sheets of limestone and shale, the salt deposits from when the Earth's ancient seabeds had once coursed their way above ground.

These long gone oceans were eventually buried as the Earth's massive plates shifted, covering them completely over the span of millions of years. It was impressive to see the result displayed so neatly in front of them.

Blalok's altered the settings, and the image zoomed in on a honeycomb cavern beneath the surface. Much smaller in comparison to the enormous aquifer, these were the Lyons salt mines. The "room and pillar" system of mining was clearly evident and stood out as an unnatural configuration. Shafts were dug to the desired depth leaving enormous salt pillars in strategic places to support the mine as it snaked deeper and deeper into the Earth.

"That's the mine?" David pointed at the checkerboard image.

"Mmm-hmm."

Blalok spun the three-dimensional diagram so they could view it from the other side. "And here's the aquifer."

He motioned toward the slick, silvery blue sheet that appeared to send out a network of probing fingers. "These are all underground rivers and streams. As you can see, right here…"

He inserted his finger directly into the 3-D image.

"The aquifer actually comes fairly close to the mine. My guess is they've tapped it and utilize a water-blast technique to tear away more mine caverns when they need to."

"Sounds kinda dangerous to me." David said flatly.

Blalok raised an eyebrow and spoke with the mock patience of a preschool teacher. "I don't believe mining has *ever* been considered the safest of professions."

David was immediately insulted. "Yeah, well neither is space-surfing tsunamis," he snapped and regretted it as soon as he'd said it. He glanced away, brushing the dark locks from his tan face. It was a habit he had when he was nervous, and the hair fell immediately back over his eyes. "Blalok…I'm sorry about that. I guess I'm just worried about them."

Blalok studied his feet. "I understand. I'm sorry too."

He glanced up. "But as long as we're imagining terrible scenarios…"

He punched a few more buttons, and the 3-D image of Kansas was replaced with an image of the *Cerulean Star*.

David gasped out loud. What he saw was beautiful and hideous at the same time. The *Star* rotated slowly in front of them like an infant's mobile, as though suspended by an invisible string in a soft breeze. The blue was indescribable, more vivid and rich than David had ever seen, even more so than a late, evening summer sky just before dusk.

The sleek, smooth, oblong body was stunning in its simplicity. The tail of it turned up ever so slightly, like a waterfowl's, and the nose flipped down. Shimmering ribbons of white and blue ran the underbelly length of it.

If he peered very closely, it appeared the surface was almost scaled, like the body of a fish. David could envision it slipping not only through space but also through time—which was exactly what the *Star* did best.

However, the beauty of it was tragically marred. Here and there, in a ragged, weblike pattern, a black thread crisscrossed the graceful body of the ship. It was ugly and vicious, like a plague, and it crackled intermittently with piercing flashes of white.

"What is that?" He was afraid to ask.

"It's the *Star*."

"No, I mean, what's that on it? I don't know, that bad looking stuff?"

"That is deterioration—the death of the hull. When it is at roughly forty percent, there will be enough exposed exoskeleton that penetration will likely be attempted."

"And we know how soon that is already, right? But how likely is it they can get in?"

"That depends." Blalok scowled. "How determined are your species to conquer and rule?"

Pausing to seriously consider Blalok's question, he said, "There aren't any species more determined than ours. We rule in that game." It wasn't meant to be funny. David was dead serious.

Blalok's eyes widened at this. "Are you exaggerating?"

David shook his head. "Look, we got sharks, gorillas, bears, lions, orcas, even giant killer bugs. And guess what? They *all* fear us. Crap is king, and not only does ours stink the worst, we sit on the biggest pile."

He spun to look his new friend squarely in the eye. "It's our nature, Blalok. We wreck stuff. I have to be honest; John Conner had it right. We're gonna destroy ourselves."

"John Conner—a philosopher?"

"Yeah, sort of. He led the resistance against the terminators." When it appeared he'd lost Blalok entirely, he added, "Just a movie, but that doesn't make it not true."

"Perhaps it doesn't have to be that way," Blalok countered.

"No? Then what do you suppose is going to happen to us when that gets bad enough?" David swept one hand through the 3-D image of the *Star*.

"We would establish a friendly alliance with your species and be allowed to return the *Cerulean Star* to space?"

When David didn't smile, Blalok sighed heavily as though he knew what the human feared was sadly true. It would be the end of the *Star* and, very likely, their lives as well.

It was just then that they heard it. The sound howled at them like a metallic machine, screaming, just for a split second. It was enough to make David clasp his hands over his ears.

"What the hell's that?"

"The shield. It's not happy about what is happening to it. That means the vasteen endoskeleton has less than fifty percent of its necessary defense left."

Blalok manipulated the monitor, and the scarred depiction of the ship changed to a precise model covered with minute numbers. They moved in waves across the surface of the *Star*. Most of the numbers were red. Some were orange, and a few were yellow and blue. However, a number of them were green—a deep, deadly green, and they flashed ominously.

"See these?" Blalok pointed at the green ones. "They indicate the areas where shield strength is dwindling to the point of critical mass. It is here that they will likely first attempt to breach the *Star*."

He stabbed at one particular area where the green was alarmingly prolific and adjusted some settings to effectively diminish the noise.

David continued to peer closely at the image, allowing his gaze to scan over the entirety of the ship. On the other end, toward the top, three dots sparkled.

"What are those?"

"Those," Blalok paused. "Are us, well, us and Cleo."

Hearing her name, the chakrat mewled softly from behind them.

David turned around to see the unusual little creature peaking out from behind the edge of the shift chamber. Her eyes were enormous and damp, as though she sensed her own peril.

This immediately drove home to David just how much Blalok and his friends had to lose. The aliens' fate would be much worse than his, he believed, not to mention taking away from them the only link they had with their planet—their *starship*. Words failed him, his eyes drawn back to the decaying *Star*.

Suddenly, David believed he and Blalok shared something very much in common…dread.

"E-I," he said.

"Yes, David?" came the computer's calm reply.

"Get me Bert."

CHAPTER NINETEEN

Δ

Sartek and Liberty hit one more yard sale before heading home. They'd been lucky enough to score a cheap hand drill and were almost back to the rental, still dragging the radio flyer. Turning the final corner, they heard a soft *beep-beep* coming from Liberty's backpack.

"Here, I'll get it," Sartek said.

It was hot outside; the sun beat down on them, and he swiped sweat from his forehead before he undid the backpack clips and slid the zipper open, just as he'd seen the human do. He carefully removed the tablet and flipped it open before passing it to Liberty. "Thanks," Liberty said.

David's face came immediately into view. "How we looking?" he blurted straight away.

"So far, we're on schedule. What's up?"

"We're running out of time. The shields are wearing out. I don't think it's gonna be too long before we start getting pummeled on, Bert. I'm worried about these guys."

"I got the black powder. If Alex and Isara make it back, we should be ready to tour the salt mine by mid-afternoon."

"And the aquifer? I saw it. It looks big."

"Yeah," Liberty acknowledged. "It's about hundred eighty feet deep there. Crazy, but the mine goes right through the middle of it."

"I don't see how," David wondered.

"They froze it. Used liquid nitrogen in giant tubes and ran them through the aquifer till it was solid ice. Then they blasted it out and lined the tunnels with concrete."

David shifted uneasily. "That's the stupidest thing I've ever heard. That can't be safe."

Liberty knew David would never admit to a fair bit of claustrophobia and tried to sound encouraging. "It's actually quite safe. This particular mine has one of the safest histories on record, that is…until later on today, anyway." He wasn't meaning to be funny. "But don't worry. I know where to place the…explosives."

By now, he and Sartek were walking up the front sidewalk of the rental. "Hold on a sec." He fumbled in his pocket for the house key, handing the notebook briefly to Sartek.

"Hi." Sartek looked anywhere but at David's image on the screen. The last time he'd spoken directly to David was when he had given him the translation ring, when they'd had that *moment*. Now David was on *his* ship, likely eating his darja and crackers.

"H'lo," was the reply, and after an awkward silence, "How's the weather?"

"Excuse me?"

"Nothing, it's just what people say sometimes."

By now, Liberty had the front door open and deposited a box of explosives paraphernalia on the kitchen table before running to the bathroom, motioning that he'd be back in a second.

Sartek set the tablet down. "Your friend…Bert, he's really pretty remarkable."

"I know, and I'd like to see him again, so we have to do this right, in pure Yoda style."

"Yoda?"

"'Try not. Do or do not. There is no *try*,'" David quoted the Star Wars character.

He was answered with a thoughtful nod by the alien. "Brilliant. A great philosopher?"

"One of the best."

"And what after? I mean, if we do this and get the *Star* back, what happens to all of you?"

David glanced off screen, then back at Sartek.

"Well, I guess we go back to *The Home*...or jail, more likely." He dismissed the notion with a wave of his hand. "But that doesn't matter. You're in this mess partly..." he frowned, "mostly cuz of us. We gotta do this; you know we do."

He glanced up when Liberty walked into the small dining room.

"So, Alex and Isara should be back any second." Liberty was in high spirits. "If they got the rest of the stuff, I should be able to get these assembled, and we go this afternoon. It'll be cutting it close, but there's a tour starting at three twenty." Noticing the expressions of the other two, he asked, "What? Why the long faces? This can *work*. I know it can!" He was embellishing their odds; they all knew that.

"It's not that," Sartek was obviously trying to remain optimistic, but couldn't hide his worry. "I was just wondering about you, when this is done."

"You know, if this never happened, I'd never be a part of it. This is the most awesome thing I could've ever imagined." Liberty motioned in the air around himself. "The universe, all the questions, wondering about things. It's like I get a free pass!" He turned to Sartek. "I'd never have met you and Isara, and David wouldn't have met Blalok. What say we pull this off and all get together over some root beers and pizzas when it's over?"

A pause, then Sartek brightened. "I'd like that very much."

Blalok inched in on the screen. "Me too, count me in."

Just about when Liberty thought he might choke up, Alex and Isara came crashing through the front door, shopping bags in hand. Had they not been on a mission to confiscate bomb paraphernalia to save an alien starship, they might have seemed like a couple of pre-teens back from a shopping spree.

"We got the pipes and the drill bits," Alex announced happily.

"And the watches!" Isara bubbled with excitement. "Mine's a mouse." She held up her wrist, proudly displaying her Minnie Mouse, one hundred percent plastic, authentic knockoff wristwatch.

"Seriously, Alex? Mickey Mouse?" Liberty rolled his eyes.

"Yeah, stupid. That's all there was, and you get Goofy." She reached into her pocket, snagged the watch, and tossed it at his head." It pinged him in the fluff of his hair and fell unharmed to the carpet.

"What is it?" Sartek secured the Pluto watch to his wrist and admired it at arm's length.

"It's a watch—means we can coordinate if we get split up." Liberty strapped Goofy on his own wrist, spread some sheets of paper across the table, and picked up a pen. He angled the tablet, so that David and Blalok could see, and swept some broad strokes across a paper. A fairly sophisticated diagram emerged, and he pointed with the pen.

"Okay, guys—here's the plan…"

CHAPTER TWENTY

Δ

Lieutenant Colonel Taylor briefed the general.

"The surface of it seems to be eroding even faster than it was before," he said with an air of gleeful anticipation. He took a quick slug from his diet Dr. Pepper before setting the can on the table, posturing with grave self-importance, his hands resting on his hips.

They were in another briefing room, gathered behind a large window of six-inch-thick ballistic glass. The *Star* glowed eerily beyond the slight distortion of the window, hovering gently against her restraints. The tethering and scaffolding looked obscenely inappropriate wrapped around the vessel, but even so, there was no denying its beauty.

"And that's not all, it—"

"I'm not sure what that means, it's *eroding*." General Jacobs tossed what was left of his coffee in the trashcan.

It was the scientist, Bennett, who replied, "What he's trying to say, sir, is that the hull of the vessel continues to decay at a logarithmic rate."

When her comment was met with a blank stare, she added, "It's like the Richter scale—*logarithmic*? You know, like an earthquake that registers as a six is ten times stronger than a level five, and a seven is one hundred times stronger than a five?"

When he just stared at her, she shrugged and muttered, "It's like that."

"And this ship is going to blow up like an earthquake?"

The general was imagining the collateral damage he would have to explain. At least he'd gotten Sylvia and her mother out of Kansas this morning.

"Sir, if I can interrupt, it's—" Taylor began.

Bennett ignored Taylor, speaking over him to the general.

"No, sir. I mean, we have no indication that a catastrophic event is imminent. But every hour, it does demonstrate an increase in its rate of deterioration. At this point, we already have several substantial areas of exposed vessel."

"And what is it, exactly, that's exposed?"

Bennett shifted nervously, glancing between Taylor and the general. "We don't know, sir."

"Well, what *do* we know about what we *don't* know about it, since that seems to be all we can figure out about this goddamn thing, other than we think it's from outer space and it practically threw itself into our arms?"

The scientist sighed. "General, please don't be fooled into false complacency. This vessel is light years beyond our capacity to comprehend it."

She pointed at the ship beyond the window.

"We don't understand the complexity of the deteriorating, helium shield or the radioactive wavelength that it emits—only that it exists. And beyond the hull?" She drew a deep breath. "It's certainly something we've never encountered before."

"This hull, is it some kind of…of super metal?"

"Uhmm, no. At least not like we know of. It isn't classified in any of our knowledge of chemistry or engineering."

"What are you saying, Miss….?" The general struggled again to remember her name.

"*Bennett*, sir. And what I'm saying is, as far as we know, this material does not exist, not on this planet. None of our rovers have picked up anything like it either. The metal is…alien."

This quieted everyone in the room.

"Then, what you're saying is…" His voice trailed off.

"It is not from here, sir. Nor anywhere remotely close to here." Bennett answered flatly and with utmost certainty. "*They…*" she gestured again toward the ship, "are not from this galaxy."

The general stood and walked slowly over to the window, absently scratching the stubble on his chin. He took several minutes to simply study the

Star. He'd been up most of the night, had grabbed two hours of sleep and yet another crappy cup of coffee.

Why could this facility not make a decent cup of coffee?

Taylor started to say something, but Jacobs waved him to silence.

The pressure was on; the Pentagon was pushing him. He'd been supplied a team of the most gifted scientists alive, only half of whom spoke English.

So why was it so hard to get answers? The technology that this ship carried could very well launch the United States decades ahead of any other country, and not just with the military. The readings they were getting from the vessel suggested an alternate energy source. Who knew? It might even launch the twenty-first century into world peace.

He frowned at the tickle that was growing in the back of his head, warning him that this thing could backfire. The alien ship could come abruptly to life, and everything could go horribly awry. Kansas could be instantly blown off the map. He had a sudden recollection of Herbert Wells' *War of the Worlds* and remembered how it terrified him as his father read it over the span of two stormy evenings. He waved a hand at the vessel.

"What about the radiation? Are we seeing any increase in levels?"

"Negative, General. Just mild fluctuations, small spikes which we believe are attributed to the decomposition of the hull, but nothing more than we've originally measured." She hesitated before adding, "But there is something else I should point out."

The general glanced back over his shoulder, one eyebrow rising. "Yes?"

"We've detected a signal coming from the vessel."

"What the *hell*? Why haven't I been informed about this? Have we tried to decode it?" Now, he was royally pissed off.

Bennett took an involuntary step backward. "We can't...yet. It seems to be a wireless signal, not unlike Wi-Fi, but we're unable to decrypt it. We do know it was being directed to the surface, although we cannot pinpoint where. It's just a matter of time before—"

Lieutenant Colonel Taylor took the opportunity just then to interrupt her and blurt, "That's what I've been trying to tell you!" He glared at Bennett, then turned his back to her. "We've been compromised, sir. Our network has been hacked."

The general targeted Bennett. "I can't accept this! We got an alien ship that's communicating with someone land side and has hacked into our classified network?" He pounded his fist on the table.

"That is an act of treason and smells like one thing to me—*war*." He spat at Taylor, "Get me the Chief, and the Pentagon, now!"

Bennett froze, mortified; Taylor simply gloated.

"We're gonna secure that thing," Jacobs hiked his thumb toward the ship, "or heads are gonna roll!"

He headed for the door.

"And if it makes a move, even a hiccup…we're taking it *down*."

CHAPTER TWENTY-ONE

Δ

Sitting across from Blalok, David realized how hungry he was. His belly growled loud enough to prompt a glance from the alien. He picked up his fork, prepared to do some serious damage to the healthy slab of lasagna that sat steaming in front of him, but just as he went to shove a mouthful in, he noticed the look on Blalok's face. The alien stared, slack jawed with wide eyes.

Even though David had yet to familiarize himself with alien mannerisms, there was no mistaking the expression of repulsion. "What? It's lasagna. Probably the best stuff ever, even better than pizza!"

"It looks…dead, like it's bleeding everywhere, like its tendons and stuff are sticking out," Blalok poked at a flake of something pristinely white on his own plate.

David stared at the lasagna, trying hard to see it from the alien's point of view. The tomato sauce dripped, glistening with the oily runoff of the ground meat. Noodles peeked out from beneath the carnage in grisly white layers. Between them, ricotta cheese bubbled and escaped in lumpy red and white glory, pouring onto his plate.

Hmmm. I guess it does look like some pretty good carnage when you think about it. I'll have to be 'lasagna man' at Halloween this year, he thought.

"I guess I see your point."

In a dramatic gesture of goodwill, David tented his napkin on the table between them, placing the lasagna out of sight of the Bettuan.

"There! Problem solved," he said and shoveled a huge bite into his mouth.

The alien attacked his own fish and some sort of leafy greens. "Thank you." He smiled politely. A leaflet of something dark stuck to Blalok's front tooth.

David laughed. "You are so much like Bert, you know." He took another bite. "So can E-I update us on what's going on down there? I mean with the military and all, like hack in and get their game plan?"

Blalok shook his head. "That is no longer possible. They have placed obstructions."

"A firewall?"

"Essentially, yes. We could easily overcome it, but because we've done it once already, we risk them discovering sensitive information from us at the same time. That would not compromise us so much, but it could super-evolve your species, if they were to gain access to our mainframe. It is an unacceptable risk we simply cannot take."

David chose not to argue with him. It appeared the Bettuan were fairly entrenched in their belief system regarding noninvolvement of alien "sub-evolved" species. It was just then that they heard it, a new noise—an unmistakable shrill violation of metal grinding against metal.

Momentarily frozen by the horrible sound, both boys jumped up in unison and ran for the door. Minutes later, they were on the bridge. Blalok quickly pulled up the 3-D holographic image of the *Star*.

David was mortified to see the blackened web effect of shield deterioration on the exquisite ship. The cuts were by now gaping maws—deep rifts of darkness that seemed to drip and slice across the vessel in a cruel, random fashion. Elsewhere, the *Star* was losing its stunning blue color as patches of it were fading to a ghastly gray.

Then, he noticed something else. "There." He pointed. "What's that?"

"That would be where they are trying to cut in," Blalok surmised.

"What?" David felt a growing, familiar pain in his gut.

A particularly deep and ugly slice of deterioration cut across what might be called the throat of the *Star*. Underneath and toward the front of the ship, it was the blackest and widest of all the wounds.

"Hold on," Blalok called and punched a control.

The front screen of the bridge morphed so that they could see the entire cavern and the ship. Scaffoldings and platforms jutted at almost every angle, and scientists and military personnel scurried here and there, all bent on studying and dismantling their extraordinary capture.

Manipulating a few more controls, Blalok pulled up a different perspective, one from directly beneath the vessel.

Immediately across the screen flashed the image of an immense device, fixed by a crane of sorts, and pressed snugly against the throat of the *Star*. From its mouth projected a probe that pressed obscenely against the vasteen hull of the ship. *This* was what made the horrible sound that seemed to come from the very soul of the *Star*.

"That's not good," Blalok said flatly and spun his chair about to pull up a smaller visual panel.

"What?" David asked urgently. "I thought you said this hull was like a billion times stronger than anything we have?"

Blalok glanced sideways at his friend. "You *are* prone to exaggeration, you realize that?" He punched in some calibrations before saying, "I said that vasteen is forty-seven times stronger than Titanium, but you do possess the technology to destroy it." He swung around to look at David.

"What is that thing?" David stared at the wicked probe that gouged into the underbelly of the *Star*. A frothy white substance sprayed in sheets from the ship into a collection trough that appeared to recirculate the material back to the weapon.

"*That*...is a water jet cutter. Your species is very clever, David. This device can eventually do a great deal of damage."

"But...but it's just water!"

"Exactly. They are directing a high pressure stream of water—one so strong it can cut through any material known on this planet." Blalok shrugged.

"But you are somewhat correct. If it were *only* a water blade, it would not likely be able to cut through the hull of the *Star,* at least not in this century. However..." He pointed, indicating the collection troughs below the giant tool.

"They are collecting runoff. Contained within that runoff are minute fragments of vasteen—a microscopic amount. If they do as I suspect they will and recirculate that particulate into the jet of water as an abrasive," he looked genuinely grim, "with vasteen mixed into the spray, they will no doubt, in time, breach the hull."

"How soon?"

"Probably before morning."

David was clearly not ready to accept this. "What kinda ship is this? You can fly through a bunch of stars and survive a cyclone—"

"Tsunami," Blalok corrected.

"But we can cut into it with a *super-soaker*?" David ignored him and hopped up, unable to contain himself.

"Blalok, you gotta do something about that thing! There's a whole lotta good about not doing any harm and all, but you're gonna lose this ship and both your friends if you don't defend yourself!"

"Just what would you have us do? Destroy those men?" The alien swept one hand at nothing in particular. "They did not ask us to come here! We came of our own accord. We were not invited."

"You came because you *had* to! You needed oxygen. And you'd leave if they let you!"

This statement, in its fundamental simplicity, sobered the alien considerably. "We had alternatives. We might have made it to another planet."

"But you *didn't*, and you couldn't have known," David insisted.

"We could have left without making contact, to whatever fate awaited," Blalok countered flatly.

"And then what, Blalok? Float through the universe till something really horrible happens? Never again have a home to go to? Never fit in anywhere?"

Blalok's eyes narrowed. "You lost your home *too*," he shot back grimly.

David swallowed thickly and tried to slow his breathing. All the while the terrible *scree* of the water cutter pierced the air around them.

"Yeah, Blalok, I did. I lost my home and my dad, but I'm not sorry. I found Alex and Bert. They're my family now. Wherever I am, as long as I'm with them, I'm home." He knelt next to Blalok, close enough that he could rest his hands on the alien's knees. "And right now they're out there, trying to make right by you."

This provoked the alien to lean far back in his chair, wide-eyed and fairly speechless. He could not know Blalok had a strong aversion to being touched. David's voice softened. "You have *us* now. You're not alone anymore, and if you have faith, we can get you outa' this. But you have to trust me on this. Donkey says, 'Where there is a will, there is a way.'"

"Donkey was another great philosopher?"

"Oh, yeah." David grinned. "Shrek's main man. Now what say we do a little damage of our own, stir things up a bit? At least slow those assholes down."

"Well, there are always infrasonic emissions? Maybe we could deter them with that?" Blalok said unobtrusively as he peeled David's fingers off his knees.

"What is that? Like a sound cannon?" He let go of Blalok.

"Then, you know of this!" Blalok was more excited than he'd yet been.

"Oh, yeah! It's what they tried to stop the Hulk with!"

"Hulk?"

"Yes—he's an *Avenger*."

"I have so much to learn of your history," the smallest Bettuan mused, then called loudly, "E-I, we need to send a signal, a two point five kilo-hertz pulse should be adequate. Please emit from all perimeters until notified otherwise."

"As you wish," was the immediate reply, and in exactly eight seconds, the terrible *screeing* against the hull stopped. The forward screen showed men and women in white coats scurrying for the exit doors like rats from a flood, hands over their ears as they ran. One rather large man stopped to vomit his lunch on the tarmac before staggering away.

"Awesome!" David could scarcely contain his excitement. "Did you see that? How long will that hold them?"

"Not very long, I'm afraid—only until they find adequate ear protection."

"Can't we up the frequency?"

"We can, but the risk of globicular and internal intestinal rupture increases."

"Globicular?"

"Eyeballs," Blalok stated matter-of-factly.

"Oh, geez." David was repulsed. He took a seat by Blalok. "You know, they're gonna come back, try to cut into us again."

"At least we've stopped them for now." Then, "Thank you David. I do appreciate your help, more than it might seem."

"Hey, if you get out, chances are, I'll get out too."

CHAPTER TWENTY-TWO

Δ

It'd been one thing for Liberty to devise the strategy—the physics and logic of the plan were sound—but when he sat at the kitchen table to build the explosives, it sickened him. Even though he was technically a child, Liberty was a philosophical giant.

It was tragic that, because of the car crash, the greatest minds in the world were painfully unaware of the rare genius that Liberty was, and only a few had ever touched upon his brilliance. And, like many of the greatest minds who'd ever lived, he'd always held strongly to a general philosophy of nonviolence. In a way, Liberty very much ascribed to the Bettuan belief system.

A grave sorrow clouded his heart as he meticulously constructed the devices, all the while trying hard not to look at it from a personal slant. Even if he'd never met Isara and Sartek, fighting for their release was the only *human* option. Therefore, building the bombs was only logical. There was no other way to assist them, to allow them a shot at freedom and the opportunity to find a way home.

It wasn't that Liberty felt aliens were unwelcome on Earth. He believed inarguably that the evolution of what was intimately human depended on allowing visitors from beyond to make contact. But he also believed that humanity was not yet intellectually prepared to allow this to happen.

Sadly, he knew that this greatest discovery—visitors from another galaxy—

would result in the end of the human race altogether. To the very depth of his soul, Liberty knew this to be true.

And so, the brilliant, eleven-year-old boy...built five bombs. And, of course, his calibrations were spot on. The explosives were dreadfully perfect.

* * *

Alex, Isara, and Sartek were gone for two hours, just as Liberty had asked them to be. They spent the time at a deserted elementary school playground, spinning slowly on the faded merry-go-round and not talking very much. Their toes dragged in the dirt until Sartek's Pluto watch *beep-beeped.*

"It's time," he announced and leapt to his feet.

Back to the house the three ran and crashed breathless through the back door. They found Liberty sitting calmly at the dining room table, head resting on crossed arms. In front of him on a dishtowel lay five identical pipes.

He looked up and said simply, "They're ready."

That afternoon, Alex stood in line at the Lyon's salt mine to get four tickets for the mine's tour. Liberty lingered off to the side, backpack slung over his shoulder, and carefully scanned the crowd. It surprised him how many tourists were prepared to seek an underground salt mine tour on a hot Tuesday afternoon. Then again, he knew that within the mine temperatures were a constant sixty-eight degrees all year long.

Alex walked back, waving the tickets. "Frick! Can you believe so many people want to see a bunch of dumb salt?" She hiked a thumb back over her shoulder at the milling crowd.

"It's not the salt they want to see. It's the mine itself."

Liberty indicated the opening, which resembled an entrance to a Wal-Mart more than it did a mine. "Down there are miles of tunnels and caves, all supported and carved out of the salt. And it stays such a constant cool temperature and humidity that some of the most valuable American artifacts are stored there. It's a tomb for some of our country's most amazing national treasures."

"How do you know that?" Alex asked with a healthy dose of skepticism and wrinkled her nose at him.

"Like what?" Sartek asked. "What's down there?"

"The original negatives of movies like *Ben-Hur, Wizard of Oz,* and *Gone with the Wind.*"

"Yawn," Alex jeered.

Liberty glared at her. "Yeah? Well, they also have James Dean's shirt from the movie '*Giant*.'"

This brought about not one visible ounce more of enthusiasm from Alex.

"And they got the original costumes of Batman and Mr. Freeze, and the suit agent Smith wore in *The Matrix*."

This was finally enough to bring a look of appreciation to Alex's face.

"I don't know what any of that is," Isara admitted.

Liberty added, "There are also some of the most important historical documents, all the way back to the birth of our country. Even the original newspaper documentation of our first presidential assassination is down there, and tons of medical research biopsies encased in wax."

Isara considered this carefully. "Bert, can we risk losing such riches, just to save us?"

"We won't. I have the subterranean map that E-I worked up for us on my tablet. Even the military doesn't have such an accurate map. We won't hurt anything we shouldn't." Then he reached into his backpack and pulled out four bandanas.

Alex tied the pink one around her neck, effectively hiding the translation collar from the public. "Speaking of which, blowing stuff up down there doesn't seem exactly safe. How do we keep it from just caving in on us?"

The others tied the bandanas around their necks.

"We'll set the detonations, then detonate them from a safe distance away." Liberty became suddenly very serious as he glanced back and forth between his friends. "Guys, this isn't foolproof. Alex is right. It carries risk. If anyone is not up for this…"

"In for a penny, in for the whole shebang." Alex elbowed Liberty gently in the ribs.

"There is no reason for you to risk your own lives going in there." Sartek countered, "Give me the map. Isara and I can go on from here, set the bombs ourselves."

"Not an option," Liberty replied with a tone of false optimism. "You need me to set the detonations. It's a delicate operation. Besides, Alex and I may have to create a separate diversion—enough to get you on the ship and out of there." He smiled weakly, his knees feeling not at all strong. "You're the most fun I've had, well, ever."

"And we're friends now," Alex added. "Friends don't abandon each other when stuff goes in the crapper."

Isara and Sartek regarded each other before extending their right hands, one on top of the other, toward their human friends. "Put yours on top," Isara prompted.

"Sweet!" Alex chirped. "A secret handshake!"

She slapped her right hand on top of Isara's, and Liberty did the same, on top of hers. What happened then was more than both humans anticipated.

Isara and Sartek closed their eyes and said nothing, nor did they move.

Liberty glanced briefly at Alex before following suit, and as the four clasped hands with eyes closed, he was overcome with a sensation he'd never experienced before. Starting at his fingertips, the tingling spread slowly into his palm, up his arm, and accelerated into a heated rush as though he'd stepped under a warm shower. It was very similar to the feeling he'd experienced previously, just from randomly touching Isara or Sartek, but multiplied now a great deal. It ran up between his ears and then down his spine, ending somewhere in the pit of his stomach. With these sensations came an overwhelming feeling of well-being and camaraderie.

Sartek pulled his hand away first. "There."

Liberty opened his eyes.

"What the bloody heck was that?" Alex asked.

"We're connected now," Isara said softly.

"What? Like we can read each other's minds?"

"No, but we will have a sense of the presence of each other, in case we're separated," Sartek said.

"Like a homing beacon?" Liberty asked.

"No." Sartek glanced at the mine.

When he didn't elaborate, Isara added soberly, "If one of us...if we...uhmm..."

"If one of us dies. That's what you're trying to say, isn't it?" Alex took a deep breath. "So we'd know if it was worth trying to help them."

Sartek nodded thoughtfully, and a hush settled over the group.

Liberty broke the silence. "Well, let's not test the connection then." He moved off toward the entrance, hiking the backpack farther up onto his shoulder. "Let's do this! Operation Phoenix!"

"Operation Phoenix!" the other three chanted back.

"Let me get that." Sartek reached for his backpack. "You've been carrying it all day."

"Negative." Liberty's hand tightened around the backpack strap. "If we get separated, I need these with me."

Truthfully, Liberty recognized the magnitude of the power each one of the explosives carried, much less five of them, and wished to guard their safety until the exact time for detonation.

Sartek reached for the pack. "It's too obvious, too heavy. Five pipes *and* the transmitters and receivers? Look at you; you look like you're moving in."

The alien pulled his own backpack off his shoulder, and Liberty finally agreed to transfer two of the assembled units to Sartek's bag. "Besides," he added, glancing over at Alex with a smile, "In for a penny…"

She shot the alien a thumbs-up.

Once inside the mine, the four hung toward the back of the tour group and were the last to enter the double elevator that would descend for just over one minute to the starting point of the mine tour. With roughly sixty-seven miles of mine, they had plenty of ground to cover, and precision would be key if they had any hopes to succeed. The plan consisted of two stages, and they had five explosives. Liberty knew that, in actuality, if they were lucky, three would detonate.

As they neared the entrance, Liberty noticed general security check at the doors. "Bert," Alex whispered urgently. "They're gonna check our bags!"

"No, they won't. Just act normal." His lips were grimly set, and he stared hard at the security guards as they approached the scanner, focusing solely on the two of them.

As he stepped past the entry garbage can, just before reaching the scanner, Liberty did something very personal. He slipped from his pocket his library card. Hesitating only a second, he passed his thumb over the beloved, worn surface before tossing his treasure—his old friend—into the garbage. It was the only thing that would verify who he was if he was caught.

After casting aside the one thing that identified how supremely civilized he truly was, he entered the mine…with bombs.

These children are just fine. You don't need to search their backpacks. They're only here on a summer-school project, an overhead voice gently suggested to the attendants.

The female guard waved the four through without asking them to send their backpacks through the scanner. "Have fun, kids. Good luck with your school project!"

"Thank you," Liberty murmured.

Sartek took him by the arm, supporting him as he'd turned suddenly very pale. Alex whispered, "I have water."

But he waved her off and said in a low voice, "I'm fine, Al. But we have to hurry." He motioned to a nearly full train where tourists were claiming their seats.

"Hurry up folks! Train leaves in five!" the tour-guide called.

They trotted to the last car and climbed in, clipping the oversized seat belts that were permanently stuck at one, extra large setting. The train resembled a tram, complete with lock and pin assembly, so that when it moved, it had the wonderful start and jerk domino effect of mildly disjointed cars, like on a roller coaster. It reminded Liberty how much he loved the concept of a train and what a thrill it'd been to hop a real one with Alex two days ago. Briefly, he considered how much he admired her raw courage.

"Move your keister over—incoming." She nearly crawled across Sartek as she clambered aboard and snuggled firmly against Liberty.

The four of them took up an entire car, and it was fortunate that the lighting was so dismally poor. The tour guide wore a miner's hardhat, complete with headlamp, more for effect than anything else, and he passed out similar hardhats to each of the tourists, only without the helmet lights. The aliens looked the other way as they took theirs.

After the guide gave them a brief orientation with a belabored discussion of emergency protocol, in the event of the tram stalling or breaking down, they started off.

Liberty pulled the tablet from Alex's backpack and opened the cover. He'd already set the display to extra dim, anticipating the darkness and not wanting to draw attention to them.

Almost immediately, he had the equivalent of a subterranean Google map and, with the long-range extender and bit of tweaking from E-I, was able to superimpose it over the layout of the military base's underground facility. It glowed dimly and eerily, a ghostlike web on the screen. The critical areas they needed to access blinked with tiny red beacons.

He worked steadily to make sure their calculations were accurate as the tour got under way, but every so often, someone's camera flashed and, for a few seconds, Liberty would be blinded.

"Do you think the flashes might cause exhibit damage?" Liberty asked.

"No," the guide responded from way up front. "Everything down here is either concrete or salt, and the equipment isn't reallyt photosensitive."

That wasn't the answer Liberty wanted; he didn't really think cameras would hurt anything, but at least the camera flashes did seem to wane a bit after his comment.

As the tour progressed deeper into the mine, Liberty's ears popped, and Alex grabbed onto his arm, her hand tightening the farther down they went.

"You okay?" Liberty whispered.

"I don't know. Does it seem hard to breathe down here?"

"You're just a little claustrophobic. Take slow breaths so you don't hyperventilate, and you'll be fine."

In the darkness, he wasn't sure if she'd acknowledged him or not, but her grasp did seem to relax a bit.

Despite the gravity of their situation, Liberty couldn't help but be intrigued by the tour. The mine was fascinating! Before the tour-guide even explained it, he knew the heavy mining equipment needed to be disassembled and brought down in pieces before being reassembled for use. And, because it was incredibly inefficient to reverse the process whenever equipment broke down or became and because there was an abundance of spare space, it became customary to just abandon the old mining machinery and vehicles whenever they died.

When they passed yet another casualty—the skeleton of an obsolete John Deere backhoe stripped of any useful parts—Liberty had the sensation that they were traveling through an underground machine graveyard. Truthfully, they were.

Finally, they were as far as the tour would allow, and the tram flipped about to head back. A short distance later, the guide stopped the rig and turned off his helmet light. "And now, ladies and gentlemen, complete blackout like you've never seen before!"

A hush fell over the group, and from somewhere in the distance the slow drip, drip of water could be heard. It was uncanny, Liberty thought to himself, how seldom humans ever really experienced true darkness, even when their eyes were closed.

The black silence wasn't there for long as confidence slowly overcame the passengers. Hellos, whistles, and jeers seemed to echo even louder than when it was light, and before long the din drowned out everything else.

It was precisely at this instant that the kids eased themselves from the car, leaving the last one empty. They tiptoed carefully back around the corner, so they would be hidden when the conductor relit his helmet light.

All the while, Liberty concentrated very hard, trying to project a single thought, *there never were four kids. The last car was empty all along.*

He wasn't certain if this helped until Sartek whispered, "I heard it."

"So did I," Alex added. "Only way more convincing that even on the bus! You're getting really good, not like you were shouting this time. Bert, you're a freakin' Jedi!"

"Yes! I even doubted we were ever in the car!" Isara beamed.

"Good." Liberty mentioned nothing about the wave of nausea that hit him again, just like the last time he'd used whatever this new ability was.

Before, when he'd used it at the mine entrance, the unpleasant after affect had dissipated fairly quickly, and this time he was determined to wait it out again and not make a fuss—see if it went away as fast as before. It didn't...

Crack went the first glow-stick. It was Alex's, and she fished around in her backpack for a few more, passing them around. Isara and Sartek followed her example, shaking them after they'd cracked them, and soon they each held a green one. And these weren't dime-store issues, either. They were industrial strength and afforded a considerable amount of light for them to work with.

Alex handed a bottled water to Liberty. "Here," she murmured, catching his eye. She didn't say anything more, but obviously knew the effect the mind trick was having on him.

The eerie green of the glow-stick made washed out Alex's features in a sickly way, and Isara and Sartek looked, well, more alien than they ever had. This only served to reinforce to Liberty that he was doing the right thing. They didn't belong here. They weren't supposed to stay on Earth, to be picked apart, analyzed, and tested until they were simply no more.

"Here." He flipped open the notebook. "This is where we need to get to— into the actual business part of the mine. If we backtrack to where the tour turned around, there's a gate. We need to get through it. Then the shaft leads to an area not being actively worked."

"It's directly under the main air exhaust tunnel of the combat operations center." He looked up. "That's where we blast, about a hundred yards apart each way."

"And the aquifer?" Isara hazarded.

"It's a couple hundred feet farther north, way beyond us. We should be okay."

No one said anything for a second, as though unwilling to acknowledge the big word, *should.*

"Let's get going. We're on the clock," Liberty said.

"Wait!" Alex held out her wrist and pressed the button on the side of her watch. The plastic round face lit up.

"Let's coordinate—make sure we're all on the same time."

Liberty smiled at her. "Good idea."

The other three held their wrists up and triggered the lights as well. They all peered closely to make sure the times were the same and the second hand was sweeping.

"What's plan B?" Alex glanced up with all the sincerity of a brand new day.

"Plan B?" Isara repeated.

"She means if…if we don't…" Sartek trailed off, at a loss for words.

"Don't worry about plan B. We've done all the right things to optimize our success. Plan B will fall into place if it needs to, only because we'll make the right decisions."

Nobody was willing to hazard what those other decisions might be. Liberty knew there wasn't likely to be an opportunity for a plan B, that if they failed, none of them were going to make it out alive. However, it was a sweet and genuine notion, so he kept his mouth shut and allowed them the dignity of optimism.

It was a longer walk than he imagined it would be as they wound their way along the tunnel, and much less entertaining than it was from the back of the tram. Liberty hitched his thumbs under the straps of his backpack as they cut into his shoulders. And one of the pipes had been poking him on his right hip for a while.

As though reading his mind, Sartek reached for the backpack, gently rearranging the bomb through the canvas so that it seemed to ride a bit better.

"Thanks."

"No worries." Sartek shot back, evidently having heard Alex coin that phrase and happy to adopt it into his own vocabulary. This prompted a smile from Liberty even though it was too dark for anyone to see it.

Now they were nearing the turn around spot of the tour route. They walked beyond it for a short distance, holding the glow-sticks high so they could see better.

"What the heck?" Alex said, as they all halted in dismay.

This section of the mineshaft was barred with heavy timbers that girded the entire span of the shaft. Filled in long ago with concrete, the only access was to one side—an iron door fixed fast into the jamb of an enormous ten-inch frame.

"Here." Sartek ran his hands over the heavy, hinged door.

It'd been so long since it was last used, and the damp air so salty, that it was obviously rusted fast. The keyed portal was eroded to the point that it was difficult to tell it from the wood surrounding it.

Leaning his head against the door, Sartek closed his eyes. They all waited, Alex with her fingers crossed. The alien concentrated hard. At one point, he opened his eyes, took a deep breath, and started again, trying his best to work the latch free. Finally, there was a faint squeak from within the mechanism, but that was all.

"Looks like we might have to blast through it, use one of the bombs," Isara sighed.

"No. It's too soon. If we blast through now, it'll draw attention before we can set up where we really need to detonate."

Liberty covered his eyes with one hand and paced gently back and forth.

"There's got to be another way."

"Turn off the tablet, and that extender thingy," Alex said suddenly.

"Why?" Isara asked.

"Just do it." Alex walked closer to the door and ran her hand across the lock mechanism.

Liberty realized straightaway what she intended to do. It was her turn to try to channel the gift the aliens' strange connection had offered the humans.

With no obvious, better choice, Liberty powered down the devices, then took them a good distance back from where they'd come before leaving them sitting on the ground next to a pillar. He also left the transmitters and receivers, wrapped in the paper bag that held them, burying them shallowly behind the giant salt pillar. Jogging back to the rest, he took Alex's glow-stick from her.

Not really having any idea what might happen next, they all backed up a ways, giving Alex room for whatever it was she might do.

She didn't close her eyes like Sartek had. She simply stood in front of the door, arms hanging loosely at her sides. It struck Liberty that she seemed very thin and small in her overalls, her wavy curls hanging long down her back, barely controlled in the faded pink scrunchy with the tiny silver stars on it.

The huge iron and timbered door was terrible and formidable in front of her as it extended up all the way to the ceiling, and her shadow cast up along it, much taller than she really was. The effect of it all held all the makings of a bad horror movie, but Liberty couldn't tear his eyes away.

Then…nothing happened.

For a long moment, it seemed like absolutely nothing would. Still, no one moved until, quite unexpectedly, the glow-sticks got brighter and brighter. Before long, they were so brilliant Liberty couldn't even look directly at one without it hurting his eyes. And, they were becoming warm in his hand.

"Alex, something's wrong with—" He didn't even get a chance to finish his sentence when the glow-stick suddenly became so hot he dropped it to the ground.

Isara and Sartek dropped theirs almost in unison. Alex seemed not to even notice what was happening behind her. She just kept…looking up at the door. Then, all four glow-sticks abruptly exploded with a splash of light, spraying droplets of burning, glowing green slime everywhere, including all over them.

"Ow!" Isara exclaimed.

With that, they were left in the awful darkness, and that wasn't all. From behind them a distant whistle was followed by a KABOOM as the tablet and long-range receiver also exploded. It was unlikely that it was enough to register as seismic activity in the mine, but Liberty jumped.

Still, Alex said nothing.

"Alex," Isara called softly.

There was no answer.

"Alex!" Sartek called out next,

"Wait!" Liberty warned in a hushed voice. "Just a sec…don't move."

Sure enough, a faint sound grew in the darkness. Then, an agonizing groan came from where the door was, a sound like twisting metal. The groan swiftly accelerated into an angry howl as rusted iron pinched and grated.

Something was moving, whether toward or away from them they couldn't be certain, but the three remained motionless until the noise finally ceased. The next sound they heard was Alex retching.

Liberty pulled out the emergency candles and cigarette lighter he'd brought just in case. He lit three, passing one to each Bettuan. When they had enough light, they could see Alex, bent over and wiping her lips with the back of her hand. Beyond her, the door was rent open toward them about a foot and a half. The twisted lock, hanging but still attached to the door, continued to flop back and forth in a bizarre fashion, like it was possessed and must be free of the door. I ground to a halt and just hung there. Beyond that, it was only black.

"Alex, you did it!" Sartek yelled.

Liberty poured water into Alex's hand so she could splash it onto her lips and tongue. "Yeah," she said in a weak voice. "But that's as good as it gets, guys."

Isara held a candle close so they could all see the black crack of the opened door. The flame flickered with the fresh air draft that greeted them.

After another minute or so of collecting themselves, Liberty went back to the pillar. The notebook was nowhere to be found. All that remained was a twisted piece of plastic tablet shell that had bounced off the ceiling and lay in the center of the tunnel.

The shallow grave for the receivers was disturbed as well. One of them jutted out, nearly free, but the other appeared to be in tact. "Thanks," he murmured to no one as he dug up the surviving receiver. He hurried back to the group where Alex was just being helped to her feet.

"Tablet's toast. But don't worry, we'll be okay without it," Liberty said.

"What? How are we going to contact E-I now?" Sartek worried.

"It's all right. All the maps, they're up here." He tapped his forehead. "Remember, we have a plan. When things like this happen, you stick to the *plan*. It's strategy one-oh-one. Blalok will know this too. "

There wasn't any alternative, really, and so, all together, they stepped through the door and into a long ago closed off shaft of the mine.

CHAPTER TWENTY-THREE

Δ

"What the hell was that?" General Jacobs poked the tip of his index finger into his right ear and withdrew it, analyzing it closely for blood.

"It's a sound pulse, sir," Bennett explained.

"So it has *weapons*?" he snarled.

"I suppose, if you look at it that way," the scientist countered.

"And what other way is there to look at it?"

"Well, if you think about it, there's a lot more damaging weapons it might've, probably *could* have, used. I think it chose to employ a weapon that would have minimal damage."

Bennett lifted her hands in appeal.

"When you consider we sliced into the hull of it, and all it does is deter us from the destruction we're so intent on? It seems fairly ridiculous to assume a ship capable of interstellar travel wouldn't have a deadlier weapon to defend itself. That's all I'm saying"

"That's bullshit, and you know it," the general countered, his ears throbbing, but he had to admit that a race this advanced would likely have the capacity to do much greater harm than a sound cannon.

"I disagree, sir," Lieutenant Colonel Taylor stepped in.

"Of course you do," Bennett shot right back.

Taylor ignored her, speaking only to Jacobs.

"They've acted in an aggressive manner. I recommend counterstrike immediately."

By then, all personnel had been evacuated from the cavern. The *Star* floated within, oddly out of place with the cables tethering it from all sides and no one around it.

The sonic pulse continued, and all access doors had been shut and secured while the general, lieutenant colonel, and Bennett, viewed everything from the overhead observatory.

Below, the people who still milled about behind the glass windows of the control room wore protective ear gear, and even behind the super thick glass of the observation room, the general could still faintly feel the throbbing of the sound cannon.

"I have a suggestion," Bennett offered.

"What? And this better not be flower garlands and welcome mats." Jacobs scowled. He was as unhappy as he'd ever been.

"Not exactly, but what if we stand down? Simply observe—try to communicate." Her face was sincere, and this caused him to look away.

Taylor took the opportunity to object loudly. "If we stand down now, after it's attacked us like that, we're only showing weakness. Then we open ourselves up to disaster. There's no way that that thing…" he stabbed his finger toward the *Star*, "…is friendly. It came here, and we have to assume—"

"Assume what?" Bennett screamed so suddenly he jumped. "That it's hostile? That it's come to take us over? Suck out our guts and eat us?" She stopped just short of stomping her feet. "You're an idiot, and you've been watching too many B-rated movies, Lieutenant!"

"Yeah, well, maybe I have!" He stepped toward her. "But how do you know if, where they came from, there aren't more already on their way!"

"What?" she exclaimed, obviously dumbfounded. "Are you implying—"

"Didn't think of *that*, did you?" he snapped. "*NOOoooo*. But you're more than happy to put our national security at risk? How do you know they didn't land somewhere else here first? Europe of Asia or something? And now they have something to gain by infiltrating U.S. securities?"

Bennett was speechless. She just stared at the man, who had an annoying habit of blinking very fast when he was excited. She shook her head and spoke to Jacobs. "Sir, I implore you, as the head of your science team, please allow us to formulate a strategy for communication, before we counterstrike. We have nothing to lose by taking the time."

"We have *everything* to lose," Taylor contradicted her.

The general weighed their words carefully, thought about what Taylor said—about if this wasn't the alien ship's first contact.

He thought about his thirty-nine years on the job, rising through the ranks, and how long it'd taken him to get to where he was today. And with global terrorism a top international issue, he realized that an incident could hurt the United States considerably, perhaps terminally.

Jacobs, arms crossed and stared so long and hard at the ship that it seemed to shimmer and sway. He had to blink to convince himself that it hadn't. He scowled, weighing their words carefully. The ship was communicating with someone landside. This brought his thoughts to his wife and daughter.

Taylor and Bennett stared at him while they waited for his orders.

He looked at Taylor. "Stabilize the zone and…prepare a counterstrike."

Bennett gasped. "You can't do that! If you attack, it could blow Hutchinson off the map!"

"Better Hutchinson than all of Kansas," he threw back, then commanded Taylor, "Prepare for complete evacuation of the base, and let's…" he spun about to have one last look at the *Cerulean Star*, "…blow this thing up."

"Yes sir!" Taylor snapped to and saluted, his eyes shining with renewed purpose.

"Wait!" Bennett pleaded, but was virtually ignored as the two men filed out, leaving her behind.

* * *

"We can't let them do this," Bennett argued.

Geller shifted his weight, allowing her to pass through the door first, and whispered back, "Yeah, I know. You're right, and I wonder if they'll let us work together in prison after the dust settles?"

She smiled wryly. Gellar had long been an immense asset to her research, and they'd developed a good friendship, even going out for pizza on occasion. The two scientists joined a grim-faced international team—a collection of the best in the world. They'd all been assembled on exceedingly short notice, and they were not just national stars; this group was an extraordinary mixture of international phenoms.

At the head of the table, the Nobel Prize laureate in astrophysics sipped a hot chocolate as he commented about how he was too old to bounce back from jet lag.

Joining him were the world's most elite in mathematics, biochemistry, molecular biology, and engineering, just to name a few. Even a first class astronomer, entomologist, and zoologist rounded out the group. None of them had slept a wink since arriving, and none of them wanted to.

Bennett herself was a biophysicist with strong minors in meteorology and thermodynamics. She cleared her throat and cut straight to business. "If they bomb this vessel, there is no predicting what will happen." She paced as she spoke, a habit of hers when she was distressed.

"Actually, we can well estimate what would happen."

All eyes turned to Nikolas Rostov, the current Nobel Prize winner in physics. He took another draw from his hot chocolate and licked his lips, wiping it from his mustache with a paper napkin before muttering, "Excellent. Why can I not get such good chocolate in Russia?"

Then, as if an afterthought, he directed his attention back to the group. "Realistically, we could have an explosion unlike any we've ever seen before. This could be worse than the *Tsar Bomba*. We might not even be able to categorize it," he explained rather too calmly.

The entire group froze simultaneously. Rostov's English was impeccable, his accent barely noticeable, and he leaned back in his chair, looking out from beneath a thick thatch of eyebrows. Everyone there knew who he was, and he'd captured in no uncertain terms the undivided attention of all.

They were staring because what Rostov so casually spoke of—Tsar Bomba—was the most powerful nuclear weapon ever made. The fifty-megaton hydrogen bomb had been dropped in an event of unparalleled terror in the Arctic Ocean north of Russia on October 30, 1961.

An event of epic annihilation, the explosion was the equivalent to one thousand, four hundred times the combined power of the bombs that destroyed both Hiroshima and Nagasaki in World War II. Mankind had been appallingly dumbstruck by the Tsara Bomba's magnitude, and a device of that power had never since been produced or tested.

What Rostov now warned of was an unthinkable possibility. Each scientist appeared to struggle with the horrible possibility.

He continued. "What we already know of the vessel is that its composition is unknown to us. Also, its structure is unstable in its current environment, but they either lack, or simply choose not to employ, weapons of extreme aggression."

"They?" the zoologist asked.

Rostov nodded. "Yes. It is my calculation that the vessel is not unmanned, or…*unaliened,* as the case may be."

"He's right," Bennett agreed. "If the vessel were simply, say, a drone, it would have initiated countermeasure at the first impact of the cutting torches. It didn't; it only took retaliatory action after we'd been cutting on it for a while. It waited, *thinking.* Only then did it defend itself. That's a *human* response." Bennett caught herself after she'd said it. "I mean, so to speak."

"So, how do we stop them?" one of the scientists, a mathematician with the face of teenager, blurted. He wasn't speaking about the aliens; he meant the military. "All of us together don't have the authority of one asshole general."

"Hold up," she cautioned, "We don't want to make them the enemy. That just hurts our cause."

"But we're only here as ancillary help," the mathematician said. "Yes, we've assembled, inarguably, some of the most impressive gray matter in the world. But when it comes down to the wire, let's face it, the ones with the biggest kahunas are gonna win out, and it isn't going to be any of us."

"It's natural selection," a geneticist added, almost comically.

Bennett shook her head. "No! That's not acceptable! We aren't going to just sit here and let a bunch of four star-idiots destroy our first…our…" She struggled, at a loss for words.

Geller jumped in. "This isn't just a leap in science, ladies and gentlemen. It's a leap in humanity! And not just that—in everything we know and believe about God and the universe!"

"This will challenge every belief system humankind has," Rostov warned.

"Or strengthen them, maybe even unite them," Bennett countered. "I won't let them destroy this." She took a deep breath. "So, who's with me?"

Silence greeted her for a few long seconds.

"Ah, what the hell."

The young mathematician's hand rose slowly, followed by another, and another, until eventually everyone in the room joined her.

"Then we're in this together." Bennett smiled widely at the lot of them.

Half an hour later, the entire team was at the door of the briefing room.

"You'll have to come back." The single security guard stood at attention, wide-eyed and gripping a rifle across his chest. He was a stalwart fellow but evidently unprepared for the rush of white lab coats that flocked against him like bleating sheep. "I'm sorry, but this is a closed meeting," he stammered.

"They're busy. You'll have to...to come back."

"Move it." Bennett grasped the rifle by the barrel with one hand and tried to reach for the door handle.

The guard held fast. "No you don't, ma'am. I can't let you do that."

"So, are you going to shoot me? Because you'll have to..."

Bennett swung the muzzle of the gun toward her own chest and glanced over her shoulder at the group of waiting scientists.

"Wait!" the guard protested, trying to pull the muzzle of the gun away from her, but she held fast, and her gamble paid off. It was all the rest of them needed, and the soldier was instantly swarmed by the determined group of scientists—mobbed like a cookie on an anthill—and he did absolutely nothing about it as they charged in, interrupting the meeting.

"Sir, we need to speak with you," Bennett announced as she was swept into the conference room in a tide of her peers.

On the overhead flatscreen was the sparkling image of the president of the United States—a live feed. It was specifically to him she directed her comment, not Jacobs or Taylor.

"Who is this?" The president's eyebrows rose in genuine surprise.

"This is our..." Jacobs explained through gritted teeth, "...our science team." Red faced and fuming, he barked at the speechless guard standing in the doorway, "Get her out of here!" But it was too. No one was going anywhere fast.

"Sir," Bennett's voice rose above the . "Mr. President, if you bomb that ship it could blow up this entire compound, could even destroy Hutchinson, and possibly the entire county. We just don't know, but it could be a domestic disaster of epic proportion, incomparable even to 9/11."

She said it quickly enough to gather the attention of everyone present, and silence overcame the chaos.

"You don't know that!" Taylor angrily protested.

"And you don't know that it *won't*!" Bennett directed a cold stare at him. "We *do* know that the ship is unstable and decomposing at an alarming rate. If we accelerate that decomposition with an act of aggression, can you guarantee we won't trigger a self-destruct mechanism?"

"She doesn't know what she's talking about," Taylor objected.

"Yes...she does," Rostov stepped in. "You know it, I know it, and on some level, we all know it." The Nobel laureate addressed everyone present. "You have them on your space shuttles, you've even put them into your land mines, and I believe in your navy you call the term "scuttling", to prevent a ship from being seized."

The young mathematician took the opportunity to jump in. "It stands to reason that a vessel capable of destroying the Drake equation to hell and back could pack a punch if it decides to terminate."

Stunned silence.

"You knew about this?" the president asked solemnly from the flatscreen.

Jacobs pressed his index finger between his eyes. He looked as though he'd just swallowed something altogether rotten. "Yes, technically...there is a small possibility."

"Why is this the first I've heard about this? Are you not collaborating with your team?" The president was clearly dismayed. "And you're willing to risk blowing Kansas clean out of the union?" He didn't give Jacobs a chance to answer. "General, get control of this situation! I will not have a domestic disaster on our hands, especially in an election year! Stabilize it or...*bury* it." He stabbed a finger in the direction of Jacobs. "And I want debriefing in..." He looked at his watch. "Two hours. Will that be a problem?"

"No, sir," was the general's flat response. "Not a problem. Two hours."

The president pushed up from his seat and stepped off screen, and the transmission went to official standby, the presidential seal unmoving in the middle of the screen.

Jacobs turned on the tight group of scientists, and the whole lot of them shrank beneath his fury.

"You!" He pointed at Bennett. "You're coming with me!"

CHAPTER TWENTY-FOUR

Δ

"What's going on out there?" David was standing on the foredeck, directly in front of Blalok, obscuring his view of the forward screen.

"If you would move your fat head, maybe I could see," Blalok said dryly.

"Fat head? You think I, compared to you, little mister alien dude, have a fat head?" David fired back playfully.

"It's a figure of speech." Blalok rolled his eyes and swept with his hand, indicating he wanted David to step aside. "Now can you please *move*?"

David couldn't resist, and he started doing jumping jacks in place, his arms swinging widely.

"Okay, boss; I'm *moving*, but I don't see how it's helping. Anything else you need me to do?"

"You are stupid. You realize that, don't you?" Blalok pushed back in his chair, crossing his arms over his chest.

David grinned. Had the situation been any less dire, he'd have milked it to boredom, but instead, he stepped aside and refocused his attention on the front screen. "So anyway, what do you think they're doing? Looks like a whole lot of nothin' to me."

The visual on the screen didn't exactly skip to different angles outside the ship; it more or less scanned as though someone were walking the perimeter from outside. When it detected movement or change, it automatically zoomed in on that angle long enough for the sensors to analyze the data. For the last half hour, there'd been no one at all moving around the ship.

The sound cannon continued, but from inside the vessel, Blalok and David were unaware of the pulse, protected entirely by the thick armor of vasteen and interior insulations.

"How do we know that the noise gun will keep going?" David asked.

"It is not a *noise gun*," Blalok said. "It's an infrasonic emission, and we know it will keep going because we have not instructed E-I to stop it." He explained this in a moderately singsong voice, not unlike how one might explain something to a child.

"But what if it breaks?"

The little alien began to look frustrated all the same. "If it had stopped, we would have heard an alarm."

"You're sure of that?"

"Yes, of at least that, I am sure."

David considered this for scarcely a moment before asking, "Okay, next question. Bert and them should be inside the mine by now, and he thinks the bombs will go off in the area of, uhmm, the commissionary?"

"The commissary," Blalok corrected. "It's like a small merchant store where people can purchase things, like everyday needs. It's strategically down the hall from the control center, which is right..." he punched a few dials, and the ship's camera focused on a pair of massive metal doors, visible from within the cavern, "here." Blalok pointed to the right of them.

Next to the doors was a row of ballistic glass windows, and beyond them personnel could be seen milling about. All of them wore protective headgear.

"Won't people get hurt in the commissary?"

Blalok shook his head. "Negative. Not likely. The tunnel approximates the back of the store. They will blast through next to a utility closet."

"And if utility people are in there?"

"The alternative is we do not free the *Star*. The collateral damage with that decision could be immense."

David gave this serious thought. "And the control room is where they'll go so they can get us freed."

"Well, yes, maybe in an ideal universe." Blalok spun his chair around so he could face him. "But, we need to consider alternative outcomes."

"Like what?" He already knew what Blalok was talking about but refused to outright acknowledge it.

"In an ideal universe? Bert, Alex, Isara, and Sartek will make it to the control center. In an even more incredible universe, they will be able to release the controls on the *Star*, Isara and Sartek will be reunited with the ship, and we will escape. *And*, you guys will get away."

Blalok seemed to have a hard time maintaining eye contact now.

"However, there is no such thing as a perfect universe, David. That is why things like black plasma and galactic tsunamis exist."

He paused. "We must answer the question of what if they don't make it? What if Bert cannot make it to the control center, and what if they are all caught? What if, eventually, these men breach the *Star*?" He flipped his hand toward the screen.

David cocked his head to one side. "Hey, I like an 'against all odds' story probably better than most, but I'm not gonna pretend that we've got the master plan here. I know the chances of us pulling this off are pretty low. So, if push comes to shove and it starts to fall apart, I need you to *trust* me. You think you can do that?"

Blalok's blank stare was all he got in return. He sighed. "Look, I get it that you guys have some history. That 'mother of all wars' story, all Vulcan and stuff. But I'm not Bettuan. I know how things go here on Earth. I'm not asking you to sit in the dark either; I wouldn't do that to you. What I'm saying is that if things get screwy—and most likely they will—I need you to trust what I know about human nature."

"Are you saying I should believe you have the human wisdom of ages?"

Leaning in, David put his hand on Blalok's knee. "Nope. I'm saying I have the experience of being shit on, and I know how these bastards will react; it's a *given*."

The alien leaned farther back in his chair, his eyes narrowing as David's voice dropped. "What they don't know is that you have a human on board. That's the key, the secret weapon, and it's gonna get your ship out of here, even if the plan doesn't go like we think it will."

"How do you know they don't know you are here?"

"I just do."

"I need specifics—facts," Blalok insisted.

"What's today?" David asked.

"Your Earth date? August four, two thousand twelve—friendship day if I am correct, which I almost always am."

David shot him a wry look. "Look up social Kansas Children and Family

Services, Foster care division."

"Yes? So?"

"Reports have to be filed every three months by *The Home*, so they can get their money and all. The deadline is the sixth day of the month.

"That report has to go in no later than today for Roxy to get her money. On it, they have to say that we're safe and present.

"So, as of today, no one's the wiser that we're missing. I mean, *The Home* knows, but Roxy's keeping her fat trap shut. She's not gonna say anything and risk not getting her wad for one more month."

Blalok seemed to consider this. "So then, you are my double-agent?"

"Yep, I'm your super secret double-agent mole, and that, my friend is our ace in the hole. So if Bert and them get caught, we're gonna shift to plan B."

"Very well. You're a hamster. Then…" Blalok's eyes widened even more. "What is plan B?"

"Plan B is…you beam me down."

CHAPTER TWENTY-FIVE

Δ

Liberty and Alex suffered the effects of using their new abilities for some time.

"I don't know if I can do that again. I might puke, and my legs don't feel right under me," Alex confessed.

Liberty didn't share that he was also not right. In truth, he couldn't be certain that it wasn't a low blood sugar, so he pulled from his pocket a handful of mini Tootsie Rolls and passed them around, tossing two into his own mouth, just in case.

Although Liberty secretly bemoaned the fact that they'd lost the notebook, there was no other way they could've gotten through the door, so he tried not to think about it. The long-range extender probably wouldn't work this far underground anyway.

"Are we going to be able to find our way now that we no longer have the tablet?" Sartek asked as though reading his mind.

"It's okay. I got the maps all here." Liberty tapped his forehead with his finger. "By the time we might need the tablet again, we won't have time to sit down and fool with it anyway."

"I think we know how awesome you thought that thing was," Isara noted.

"Yeah, it was. But like you say, it's just a *thing*. I'll get another one someday, or maybe even something better."

Finally, feeling like they could travel, the four got to their feet. They wandered for a bit, following Liberty as they snaked this way and that, deeper into the belly of the mine. On several occasions, he made them turn back and reroute themselves, but eventually they neared the margin of where he knew they needed to deploy the first of the bombs.

"This is the spot. We'll set the first one here."

"Is this under the commissary?" Isara's pale skin and sparkling eyes were ghostly in the low light of the candles. The good news was the wicks of the candles flickered, indicating that there was airflow in this section of the mining shaft even though it had been barricaded off several years ago.

"No, we're about a city block west of it," Liberty said.

"I don't understand; then why are we blowing one here?" Sartek asked.

"We drag attention here." He pointed up. "And then, when we're sure we have it, we blow the second one under the commissary." Liberty had to lick his lips to finish. His throat was really dry, and he had a sickening feeling in his belly just thinking about detonating a bomb. It was the same feeling he'd gotten earlier that day when he'd assembled them. Bombs were, in his mind, just *wrong*.

"How many do we set?" Sartek glanced up from between strands of alien hair as he fished through his backpack for the first of two pipes.

"Two," Liberty said.

"Why two?" Alex asked.

"Because, we want to shake them up; two ought to do it.

"Just how seriously will we get their attention?"

"Four point one eight four times ten to the sixth joules…times two."

"Uhmm…" Sartek began.

Liberty smiled. "Yep, we'll stir things up, mostly because we're gonna set it correctly."

"What if we hurt someone by accident?" Isara wondered.

He'd been unwilling to entertain this thought openly and had hoped they wouldn't even ask. He shrugged. "There's no way of knowing for sure. But, if I'm correct, this spot is directly under a service hall, and a dead-end one at that. There's not likely to be much traffic there. That's why I picked it."

"But we can't be sure."

"No. It's the best we can do, I'm afraid. And we don't have much choice. The only other option is to abort."

"Not really an option," Sartek said.

"No…it isn't." Liberty gestured that he needed Alex's backpack. She knelt, pulling it from her shoulders, and laid it gently on the ground in front on him. Fetching from it the hammer and chisel they'd gotten from the hardware store, Liberty gazed overhead, squinting as he calculated just the right spot.

"Somewhere just about…" he murmured more to himself than to them.

Peering up at the dark, grainy, salt wall, he scanned the micro-fissures, slope, and color. When he couldn't determine just the right spot, he wandered a bit farther to a bend in the wall. Alex fidgeted, but he ignored her. Liberty was nothing if not meticulous about his calculations and took his time, running his hands along the wall. When he was at last satisfied, he spun about and paced fourteen long steps before stopping and facing the wall.

The others watched in awed silence as he mapped out the bombing strategy.

Placing both hands flat upon the gritty salt surface, Liberty closed his eyes and rested his forehead against it, then pressed his ear to the surface and plugged his other ear with his pinky finger.

"What are you—" Sartek began.

"Shhh! He's trying to listen!" Alex cut him short, "And your yackin' isn't making it any—"

"Like you're doing right now?" Sartek glared at her.

She narrowed her eyes and jutted her jaw at him in a mock threat.

After what seemed like an eternity to the other three, Liberty pulled his ear from the wall. He then picked the chisel and hammer up from where they lay at his feet. Truthfully, he had never used a hammer and chisel before, and he pulled from his pocket a grimy pair of safety goggles, pushing them up and over his glasses. They barely fit.

He gave Isara a nod, and she headed back down the tunnel about fifty yards to keep an eye out for any unwanted visitors. Once she was in place, Liberty reached up as high as he could and positioned the chisel. Then, he swung the hammer.

Missing the chisel altogether, he narrowly missed his hand. "Must be a little more nervous than I thought." He laughed shakily and went to raise the chisel again.

Sartek reached wordlessly over Liberty's shoulder and gently took the hammer out of his hands. He held out his other hand, gesturing for the chisel as well.

Liberty yanked the goggles off and handed them to Sartek, relieved to hand over the task. "Thanks. We need a hole, hardly bigger than the two pipes together, and just as deep. And it needs to be accurate."

Sartek nodded as he pulled the goggles down, settling the elastic above his ears, around the thick, dark ropes of sleek hair. The band snugged his hair tighter against his head, accentuating the serrated ridge.

"Right, captain."

He winked at Liberty from behind the goggles and faced the wall.

Liberty stepped back a few paces as Sartek lifted the chisel to a spot on the rough salt surface of the wall, about a foot and a half above where he'd tried to chisel. "This okay?" he asked, and Liberty nodded 'yes'. The alien gently twisted the chisel until he seemed satisfied with the placement of the tip, then swung the hammer very hard.

Thinking he'd used way too much force, Liberty winced, involuntarily scrunching his eyes closed, and only heard the sharp *crack* as the hammer connected solidly with the chisel.

Salt fragments sprayed in a fan away from the mark and showered the others. They stepped back another few yards and watched in amazement as Sartek chiseled out the hole.

His tall, strong body arced as he swung the hammer again and again. Now he was getting into the rhythm of it, and his shoulder came back as he set up and followed through with each swing, his head dipping after each pull. He did it without fear and with supreme accuracy. The chisel obeyed, sinking its bite deeper and deeper into the salt wall.

He's like David, Liberty thought to himself. *David could do that.*

The random thought made him miss his friend very much, and it bolstered his courage that he might see David again, very soon.

Between swings, Sartek twisted the chisel so that it pulled salt out each time he extracted and replaced it for another blow. Before long, there was a rough cylinder cut from the wall, twice as wide as it was tall, just right for the two pipes to fit into.

"You're really cool," Liberty said with all sincerity as he handed over the first of the two pipes.

Sartek only shrugged as he slid the bomb into the hole, twisting it gently when it hung up on salt fragments. Holding the pipe in place with one hand, he next fit the second one against the first, tapping the end cap firmly with his palm to squeeze it into place next to its twin. In a remarkably short amount of time, both pipes were snugged into the hole, about two inches sub-flush with the surface of the wall.

Now Sartek dropped to one knee so Liberty could stand on it. Alex stabilized Liberty by holding either side of his belt loops.

"This'll be the one and only time I let your skinny butt be in my face," she joked. She couldn't see him grinning, his cheek pressed against the wall. He steadied himself as he gently threaded the fuse from each pipe before winding them together.

When it was all completely assembled and to his satisfaction, he dangled the fused to within reach. Now, everything was strategically in place, and he slapped Alex gently on the shoulder, indicating he was ready to get down.

"So how far do we want to be from this when it goes off?" Isara asked as she walked urgently back toward her friends.

"I should be able to get at least a hundred twenty feet from it," Liberty explained, peering farther down the tunnel. Looking briefly over their handiwork one last time, Liberty headed out. "C'mon guys. Time to set the next one."

It was slow going. He'd previously measured his stride and was careful to count them out as he walked. In addition, he had to hold the candle just right to read his compass. Pausing for brief intervals, he made quick calculations in his head. They were about three hundred feet along when he stopped, having passed a half-dozen long bends.

"Are you sure?" Alex wondered aloud, "I mean, it's so dark in here; I can't find my ass with both hands. It seems like we've gone too far."

"Yep, we're good," he said. "Just have to count steps and adjust for the bends—use the triangular hypotenuse."

"Huh?"

"You know, Pythagoras and his theorem."

Believing that would explain everything, he went back to work. Just as before, he walked to the wall and paced backward in long, calculated strides before listening with one ear to the face of the surface—for even longer this time.

"Hurry up, Bert, I'm getting the heebie jeebies," Alex shivered, peering forward then back down the tunnel.

"I don't know what that is, but if it means nervous beyond all reasonable comfort, that's me too," Isara said.

"Yeah, my belly doesn't feel right either," Sartek mumbled his agreement.

"It's gotta be exact, guys," Liberty warned. "We have one chance with this. We need to bust through without bringing everything down on us."

He ran his gaze along the roof of the mineshaft, measuring the engineering moments in his head.

"Yeah, let's not do that." Alex remarked sarcastically, "I like living."

"Here," Liberty pointed higher on the wall, giving Sartek the go ahead.

Sartek chiseled out the wall again, a hole just big enough to hold three of the pipes this time. He also fashioned a small shelf, per Liberty's instruction, about the size of a small, hand-held walkie-talkie. The space wound up being farther up, as far as Sartek could comfortably reach and yet swing the hammer. When he had it prepared to specs, he reached for the pipes, one by one and, just as before, slid them into the. This time, however, instead of kneeling, he boosted Liberty up onto his shoulders.

Liberty steadied himself before tucking the receiver onto the shelf. Next, he gently threaded the receiver wire and alligator clips up to the pipes, carefully wrapping both of the fuses in candy cane style around the nichrome wire, all the while being very cautious not to break the fragile filament.

Finally, he stabilized the small receiver and flipped the *on* toggle so that it was engaged. "It's live, folks. Let's be careful not to accidentally bump this."

When Liberty crawled down, he wiped his hands on his pockets and said, "That's it, guys. First stage of *Phoenix* is armed and ready. He laid the transmitter gently on the ground and backed away. "Now let's go over this again before we get started."

They crowded around, leaning in to listen as Liberty went over the plan one last time. The others were to go a hundred twenty feet away, the far end of what the transmitter would trigger the bomb, Liberty explained, peering farther down the tunnel. He would backtrack set the first bomb off by hand.

They'd argued with him, said that they should stay together, but he'd held firm in the end. If a cave-in occurred with the decoy explosion, the other three would still be able to set off the second and storm the commissary.

"I can't see us splitting up and leaving you behind!" Alex insisted. "It makes no sense. What if we get in there and don't know what to do?"

"She's right," Sartek agreed. "If there is a cave-in, you should be on this side to make sure the rest of the plan goes like it should. You're the…well, smartest one."

"Nuh—uh," Liberty countered. "You and Isara have to make it in, no matter what. That's priority. The best odds of that are if the two of you are together. Besides, if push comes to shove, you're stronger and faster than I am—all of you.

"Besides, I can hardly wait to see what setting off the first one does. I really deserve to be the one to fire it." His mock chivalry was charming, but his eyes were enormous with fear and anticipation.

Alex hugged him, long and hard. Then they all double-checked their fake Disney watches one last time.

"Hey, how come these didn't blow up when Alex busted through the door," Sartek wondered aloud.

She smiled, "I dunno. It's weird, like I'm starting to grab what energy I want from something in particular, or something. It's hard to explain, like if you listen real hard to just one thing, you can drown other stuff out."

This fascinated Liberty, but he knew they were running out of time. "Okay. I detonate the Alpha bomb first, got it? At four-ten, whether or not I'm back, you fire Omega." Liberty checked and checked again to make certain they had it straight. "Flip the toggle." He looked at Sartek as though giving him this most critical job. "That means it's live. It'll glow green—red button means 'kaboom.' But not till about five seconds before you really want to detonate, just in case."

When they all had a good understanding of the strategy, he added, "And no deviation from the plan, got it?"

They agreed, reciting it back to him two times straight, and so he packed up to backtrack to the first bombsite.

"Wait, Bert…just a sec," Alex said softly. She pulled from her bib overall pocket her fishing string and Swiss army knife, and she took his right hand.

"Alex, wait, that's your lucky line," Liberty protested.

"Shut up," she murmured. Tying around his middle finger a triple loop of string before finishing the ring with a cool double fisherman's knot, she cut the extra off with her pocketknife.

Liberty examined it closely in the dim light. "Thanks. I like it. I…"

"It's so you come back." Alex said abruptly and stared at her feet. "Like you said, it's lucky. No fish I ever wrangled with it ever died. And no fish ever got loose, not till I wanted 'em to." Her gaze met his. "I don't want you to, ever. I…" She was too overcome to continue.

He wrapped his arms around her and pulled her tight. "I'll come back, Al. I promise. We're together, forever, okay?"

She was too choked up to say anything else.

He glanced over Alex's shoulder at the aliens. Faith and sincerity shone from their faces as they watched the sweet exchange between their human friends. Liberty struggled to say next what he felt he must.

"If we are separated, if it falls apart, get away, in any way you can. Then, no matter what, even if it takes forever…I'll find you. Somehow, I will."

"How? Where?" Isara wondered.

He looked over her shoulder to the blackness of the mine beyond. "I don't know. But if the time comes, we'll know."

Sartek was very somber. "I agree. We never give up. We're …family."

This struck Liberty in a profound way.

He'd known Alex and David for not quite two years, and Sartek and Isara scarcely three days. But there was no denying the bond they already held with each other.

Alex could only nod. Liberty hugged her again, then hugged Isara and Sartek in turn before heading back the way they'd come.. The last thing the three saw was the white halo of Liberty's hair…as he disappeared down the mine

* * *

By the time Liberty was positioned correctly at bombsite alpha, it was just a few minutes before four o'clock. He intended to blow the bomb right at four, according to the plan. Then, he would sprint as fast as he could, back to his friends, and they would set off the second bomb when just enough time had passed to create the diversion.

He'd calculated the time meticulously, even studied historical events of mass evacuations. He knew that within three minutes, there should be considerable attention gathered at the site of the alpha explosion. Within four, strategic personnel would also have made it to the area.

Liberty dug a miniature volcano in the dirt and nestled the candle in it. It was unnerving to be alone in the darkened mine with only the dim light of a single flame and terribly quiet. He tried to hum a song, one of his favorites—a Mozart violin concerto, but his throat was too dry.

Kneeling, his legs tucked under himself, he pressed the button on the side of his wristwatch that would light it up for about five seconds. Pushing his glasses up with his index finger, he peered closely as the second-hand swept past Goofy's snout. It was oddly comforting to touch it, knowing Alex had picked it out for him.

He groaned—his belly wasn't yet right. Suddenly, he was so nervous he doubted he could even stand. Fishing one more Tootsie Roll from his pocket, he tossed it into his mouth, just in case.

Now, he closed his eyes…and waited

At precisely thirty-seconds before four o'clock, Liberty pushed unsteadily to his feet. The Tootsie Roll had by then become a thick glob in the back of his throat and was going nowhere fast. He turned and spat what was left of it onto the. Then, he pulled from his pocket the lighter and flicked the tiny flame to life. Reaching, he lifted the flame to the end of the foot long fuse.

"Okay, Liberty…here we go."

He took a deep breath, closed his eyes, and lit the fuse.

CHAPTER TWENTY-SIX

Δ

"Get ready." Blalok leaned in more closely to his console as though it would help him to analyze the readouts better. "If things go as planned, any minute now, Liberty should detonate the first stage."

"We don't call him Liberty, we only call him Bert. It's short for Liberty, but that's his name. *Okay*? Bert," David reminded him.

"Very good." Blalok seemed to consider this before saying, "Bert is very…courageous, wouldn't you say?"

"Uhmm…" David hesitated.. "Liberty? *Brave*?" He was unaware that he'd called him Liberty…

* * *

Once, about a year ago, they'd tied a rope onto the overhead branch that hung alongside the lake—the same lake that they'd been fishing from three days before.

On one side of the lake, the bank rose up in a small cliff cutaway, and a big tree grew smack on top of it. Liberty thought it was the biggest tree around, perhaps even the biggest in all of Erie—probably because of its endless water supply.

One of the tree's high branches snaked sideways, perfect for tying a swing rope to. Below the cutaway embankment, the water was deep—a perfect spot for swinging out and letting go of the rope, Tarzan style.

Alex shinnied up the tree. She was always the best climber and had absolutely no fear of heights. It had terrified David how she'd walked, like a tight-rope walker, out onto the branch before jumping, grabbing the branch as she did, and swinging to sitting. She then tied a bowling knot so that the rope wouldn't gradually tighten as the branch grew, hurting it—at least that's how she'd explained it later. Then, instead of crawling back down the tree, she simply leapt off the branch, howling as she fell a good twenty-five feet before splashing feet first into the water below.

Her jumping from the tree had freaked Liberty out completely, and he'd been genuinely upset with her, counting off on one hand with his fingers the ways she could have been "hurt or killed."

She thumbed her nose at him and called him a *scaredy-cat*.

David remembered another occasion when a bat had flown into the attic at *The Home*. It was a hot summer night, and the little brown bat came right inside through an open window. He and Alex chased it around for a couple minutes before they were at last able to herd it back. Alex had a broom, and David was swinging a jacket at it. Liberty was under the bed with Goo, eyes wide in terror.

Lastly, David recalled that afternoon when Alex had stolen the remains of a birthday cake. It wasn't her cake; it was Hog's. He and Roxy brought it home from *The Boneyard*, a bar they frequented more evenings than not.

The bartender made the cake for Hog, and it was shaped like a motorcycle. In icing, a girl with big titties straddled the bike, and it said, "Happy Birthday Hog! Ride Hard!" across the top of it. Only it'd been eaten down enough that now it just said, "Hap—Hog," with only the fender, handlebars, a half-rack of titties, and part of the front tire left.

Stealing the cake right out of the fridge, even though they'd all been warned to "keep your mitts off," Alex took it out back with what was left of a gallon of milk. Then she'd shared it with Charlie, Julian, and Sage. It was also Sage's birthday; she was five.

Alex divvied the remains up for the three youngest kids at *The Home*, and they'd scarfed it down and passed around the milk jug until they were all blissfully sick and chock full of cake.

When Roxy and Hog found out, it was a royal disaster, but before anyone could begin to deny anything, Liberty stepped forward.

"I took it," he said flatly. "My blood sugar was low."

Hog was furious. He threw his unopened beer can at Alex.

She dodged it, and it hit the wall instead and exploded, fueling Hog's rage further, and he lifted his hand high over Liberty. It hung in the air for a terrible, long moment, and Alex screamed for him to, "Stop, you big ape!"

Hog didn't hit Bert, only turned on her and stomped, chasing her outside.

"You would've thought Bert wrecked his lame-ass motorcycle or something!" David shouted at Roxy, which didn't serve to help the situation at all.

"Now see what you've done? You've gone and upset him!" Roxy narrowed her beady pig eyes on all the kids. "Get out! All of you!"

The children scattered for the doors like roaches with the lights flipped on, but she zoned in on Liberty, cornering him. "Not you, you, you little frea*k*! You're getting what for."

Roxy used the belt on Liberty, and when he crawled out the attic window some time later to sit by himself on the shanty roof, they kids called softly to him from below, from behind the corncrib.

"It's okay, guys," he called back. "I'm all right." He waved cheerily at them before hobbling back through the window.

David, however, had really sharp eyesight—twenty-ten he'd been told once by the school nurse. "You could be a jet plane pilot, *easy*," she'd cheerily informed him.

So, even from the distance to the corn bin and with dusk set in, David could see how red Liberty's eyes were, and the marks on his legs were dreadfully obvious as he shinnied back through the window.

It was that night that David first decided that he could truly *hate* someone. It was also the first time he'd ever thought of Liberty as truly…brave.

* * *

"Uhmm." David pulled himself back to the present and cleared his throat. "Yeah." He looked away and said huskily, "He's pretty much the bravest kid ever."

"You are fortunate to have him as your friend," the Bettuan murmured reverently.

They sat together, waiting, their attention riveted to the monitors and the forward screen. There really wasn't anything that should acutely happen within the cavern when the first of the two blasts went off. That is how E-I had explained it. The *Star* would simply pick up a shockwave on its sensors.

However, the second explosion should "kick the skorpin nest," Blalok thought. He then pronounced them on "standby" and instructed E-I to notify them of anything significant. Now it was nearly four o'clock.

The doors to the hangar bay suddenly opened, and even though the sonic pulse continued, men filtered back inside wearing flack suits and insulating headgear.

"Let's up the pulse," David suggested.

"Negative. If we increase it enough to breach their protective gear, they would be at risk for mortal damage as well."

"You *care* about those guys?" David was incredulous. "Those guys will destroy you. Do you get that?" He wasn't angry. In fact, he was more concerned and sincere than he'd ever been.

Blalok looked away, evidently not impressed.

David slammed his hand down on the counter. "Hey! Look at me! I'm not playing around! Those guys will dissect you into little bitty pieces, homeboy, and Isara and Sartek! Is that what you want?"

The outburst startled the alien quite a bit, his expression stricken. "How do you know these things? And how can they be so horrible when you and your friends are so—are…"

David softened a bit. "Blalok, look, there are tons of humans out there who are kind, and good, and, well, Liberty and Alex are two of the best you could ever want to know. But those kinds aren't *these* guys."

He hiked his finger toward the screen. "These guys are the muscle, and they have orders. Those orders come from some serious assholes. You get that? They'll do as they're told, even if it kills them. And you will never get out of here; you, Isara, and Sartek will never make it out alive if you don't listen to me!"

Blalok studied him seriously, his enormous eyes showing such an expression of pain. "Is there not another way other than hurting them?" He gestured toward the humans just as the giant water knife started up again.

"I'm not asking you to hurt them intentionally. I'm asking you to defend yourself. And, if you can't, please, let me. Look, we got this dude, the 'Dolly Llama', that's so much like you. Bert taught me about him—he'd never scratch a fly—but he doesn't have to, and neither do you. I can do this *for* you."

The Bettuan seemed to consider this. "You…you are very much like Sartek, you know."

"Well, I'll take that as a compliment, and I'd love to kick it with him, but that's not gonna happen if the *Star* is lying in a scrap heap and you're strapped to a lab table, now is it?"

The alien shook his head.

"Blalok, send me down, now."

The alien caved, but just before David had a chance to shift, an alarm sounded on the console, and E-1 announced seriously. "The first detonation has been discharged. It has successfully breached the base."

"What? What is it?" David demanded, "What does that mean?" He stepped closer to the front screen as though he might see something.

Outside the *Star*, service personnel sprinted away, leaving the cavern and the bay doors slammed tightly shut so that the ship was once more alone. Behind the thick glass windows, soldiers and scientists could be seen frantically running about as confusion and panic set in.

"It's the first bomb," Blalok explained as data filtered in. "They've detonated it and blown a hole into Hutchinson air base." He looked up, an expression of fear and exhilaration on his face.

"David...it's *begun*."

CHAPTER TWENTY-SEVEN

Δ

"What the hell was that?" General Jacobs grabbed the edge of his desk as a pencil holder rattled and tipped over, scattering pencils to the floor. He reflexively grabbed a couple as they fell, then just pitched them angrily at the garbage can.

Lieutenant Taylor stared dumbly at him, eyes wide. Then, both shot out of their chairs and out the door. A security specialist met them in the hall. "There's been an explosion sir, below level two. Initial assessment is a mishap from the salt mine."

"I thought that mine wasn't active anymore?"

"The word I have is that it's quite active, sir, just not directly beneath the base. That section's been shut down a long time." He shrugged. "Looks like someone didn't get the memo."

"I want to see this hole," the general commanded and was led to the Eastern wing and shown the small fissure in the flooring. The industrial grade linoleum had burst up and outward as though someone popped a grape. Beneath it, the concrete was shattered into enormous chunks with pieces of rebar snaking through them like industrial pick up sticks.

Center of the rubble was a long, open crack with nothing but blackness beyond, and it was spewing a cool, dusty breeze up into the hallway.

"Get that open," he ordered. "I want men down there, now!"

Within minutes, there was a considerable amount of excitement around the small opening as men removed the sub-flooring and loosened chunks of concrete and rebar just enough so that a man could slip through. A plume of dust drifted up through the draft, and the hallway fast became a thick, hazy gray under the fluorescent lights.

An armed escort ushered the director of mining operations to the general's side. Thoroughly dismayed, the man defended his operation's innocence openly. "There's no drilling going on in that vein! We tapped out..." He did some quick mental calculations. "...a good sixteen months ago—not productive enough and too close for comfort to, well, *you* guys. We don't even have any men down there."

"And is it closed off?" the general asked.

"Yeah, barricaded. And the door's pretty rusted up. It'd take a pretty damn good team to bust through, but no, we haven't blasted there for nearly two years. This mine brings out close to four hundred fifty tons of salt a year. That's over a ton a day, on average. We got no use headin' down the jigsaw. It's a dead shaft and too risky."

"Jigsaw?" Taylor asked.

"That's that closed leg of the mine. It loops down then seesaws back on itself."

By then, the excavation crew had opened a hole big enough for a man to get down and through, and the general gave the go ahead. Several special tactics officers, outfitted with rappelling gear, headlamps, and...weapons, clambered down and disappeared into the dusty darkness beyond.

The general was on standby to follow when he got the confirmation that the area was secure. Then, down the hole he went.

* * *

The concussion from the explosion hit Liberty full in the back. He'd stumbled as he ran, and, even at nearly forty feet, the blast was significantly more powerful than he'd gauged it would be. Enclosed in the tunnel like it was, the kickback force swiftly channeled itself down the tunnel, both directions and...directly over Liberty.

What thumped against him was more like an air blast. There wasn't any immediate debris, yet, but it was enough to unbalance him again, sending him tripping forward onto his face. He might have been all right, but before he could assemble his wits enough to get up and move again, the dust wave hit him.

There were strong air currents down in the mine, ventilation shafts that assured good circulation for the miners. This, along with the blast wave, provided a sweeping gale of wind. The strong current carried the dirt and salt dust directly across Liberty like a tidal wave. And because everything was so dark, he couldn't see the billowing surge as it swept over him. He was breathing in...just as it hit.

After his first choking gasp, he yanked his T-shirt down past his elbow, sheltering his nose and mouth in the crook of his arm as he tried to breathe through the fabric. Pushing himself back to his feet, he began to trip his way toward his friends.

Forced to stop after only about twenty feet, his breathing was getting rapidly worse. Increasingly unable to catch his breath, he wheezed enough that it echoed down the mineshaft. The blast had blown out the candle, and with pitch-blackness all around, he desperately fished around in his pocket for the cigarette lighter.

Just when he thought he'd lost it, his fingers wrapped around the smooth, plastic barrel, and he pulled it out, clicked it to life, and looked about in dismay. The salt particles floating in the air around him funneled like a snowstorm, and the mica flecks glittered brilliantly.

He swished his hand in front of himself. The dust swirled in beautiful, dizzying, deadly patterns. *Oh God,* he thought to himself.

Liberty held the lighter in one hand, his lungs on fire, and unshouldered the backpack, laying it on the ground. Digging through three pockets before his fingers found it, he pulled out his inhaler and shook it weakly for a few seconds, then pulled a shallow draw as he dispensed the medication.

His lungs shut down, the rescue inhaler just effective enough to keep him barely breathing as he sagged to his knees, his chin tucked to his chest. He tried to raise the inhaler one last time as his lungs tightened even more, but he was just too weak. His hand fell limply to his lap, the inhaler and lighter clattering away in the darkness.

Liberty's last thought was that he hoped his friends made it home—all of them. He also hoped Goo would forgive him for not coming back and begged the great unknown to allow the little dog to be okay without him.

Then, he was vaguely aware of a soft thump as he lost consciousness and pitched face forward into blackness.

* * *

"Where *is* he?" Alex was beside herself. It was four minutes after four and there was no sign of Liberty. "He should've been back by now!"

"Maybe he got caught up in a cave-in or something." Sartek was pacing worriedly and stopped abruptly, hands clenched.

"I'm going back after him." He swiftly unshouldered his pack so he could run faster.

"No!" Alex barked, before he could step away.

Isara and Sartek gawked at her with surprise. "But Alex! It's Bert. We can't just leave him."

"He made me promise," she said, wringing her hands as tears threatened.

"What? He made you promise *what*?" Sartek took her by the shoulders.

"He made me promise in the parking lot that if something happened down here, and he couldn't get back to us, that I'd," she hesitated, wanting to quote Liberty accurately, "'Blow the heck outa' that cave and get them into that base.'"

She shook her hands, as though she could shake it all away.

"He told me everything's timed, and we can't mess up the schedule. I promised him I'd follow through. He made me…" Her words were strong, but her voice quavered, and she blinked back the tears. "He made me promise, said you might not follow the plan."

"I'm going to find him," Isara said flatly and started back.

Sartek grabbed her by the arm. "Wait! This might be part of the plan. We don't know."

"Bert would've told us. I know he would. Something's wrong, and I'm not leaving him!"

"Hold on," Alex bit her lip hard. "Bert's gonna kill me for this." She glanced at her wristwatch. "We have one minute, and we're supposed to blow the second bomb." She looked at Isara. "I'm gonna catch all kinds of hell for this, but…go back. Get Bert. If something's happened, you're the best one to help him."

Then, Alex focused on Sartek. "We'll blow stage two and get into the base. We can get stuff sorted out once we're inside—find David and figure out what to do. Then maybe we can send someone back for a rescue or something."

With no better option, they agreed that leaving Liberty to his own resources was simply not an option.

"Okay." Sartek glanced at his watch then at Isara. "You have ninety seconds to run fast as you can." He nodded back in the direction from which they'd come, then fixed a hard stare on Alex. "And we have ninety to run this way before we need to detonate it."

He indicated deeper into the mine.

"Ready?" They nodded. "...Go!"

A minute later, Isara was backtracked a good ways, well beyond where she might be hurt by the second explosion. She ran as fast as she could, holding a hand up to shield the candle from blowing out.

Sartek pulled the receiver out of his backpack and flipped the toggle on as he ran. He and Alex were, by then, at least a good hundred feet beyond where the second explosion would occur. They stopped, both staring at the glowing, green light on the receiver. Then, Sartek turned his back to the direction that the blast might come from and knelt onto one knee. Alex crouched beside him.

He put his arm around her shoulders, and pulled Alex close. "You ready?" he asked in a low voice. When she nodded, eyes wide in anticipation, he reached with his free hand, and...triggered the bomb.

* * *

A tremendous concussion rattled everything as glass shattered and fell from the commissary windows. The two sliding doors remained intact but they immediately whooshed shut, and an alarm light flashed red silently and ominously above them.

There were only two people in the little store: the clerk—a smallish woman in her fifties who wore civilian clothes—and a soldier who'd come in to pick up a belated birthday card for his mother. The soldier was spinning the revolving stand of generic "Cards for all Occasions" for a second time around when it happened.

The ground shook for only a second, like an earthquake gearing up, and a loud boom came from somewhere close by. The soldier dropped into a battle-ready stance and looked around, pulling his sidearm out just like he'd been trained to do.

Suddenly, rubble fell downwards, disappearing into a hole about the size of a couch that opened up in the floor, right next to a utility closet. A stand of potato chips teetered and disappeared down the hole and was followed, ironically, by a display of pain-relievers.

Somewhere in the darkness below the commissary, a handful of *Tylenol PM* caplets crunched beneath Sartek's boot as he scurried toward the slide of rubble, holding his breath as he grasped onto boulders of rock and salt, pulling his way up through the hole

Alex was fast on his heels.

The dust was horrendous, and she held her breath until she could bear it no longer.

Sucking in a lungful of salty dust, she coughed violently, stumbled, and snatched at the back of Sartek's jeans just fast enough to save herself from losing her footing altogether. She was immediately surprised at how strong the alien was. Still holding his breath, he reached back and grabbed her hand, then bolted up the steep pile of debris, half-dragging her along.

Briefly, Alex thought of David and wondered if he and Blalok were aware that Phoenix was well under way in grand, "opened up a can of whoop-ass" style. They'd been blind to communication for so long now that it'd become a delicate matter of timing and following the master plan. Next she worried about Liberty and Isara, and it gave her a pain in her stomach she'd never experienced before.

But before she could worry any more about it, she blinked against the fluorescent light that illuminated the whirling eddy of sooty air. They were nearly into the commissary, both covered so liberally with white dust that they could have been a couple of adolescent ghosts, rising from the dead.

Alex coughed again and rubbed her eyes, a mistake as the salt dust brought tears streaming in muddy gray rivers down her ashen face.

"You held your breath for such a long time," she sputtered, "when you were dragging me up."

"All Bettuan can do that. It's because we are swimmers." Sartek shrugged it off, his green features now so caked in salt dust that he was exceedingly zombielike, Alex decided.

Evidently shocked by the blast, the clerk cowered behind the checkout stand, her out of date bouffant sticking up as she peeked over the edge of the counter. Behind her, on the wall, someone had penciled a ridiculous drawing of two space creatures, one holding the decapitated head of a human by the hair. Below it read, "Stop the Aliens! Buy American!"

Alex hadn't noticed the soldier yet but possessed such immediate composure that she pointed first at the woman and then at the sign. "Take that down," she ordered grimly.

The woman scarcely moved.

"I'm not gonna hurt you…unless you ignore me. Now, I said take it down."

Standing only just tall enough to reach the sign, the woman snatched it off the wall and dropped out of view behind the stand.

The soldier remained kneeling, peeking over the end of the counter, his left hand resting on it while his right hand steadied his unholstered gun.   His gaze was fixed on the two figures who had risen up from the rubble.

"Halt! Who goes there?" The soldier slowly straightened, two handing his service pistol as he pointed it at the peculiar pair.

Sartek stepped halfway in front of Alex, but she strong-armed him, shoving him aside. Covered with white dust and salt as he was, she hoped it would be difficult, at least for the moment, for the soldier to tell that Sartek wasn't human.

"Don't shoot! We're kids!" She appealed with both hands up. "We were on a tour of the mine and got separated from mom n' dad." Only half faking a fairly pathetic cough, she added, "There musta' been like an earthquake or something! Lots of bodies, and some old people and kids are trapped. It's crazy! You better get down there right away." She gestured toward the hole

The man dropped his sidearm and reached for his radio, holding the mike up to his mouth. "I have a situation. There's—"

Alex dropped her hands to her sides.

Before the soldier could finish his report, the overhead lights flickered and the radio jerked from his hand, wholluping him a good one on the lip as it flew across the room and crashed against the only intact glass pane window in the commissary.

"Sorry about that," Alex apologized. "I can't let you do that."

The soldier started to raise the firearm again, but the lights flickered once more. This time, he hadn't time to aim properly when the gun discharged, sending a bullet mere inches above Sartek's head. Then the gun jerked from the soldier's hands and flew, smashing brilliantly into an overhead fluorescent light.

The room darkened as the pistol fell only inches from Alex's feet, along with a shower of fluorescent tube glass.

"What the hell!" Alex yelled. "I said we're kids! Jesus Christ!"

The soldier spun around.

"Stop!" Alex called, "or…I'll shoot."

The soldier froze, his back to Alex, and carefully raised his hands in the air.

Perhaps he sensed the desperation in her voice, but he was clearly convinced her threat was genuine.

Alex knelt and picked up the pistol. It was cold, and heavier than she anticipated, and she thought how quickly things had moved right along. "I'm sorry to mix you up in this, I really am, but I can't let you leave."

"I know you're not kids, I mean, you might be, but those collars..." Hands still in the air, he nodded over his shoulder toward the translation rings that glimmered, now only poorly concealed by the bandanas. "I've seen that stuff before. It's on that ship, isn't it? At least, what's left of it."

"You've seen the ship?" Alex took an involuntary step toward him.

Sartek said nothing. He could only understand Alex's half of the conversation with the guard, and he knew the guard wouldn't have been able to understand anything he said.

"Yeah, they're cutting into it right now, but after this..." The soldier jerked his head in a direction somewhere down the hall, "I'm guessing that other alert has something to do with the two of you as well."

"Okay, I didn't exactly lie." Alex shrugged. "We are kids, but you know we're not here on account of a salt mine tour. So let's just pretend you're smart. I'm guessing you probably are, so if you'll please just turn around." She waved the gun in a loose circle.

"You'll never get away with this—" the soldier started to say just as a bullet struck the floor, pretty much right between his feet. "Fuk'n A!—" He leapt straight up and landed, legs splayed apart.

"Oh, geez! Sorry 'bout that!" Alex apologized profusely. "Never held one of these before, and you're making me really nervous!" It was the truth, and she tilted her head back, peering down her nose at the gun. "Thought that was the safety," she muttered, now keeping the barrel pointed carefully at the floor. "And heavier than it looks in the movies," she added, her gaze now pinned on him. "Listen, this can go really good, or it can go really bad. I've seen guys like you—guys that want to do the right thing but get caught up in the game."

"Game?"

"Yeah, like chess. You know, you're the pawn, and the king is somewhere safe, I'm guessing on vacation or something. And guess what that means?"

"I get to die first?" The soldier was indeed a quick study. "They won't negotiate with you, you know. This isn't a civilian situation." He dropped his hands just a small bit and spread them, appealingly. "You can take me hostage if you want, but I'm disposable—Government Issue, as you've already pointed out. They won't—"

"You're right," Alex interrupted him. "And I totally get it, so don't act like I'm stupid. 'kay?" This time, her voice wasn't as calm as it'd been seconds before.

"I'm one of those lost souls too. *Disposable*. Have been for a long time." She laughed when she said it, but there wasn't an ounce of humor in her voice.

"So, let's just get down to it and make sure neither of us gets caught in the crossfire, Mister...?"

"He's an alien, isn't he?" The soldier scowled, indicating Sartek.

"Yep, Einstein." Alex didn't miss a beat. "He is, and he's a friend of mine. And your name is?"

"Are you one, too?"

"*Seriously*? No! I'm Alex, and you're seriously testing my patience." She barely raised the gun.

"Prince," he blurted.

"*Mr*. Prince?"

"Private. I'm first year."

"Hmm." Alex's eyes narrowed. "My brother's army too, you know. Been in over two years."

Sartek shot her a glance, surprised by this new bit of information.

"That right? Does he know what baby sis is up to these days?" The soldier seemed to relax a bit, letting his hands drop even more.

"Don't do that," she warned, waving with the gun. "And to answer your question, I doubt it. I haven't seen him since he joined, but I figure he must be alive, since I haven't got the letter or anything." She peered at him with slitted eyes. "You *do* still get the letter, don't you? You know, if..." Her voice trailed off.

The soldier listened intently but said nothing.

"How'd you get in on all this?" Alex waved the gun lazily overhead and glanced around the commissary as though she might see something astounding. "Seems like a lot of super top secret mumbo jumbo to have a private all involved and stuff. I'm guessing you gotta be pretty special."

"Right place, right time, or...wrong, I guess." He indicated the gun.

Alex stared for a long moment at the gun in her hands.

"You know, I've never held one of these before," she said with all honesty. In truth, although seeming so fiercely composed on the outside, Alex was crumbling on the inside. Here she was, the girl who rescued turtles from hostile traffic and released wrangled catfish, now pointing a gun at another person. It simply went against everything that she believed about the sanctity of all life, even though humans were not her favorite species by a long shot.

Without warning, she flipped the gun around, holding it out by the barrel. "Here. Last thing I want is for you to get in trouble cuz of us." She indicated Sartek as well.

"Alex, no!" Sartek exclaimed.

The soldier's eyes shot wide in mild surprise. Alex couldn't be sure whether it was from her turning the gun over or from Sartek speaking.

She cautioned the private, "But let me warn you. If you pull it on us or even try to follow, it'll do something you'll wish it hadn't."

She advanced slowly toward Private Prince. "Stuff seems to get a mind of its own when I get nervous, so let's not make me nervous. Deal?" Alex added as an afterthought, "And my friend here? He's a kid, like me, and he's lost. Got two friends too, his age—best friends, as a matter of fact. One of them's on that ship, the other's down there somewhere." She swung her arm back toward the gaping hole in the commissary floor.

The soldier seemed unsure of himself; he just stared at the pistol the dusty little girl was giving back to him as though it was a gift. Private Prince reached out and gingerly slipped it from her hand.

As he palmed the pistol, Alex explained further, "Now, we've already had our share of bad luck, and the odds are stacked pretty awful against us. You probably already know that. We could sure use for you to not make things worse."

The private flipped the gun safety on and holstered it. "What's your name?"

"Alex, and this is Sartek."

Private Prince rubbed the back of his neck with one hand before running it through his short hair. "Alex, we have a situation here. You see—"

"Like I said, we don't have time for this," Alex pressed two fingers between her eyes.

The gun tugged in its holster seemingly all by itself, and the private glanced at his hip with an expression of rising alarm.

"Now we're gonna walk out that door." She pointed at the commissary exit. "And the two of you are gonna just sit here and wait this out. Have a soda, bag of chips, or something; on the house."

She glanced first at him and then toward the store-clerk, still cowering somewhere behind the counter, then smiled brilliantly.

"Then give us, say, five minutes?"

Alex's face was ghost white with salt-tear streaks down her cheeks, but she was practically beaming. "Then you get to live to tell all the little Prince's about the day you met a true, green, bona fide alien dude."

Her smile vanished abruptly.

"But if you don't, well..." She put her fingertips to her lips and made a "poof" gesture outwards with her hand.

"You wouldn't really wanna' be responsible for blowing up some death-star or anything, now would you?"

Private Prince started to tremble. "Could it?"

"It could," she said flatly. "So...we got an understanding here?"

"Call it a solid? Go our separate ways?" Prince asked.

"Yep...just like that."

Sartek stepped next to Alex. Nearer, and in more direct light, his alien features were greatly evident, even dusted as they were with debris and white salt.

The private considered them thoroughly before looking over at the empty counter. "I think I'll have a soda, fountain orange for me," he said loud enough for the whole room to hear. "Tina, what would you like?"

Alex grinned, took Sartek by the hand, and headed for the door.

"That was amazing!" he whispered as they shuffled from the commissary out into the hall.

"Yeah...save it for the memoirs."

* * *

When the special tactics team, guns pulled and ready, turned the corner of the mine, the dust was swirling in snowy circles in their headlamps. The first thing they saw was a small boy lying motionless on his back, arms outstretched, eyes closed.

Close to one limp hand lay an uncapped albuterol inhaler.

Another child, thin and willowy, perhaps a girl, knelt over the boy. She was covered with the same white dust and coughed at intervals. Her hands were around the unconscious child's neck, and her eyes were closed very tightly.

Around the boy's neck, and hers, were metallic rings. Despite the dusty light of the head-beams, these collars shone brilliantly as though of their own accord. They resembled very much what the captured spaceship was slowly becoming as its milky shields eroded away.

"Freeze!" the closest officer yelled, which was fairly ridiculous as neither of the children were moving.

In seconds, a small, special-tactics army was gathered around, weapons drawn on the two locked in such a strange embrace.

"Move and we'll shoot!" someone shouted.

"You!" General Jacobs pushed past the soldiers, his own weapon drawn. He pointed the M1911 pistol at Isara's head. "Move away from that boy! *Now!*"

* * *

Isara could hear them, but their voices were so far away, barely tickling the edges of her mind. What's more, they were insignificant, *very* insignificant. On the other hand, what was important was the other sound, the *thump-thump* that barely beat within her own head—the heartbeat of another—the life-thread of a boy called Liberty. Everything was overshadowed by the dead quiet that was the absence of any breathing coming from the body of the human child.

When Isara's essence, the very fabric of her being, reached out and touched the fringe of Liberty's soul, the healing trickled into him terribly slow, like precious lifeblood. It was so slow at first that Isara was certain she'd lost him. Subconsciously, she compared her efforts to sprinkling water on a neglected plant, one terribly withered and nearly, but not quite, gone.

The whole experience was very dark, pitch-black, in fact, blacker even than if one shut their eyes very tightly.

When she believed all was lost, when she almost sobbed her failure, a pinpoint of light appeared a great distance from her. At first, she thought she only imagined it, a candle flame, only miles away. Then very gradually, the spark of the human boy flickered again and slowly grew.

The fragile tapping of his heart, as frail as a bird's, suddenly appeared beneath her fingertips. *Tap-uh, tap-uh, tap-uh* it went, terribly thready and fast, but as it became a more substantial pulse beneath her touch, it slowed and strengthened.

Lastly, he began to breathe, squeaking and agonizing at first, a few dreadful gasps, but then his throat and lungs squeaked open. His thin ribs drew the air in by fragile, gasping lungfuls between a few weak fits of coughing.

Isara sobbed out loud as she realized her friend was alive and stepping back from harms grasp.

Liberty, she whispered to him through the healing connection that she maintained, *I have you now. You're okay.*

Isara?

He lay very quiet, too weak yet to move, but she heard his voice in her own head as though he had spoken out loud. He was back. Death would not claim him just yet.

His bloodshot eyes flitted open as a flashlight beam swung wildly over him, and all he said was...

...Run.

It was just then that someone hit Isara very hard on the side of the head with a baton, and the Bettuan child-healer collapsed next to the human boy.

CHAPTER TWENTY-EIGHT

Δ

Just like Liberty said it would, the first explosion gathered a great deal of attention. By the time the second blast went off beneath the commissary, the general and a significant handful of the base's security forces were preoccupied with the tunnel that had been chiseled out from the first one. However, the most effective diversion was clearly the discovery of two children, one of them very odd indeed.

The boy seemed to have been nearly fatally injured by the alien but was recovering and could almost talk, *almost*. When he could talk, though, there was surely going to be a great deal he could share with them.

The alien, who appeared to be female, remained unconscious from the blow to the head.

No one was willing to touch the alien, or the human child for that matter. Who knew? Contamination and all, and personnel were just arriving with Hazmat suits when the second explosion went off, farther down the tunnel.

"Get them secured," the general barked. "And get a dispatch to that second explosion!"

He double-timed it back to the hole and struggled to climb back up the small mountain of debris, back into the base.

By the time Isara and Liberty were wrapped in decontamination blankets and secured on stretchers, Alex and Sartek were already well inside and much farther down the hall, standing behind a corner just outside the very critical control center.

* * *

All doors within the compound had automatically closed when the second explosion beneath the commissary went off, and several guards were now posted just outside of the control center. They were older men, older than Private Prince, and both had the deadly appearance of military authority.

Alex peeked swiftly from behind the corner and ducked back again.

"How do we get past them?" Sartek whispered.

"Here's the deal; I'm not sure how this secret power works." She held up both hands and wiggled her fingers. "I can't even be sure if it'll always work in our favor." She was remembering minutes before, in the commissary, when Sartek had nearly been shot in the head.

"I'm gonna try to use it again to get us inside." She pointed farther down the hall, past the control center. "Bert said the ship is beyond here, just around that bend in the hall."

When Sartek shifted nervously, she added, "Unless you got a better plan?"

"We should have kept the gun," Sartek said regretfully. "We have no way of defending ourselves now."

"Don't worry. I've dealt with stuff like this all my life."

"Really?"

"No…" she answered, the corner of her mouth trembling in a small smile.

Sartek shot her a look of mild surprise.

She elbowed him gently in the ribs. "C'mon, trust me. This is gonna be fun." Nowhere in the core of Alex's belief system did she think it was going to be fun.

Before he could answer, she moved casually around the corner and, with hands out, walked straight up to the guards. Both drew on her, rifles pointing at her chest.

"See, here's the deal," Alex announced simply. "I have an alien with me, and he needs his ship back."

"That's it? That's your strategy?" Sartek said in a low voice as he walked out and took his place at her right shoulder.

"Stay right there!" one of the guards ordered, swinging his rifle now at Alex's head.

The other man reached for a small microphone attached to his lapel.

Before they could report anything, the overhead lights flickered and the small mic zinged out and away from the soldier's flack jacket, pulling with it the wire that attached it to a small receiver in his right ear. It circled dizzyingly in front of the man's face, its thin cord zipping back and forth behind it like an angry serpent's tail, before poking him sharply in one eye.

"Ow!" the officer exclaimed and slapped the angry device away as though some crazed, electronic bee was attacking him.

The other guard, mesmerized by the tiny device that appeared to have come so abruptly to life and take issue with its owner, dropped the muzzle of his gun for a split second. "What the…" he began as his rifle dipped even more.

It was at just that instant that the overhead lights flickered again and both guns were yanked from the men's hands. They clattered to the ground in front of Alex and Sartek.

"Don't move," Alex said calmly. "If you do, I can't be responsible for what happens."

Sartek bent down and, even though unfamiliar with the weapons, shouldered one comfortably, pointing it at the knees of the second guard.

"Here's what we're gonna do," Alex explained. "We're gonna walk past these doors…" She tilted her head toward the control center. "And go on around the corner to let him…" she nodded at Sartek. "Go in to where his ship is. *Got it?*"

The guards wisely raised their hands.

"And you probably realize that those communication thingies won't work anymore—they're fried," Alex added casually as she leaned down to pick up the other assault rifle.

"But *these* aren't electronic. They'll work just fine, and I might look like a sweet little kid, but I'm a kid with nothing to lose. And I sure as hell don't wanna' go back to where I come from."

The guards said nothing, just stared, hollow-eyed, as Alex shrugged her small shoulders. "So let's just all play nice and make this a happy ending, 'kay? Cuz the way I see it, I'm going to jail anyway, and I'd hate to make you two a bigger part of my problem…." She now leveled the rifle directly at the first guard's chest. "But if I have to…I will."

On the outside, the little girl in overalls was cool as tile flooring beneath bare feet. On the inside, however, Alex's heart thumped so loudly she could scarcely hear what she was saying, and she trembled so badly she worried she might drop the rifle.

She tipped the point of the rifle toward the guard's knees. "Let's just all move that way and—"

The older soldier interrupted her. "You'll never get—"

"Shut up!" Alex snapped.

The guard puffed up a bit, perhaps unused to being taken prisoner by a thirteen-year-old girl.

"I've already killed Private Prince," she added matter-of-factly.

The guards' eyes flew wide.

"He made the unfortunate mistake of being in the commissionary. I feel real bad about that, but..." She lifted her chin. "I could get used to it." Truthfully, she thought she could never get used to such a thing, even if it was just a lie.

The guards stared at each other with genuine concern.

"Sidearms, guys." Alex tapped the toe of her sneaker on the concrete floor, not giving them a chance to dwell too long on her story.

Sartek shot her a surprised glance. In any galaxy, hearing someone bluff so eloquently was rare. He was just realizing that Alex possessed quite a bit more courage than he'd first thought. Earlier, before they'd fired the second bomb, he'd asked her if she was "ready."

She'd replied, "Guess you never know your mettle until you put it to the fire." Well, they were certainly well into the blaze now, and Alex's mettle could challenge vasteen.

The guards slowly unholstered their sidearms and knelt, sliding the pistols across the floor to them. Alex kept the rifle leveled at them both as she kicked the pistols off to the side, well out of reach of the guards.

It was a very peculiar situation; the girl with the dusty, sun-streaked ponytail and freckled cheeks barely showing beneath the grime, her sweet cherub mouth, and the hands that looked so tiny grasping the MK-17. She had to twist the weapon in the crook of her arm just to carry it.

However, her eyes spoke something entirely different. They burned with fearless. "Gentlemen," she repeated, pointing her chin down the hall. "Shall we? Or are you willing to lay it down for a couple stupid orphan kids?"

They hesitated but, in the end, turned and headed down the hall, past the control center. Alex glanced sideways as they walked by the big, glass pane windows, hoping nobody noticed them.

A small woman with black hair, wearing a white lab jacket, was pacing and yelling into a cell phone when she caught the movement out of the corner of her eye. There was an instant when she turned and gazed straight at Alex with the most startling blue eyes that Alex believed she'd ever seen. The woman's mouth opened in silent alarm, but strangely, she didn't call out. She just stood there, frozen, and slowly laid the phone on a counter.

There was something about the expression on her face, as she looked first at Alex, then at Sartek, then back at Alex. It seemed to her almost…sad.

Alex shook her head softly, her eyes begging the woman as she held her finger up to her lips.

And then, just like that, the four stepped past the glass windows and out of sight. Just beyond the windows, about twenty yards farther, lay the double closed doors. Behind them would be the *Cerulean Star*.

"Open them," Alex commanded just as the overhead alarms started to shriek in earnest. It had been less than five minutes since they'd crawled out of the hole in the commissary floor.

"Well, we knew *that* was going to happen," Sartek said wryly.

When he spoke, both the guards stared at him, uncomprehending.

"Doesn't matter," she replied, then repeated with grave authority, "I said *open* it."

"I can't," the younger indicated. "It's security coded and—"

"And you're a *security* guard. Now how 'bout that!" Alex flipped the rifle safety off, just as Liberty told her she might have to do.

Alex was by now convinced that her heart had climbed right up into her throat and was going to explode out of her ears. She would've given anything to be back on the side of the little pond. Then she could catch catfish, watch David dive so perfectly from the cliff, and listen to Liberty go on about some dumb thing or another.

Instead, she steadied herself and raised the tip of the assault rifle in line with the guard's head. "I will blow your head off before I get your friend to open it. I don't want to…but if you make me…I goddamn-sure will." Her finger slid onto the trigger.

"Wait! Wait, hold on! Just relax, kid." The soldier held trembling hands up and glanced over at the other guard as though he'd just crapped his pants.

The older man was biting his own lip to the point of drawing blood. He nodded the 'go ahead,' and the younger soldier went to reach slowly into his vest.

"I'm just getting my access badge." He pulled it gingerly out, showing it to

Alex first before reaching over to the access panel and sliding it across the surface.

The red, luminescent bar flickered to a happy green, and a metallic *kachunk* rattled in the heavy doors' hardware just before they lurched into motion, receding back into the wall jambs. Then, the underground vault opened enormous and spectacular before them.

"Son of a..." Alex gasped, as the doors slid apart.

Beyond them opened the biggest cave she'd ever imagined, and hovering within was her birthday present. Only now the *Star* wasn't elegant and breathtakingly blue like before.

The *Cerulean Star*'s shell looked ravaged by a terrible plague. Ghastly, black gashes were slashed into and torn across it, exposing in a vulgar way the vasteen beneath. The helium shield was depleting even faster in rivulets that dripped in an ominous, black vapor, disappearing just before hitting the ground. The frame beneath glowed a brilliant and metallic orange, just like the collars that the two children wore.

Alex stepped forward.

"What the *fuck* have you done to it?" she screamed.

Just then, the awful pounding of the sound cannon assaulted them, forcing the two guards and Alex immediately to their knees. She straightaway clutched her hands over her ears, and her rifle clattered across the concrete floor.

The older guard reached one hand for the MK-17.

Sartek managed to maintain his footing despite the horrible, crushing hammering that pounded upon him. He cried out as he fired a blast of shots between the rifle and the guard. The man cowered, hands over his head.

Then, just as suddenly, the sound cannon ceased. The stark, abrupt absence of it was almost as deafening.

It'd been too much for Alex. Doubled over, she dry-heaved onto the tarmac. Sartek held the gun on the guards and waited patiently until Alex was done retching. The dry heaves eventually ceased, and she reached for her own fallen rifle.

Sartek grabbed her by the elbow and gently helped her, staggering, to her feet.

"Get out," she gasped, regathering and pointing the rifle at the guards while motioning back out the doors. "Get the hell out, and close them behind you!"

The men didn't hesitate. They half stumbled, half crawled, back from where they'd come. As soon as they were out, the doors whooshed shut.

Sartek and Alex stood alone, the assault rifles dangling in their hands.

Alex glanced around the cavern.

Off to one side of the *Star* was a terrible device, perched on a platform like a wicked mantis. It looked as though it spewed something terrible from its mouth…into the throat of the ship. Safely outfitted in protective headgear and back at it, the technicians sliced away at the *Cerulean Star*.

The cutter made a wretched screeching noise as the frothy, white beam ground into the lovely belly of the ship.

"Make them stop!" Sartek cried.

Alex glanced at him before whistling, very loudly, between her front teeth. Nothing happened. She then sprayed the cavern ceiling with bullets.

One of the technicians, the one standing closest to the giant water knife, looked up as rock debris rained down on him. He glanced over his shoulder and nearly fell from the platform when he saw the little girl and alien with guns in their hands. The man reached up with both hands and carefully removed the helmet from his head, indicating at the same time that he wanted no trouble.

It would be alarming, Alex thought, to see two kids with automatic weapons in their hands—much worse than firecrackers or cigarette lighters. This brought the trace of a smile to her lips.

Other personnel—scientists mostly—came hurrying from a temporary workstation set up on the other side of the *Star*. On seeing the children, and most noticeably the MK-17s, all of them raised their hands. Curiously, there were no soldiers stationed in the cavern, and this lot did not seem prone to outright confrontation.

"Get out," Alex said in a ragged voice.

When not even one of them began to move, she screamed hoarsely, "Get the *fuck* out!"

The gaggle of scientists and technicians sprinted for the exit doors, disappearing beyond.

Alex glanced around the empty cavern, the only sound the scream of the water blade as it still ground against the *Star*. She thought how the ship looked enormous in the cave, much larger than it had seemed even in the little meadow. Such a magnificent creation the starship was, and now so wounded, so defiled. She turned to Sartek.

"Oh, my God…I'm so *sorry*," she half sobbed.

Blood, so dark green as to appear black, trickled from her friend's left ear. Sartek's eyes were huge and damp, but not from the sound cannon. His eyes grieved the awful destruction wrought upon the *Star*, *his* ship—the only thing that connected him to his home.

He let the rifle sag, pointed to the ground at his feet and took one staggering step forward, then whirled on Alex.

"Make it stop!"

Alex took two steps toward the water blade, dropped her chin, and closed her eyes. For a long moment, nothing happened. She raised both hand slowly, her right arm extended, reaching as her left hand swung in an arc about her, collecting what it was she required.

All the overhead lights shattered at once, raining glass shards and sparks down on the beautiful ship in a magnificent way.

The entire cavern darkened, only making the glow of the Star that much more intense. The water blade ground to a halt, and screamed no more. Stumbling, Alex fell backwards, her eyes rolling back as she dropped...into Sartek's arms.

"You did it," he whispered. "Alex, thank you."

Blinking slowly, Alex saw from the corner of her eye the woman with the black hair.

She stood behind the glass observatory window, pounding her hands against the glass. Her lips moving in a silent scream, and Alex understood the word..."*Run.*"

"Sartek..." Alex began, but before she could finish the sentence, her vision paled and was clouded in brilliant color.

The glorious gold of the *Star*'s endoskeleton shimmered so brilliantly that it seemed to radiate heat. In an instant, two shift beams dropped from empty space and engulfed the children.

When they materialized, Alex, still dazed, vaguely noticed the interior of the beautiful ship. But then she saw David standing on the opposite side of the bridge, beautiful eyes damp with relief. Scrambling from Sartek's arms, she ran to him, throwing her arms around his neck. She hugged him tightly, tears streaming from her eyes. "David, oh God, we made it! We made it!"

Sartek watched the reunion with a curious expression and circled wide around the two.

"Alex..." David choked and hugged her back, hoisting her above the ground, then put her down and held her at arm's length. "Where's Bert?" He shook her gently by the shoulders. More urgently, "Alex...where's Bert. Where is he?"

"I...I don't know," she stammered. "He went back. Isara—"

Sartek finished for her, "We lost him after the first explosion. Isara went back for him."

David released Alex and spun on Sartek, seeing for the first time since they had met in the meadow the tall male alien with the darkest-green eyes.

"What the hell do you mean, you lost them? You can't *lose* Bert! He's not the one you lose, ever! Do you hear me? *Never!*"

He stepped toward Sartek.

Sartek's eyes narrowed, and he likewise stepped toward David, the tension immediately thick between them. "Isara is down there too!" he countered in a low voice. "We both have lost friends right now. Not just you."

"Whoa, whoa, slow down, David!" Alex said, swiping the tears from her eyes with the heel of her hand. She stepped between the two. "He didn't do anything! We had a plan and—"

"And that plan was to leave Bert *behind*? Sorry!" David stabbed at the air over Alex's shoulder, toward Sartek, "Not a good enough plan, genius! As a matter of fact," he shouted at Sartek, fists clenched as he pushed Alex aside, "that is the *opposite* of a good plan!" David poked at Sartek's chest with his index finger as he spoke.

Sartek slapped it away. "*Yeah*? And if Isara hadn't thought it was a good idea to meet you to begin with, we wouldn't all be in this mess!"

Alex jumped between the two, arms extended. "We don't have time for this! We gotta figure out where they are and what the new plan is. Bert would want us to do that." She let her arms fall to her sides. "And so would Isara."

David scowled at Sartek. The alien glared back.

CHAPTER TWENTY-NINE

Δ

Liberty struggled to sit, to get his senses about himself. Something had slipped over one eye, and he squinted to focus through the other. Reaching up, he pulled the bandage off his forehead.

He lay on a hospital gurney in what appeared to be a temporary medical bay. Plastic sheeting surrounded him, strung in tight panels from floor to ceiling. He remembered seeing just such a setup in movies—movies about terrible viruses gone crazy, contaminating whole populations in a matter of hours. Realization dawned on him that they must think he was infected, that he might risk spreading whatever horrors they thought the aliens carried.

Just then, he thought of Isara.

"Where is she?" he said to no one as he tried again to sit, tearing at the EKG patches and yanking at his IV. "Is she okay? What did you do with her?" He reached for his neck and was aghast to discover the translation ring was gone.

They must have taken it!

"Whoa! Whoa, calm down," the nurse prompted, his voice muffled by the Hazmat helmet he wore. "You're okay now—we saved you. Just relax, little buddy."

Liberty possessed the natural resolve to calmly pull himself together and assess his situation. He was briefly grateful that it was he, and not Alex, lying on the hospital bed. Even so, he struggled to keep panic from returning.

"I'm sorry, I must have blacked out. Where am I?" he asked with forced control.

"You're in Hutchinson Air Base—the infirmary. You're okay, but that thing almost killed you."

"What are you talking about?" Liberty tried to lead with his question.

"That thing—the alien. It had you in the mineshaft and was sucking the life right outa' you. We barely got you out alive."

Liberty swallowed thickly, even now feeling the residual effects of the acute asthma attack he'd suffered after the explosion. Breathing remained an everyday chore for him. Seldom did he ever not feel the familiar tightness in his chest, like a vise—a monster always there, waiting to close in on him. The dirt and salt dust of the explosion had simply been too much. Left to his own devices, Liberty would have died in the mineshaft. Isara saved his life, and in return....

He closed his eyes and tried to quiet his mind. A calm settled over him, and he searched for her, ferreting about in the recesses of his being until he felt it, felt *her*, just as Sartek said he would. He saw her as though a glimpse through a foggy screen, and it was familiar, like an awareness of himself.

They were *all* there: Sartek, Isara, and Alex. They were still alive, as much as his left hand or foot was.

"You diabetic?" the nurse asked without warning.

"Huh?" Liberty was still a bit dazed and almost answered, "Yes," but instead said, "Not exactly."

"Cause your blood sugar came back over three hundred. That's pretty high. We weren't sure if it was something that thing did to you or not. Other labs are coming back pretty clean, though."

Liberty blinked hard and glanced around the room.

"Got you on a sliding scale," the nurse said. "And looks like you're better now. Feel like some pudding? Think you can swallow something? Nothing too coarse or anything, not so soon after what happened."

The nurse seemed too casual, given the situation.

"The alien, where did they take...it?" Liberty almost said "her".

"Oh, it's in lockdown. You can be sure of that. They got a probe so far up its ass by now it'll think it's turned into shit on a stick."

Liberty was immediately outraged, but it didn't slow the nurse down.

"There's no way it's getting out. Its ass is grass."

The nurse set a tray down on the bedside table and slid it closer to Liberty. "You should try to eat something. The general's gonna be here soon. You'll need your strength. They've got some questions, but don't worry. You're safe now, and a *hero*!"

Liberty shook his head. "I'm not hungry, but I'm ready to speak with the general. Can you call him please?"

He swung his legs over the side of the hospital bed.

"Whoa, whoa there! Slow down, champ; you're not goin' nowhere. You just had an alien try to choke the life outa' you, and besides, this is decontamination. We still got a lot of tests to run on you, but you're gonna be all right. And you'll get your chance to tell the general exactly what happened, in your own words."

"I'm *not* fine, far from, and it's only going to get worse," Liberty insisted in what he hoped was an ominous voice. "I need to talk to the general, *now!*" He tried to shrug the nurse's strong hand off his shoulder. "Human life, maybe even the whole human species, depends on it."

The nurse peered at him a bit suspiciously. "What kind of information?"

"It's classified. I'm so sorry, but I can only speak to the general, or the President."

"Of the United States?" The nurse laughed outright. "Look, little bro, you got yourself in a pretty bad pickle, almost getting choked to death by that thing and all, and your story's sure to make headlines. Who knows, maybe even a spot on Leno. But you're kinda government property for a while."

Liberty stared as he rambled dumbly on.

The nurse slid his hand from Liberty's shoulder, patting it as he did, and indicated the plastic sealed room around him.

"All this? This is to make sure you're doing okay and everyone's safe, no offense. You could be carrying something, you know, contagious and all. Who knows what those bastards can do. We've already seen some of it, now haven't we?"

Liberty bristled at the continued crude evaluation of his Bettuan friends, and his eyes narrowed. "That's what I've been trying to tell you. I *am* contaminated, and so are you, if you've spent more than..." He glanced at the clock. "How long have you been with me?"

The nurse lapsed into silence, for the first time since Liberty gained consciousness, and fumbled absently with the zipper of his HAZMAT suit, drawing it snug beneath his chin.

"The infection attaches to…*light*, the particles of it, I mean. So it doesn't ascribe to ordinary barriers. If light can get through, so can the disease." Liberty became more animated.

The nurse held his hands, with their semi-transparent gloves, up in front of his face.

Glancing at the clock—it was five forty-five—Liberty went on to elaborate gory specifics of the imaginary infestation.

"I was captured by them for a good while, poked, prodded, and *exposed*. It starts out with a terrible thirst, worse than anything, then the bleeding begins, out of…*everywhere*, until gangrene sets in and things, well, you know…start to fall off."

The nurse swallowed heavily. It was fairly evident that, until this moment, he'd not really considered himself at any real risk. He backed slowly away as Liberty continued, expounding about such things as pus, vomiting, and…loss of erections.

"And I'm not the first one it's happened to. I've seen it at least a dozen times before; they're all dead. However, the exposure incubation is long. There's still time for you, but the clock is ticking."

He appealed with outstretched hands. "Look, my folks are dead. I have no one who will miss me, absolutely no one." He allowed his hands to fall pathetically into his lap and dropped his chin forlornly to his chest. "I'm a goner, but I need to do the right thing."

Coming abruptly back to life, he reached a hand, clawing at the nurse's arm. The man jumped back as Liberty croaked, "And that's why I need you to call the general! The plague has to be stopped! You have to call him, *now*!"

The nurse stepped farther away from Liberty's outstretched hand and shot a nervous glance at the overhead clock. Suddenly, he was not nearly as cavalier with the young patient as he'd been just seconds ago.

"Okay," he said, both hands held out as though he might keep the infection at bay. "Okay, look, just relax kid. I'm sure everything's going to be fine."

Liberty squinted to make out the nurse's nametag. "For you, Larry, maybe…if it isn't already too late. But I know it's too late for me." He coughed dramatically right at him, without covering his mouth.

The nurse backed away, hands remaining up. "Listen, kid. Just hang on. I'm gonna go…" he motioned toward the plastic zip door, "out, and I'm gonna let the general know. So don't freak out or anything. Just stay put, and I'll be right back, okay?"

Liberty stared at him and coughed again.

Larry couldn't back out of the isolation room fast enough, and he zipped two layers of plastic film closed behind him.

Through the blur of the two plastic layers, Liberty watched Larry strip violently out of his isolation suit before stepping naked into a decontamination shower. It was his guess that this wasn't normal protocol when someone exited an isolation room.

With his legs swung over the side of the bed, he just sat there, allowing his equilibrium to settle and his head to clear while he waited. It made him dizzy just to sit up.

Reaching for the bedside equipment stand, he grabbed the cool steel edge of it and dragged it closer. Rummaging around on the stand, he found a two-by-two gauze and piece of tape, then slid the roller clamp on the IV tubing until it was pinched off. Peeling the clear dressing off first, he pulled the IV out of his arm, then slapped the gauze and tape over it, pressing down for a few seconds until it didn't bleed anymore.

The nasal cannula and blood pressure cuff were the next to go. When he was at last free of all the monitoring devices, he hopped barefoot to the floor. Evidently, they'd never anticipated a pediatric patient because his hospital gown hung nearly to the floor and was so big that, even tied up, it flopped open behind in the breeze. At least they'd allowed him the dignity of his Superman briefs. They were really three-year hand-me-downs from David, and Liberty smiled at the thought.

It would have been ridiculous for him to try to exit the ward. He could see the guard posted outside the two sheets of isolation plastic. The soldier was fitting himself with a gas mask now, evidently alarmed by nurse Larry's freakout.

Pulling up a chair and dropping the bedside table, Liberty popped open a chocolate pudding pack and dove into it with a spoon. He glanced again at the overhead clock. Five fifty-two. Returning his attention to the pudding, he waited and, just as expected, it took less than five minutes before the general showed up outside the isolation unit.

Liberty couldn't see the general's face clearly through the plastic sheets, but he did recognize the patch on his shoulder. The four linear, gold stars indicated his rank, and just below them was a sleeve emblem—a green shield with three gold lightning bolts and a sword across them. This meant the general was also a member of the army special forces Green Beret.

It wouldn't do to underestimate this very worthy opponent.

Liberty watched as the general, his eyes fixed on the boy, deliberately flipped the light switches, one by one. The room gradually darkened until only the monitoring equipment illuminated the space in a weird way. Then, the general looked over his shoulder to study Liberty for an uncomfortable length of time, all the while remaining on the other side of the two plastic sheets. He darkened face was unsettling.

"H'lo," Liberty said simply.

"Hi, young fella. I hope you're feeling better. Looked like that alien put the screws to you pretty good. How 'bout we call your momma and daddy and get this situation figured out?"

"Don't have any," Liberty replied simply, focusing on the last of the pudding, scraping the cup clean with the little, white, plastic spoon. "I live..." he faltered, perfectly, "I live...uhmm..." His face crossed with worry. "I-I don't know where I live!" He dropped the pudding cup and his hands went up to his face as though to make sure it was still there.

"It's okay, son. That's just residual from the choking. It'll probably pass." The general seemed to want to calm him, but his expression remained unclear as he tilted his head back and studied Liberty a bit longer. "I understand you have some information you need to share with me?" Jacobs pulled up a chair and sat backward on it, his elbows resting on the back. "I'm all ears, uhmm, what did you say your name was?"

"I didn't; my name's Liberty."

The general nodded and waited. Liberty was aware that he was being interrogated. Significantly, there was no child advocacy group present, not even a doctor. Regardless of how genuine and kind the general was trying to come across, Liberty's rights were not paramount, and he knew it.

"That's a fine, strong name, son. All right, *Liberty*. Suppose we talk about what's on your mind?"

Liberty cleared his throat. "I've been infected. And the alien species' viral contamination is slowed by the collar."

The general's eyes shot wide, and he shifted in his chair. "Well, now that's a mouthful. And how exactly do you know this?"

Liberty slowed down, picking his words more carefully. "They told me when they had me aboard the ship, and I can already feel the effects. Plus, I saw the others die."

"You? You were aboard their ship?"

"Yes, sir, and my best friend's still aboard it. You might remember him? Dark hair—the kid that ran across the meadow when you first captured it?"

There was no disputing the accuracy of Liberty's claim. The capture report contained within it the video of a dark-haired boy, sprinting across the meadow before disappearing as though he'd been sucked into a beam of sorts. It was exactly like when the two within the cavern—the little girl and the alien—disappeared. That'd happened just over an hour ago, about the same time as when they'd found the boy with the alien wrapped around his neck in the mineshaft.

The general shifted uneasily in the dark. "And the little girl? The one with the ponytail and pretty eyes who was with another bigger one of them?" he asked flatly, almost sarcastically.

He knew the general meant Alex and Sartek, and he was right—Alex did have pretty eyes. Liberty hesitated, knew that reasoning with Jacobs would prove futile. The military, the government, and the world for that matter, would do as they pleased with this vessel and its inhabitants, and considering Earth's short history of humanity running the show, it probably wouldn't end well.

There was one more thing Liberty knew—the general was no idiot. To win his case, Liberty needed to be perceived as an ally, not a foe. If the general determined it a national security issue, it would preclude the loss of a singular child, or several. So, he decided he needed to keep his cards close to his chest to prevent compromising the deception he was trying so valiantly to present.

"Is Alex okay?" he asked urgently as he slid from the bed. "Where is she? Did she get infected?"

General Jacobs eyes widened.

Liberty knew the man would pick his words carefully.

"Liberty…"

"You can call me Bert, General." He knew the tactics of special-ops interrogation, that the general would attempt to coerce him, gain his trust to draw information from him. If this failed, he would employ advanced interrogation techniques, what they termed "unconventional warfare". And…Liberty intended to do the same, only more subtly. The man wouldn't anticipate such tactics from a boy and had no way of knowing how brilliant this particular eleven-year-old was.

"The girl is Alexandra, but she likes to be called Alex. She and David are all I have. Is she all right?" Before the general had a chance to answer he said, "If they've taken her too, I…I…?"

He let his voice trail off and wrung his hands.

"Hold on Bert, calm down."

Jacobs stood up, flipped the chair around, and sat down again, elbows on his knees with his fingers tented in front of himself.

"Bert, my name is Alan, you can call me that if you—"

"The ring!" Liberty interrupted him again. "Did Alex have one on? On her neck? If she didn't, oh, *God*." Liberty grabbed his stomach and leaned over, staggering forward a step. This was only half faked as he remained fairly dizzy from the near death incident in the mine.

Jacobs jumped up and stepped back, even though he was on the other side of the plastic sheet. "Sit down, son, before you fall down."

Liberty returned to the bed and scrambled up onto it, his faded Superman briefs flashing. He twisted around to face the general, skinny legs crossed, boney knees sticking out from the edges of the hospital gown. He tried hard to think of Goo, seriously wondering if his little dog was okay, and this singular thought brought very real tears to his eyes.

"We don't know about your friends. What we do know is the girl, Alex, disappeared with one of them after getting into the cavern."

"Did they hurt her? Did they make her do things? *Bad* things?"

So, Alex and Sartek made it to the ship. Liberty was aware that she would've had no problem taking the initiative in that process, and he assumed she'd hurt a few feelings along the way. She was *queen* at that. He tried hard not to smile.

"They'll make you do things you shouldn't; they made me blow up the tunnel!" Liberty gestured with his hands over his head, then asked again, "Alan, did she have a *ring*? Around her neck?" Liberty manipulated counter coercion magnificently. "If she didn't, she will die sooner." He choked back another fairly convincing sob.

The general seemed unsure where to go with this but was ultimately sucked in. "She did, Bert, she did." Then, "What exactly does that ring do?"

Liberty already had his answer prepared. "Like I said, she's all I have left, her and David. The aliens, they took us from the forest. The rings protect us from getting sicker, but they can't save us. *They* know that. I'm already infected, Alex is infected, and I'm guessing by now David is too. Problem is, without the ring, and one of them to run it, we'll die quicker."

"Tell me about this infection."

"Light carries it. You're smart to sit in the dark." He winced. "The collar helps, they said. So they can study us longer. I overheard them. It takes a while for the infection to break through our immune systems. You need to get everyone out of here, and let the ship go."

"Just how long does that take?" The general leaned back in the shadows, arms crossed over his chest.

Liberty shrugged. "Two, maybe three days. It probably depends on exposure."

"Bert, what is your last name?"

This was a dangerous question. If the general gained access to Liberty's previous records, they would know about his asthma and diabetes. It would be harder to feign the fabricated illness that was his ace in the hole. They would also discover that he'd been classified as brilliant.

"There's one more thing," Liberty added quickly. "If I have the ring, I can understand them…"

The general forgot, for now at least, that he'd tried to get Liberty's last name and leapt up, bolting from the room.

Hmm. So much for his concern for the child in the infirmary, Liberty thought to himself.

CHAPTER THIRTY

Δ

Isara lay on a stainless steel table in an observation vault, tethered with leather bands about her ankles and wrists. A large strap was cinched tightly across her waist and another, across her neck, made it difficult for her to raise her head or look around. The temperature in the observation room was a cool sixty-eight, and Isara shivered.

There were monitors connected to her; blood oxygen was ninety-three percent, blood pressure was eighty over twenty-eight, respirations nineteen. This is what the technician outside the vault recorded as he watched very closely the alien.

* * *

The alien groaned as though in pain. Large eyes blinked slowly as it tilted its head to one side, away from the laceration on its scalp, before closing its eyes again. Blood, a deep, greenish-black, had pooled on the steel table and dried sticky across the creature's temple. Gone was the ring from the alien's neck. It had been confiscated along with the one from the human boy.

"It doesn't appear to be aggressive. We can at least remove the restraints. Don't you think?" Bennett argued. "It's hardly the size of a child itself. Can we at least free it in the room? Perhaps give it something to sit on?"

"Negative." Lieutenant Colonel Taylor stood very tall, literally looking down his nose at her. "We cannot underestimate the capabilities of the enemy."

Bennett wasn't sure if he smiled or not; it was one of *those* smiles, and he spoke to her as though she were an imbecile.

"If you've never seen a snake, you might make the same assumption, that it isn't dangerous because it's smaller, or..." he looked Bennett up and down, "pretty." The smile faded. "And you'd be wrong."

Bennett groaned. There was no communicating with him, and she decided to turn her efforts on Jacobs. She didn't have to go far. The general busted through the door before she had a chance to turn around.

"Get me those rings!" he snapped. "And turn off the lights."

The technician obeyed, and the room dimmed, lit only by the bank of computer terminals in the observation room. Taylor saluted with all the enthusiasm of a trained monkey and left, evidently to confiscate the rings.

"What? What is it?" Bennett asked. "And why turn the lights off?"

"The boy. He claims he's infected; says the ring helps keep him alive." He looked squarely at Bennett. "Says the infection attaches to light. *And* he says we can communicate with it if we wear the rings."

She was stunned and said first, "We need to get the ring back on the boy!" Then she seemed to grasp the item of bigger importance. "You mean with her? You can talk to her?"

"*It*, Miss. Bennett. It is an invading species and non-human. It is an *it*. And it is carrying something contagious, has invaded our planet, and tried to choke a ten-year-old boy to death."

"Wait! Please...just wait. I volunteer to communicate with it," Bennett offered straight up.

"What?"

"I volunteer. I'll do it. Let me put the ring on. Let me speak to it."

"Did you hear me right, Ms. Bennett? Because I'm not entirely convinced of any of it. What I do know is they have two human children captive aboard their ship, and they might be capable of mind control!"

This gave Bennett much to think about, but primarily she wished to communicate with the female alien. And, that little human girl—the one with the alien in the hallway outside of the control center—there was just something about her face, the way she'd made such a silent appeal. A piece of the puzzle was missing.

When Bennett was a child, her mother told her about the little voice in the back of her head, and she could still hear her mom as though it was yesterday.

Sometimes you'll barely hear it. Sometimes it will scream bloody murder at you, and you'll just be annoyed and want to push it away. That little voice is what humanity classically conditions you to ignore, since day one. But don't listen to them. Pay attention. One day it could save you.

Now the little voice pounded on the back of her head like a jackhammer, and Bennett, much to the credit of her very wise mother, was very good at listening to it. Consequently, she believed there was much more to the situation than there first appeared to be.

"Give me the ring. I'll speak with the alien. If I become infected, it will give us a bigger control group to evaluate the disease process and prevent further outbreak."

"We already have the boy for that," the general countered. "You can go in, but you're wearing Hazmat."

Taylor appeared with a lead case. Inside were the two rings taken from Liberty's and Isara's necks.

"Don't move; I'll be right back!" Bennett swept a stray, dark lock of hair from her eyes. Hardly able to control her excitement, she ran to go change into a Hazmat suit.

* * *

As soon as she was gone, the general entered the interrogation vault room alone, without a Hazmat suit, with both the rings in his hand.

"Sir?" Taylor started to object.

"Shut up," Jacobs ordered, closing the door behind him. He indicated with a sweep of his hand that he was not to be interrupted and approached the alien.

The creature was lying as though dead, its eyes closed. The general wasn't sure if it'd even heard him enter. He squinted as he studied the delicate ear, the flat nose, and smooth skin. Removing a pencil from his uniform shirt pocket, he hesitated, clearing his throat.

No response, so he poked the tip of the pencil sharply into the ribs of the alien, burying the lead in its flesh.

Brilliant turquoise eyes flew open, and he was astonished with how liquid they appeared. He remembered, once, swimming with dolphins on a Hawaiian vacation. The dolphins' eyes seemed so deep, clear, and liquid—just like the alien's appeared now, only these seemed too large. Jacobs backed away as humans will do when confronted with something...*alien*.

It didn't move, only looked at him, tracking him as he moved around the room to the other side of the bed. It had a mouth and thin lips, but no sound escaped; it almost appeared closed too tightly. Even with the lead tip of the pencil broken off in its side, the creature did not cry out as a human might.

Freak, Jacobs thought to himself.

He laid the lead briefcase on the table with a heavy thud and flipped the catches, opening it with the back toward the alien. There was no way the creature could know what lay inside. As the general slowly removed one of the rings, he studied the alien. Its eyes opened even wider, thin lips parting though no sound came from it.

"You know what this is, *don't* you?" the general asked.

The alien remained silent.

He peered closely at the ring. It felt warm in his hand, as though it had a life of its own, and as delicate as the band was, it was heavy, with a significant weight to it. Briefly he wondered if it emitted radiation and then was sorry he'd handled it so carelessly. He would hate to lose a hand or something.

"You *want* it, *don't* you?" The general studied the alien from between narrowed eyes. "What is it? A weapon? Does it give you your power?"

The creature's breathing quickened, and so did its heart rate. The monitor bleeped rapidly and urgently in the background.

Jacobs was trained to notice things such as these, and he was aware that he'd gotten the alien's attention. "Fuck it," he muttered more to himself than the alien and reached up to slip the ring around his neck.

The metal was easy to pull apart—had been when they removed it from the boy—but as he released it, the ring formed comfortably around his neck. As a matter of fact, it was as if it'd instantly become part of him—he no longer even perceived its weight.

He staggered, the room swirling about him as he swayed, but the effect faded almost immediately as the translation device calibrated to his system. Steadying himself, he stared at the alien. "You can understand me now, can't you? This is how it works, isn't it?"

The alien said nothing, only looked at him.

He grabbed the other ring, yanked it open, and situated it roughly about the neck of his captive. "Talk, goddammit!"

Nothing. The alien only stared dumbly at him. He waited for only a few seconds longer before saying coldly, "I *killed* Liberty..."

Still nothing. The alien only gazed at him, its liquid eyes fathomlessly blank. From everything the general could glean from its expression, it either couldn't understand or didn't care. And in that one moment...he *hated* it.

He snatched the ring too roughly from her neck, pulled his own off, and stuffed them back into the lead case. Stomping from the interrogation room, he didn't even explain himself as he stormed past a confused Bennett, who'd just arrived outfitted in her Hazmat suit.

"Sir, I—" she stammered.

He charged on. Moments later, he was back in the infirmary.

CHAPTER THIRTY-ONE

Δ

"You said I'd be able to talk to it!" The general burst into Liberty's room, pulling the plastic sheeting apart. He halted next to his bed, enormous over the boy.

"No, I didn't say that. I said *I* would be able to understand them. It's *my* collar; it was made for me. They created it to fit my condition, to slow the illness." His reaction was immediate and controlled.

"How do I know what you say is true?" Jacobs was obviously approaching the end of his willingness to be duped.

Liberty slid from the bed. He was only mildly relieved. Isara had evidently refused to speak. It bought them a little more time, however, that was a small luxury. The interrogation methods would escalate, and she would talk, eventually.

"Take me to it. I can make it talk," Liberty encouraged the general. "I promise, and by letting me have the collar again, it will prolong my life. *Pleeeze.* It's the right thing to do."

The general hesitated, scratching his chin with his thumb and forefinger.

"You have nothing to lose, sir, and I have everything to gain. It will look good for the military if you take good care of me, until I…die." Liberty was valiantly playing the public image card now, but it was obvious he'd shown too much of his hand.

Jacobs refused to bite, and the tables turned abruptly. "Look here, Bert, Liberty, or whatever your name is. I don't know if what you're saying is true or not, but I do intend to have a go at this. So if you can get this thing to communicate, it will go well for you. If not..."

He reached out and grabbed Liberty roughly by the wrist. His previously concerned and compassionate demeanor was entirely absent.

"It won't matter a damn what the public thinks because they'll never know you even existed. Kids like you disappear all the time." He dragged Liberty from the bed and out the infirmary door.

The boy could barely keep up as the general pulled him down the hall. He struggled not to trip over his gown. There were whispers and looks of concern as the general half dragged the *white-haired boy that the alien almost killed* through the base.

Jacobs seemed oblivious to the stares. Minutes later, he shoved the boy into the small observation chamber, outside of the interrogation room where the alien still lay bound.

Liberty could see Isara strapped to the stainless steel table just on the other side of a narrow glass window. His heart caught in his throat and he took an involuntary step toward her.

C'mon, be smart and keep it together. Don't screw this up now, he thought to himself.

"May I have the ring, so I don't get sicker?" Liberty asked with as much despair as he could muster.

The general indicated the lead briefcase. "Knock yourself out."

Liberty walked over to the table, flipped the catches, and exposed the two rings. He glanced over at General Jacobs.

"Go on. Put it on—that's what we're here for," the general prodded.

Liberty slipped a ring on, closing his eyes as he adjusted to it. Then he lifted the other ring and walked to the door, looking back over his shoulder as he did. "Will you come in with me? In case, in case I get scared?"

"Yes, and the routine is this; you say only what I tell you to say. Anything it says, you translate exactly as it speaks. Got it?"

"Mmm-hmm," Liberty agreed, and through the door they went.

Isara didn't stir until she felt the gentle hand on her shoulder. Her eyes flew open—the connection was immediate.

Shh, Isara, it's all right. I'm going to get you out of here.

Liberty tried to carefully think this only to himself, hoping no one heard it besides Isara. There was no way to be certain he could control it, that she was the only one to understand his thoughts.

"Ask it why they're here," the general commanded.

Liberty slipped the other ring around Isara's neck, and it broke his heart when he saw how the leather restraint cut into her throat.

"It can't talk if that strap is so tight." He immediately reached for the buckle beneath the table.

"No you don't," The general grabbed his hand. "Sorry, kid. Can't risk it."

Liberty's eyes didn't leave Isara's. He was so incredibly sorry.

"I'm okay. It's all right," she said, hoarsely.

"What did it say?" The general's eyes flew wide at hearing the singsong voice of the alien for the first time.

"It said its throat hurts."

The general hesitated but finally reached over, loosening the strap a small bit. Isara twisted her head left and right, obviously stiffened from being immobilized on the table for such a long time. Liberty saw the gash on the side of her head and the pooling blood—a dark, green goo, on the table.

"She's hurt," he said without thinking.

"You can't appear as my friend. If you do, they'll imprison you as well," Isara warned without calling Liberty by his name.

"Translate," the general commanded.

"She said 'thank you' for releasing her throat. It makes her head hurt less."

"Why are you here?" the general asked Isara directly.

"Did they make it to the ship?" Isara ignored the general's question, speaking to Liberty instead.

"She says the ship was harvesting water, just stopping by our planet," Liberty explained but, at the same time, nodded slightly to let Isara know Alex and David made it to the *Star*.

"How many more are there?" the general demanded. "How many more ships and how many aliens on this one?"

Liberty repeated the question, his eyes begging Isara to play along.

"What do we do now? We have to get the *Star* out of here, and if they must leave me behind, it has to be!" she said, again ignoring the general's question.

There are two hundred twenty of them, and they carry a virus that can wipe out the entire human race within a month. She says, however, that that was not their intention; they did not mean for all this to happen. Their mission was peaceful.

Liberty no longer spoke out loud. Instead the voice that everyone heard was telepathic, and very strong. It spoke to everyone—the general, the colonel, Bennett, and the guard within the room. And the information wasn't only presented to them, it commanded them to listen; it was that convincing.

Liberty staggered, grabbing the side of the table.

"No! You can't do this again. You're too weak!" Isara begged him. "Bert! Stop it!"

The general's head snapped as he realized the alien knew Liberty by name.

You have one chance for survival—return the alien to the vessel and release it. Send the human, Bert, with it.

The voice was now even louder, as though spoken over a loudspeaker, and Liberty faltered, his knees giving way. As he crumpled to the floor, he projectile vomited chocolate pudding mixed with bile. It had the horridly convincing appearance of a slow, bloody death, although this wasn't the case at all.

The general jumped back, eyes wider.

"Don't do this!" Isara pleaded out loud, but the overhead voice came again, more convincing than ever.

You need to put the alien back on the ship. You're time is running out. Release the ship or you will all become infected.

Liberty stopped retching but not before it had been a very dramatic display. Severely weakened, he pushed himself up, staggering with some effort to his feet, and reached to undo the bonds at Isara's wrists.

"I'm dying," Liberty said in a ragged voice. His statement was directed at the general, and he motioned towards the door with his head. "Get out of here before you increase your exposure. *Pleeeze*, no one else needs to die." He was stunned when instead the general pulled his pistol from its holster and pointed it at Isara.

Everyone froze.

"Okay, *Bert*. Here's the plan," the general smashed the nose of the gun into Isara's temple, "It goes, but you stay. And if this bitch makes trouble for me? Then you can kindly explain to it what will happen if I get upset and happen to pull this trigger."

"No!" Isara said to Liberty. "I can't leave you behind!"

Liberty yanked her ankle straps until they slipped free. He wasn't sure if he could do it, but his thoughts were now meant just for Isara.

This was our plan all along, that once we got inside, maybe I could open the gates to get your ship free. You have to go! Sartek and Blalok won't leave without you.

"It wasn't the plan, to lose you," she sobbed.

The argument was heartbreaking but pointless because right as Liberty had the bonds freed, the general grabbed and pulled Isara from the table.   She sagged to her knees, but the much stronger human yanked her back to her feet and pressed the nose of the pistol harder against her head.

Now Liberty commanded aloud, "You must go with the general. If you don't, he will destroy you with the weapon he holds." Then he directed his attention back to Jacobs. You should have no trouble taking the alien back to the ship now."

"That'll do." General Jacobs said between gritted teeth as he dragged Isara easily toward the door. Bennett stood with her mouth open, obviously shocked by the awful turn of events, as Jacobs snapped, "Confine him now!"

"Wait! Where are you going?" she asked.

"Putting this thing…" he shoved Isara hard out the door, "back where it belongs."

CHAPTER THIRTY-TWO

Δ

Sartek studied the virtual map of the base. Alex and David crowded around the table as he pointed. "I think I found it. Their stockade is here."

"Hey…guys." Blalok said. When he was nearly universally ignored, "Hey, *stupid* heads!" The others looked up all at once. "If I can have your attention for just a minute." Blalok motioned toward the bridge deck.

There, larger than life and splashed across the front screen, was Isara. A man, roughly sixty years old, held her arm tightly and was half walking, half dragging her into the huge chamber, a gun pressed to her head. She appeared weak and stumbled as though she'd been hurt.

"Assess situation," Blalok called to no one in particular.

"Unable to engage her without receiving the human as well," E-I responded instantly. "Dis-advise shift."

"What does that mean?" David looked anxiously up, speaking to E-I. "What are you *saying*?"

"It means if we shift Isara, that man will come with her. The weapon will too. I assume that is a weapon?"

Blalok's left brow rose.

"Yeah, it is," Alex said grimly.

Sartek walked over to the console and studied the readout.

"It's a gun, and it will kill her if he deploys it. But if he shifts aboard, he is not only on our ship, he's on our ship…armed." His said it miserably, his voice catching.

"Are you certain? Will he try to engage us?" Blalok asked.

"Yep," Alex replied urgently. "After what I did, it's pretty much a given; he will."

"I'm not leaving her down there," Sartek said flatly.

Before he could say or do anything, David jumped in. "Nope, you're not. Cuz I'm going down there. I'm gonna get Isara, and I'm gonna find Bert." David glanced at Blalok. "Time for plan B." He picked up the rifle Sartek brought on board. Everyone else was speechless.

It was Blalok who had something to say to his new friend. "You won't need that, David."

David paused. "What do you mean?"

The smallest alien crossed his arms in a "dun deal" fashion. "You only need to be near Isara."

"What are you talking about?" It was Alex's turn to be puzzled.

Blalok rose from his chair and stepped up onto the main level of the bridge, gazing earnestly at Alex. "I gather you have experienced certain phenomena in the presence of Isara and Sartek?"

Alex's face brightened, "Yeah, things move and electric stuff quits. But not like I have much control over it. It happens mostly when I'm scared or mad."

"And Bert?"

"Situation escalating," E-I interrupted, zooming in even more on the front screen where the man forced Isara roughly to her knees. He seemed angry, was saying something and holding the gun to the back of her head, stabbing at it as he spoke.

They could see Isara's head jerk forward with each word every time the gun struck her.

Blalok ignored the screen. "*Alex!* Focus. Bert developed something too, didn't he?" When she remained fixated on the screen, he took her by the arms and shook her. "Didn't he?"

"I don't see what this has to do with Isara!" Sartek interrupted.

"I think I know what he's getting at," David said, giving his entire attention to Blalok. "You're talking about what happened in the sleep room, aren't you?"

"Yes. You simply need to step close to Isara, then…*push* him."

"Push him? I think that's risky." Alex shook her head. "One of them could get shot."

"Unlikely," E-I explained. "David will be interpreted as an exchange for Isara. Seeing a human boy, the adult male will be taken off guard and likely drop his weapon, even if only momentarily. It would be the window of opportunity. Blalok is right. It is the most logical strategy."

"We only need him to let go of her, break even the smallest contact, and we can get her, and you, back," Blalok added. "And that is not likely to happen if you are carrying a rifle."

"I'm going." David moved toward the shift module. "I can do this. I'll get Isara back aboard, then go find Bert."

"David," Blalok stepped near to him. "Remember what I said. You moved that chair. I am convinced of that." Then, very unexpectedly, he slapped David quite hard across the face.

"What was that for?" David rubbed his cheek, seemingly more dismayed than angry.

"Remember? You were agitated, in the sleep room. I am assisting you." Blalok lifted his hand again as though he would like to assist again.

David held out both hands in defense. "Whoa, hold up there. I'll be plenty agitated."

Blalok lowered his hand. "Good. Then let us get on with this before Isara is hurt…" then under his breath, "or killed."

David turned to say something to Alex but was met squarely with Sartek's fist. This time, it wasn't an annoying tag as when Blalok smacked him. This time he was sent sprawling backward across the bridge floor, sliding on his back from the impact. He struggled for a second to regain his feet, then lunged at Sartek.

"Wait! David, wait!" Alex threw herself in front of him.

"Just making sure about that *agitation*." Sartek grinned, brushing his hands together as though he would brush the human from him. "Besides, you needed some special effects." He pointed at David's nose, now freely dripping blood. "That's a freaky color, by the way."

When David smeared the back of his hand across his nose, it only made it worse, in a very convincing way. He paused, wiping the blood from his hand across the front of his T-shirt for added effect. "You've got a pretty good arm there, slick." He sniffed and glowered.

The amusement left Sartek's face. He said, very seriously, "Get her, David. Get Isara."

* * *

Seconds later, David shifted to the cavern floor. He materialized nearly thirty yards in front of the general. Staggering forward as though dazed or hurt, he even allowed himself to limp a little. It was perfect. He looked like he'd been shot through an alien ringer and was on his last legs.

"Hello? Son, are you okay?" General Jacobs squinted as the obviously human boy, liberally smeared with blood, approached him.

"Help…" David gasped as he stepped closer to the general, one arm extended, the other dangling limp at his side. He dragged one leg even more, trying to mimic what he'd seen in every bad zombie movie.

"David? Is that you?" Jacobs asked. At just about ten yards, the general dropped the pistol from Isara's head and took a small step toward the boy.

It was at that precise second that David grit his teeth and lifted both hands, shoving the air in front of him, in the exact direction of the general's chest.

Backward, the general slammed, his pistol flying from his hand. He crashed with a hard thud and a gasp, and remained on the ground, unmoving. It surprised even David how hard the man flew.

The two guards stationed just inside the doors raised their rifles, but before they could even get a shot off, the silvery, oily shimmer engulfed Isara and David. The guards fired, but it was too late. The bullets ricocheted harmlessly off the concrete floor.

As Isara materialized onboard the *Cerulean Star*, she buckled. Sartek grabbed her and hugged her close. She sobbed, struggling to regain some composure. "Bert…" She gestured weakly toward the screen.

David, who was starting to get the hand of shifting, targeted Blalok. "You were supposed to leave me! I have to find Bert!"

"Negative," Blalok answered almost too calmly, "You cannot wield that power if a Bettuan is not present. We haven't adequately tested the range of it, and Isara is in no condition to return with you. As brilliant as you were, you are no match for them by yourself."

"You're not listening!" David insisted. "Leaving Bert isn't an option! We're a *team*, okay? If one loses, we all lose!"

"I'll go." Sartek extended his hand to David just as he'd seen Blalok do earlier with Alex. "I'll go with you. We'll free the *Star* and find Bert, together."

David was breathless from the encounter with the general, more from adrenalin than fear, but stepped back toward the shifter platform.

"Damn straight, we will."

"Wait!" Alex called. "We have to have a plan. Bert wouldn't like it if we didn't. Remember? He says only stupid people don't have plans."

Blalok pulled up a holographic image of the internal layout of the underground base. "I must agree." Spinning the image ninety degrees, he pointed. "Bert is here, in the infirmary."

"He's right." Isara massaged her wrists where the restraints had rubbed them raw. "I can feel it. Bert's alive."

"Me, too," Alex chimed in. "Ever since we linked, I have a feeling where we all are. It's like, weird!"

"Okay." David was even more determined and studied the image carefully to make certain of Liberty's whereabouts. "Then the plan is I'm going back to get Bert."

"David, you can't! That's not a good plan!" she pleaded. "Chances are they'll just shoot you. And then Bert just goes back to *The Home* anyway."

"Not if I can help it." He reached for the rifle. "Bert's a domestic terrorist now. They'll never let him go. And as soon as they figure out he's an orphan, they'll have no need to spare him. I'm not gonna leave him to rot in some underground prison."

Sartek laid his hand on David's arm and gently removed the rifle. "You won't need that."

David stared at him.

Sartek added gravely, "I'm going with you."

"That is a better plan," E-I advised, very humanlike.

"You don't have to do that," David said.

"Yeah...I do. Bert's my friend, too," Sartek explained. "I feel like maybe I've known Bert my whole life. But only just now have I gotten to meet him."

David smiled. "Yeah. He does that to you, huh?"

Seconds later, two boys shifted to the back of the cavern, away from the huge entry doors.

CHAPTER THIRTY-THREE

Δ

In the few short minutes that Isara was back on the *Star*, the general ordered the vessel buried, just as the president had ordered.

"You can't do that!" Bennett yelled outright. "Those are intelligent life-forms!"

"And they just tried to kill me." Jacobs grimaced as a guard helped him to the infirmary. His right arm was worthless, badly dislocated at the shoulder. He held it against his abdomen, cradled with the left. From his hairline, blood dripped down his face.

"You can't take what they did personal. They were just trying to rescue the female," Bennett argued.

"It doesn't matter!" He spun on her, grimacing from the motion.

"Look, I know you're hurt, and maybe it's hard to have a perspective here, but it was pretty obvious—"

"Shut up!"

She persisted as the scrub-tech ushered her from the room. "You'll destroy the greatest discovery mankind has ever known if you do this!"

The doors whooshed shut as the general eased onto the O.R. table. The flight surgeon scrubbed in the corner as anesthesia started the I.V. Moments later, Jacobs drifted off to sleep, and his shoulder was popped into place. It was all said and done—his arm immobilized and his scalp laceration repaired—in less than ten minutes. It would take Jacobs a while longer to shake the effects of the anesthesia.

This was Bennett's one chance, and she gratefully accepted it. She went to find Liberty.

* * *

"I know you're aware of what they are—what they're doing here," Bennett said flatly.

Lying on the bed, still weak from the continual insults his fragile frame had endured, Liberty gazed at the scientist with pale blue eyes.

"The general thinks they're using mind control, and that they want to—"

"Please turn on the lights."

"I...uh. Liberty, you're ill. The contamination."

"I lied," he said. Her open mouth snapped shut, and Liberty shrugged. "I'm sorry. I had to say that. He wouldn't have let Isara go if I hadn't. I'm not proud of it, but I had no choice."

"Isara? You know her name?" Bennett asked.

"They're kids, and they're here because they had to be." Liberty pushed himself up in bed as he pulled the nasal cannula off, tossing it to the side. "They needed water, oxygen. They're lost. It was first contact, but you know the military won't ever let them leave."

This seemed to set Bennett back not a small bit. "Why here?" she asked suspiciously.

"Why not?" Liberty snapped, then dropped his head. "Sorry, it's just that I know how this goes. I'm not stupid. When they saw us, they made the mistake of thinking they could befriend us—a plan B, if you will. And we've let them down in perfect homo-sapien fashion."

"It doesn't have to go poorly. The world's best scientists are here to—"

"And I play chess against one of them! He loses, miserably! You're wrong. The good guys don't win here!" he countered. "Take the empirical evidence and analyze it. Then compound it with our history." Pulling his feet up, he rested his chin on his knees.

Surprise flashed across her face. She sat down next to Liberty. "Liberty..."

He shrugged. "All your good intentions and best efforts won't make any difference. I told you, I *know* how this will go."

"You're wrong. We'll reason with them."

"Excuse me, but I don't have time for this. I might look like a kid, but like I said, I'm not stupid." He glanced up at the wall clock, then at her. "If you really mean to help, then *help* me. If not, then please leave me alone so I can think."

Bennett chewed her lip. "I really can't—I..."

She seemed unsure of herself.

"Your friends, the girl and the alien, I saw them. They were armed. They took hostages—two soldiers."

He smiled. "Good."

"Good? You think that is *good*? That was an act of terrorism!"

He locked her with a dead stare. "How about we consider what this really is. Think with your frontal cortex for one second." He wasn't meaning to be rude, was really very serious with his request. "We, and when I say *we*, I mean humans, took their ship. Okay? We took it, stuck it in a cave, and we will brutally dismember it. And then, when we have dissected the complete essence of what it is, down to its complete nonexistence, we will do the same...to them."

She gaped at him. "And what exactly *are* they, Bert?"

He rethought his initial intuition, that Bennett might help him. "They're kind, peaceful, more peaceful than humans, anyway. And now they're our prisoners, our glorified lab rats."

Bennett glanced nervously behind her. Beyond the plastic was the hazy figure of two guards.

"The general said Alex and Sartek got on board. You said you saw them. Is that true?" He shifted the narrative again.

She nodded.

"Good. Can you get me to the control center?"

She readjusted herself on the bed but finally agreed with him. "You're right. This isn't going to end well." She let her hands fall into her lap and shook her head in the direction of the door. "The general ordered a strike."

"That's why I need you to get me to the control room."

"I can't do that. I'm your friend. Truly I am. But they have guns." She nodded barely at the guards.

Liberty sighed. "Can you get me a computer? Laptop, cell phone, anything with internet access and Wi-Fi."

Bennett slowly slipped her hand beneath her lab coat into the pocket of her suit jacket. Pulling out a smartphone, she palmed it and slid it along the blanket to Liberty. "Password to unlock is Halley 1705," she whispered.

"Year the comet was first discovered." He smiled to himself.

"It's already linked in. Just accept. They'll think you're me." She paused.

"I need codes to the doors, the service entry doors of the main tunnel, the one the ship came in through." He said it like he was ordering a pizza.

"I'll try." She glanced away. "Liberty, you're smart, aren't you?"

He ignored her, tucking the smartphone beneath the corner of his gown.

"I mean, you're *really* smart. Did the aliens contact you because they knew how intelligent you—"

"Ms. Bennett, we haven't much time. I can do this with you sitting here, but it might incriminate you if we're caught. I'd strongly suggest you leave. Oh, and how long before the general comes for me?"

She nearly smiled. "Your friend, the dark haired one? He did a little number on the general."

"Sartek? The Bettuan?"

"Bettuan? Is that what they are?" She buttoned her lab coat and stood up. "No, it was a human child—black hair, taller than you—came down from the ship when Jacobs took Isara into the cavern."

"David…"

"Is that his name? Anyway, he seemed hurt, with blood on his face. But when the general dropped his guard…" she paused, glancing away from him, "the second he did, your friend just lifted his hands and sent the general flying…nearly twenty-feet. Dislocated his shoulder and shook him up pretty good. It's a miracle he wasn't hurt worse."

"Proximity to Isara," Liberty said flatly.

"Huh?"

"Nothing. But what happened?"

"They disappeared. Beamed up, I guess, but it opened up a shit storm, and there's not much time now. He *will* come for you."

"How long?"

She hemmed. "I don't know, but he's ordered the strike and should be out of recovery soon."

"You mean *destroy the ship?*"

"Yes, bury it." Her eyes were filled with apology.

Instead of panicking, Liberty went straight to work. "Can you stall them?" he asked as he activated the phone.

She lifted the heavy plastic drape aside, glancing back over her shoulder. "I'll try."

He pulled himself away from his very urgent task just long enough to say, "Thank you. You're doing the right thing."

"I hope so," she murmured and was gone.

He exhaled deeply. Perhaps Miss Bennett was an ally after all. This was a relief, because truthfully, he was running out of options.

CHAPTER THIRTY-FOUR

Δ

David and Sartek were busy. They'd shifted to the cavern floor, out of sight of the bay doors. From where they crouched, they could see the water saw, the arm of it still pressed obscenely against the *Star*.

The winches that held the ship were immense with enormous cables strung from the *Star* to the walls of the cave. There was no way to disable them directly; they were computer controlled, and the cleats that the cables were fastened to were also incredibly fortified.

"Can't we just pull them out of the wall?" David asked.

"Yes. It'd be a mess, but the ship has nowhere to go. The bay doors are still closed."

Now they were approaching the cutting machine, sneaking stealthily along even though all personnel had been evacuated from the cavern. What they did not know was that the annihilation strike had already been ordered on the ship.

They could not see how a thermobaric device was, at that very moment, being brought into the base, and everyone of last minute, non-urgent status was being evacuated. The *Cerulean Star* was about to become an underground, apocalyptic wasteland in the name of ignorance and humanity, but they were focused on the doors.

"I wonder where everybody went?" Sartek mused aloud.

David didn't answer. He was far too preoccupied.

Sartek turned just in time to see David drop his chin and close his eyes. It was a bizarre picture, the gangly, twelve-year-old adolescent with all the potential in the world. He stood braced, his feet too large for his body, beautiful hands lifting slowly out in front of him, dark hair falling over his eyes as he concentrated with everything he had.

Then, David shoved both hands toward the wicked cutter. For an instant, nothing happened. It was almost as though the effort needed to be primed, but then, sure as could be, the machinery groaned. It slowly teetered from its scaffolding and started to move back and forth on its stabilizing platform. Swaying only a small bit, it all of a sudden wrenched violently, shuddered, and launched as though a bomb exploded from beneath it.

Sartek and David were standing too close. Neither could have expected the force with which the cutter would be dislodged. The shrapnel that flew, as the machinery cut loose, hurled in every direction, and a piece struck Sartek cleanly across his temple. The blow twisted him about, and he fell, landing hard onto his side.

"You okay?" David was at his side immediately, even as the physical effects from using his *gift* washed miserably across him.

Sartek shook his head, obviously stunned by the blow, and pushed himself up onto one elbow. Inky-green blood spurted and ran down across his right eye, then trickled steady, dripping from the ends of his dark strands of hair.

"We need to get you back on board."

"No!" Sartek held his hand up. "No…just give me a moment. I'm all right." He pressed a hand against the wound and struggled to focus on David. "We do this, all the way. Okay?" Reaching up with his other hand, he smeared the blood from his eye, flinging the excess from his fingertips. "No going back."

The blood was so dark, almost black, and David, for an instant, couldn't take his eyes from it. Because the wound pulsated slightly, sending small spurts from Sartek's temple, he knew this meant it was an arterial bleed. The Bettuan wasn't small for his species or age, but blood loss wasn't something he could compensate for indefinitely.

"Sit up. Let's get your head up." He helped Sartek to a more upright position, then pulled his T-shirt off and ripped it up the seam. The shirt, one of the first Hulk Hogan issues, was a favorite foster child hand-me-down and already worn beyond practical purpose. Had it been in better condition, it would have been a vintage score on E-Bay. Now it tore easily, and in seconds David had a good handful of it and was holding pressure on the wound.

His own dried blood mingled with the fresh blood from the alien.

"Press here," he instructed, remembering when the boy on the B-league football team took a cleat to the face. That's what the adults did for him.   A long time ago, it wasn't long afterward that David ran out of money and resources. His father went to prison, and he went to oblivion-land and dropped out of sports altogether.

Sartek didn't reply but pushed firmly against the makeshift dressing, staunching the blood flow as he'd been directed. Holding the rag against his temple, the alien eyed his now half naked compadre and watched him stuff the remainder of the T-shirt into the waist of his pants.

"You're mighty pale, you know."

David glanced down at his own bare midriff.

"Me? I'm Italian! This is a *good* tan. You should see Bert. He looks like he bathes in *Clorox*."

There was no way Sartek could know what *Clorox* was, but the statement brought them both to wide grins. There was no disputing the fact that Liberty was so pale as to be practically clear. It also acutely reminded them of their immediate task. Their friend remained somewhere within the belly of the compound, and they were still stuck in the cavern and none the closer to escaping it.

"This way." David motioned, and they crawled, skirting under the bow of the *Star*. They were soon more able to visualize the enormity of the cavern, including the long runway on which the military had towed the *Star*.

"We have to get the bay doors open," Sartek said as he pulled the rag off his forehead, gently touching the wound, checking to see if the bleeding was lessening.

David shook his head. "Not yet. Here." He pulled the remainder of the T-shirt from his waist, tearing a longer strip to tie around Sartek's forehead. Wadding up a fresh piece of cloth, he stuffed it under the headband. This applied more pressure directly over the wound. David thought Sartek had a Rambo look to him and grinned. "Better. You okay?"

Sartek nodded.

They were squatting down behind an oversized supply crate, eyeing the main entry, both breathing hard. Nothing. There wasn't even a guard, posted inside.

"It's quiet...too quiet." Sartek glowered through slitted eyes.

David's eyebrow shot up and he nearly smiled. "Let's try to get out of her and find Bert first. He'll be able to get the doors open if we can get him to the control center."

Secretly, he just hoped Liberty was all right. What if he'd been subjected to interrogation? David was also convinced that Bert would not fare well with interrogation, and he suddenly imagined Bert hooked up to shock probes.

If they hurt him, I'll ...

This thought didn't capture him for very long for the cavern doors cranked open at precisely that moment. David's jaw dropped. Strapped to the bed of a ballistic missile carrier was a MOAB warhead with a detonation device attached. A semi truck, with armed escort, rolled to just inside the bay.

The two boys crouched down further and peeked out. Soldiers scanned the cavern, the noses of their rifles swinging ominously to and fro, but they seemed unaware of the two kids, hidden so nearby.

The truck stalled and the driver jumped from the vehicle. General Jacobs stepped from the other side, one arm in a sling, an assault rifle in his other hand.

"Hey, that's the guy I shoved," David whispered, still hunkered down behind the supply crates.

The general and driver walked along the long bed of the bomb. Jacobs handed his rifle to the driver and ran his good hand over the exterior of the bomb. He smacked the smooth surface of it, glancing back only once before exiting the room along with the armed escort.

The doors whooshed shut, and from a distance, strapped to the side of the MOAB, a flashing red light caught David's attention. It wasn't hard to figure out that a chronometer was counting down time.

Sartek stood up slowly from behind the supply crate. From his hand a shred of David's dark stained T-shirt slipped to the floor. "That's a bomb"

"Crap, that's not just a bomb, that's a big-ass bomb!" David was incredulous. "This is insane! There's no way they're gonna blow this base up, *right*? They can't!"

Behind the observatory windows of the control center, the few remaining personnel could be seen hustling frantically out. Both boys were in plain view now. There was no reason not to be.

A look of horror was plastered across Sartek's face. "They're going to blow the *Star* up." He took a staggering step toward the weapon.

"Don't; wait a minute!" David reached for his friend's arm. "We need to figure out what to do!"

"With what? That *bomb*? What are we going to do about it, David? *What*? Answer me that!" His voice choked and he staggered.

David couldn't be sure if it was from the head trauma, the horrible turn of events, or both. "Bert, that's what we do. We find him. He'll know how to get us out of this."

Sartek seemed to give this only a microsecond's worth of consideration before agreeing wholeheartedly. "You're right. We have to find him."

* * *

Back aboard the ship, Blalok was very busy.

"Analyze," he demanded of E-I.

It wasn't long before the computer explained that MOAB was short for Massive Ordnance Air Blast Bomb. It was a thirty foot long piece of warhead that was the equivalent of a warhead nuclear bomb, only without the radiation.

"Can they seriously think it would be okay to blow us up?" Alex was obviously horrified by the thought.

"Assuming they perceive us as that much of a threat, I suppose they might," Blalok admitted. "And it makes sense. If they think we're mounting an attack of our own, what better place to be proactive than underground. Instant burial, minimal collateral damage, and if they do it right, almost no public scrutiny."

Alex looked at him as though it was last down of the Super Bowl and he'd just flipped the station to a cooking channel. "Do you hear yourself when you talk?"

"They would have to evacuate the entire mine and base," Isara argued.

"Hypothetically, yes, one would hope so," E-I replied, "However, human history has many examples of acceptable fatality. Even the personnel in the mine might be considered reasonable loss, comparatively."

"Shut up already!" Alex exclaimed, then said in a flat voice, "We need Bert…"

"It would seem Sartek and David agree," Blalok indicated.

They all directed their attention to the forward screen. The two boys could be seen running toward the bomb and the cavern double bay doors beyond it.

Isara squinted. "Sartek's hurt."

* * *

The boys approached the bomb. David ran his hand along the sleek body of the enormous weapon. The cool, glossy surface seemed ridiculously out of context with the weapon's ultimate destiny. It was beautifully detailed, but if it did what it was supposed to do, the elegant orange body with the black pin stripes would be destroyed. "What is wrong with people?"

"What?"

"I was just thinking how it seems that more people are assholes than not. Makes it hard to believe in humanity, I guess."

"Well, if it's any consolation, that hasn't been my experience at all."

David halted, glancing over his shoulder at Sartek. "How do you mean? Look what we've done to you, and a happy ending isn't looking like it's in the cards."

"Not you. You didn't do this." He waved his arms around the cavern. "The military and government of a world that still has much to fear did this."

"You're not making any sense."

"Think about it. That's what Blalok is always trying to get us to realize. Look what the three of you have done. You've jeopardized everything, including your own lives, just to help us try to escape."

"Yeah?"

"Well, if we do escape..." Sartek gestured at the ship, "that's awesome for us; we're free to continue our search for a way home, but where does that leave you?"

David didn't say anything, only rested his forehead on the smooth edge of the flatbed that cradled of the bomb. It was all too much for him to even consider.

"What you've done is...it's more Bettuan than anything I've ever seen," Sartek murmured.

Spinning around, David countered, "It's not so great, Sartek. It's-it's..." He was overwhelmed with how ridiculously kind the alien was, even as humans were about to blow up his ship. "There wasn't anything else we could do. It was the only *right* thing to do."

"You could have walked away."

The alien gazed back at the *Star*, at the horrible devastation that was upon it and the jagged cut across the smooth throat of it. It looked as though it was being ravaged by a terrible illness, and he pulled his gaze away from it.

"You could have walked away."

"No...we couldn't."

Sartek smiled wryly. "I know about cruelty, David. Our planet has thrown its hand into a good share of it, but nowhere, in anything about my own history, have I ever heard of anyone as amazing as the three of you have been to us. And we're not family. We're not even the same *species*."

David was moved by what Sartek was trying to say. "But we're friends. And…and more family than anybody I've ever had, except Bert and Alex."

He tried to shrug away some of the burden of what the alien was obviously carrying, tried to sound more lighthearted.

"Hey, I'd rather do this any day than sit another day at *The Home*. Besides, I got this awesome superpower to play with now. Now what's say we see if we can get these doors open?"

Sartek grinned again, the tail of the bloodied headband partially obscuring one eye. It prompted a slow grin from David.

Yep, very Rambo-esque.

Then the human turned to face the towering doors, side by side with his alien friend.

CHAPTER THIRTY-FIVE

Δ

The base and the mine were close to being evacuated. Personnel streamed from the gaping, underground entry of Hutchinson like ants swarming from an anthill. They'd all heard the alarm, and the countdown was being broadcast.

The awful device, MOAB, was scheduled for detonation below the surface of the base in less than forty-five minutes. The goal was to obliterate ship along with the deadly virus that the species might be carrying. Never mind the technology, never mind the social, political, and even religious ramifications of their find. The vessel would be destroyed. Then the cover-up could begin.

Liberty remained in the isolation room while they prepared him for evacuation. He would be kept in an isolette and transported to the Munson Army Hospital in Fort Leavenworth. There he would be studied and debriefed to the core of his being.

Having nowhere on himself to hide Bennett's cell-phone, he crushed it to bits under the metal toilet seat lid and flushed the fragments away. When they came for him, he crawled, at gunpoint, into the military issue medical isolation unit, or "Bubble Bunker" as they called it, for evacuation.

Liberty wasn't surprised at all that this was how it was going down. Discovery of the spaceship would cause a power struggle, war, death, and catastrophe. Earth was simply not ready. Shaking his head, Liberty briefly considered humanity's conception of an alien species.

Sadly, he knew that if he Google-searched the word "alien" and viewed images—and he'd done this before—that all he would see were grotesque and terrifying depictions, all of them ready to destroy humankind in horrific ways.

He scrunched his eyes tightly and willed these images from his mind, replacing them with the memory of Sartek and Isara laughing at Homer Simpson and enjoying ice cream. *I'm so sorry,* he thought to himself as he crawled into the isolation carrier.

The soldier wearing the Hazmat suit sealed the isolette, and Liberty, in his Superman briefs and oversized hospital gown, was taken from the room on a trolley cart.

"You can't do this!" Bennett argued. "I'm telling you he *lied*! To protect the aliens! There is no contamination; there is no virus! He said that only to get you to return that alien child to its ship!"

"That is not my observation, and your opinion is no longer of value to military intelligence!" the general yelled at her. "Do I make myself clear? Whatever that, that *thing* was that attacked me, it wasn't a human boy! Do you fucking get that?"

"I-I…" she stammered, unable to explain what had happened to Jacobs when the dark David had approached him in the cavern, slamming him ass over teakettle.

General Jacobs gave her no time to respond. Instead, he turned on his heel and continued to organize deployment of the bomb, even personally driving into the cavern with it.

MOAB stood for "mother of all bombs," and it was considered the most powerful, non-nuclear weapon of its time. Also, it had never been deployed either offensively or defensively. As a matter of fact, it had only been tested twice, and Jacobs had been present for both.

Now one of them lay inside the cavern, all twenty-one thousand pounds of it, with a very civil detonation device strapped to it and calibrated to a timer.

It would destroy the starship and anything aboard it. It would also turn Hutchinson underground base and the entire salt mine into dust.

Above ground, there wasn't anything in significant proximity to the air base. Years ago, it had been zoned in a very secluded area south of the city proper. Consequently, evacuation was limited to base personnel. The town had also been alerted that there may be a "drill" and to expect possible seismic activity.

The situation was militarily considered an FPCON Delta alert, which meant that an actual terrorist attack was taking place, and after 9/11 attack on New York City—the *last* such FPCON Delta alert—military personnel took it very seriously. The base was empty within the half-hour.

* * *

Back in the cavern, David sagged to his knees. The massive iron doors now carried several impressive dents on them, but their mechanisms held fast.

"Nothin' left." David sat with his head hanging after throwing up for the third time. He wiped his lips with the back of his hand.

They'd even attempted to smash in the windows at one point, but the impact simply bounced back as though off a rubber wall—the safety glass had been much too thick.

* * *

Back on the bridge of the ship, Alex paced. "Don't you have a weapon or something that can blast through that?"

"Negative," Blalok replied. "We do not carry anything capable of inflicting offensive damage or harm. We would require sub-time momentum to disintegrate the structures, something we cannot obtain from a standstill at this short of distance."

"Well, for Hell's sake! What about that cutter thingy? Can we use that and cut through the door?"

"I believe David has decommissioned it," Blalok replied. "Even if we could get it working again, I think it would be too late—not enough time." Chances were, Blalok felt just as awful about the situation as Alex, but honesty was inbred with him, and he simply had no good news.

It was fairly easy for them to coordinate with the MOAB detonation timer. Straightforward military time, it was scheduled to count down in hours, minutes, and seconds. And in approximately forty minutes, the bomb would detonate.

"That's not good enough!" Alex cried. "I'm going down. Send me down, now!"

"I can't do that. If we're to survive this blast, the best odds are onboard the *Star*. As a matter of fact, I will be bringing David and Sartek back aboard very shortly."

"E-I," Isara asked. "What kind of bomb is that?"

"It is a GBU-43/B Massive Ordnance Air Blast—a large yield, conventional bomb designed to—"

"Can the *Star* survive it at this range?" she interrupted the computer.

For the first time, ever…E-I hesitated. "Ordinarily, at atmospheric conditions, the *Cerulean Star* would survive the exterior impact of the device. However, considering the erosion of our external shields and the confined surroundings of the cave, and given the proximity to the device to the ship, survival of the vessel with acceptable recoverability is zero point zero, zero, zero, one, seven percent. Odds for survival of crew members are…*zero*."

Stunned silence settled over the kids.

Isara cried, "So we're just supposed to all get back on board and hope for that ridiculous statistic to be somehow wrong?"

"Let me go down. Please! Maybe I can do something, short it out or something; you know, help David and Sartek." Alex felt the fingers of desperation claw at her.

Blalok, still reeling from the information E-I had given them, asked E-I, "Advise…please."

The computer then did something it had never done before. It answered Blalok in a very mortal way, calling the smallest alien by name. "Blalok, we have lost our connection to a more suitable outcome, namely Liberty. Bring David and Sartek back aboard, go to your sleep quarters, and inhabit stasis."

The statement was so appallingly compassionate, so devoid of struggle that it fell upon them all in a hideously suffocating way.

"He's right, you know," Blalok conceded. "If we are going to die, this would be a painless way to go, like falling asleep."

"That's not going to happen!" Alex was furious. "First of all, if we're going to die, we're dying together, you got that? You got that E-I!" she screamed to the faceless entity overhead.

"I agree," Isara added immediately. "Blalok, bring them back aboard."

Seconds later, Sartek and David, were back onboard the *Star*, both battered and exhausted. David refused to give up. "Beam me into the control center!"

"I can't," Isara explained. You can't shift through a solid object beyond the *Star* unless it's another vessel with the same capability. It must be air to air only."

"She's right," Blalok explained further. "You aren't de-assembled and then re-assembled, you are simply slid from this dimension to another, and then back. All dimensions have..." Isara shot him a look. He finished lamely, "...barriers."

Out of options, exhausted, and emotionally spent, they realized there was no obvious avenue left to explore. One by one, each succumbed to the horror of the moment and gathered around one another to wait out what would be.

* * *

The minutes ticked down as a temporary control tower was set up to monitor the explosion, including live video feed of the ship and cavern. Technical specialists brought to life the fate of the Star on a dozen screens, one very large front and center. Everyone watched in amazement as David tried to smash through the doors. A tank mortar wouldn't have been able to penetrate the RHA steel doors, but the dents left on them by the humanoid child were impressive. It lent them all to believe that David was, in fact, not human, and there were hushed gasps as they observed the two figures finally disappear, evidently back aboard the vessel.

* * *

On board the ship, with just over four minutes before the bomb would detonate, the children convened closer together, sitting in a circle on foredeck of the bridge. Blalok was the only one who sat with his hands even now on his precious controls. On the view screen, a clock counted down.

"I can't watch any more" Isara turned away, burying her head into Sartek's shoulder.

"Me either," Alex dropped her chin to her chest, a tear running down her cheek.

David reached an arm around her and pulled her tight, brushing the tear away. He had no words, and only pulled her closer.

Then...something extraordinary happened.

CHAPTER THIRTY-SIX

Δ

"*Merry Fucking Christmas!*"

The words flashed enormous across every monitor screen in the remote military bunker, even those displaying the fate of the *Cerulean Star*. Along with the image played a booming rendition of Three Doors Down's *Kryptonite*. Blank faces looked around the room to see if everyone was experiencing the same phenomenon.

"Is this some kind of joke?" Taylor screamed, his voice cracking at the high end of the register. Reaching over the shoulder of a technician, he punched the keyboard, trying to disable the blaring music, but there was a system override in place no one could have cracked, even on a good day.

As the music boomed, boasting of superhuman might, and 'Merry Fucking Christmas' scrolled happily back and forth across the screens in a cheerful, bouncing style, another image slowly appeared in front of the words. It was that of a very unusual boy. He was, perhaps, fifteen years old, slight of build, with short blondish-brown hair chopped unevenly and the sparkling, white eyes of youth. He was crump dancing, and his jeans sagged enough to display *Down With The Man* printed in *Sharpie* across the back waistband of his boxer shorts.

"What the fuck is...*that*?" demanded General Jacobs.

"I'm not sure, sir, but I think we're about to find out," Bennett replied, her eyes dancing with joy despite her somber face.

Way to go, Liberty!
Suddenly, she didn't miss her smartphone at all.

* * *

On board the *Cerulean Star*, the same dancing youth flashed across the magnificent front screen of the bridge. None of the children had ever seen him before, but below the image of the teen flashed the simple words, "Time to bounce, kids."

"Who's that?" Sartek asked what everyone wondered.

Alex jumped up, shoving David aside. "It's Vole! Bert's friend! Has to be!"

"Holy shit!" David exclaimed, scrambling to his feet.

Blalok leapt into action, bringing the *Star* from hibernation into active flight mode. The feeble remnants of her shell glowed fiercely, and the Vasteen frame came to life with a brilliance all its own.

"How do we get out?" Sartek furiously scanned the ship's controls, but just then the bay doors slid open. Vole had taken care of that detail as well, hacking and overriding the military's base's complex computer security system before inserting the codes. The only remaining obstacle, sitting between them and the open doors…was the MOAB bomb.

"We gotta move that truck!" Sartek yelled.

"I got this," Alex jumped up and hopped onto an advancement portal.

"No!" Isara cried.

David stopped her. "She can do this. I've seen her do it before."

"It's our only chance," Alex said swiftly. "Just like train-hopping—piece of cake."

Isara was unconvinced. "Alex—"

"*Don't!* Just…just don't. We'll catch up when I get back." She tried to smile, but her lips trembled, and she swept at tearful eyes. Seconds later, a small, human girl materialized onto the tarmac, right next to the MOAB bomb.

Alex sprinted for the truck cab and clambered up the steep steps into the semi's cab, fumbling around for the keys.

No go. "Asshole," she muttered, convinced the general had pocketed them.

Mashing the clutch, she made sure the gearshift was in neutral before flopping down onto her side on the bench seat. Shoving her hand into her pocket, her fingers grasped, curling at last around her Swiss army knife. "Thanks, Jimmy," she murmured as she flipped out the short blade.

Reaching behind the dash, she fished around before grasping what she was looking for. She pulled the wires down, blindly swept the blade across all four, and she cut her thumb.

Two of the wires slipped from her wet fingers. "Shit! Shit!"

Reaching, she re-gathered them and held on firmly, two in each hand.

"Battery hot…ignition…accessory…starter," she muttered out loud as she stripped a half inch of plastic off the ends of the four wires, one at a time. Then, reaching up, she flipped the radio to on.

"Which one, which one?" she wondered out loud as she quickly twisted two of the wires together.

Johnny Paycheck blared from the cosmos.

"Oh hell, no," Alex said on two counts. First, she never did appreciate the twangy country music that dominated Kansas' radio stations, and second, the wires were wrong. She flipped the radio off before untwisting the two wires. Abandoning one of them, she then twisted two more together.

"Please God, please," she murmured and touched a third wire to the two already twisted ones. Even though she expected it, the tiny spark made her jump, and the engine spat and died.

"Yes!" She sat up. This time she steeled herself and held the third wire firmly against the two twisted ones, even as it sparked. The starter cranked, and the already warm diesel engine roared to life.

Sliding her butt to the edge of the seat, she reached her feet for the pedals. She wasn't familiar with the parking brakes, pushing first on one pedal and then the other, but they failed to release.

"*No!*" she screamed, stomping both of feet onto both pedals at the same time. That was the ticket, and the brake released with a jerk. "Yes!" she screamed triumphantly, for the second time.

Mashing on the clutch, she slid the shifter into first gear, then eased up on the clutch. The big rig lurched and immediately died. "C'mon, Alex. You can do this."

Many years before Alex had been forced to drive a drunken foster dad home from the bar. After spending countless evenings sleeping on the bench seat of the Dodge diesel, the man would eventually stumble from the bar and slap the roof of the truck cab to waken her. Then, she would drive him home.

Now, she touched the single wire to the other two again, and the engine rumbled to life just as before. This time, she put the truck into *second* gear before easing out on the clutch.

The semi crept forward one inch, then another. As soon as the rig engaged the hitch of the cradle trailer, it jerked slightly under the immense weight of the MOAB, but remained running, settling into its load, doing what it was made to do as it eased forward.

The steering wheel was heavy and slick. Alex two-handed it as she turned the rig first to the right and then the left, maneuvering the bomb away from the double-door entry enough that the *Cerulean Star* might make her escape.

With only forty-two seconds until detonation, Alex mashed the brakes of the semi, allowing it to stall and die, its deadly payload barely out of the way of the exit. She leapt from the cab and motioned to the ship, frantically swinging both arms overhead toward the bay doors that the coast was clear.

The Vasteen framework of the ship shone so brilliantly Alex could barely look at it. One by one, the cables melted, crashing to the floor in heaps of coiled steel. The heat was nearly unbearable. Then, a rumble, like a gearing up, grew to a deafening crescendo, threatening to shatter her eardrums. Throwing her hands over her ears, she turned her face aside and closed her eyes, sobbing a single cry…just as she was shifted back aboard the *Star*.

Now, with scarcely under thirty seconds to go, the *Cerulean Star* powered up even more, glowing a stunning mottled pattern of Vasteen orange and helium shield blue. With a roar, it swept from the cavern, but there was no way the ship would make the flight from the underground cave on autopilot. They were two long miles down.

"Override! Override!" Blalok pounded the navigation console.

He would not use the automatic sensors for this flight, for the computer would have interpreted the narrow flight path as too technically dangerous, maintaining a more conservative speed. There just wouldn't be enough time. Everything rested on the shoulders of the smallest alien now.

E-I complied, shifting to manual mode, and Blalok navigated the starship dangerously fast through the tunnels. The path was treacherous as the *Star* sailed from the belly of the base. Vole had opened each door on every level, allowing their escape. Even so, it was spectacularly perilous!

The ship flew with rough precision, gaining speed as it went. On several occasions, the hull came precariously close to the walls of the tunnel. What was left of the shields tore massive chunks of concrete away in sprays of dust, rebar, and gravel.

Up, up, up the enormous underground passage the *Cerulean Star* soared. The children clutched at each other as Blalok worked his magic. There was an awful sound, inadequate shield against raw material as the beautiful little ship struggled, careening against the walls of the tunnel, left, right, trying desperately to reach the surface.

As the seconds counted down—five, four, three, two—five children screamed. Then…

…the bomb exploded.

* * *

"What the fuck just happened!" General Jacobs, insane with fury, pounded both fists on a table.

Behind him, Private Prince, from the commissary, gave a small fist pump and worded a silent, *"Yes!"* Bennett noticed.

Vole was still dancing across the monitor screens. Behind him an impressive flash of fire shot out the entrance of the base. The sensors were restored enough for them all to hear the terrible explosion, then the surface above the underground compound heaved as though a giant had shoveled it up and dropped it again.

Dust and debris shot in a vortex from the mouth of what was left of the base, and the earth was so impressively lifted and resettled that it left a perfect, dusty mushroom cloud in its wake.

Vole stopped dancing, faced them seriously, and crossed his arms. With the first two fingers of his right hand, he reached up and touched his temple, lazily saluting everyone, then turned and walked away, fading into the dust storm.

Replacing "Merry Fucking Christmas," new words appeared. "Keep it chill, assholes."

Then, Vole disappeared, all the screens went blank, and the mainframe of the military's security center crashed.

The mousy voice of a computer specialist squeaked, "It's Vole, sir."

"Who?" The general fixed him with a stare.

"Vole." The specialist flinched. "He's security risk AKE red 78, considered beyond critical. He's been off the radar for twelve months." The specialist struggled to wipe the star-struck grin that threatened.

"I guess…he's back."

CHAPTER THIRTY-SEVEN

Δ

The military air ambulance arrived at the secure army medical base within the hour. As the bubble bunker was eased from the helicopter and secured on a gurney, Liberty wept. Silent tears streamed from the corners of his eyes, dripping to the rubber pillow. He was exhausted, ill, and, most critically, no longer sensed the presence of his friends.

Liberty didn't know what the outcome had been at the underground base. No one knew. The explosion was monstrous, destroying not only the base but the Lyons salt mine as well. Where a military installation had once existed now coursed the underground aquifer, sweeping all remnants of the terrible catastrophe away in an enormous network of subterranean rivers.

Liberty asked, then begged for information but was declined any explanation. And so, naturally, he imagined the worst. Before long, he was the only patient in a maximum-security ward on the fifth floor of the hospital, complete with armed guards at all the doors.

Actually, this wasn't entirely true. There was a terrorist suspect on another wing—an adult male—but this man was quickly evacuated as Liberty was considered the higher priority risk. He was terribly alone.

As the nurse hooked him up to the monitors, she gazed from behind her isolation hood at the frail child that commanded so much fear and attention, and shook her head. "I'm Kailey, Liberty. I'm going to take care of you."

"Bert," he whispered, "my name's Bert," and closed his eyes.

"Okay, Bert. You're going to be all right now. I'm just getting you hooked up to some monitors."

Liberty said nothing, but before he could object, he felt something slide between the fishing-string ring and his middle finger.

"There, that's gotta feel better." The nurse smiled sweetly, pocketed the scissors, and tossed the ring fragments into the trash. And with that one gesture, Liberty was broken.

The tests started the next day. They began with bio-physiology profiles, chem screens, tissue biopsies, MRI's, and scores of x-rays, EKG's, and ultrasounds. All personnel wore maximum protection Hazmat suits.

Most of the time, Liberty simply tolerated the invasions, mutely numb as he resigned himself to his fate. Sometimes, it was too much, and when that happened, they thought he'd lost his mind. Then the sedatives were infused. The Bard infusers would trickle oblivion into his veins, and he would check out for a while.

It was at those moments that he would sink into merciful catatonia. Then he would have the dreams. Sometimes he would be burying his parents, sometimes it would be his friends aboard the *Star*. Once…it was Goo.

Eventually, he'd be roused again, and the pain of not knowing would return, the terrible cycle starting all over again. Still, no one would or could offer an explanation. Eventually, he stopped asking.

He remained hospitalized for three months in maximum security. After countless tests and procedures, humanity's best physicians ultimately determined that Liberty was, in fact, neither infected nor dying.

What they discovered, instead, was that they were harboring a fragile and incredibly bright twelve-year-old child with fairly severe asthma and brittle juvenile diabetes. He was determined to be in the fifth percentile for height and weight and the ninety-nine point nine seven percentile of IQ testing—all *known* IQ testing.

One afternoon, he went for the last time to the interrogation room, the one with the scratched one-way mirror and metal subway chairs bolted to the floor. He sat in the empty room, waiting until Jacobs, somewhat leaner and a bit bent, wearily took a seat across the table from him. Rubbing the significant stubble on his drawn face, the general sighed and flipped a manila folder open.

"Okay, Bert. Let's go through this one last time."

Liberty stared down at his folded hands, just as he'd done countless times before, and mumbled, exactly as he did every other time, "I don't remember...anything."

He would never again confirm the statement he'd made to Miss Bennett, that the aliens were just children come to harvest water. Instead, he maintained that perhaps the aliens made him say things with mind control tactics to get him to appeal to Miss Bennett for assistance, but he just couldn't be sure.

Before long, everything was tidily categorized, nobody asked any more questions, and Liberty was slipping away.

Then, one day, Ms. Bennett visited him.

Liberty was lying on his side, the sun coming through the window in a late afternoon slant against his frail frame as he rested with his eyes closed. The all of him was as white as the sheet he lay under.

She was just about to turn and leave when he murmured, "I'm not sleeping."

He flipped onto his back but didn't sit up, only pulled the hospital blanket farther up his chest, under his nose, and stared at her over his clenched fists.

The effect was immediately endearing, and she smiled and took a seat by his bed, edging the chair near as she could.

"They wouldn't let me see you—said they'd traced contact with someone named Vole from my phone records. I'm being investigated for espionage, but that appears to be all they can muster up against me." Bennett glanced briefly at the ceiling corner camera as though to say, *We are being monitored. Speak carefully.*

"I see." He nodded imperceptibly and said in a stronger voice, "I'm so sorry I stole your phone; that was terribly rude of me. I think the aliens made me do it."

She smiled weakly at Liberty's attempt at exonerating her from blame, and brushed the issue aside with a sweep of her hand and a soft laugh. "Oh, Bert, it's okay. You did what you thought you needed to do."

"And the ship?"

"Gone—destroyed. They buried it, what's left of it anyway, beneath Hutchinson. Oh, you might be interested to know that the people there in Reno County experienced the largest earthquake on record. No casualties though."

"So they are all dead, the aliens, I mean?" Liberty didn't ask about Alex and David; he knew their fates would simply be the same.

"Yes," she murmured. "I'm so sorry."

Someone may as well have slammed him against a stone wall—he was that devastated. He swallowed thickly, tears welling up, and pulled his glasses off, tossing them onto the blanket between his knees. He wiped at his eyes with the corner of the sheet.

Bennett changed the subject.

"I can't stay long—my nephew is coming in from Switzerland."

This gained only the smallest amount of attention from Liberty. He said politely, "That's nice."

"Mmm. Yes…he's a little older than you, 'bout fifteen—Elov is his name."

Liberty stopped crying. eyes frozen on Bennett, begging her to continue.

"He's into physics and computers. Loves model rockets too," she said casually.

"So do I" Liberty said truthfully in the faintest whisper.

"Yeah, I figured so. Elov gets himself into a fair bit of trouble with it sometimes, though. He just launched a big one. Huge success, he thinks, but got into a fair bit of trouble with it."

"He should've had passengers on it. You know, like lab mice or something, to see if he could do it safely. That would've been the best test." This was the most communicative Liberty had been in days.

Bennett pushed up carefully from her chair and stood so that her face was evident only to Liberty. With grave seriousness, she said, "He did."

"And?" Liberty's eyes pleaded.

"No one really knows. He never found the rocket. Lost it, I suppose. But, who's to say they didn't make it?"

He was stunned.

Her eyes softened as she leaned against his bedside, resting a hand on his knee. "Good luck, Bert. I think you can put all this behind you now."

"Thank…" Liberty choked on his words. "Thank you, miss…" He'd never known her first name.

"Debra, and don't mention it." Bennett walked to the door and hesitated, glancing back over her shoulder. "Bert, I want you to know, I've never met anyone like you. You're going to do amazing things in your life. Matter of fact, you already have."

Liberty said nothing as Bennett waved *bye* and left.

This brought the first smile to Liberty's face since he'd been admitted to the hospital. Vole, or *Elov*, had come through after all.

Who's to say they didn't make it

He pulled the blanket all the way over his head and cried tears of joy.

After his visit from Bennett, the psychiatric evaluations continued. The tests were ridiculous, really, because there were no psychiatrists talented enough to properly evaluate someone as brilliant as Liberty.

He played them supremely, not because he considered it a game, but to spare collateral damage to Debra or Vole. Dully answering the questions in just the fashion that might be expected of a twelve-year-old boy, he manipulated them brilliantly, all in an effort to give closure on the bizarre incident and optimize his chance for freedom. Ultimately, he was released under observation.

When he was at long last returned to *The Home* in late October, he was thoroughly exhausted and considerably depressed. It was one thing to believe the *Cerulean Star* might have made it, but entirely another to not really know.

A government issue Cadillac slid sleekly into the gravelly back drive of the foster home. Shortly, two men approached the house with the fragile shell of a boy between them.

Roxy stepped onto the back porch and squinted through the screen. Taking a final drag from her cigarette, she pinched it out between her blackened finger and thumb. The ash drifted to the floor, and she stuffed the butt into her front shirt pocket.

"Well, ain't you a mess?" She scowled at Liberty, then asked the officers, "Any sign of them other two?"

The major motioned for her to move inside. "There are some things we need to go over with you ma'am. If we can just step back into the house?"

In the kitchen, Roxy flopped down at the kitchen table. "Let's get this over with." The major pulled out a very official looking stack of papers from a briefcase, the guards remaining posted at the door. Julian, Sage, and Charlie peeked from behind the living room couch and disappeared when Roxy, beady eyes flashing, shot them a scathing glance.

"Do I need to be here?" Liberty wondered, head hanging, hands limply at his sides.

"No, son. You can go. But don't leave the house." The major had grown sweetly accustomed to the strange little boy, having been assigned to his security detail over the past several months. He'd developed a familiar kindness born of true likability for the frail child with the obnoxiously awesome hair.

Liberty started up the two flights of stairs. The climb seemed somehow longer to him, and he was fairly breathless when he topped the attic landing. The door was about two inches ajar, and he swung his small duffel to open it.

Nothing, absolutely *nothing*, was changed. Even their bunk beds were yet unmade from the last time they'd piled out of them, and one side of the sheet fort was still tucked under the edge of the Alex's mattress. Dust wafted as he dropped his backpack to the floor, and he swallowed thickly, surrounded by the ghosts of those he loved.

Walking to his bed, he was too exhausted to think about his friends and too lonely to consider how life would be without them. He chose to believe they'd escaped Hutchinson and *The Home*, but it was not lie that he lacked the will to go on without them. And now it was terribly bittersweet to be amongst the relics of their past.

For just a second, he wished Debra Bennett had taken him with her.

Liberty sat down on the edge of his bed, his chest suddenly tight, and he wept again. The last time his heart had heart like this was when he'd awakened from the accident, when he'd realized his parents were gone. Today was just as then, and it was almost more than he could bear.

He sagged onto his elbow and eased himself down onto the flat mattress, curling his knees up under his chin as he closed his eyes. Tears ran silently, dripping from his cheek onto the thin pillow with the *Power Girl's* pillowcase.

Just go to sleep. Go to sleep...forever.

He hugged his knees even tighter. Liberty was, for the second time in his life, "disappearing" as Alex had called it.

Then...something stirred at his feet—a wiggle, and then another one.

Liberty's eyes flew open. Too afraid to believe, he simply lay there as, beneath the sheet, something long and tubular wriggled, working its way to the head of the bed. A few seconds later, a very relieved wiener dog stuck its gaunt face out from under the sheet and crawled up against the chest of his human.

"Oh, Goo! *Goo!* Oh God, I'm so glad to see you!" He hugged the little dog so tightly, laughing and sobbing. "Oh, you're so skinny! Didn't they feed you? Of course they didn't! Wicked humans!" Liberty sat up, cradling the thin dog in his arms like a baby.

Goo smiled wide and wriggled from end of nose to tip of tail. Liberty could scarcely hang on to him. "Who's a good dog? Who's a *good* dog? Who is he? Goo! Goo's a good dog, that's who!" Liberty rolled onto the floor, and Goo ran circles around him, tail wagging, face-licking him, jumping onto and off of him. It was a perfect reunion that ended with a small boy clutching his dog as he wept tears of joy.

A short while later, hopping two steps at a time, Liberty burst into the kitchen. The adults looked up from their paperwork, but he went straight to the fridge and pulled the door open. "You coulda' fed my dog while I was gone," he muttered aloud as he searched the refrigerator. Settling on a half-spent package of hotdogs and three slices of American cheese, he grabbed the spoils and ran back upstairs, shutting the door behind him.

Goo danced, one paw up as he watched Liberty make a blanket nest in the middle of the floor, smack center in the late afternoon sunbeam. Arranging the pillows just so, the boy settled into the nest with Goo and watched the autumn clouds through the narrow attic window as they filtered across the sky. For a long while, he just lay like this—Goo curled up against his stomach—and shared raw hotdogs with his little dog. Whispering to him about his fantastic adventure and how much he'd missed him, he apologized for making him stay and told him what a good and patient dog he'd been. He also promised he would never again allow them to be parted again.

Presently, the sun moved west and the sunbeam shifted away from the frail boy and his thin dog. Liberty's eyes grew heavy, and he drifted off to sleep. Then, for the first time in many weeks, he slept uninterrupted, unmonitored, and without dreams.

* * *

The next time he awoke, it was morning, and the sun hung three fingers above the horizon. That's how Alex always described it. Four fingers was an hour if you extended your arm and held your hand sideways. The sun moved four fingers an hour; that's how they'd always known how long they could play until it would be dark.

Yawning, Liberty rolled over onto his back, stretching his legs out straight. He'd scarcely moved since he'd fallen asleep, and neither had Goo.

Slapping his owner with his tail, the dog seemed completely content to lean against the warm side of his human, perhaps thinking he might stay there all day. He rested his chin on his human's hip, clear eyes dancing with happiness.

Liberty reached for his glasses and patted Goo, pulling him closer so he could hug him. He was again overwhelmed with joy that Goo was alive and with him, but then his heart shifted that sad direction as he realized that there would be no David and Alex waiting for him at the bottom of the stairs.

What to do now? It was Saturday morning, at least he thought it was. He wouldn't be going back to school until next Monday the major had explained to him on the long drive back to *The Home*.

There was a lot of time to kill and no one to kill it with. He toyed with the idea of spending the whole day in the attic and rolled over onto his hip. He'd slept dressed and with his socks on—a peculiar habit he'd insisted on when he was held at the military hospital after the *incident*.

Sitting up, he pulled his shoes on, then shuffled over to the dresser, pulling the top drawer open. Standing on tiptoe, he could see inside. There they were, David's T-shirts, stuffed in haphazardly. Liberty smiled to himself. David never folded anything, but mixed altogether as they were, the shirts were aesthetically very colorful and pleasing. It was like cloth soup, and the recipe was David. He could even smell his dear friend, the dusty, musty smell of that particular twelve-year-old boy. Sifting through them, Liberty finally found it—David's favorite.

It was white with green stripes and said *East Valley Hornets* across the chest with the number nineteen on the back and arm sleeves. It'd been David's baseball jersey way back when he'd played kiddie league. He'd been pitcher, and even though he'd long outgrown it, he kept it around for sentimental reasons. Liberty knew how proud David was of it.

Peeling out of his own government issue T-shirt, he pulled David's on; it fit perfectly. Glancing out the little attic dormer window, squinted into the early sun, his hand shielding his eyes. There, parked on the edge of the cornfield, was a dark van—two government agents sitting in the front seats. One of them had a rifle propped lazily across his lap, the nose of it sticking out the open passenger window.

Liberty had considered going back to the lake today, but evidently *that* wasn't going to happen. He turned, and that's when he saw it. Stumbling backward, he caught his elbow hard on the edge of the dresser. "Ow!"

The dresser wobbled, and three plastic horses—cheap ones, not the nice Breyer ones Alex really wanted—tumbled off, onto the floor. It was enough racket that the dark-haired boy wrapped in only a sheet mumbled and pulled the corner of it more over his head.

Liberty rubbed his elbow and slid his glasses up his nose with his finger. "Hey! Hey, you, in David's bed. Who are you?" Still zinging from the blow, his hand tingled as it hung limp at his side. "Hey, wake up!" Liberty had decided, during his long incarceration at the military hospital, that he didn't like strangers.

The figure didn't stir.

It was only after he repeated himself that the boy rolled over, eyes still tightly closed. Liberty squinted. The stranger was maybe fifteen, jet-black hair hanging uneven about his pale face. The teen stirred and blinked twice, oddly, as though he had difficulty focusing.

It was then that Liberty noticed the stick leaning against the corner of the bed frame—the walking cane with the red tip. The boy was blind.

Dropping his hand to the floor, the teen fished around for a few seconds before locating a pair of dark glasses. They were nice—not the lame ones some blind people had to wear. As though he'd done it a million times before, the youth slipped them on one handed with a sleek flip of the wrist. In truth, they made the youth look pretty outrageous in a cool way.

The boy sat up. He was thin and pale and wore only boxer shorts. Untangling himself from his sheet, he stretched then turned his head abruptly sideways as though suddenly aware that Liberty and Goo were standing motionless on the other side of the room.

"Hey! Who's there?" The boy fumbled for his cane and rested it between his knees.

"Hi." Liberty walked across the room and sat on his own bunk. "I live here. I've just been away for a while."

"Vacation?" the boy wondered innocently.

"Uhmm…no. Not really. Just…"

"Oh, I get it. Court stuff? Yeah, I know how that goes. Sucks." The boy seemed entirely comfortable filling in the missing details of Liberty's absence.

"Yeah, something like that."

"I'm Cole. Been here 'bout a month. I came up to bed last night, but you were already asleep. I could hear you and the mutt snoring on the floor, and they told me some kid was coming back, so didn't want to wake you. Who are you?" The boy slid his hand up the cane. Whipping it expertly in front of himself, he used it to help push up from the bed.

"Liberty. My name's Liberty, but my friends…" he paused, "they just call me Bert."

"Huh. Weird name—*Liberty*. I like it though."

Cole swung the cane easily, back and forth in a controlled arc, about two feet wide and gently scraping the floor. On his way to the dresser, he whacked one of the plastic horses in the head.

"Oh, sorry!" Liberty jumped in front of Cole and scooped up the three horses, setting them back on the dresser just as Alex had arranged them.

"Okay, first things first?" Cole said, "*Don't* apologize. I'm blind, but I'm not impaired. I can figure things out, get around fine.

"It just takes me a little longer sometimes."

Liberty instantly liked the boy. "I kinda get that too. Not because I'm blind, but…" He grimaced having just compared his own disabilities to that of the blind kid.

"Yeah, I can tell you're a runt." Cole smiled as his hand slid down the bureau to the second drawer.

This pulled a grin from Liberty, and even Goo wagged approvingly. "I gotta go shoot up," Liberty said. "Be back in a minute. Want anything from the kitchen?"

"Nope. Don't really have a morning appetite. But I'll take coffee if there is some? Roxy's a total bitch, though. If she catches me drinking her coffee, she totally wigs."

This delighted Liberty even more. "Be right back," he promised and slipped from the attic, going first to the bathroom, then down to the kitchen.

Roxy wasn't up yet. No one was up yet.

Pulling his insulin from the fridge, he shot up before making two pieces of toast from stale bread. He slathered them with cheap peanut butter and gave one to Goo. Musing to himself how Goo never had any problem with peanut butter, he poured what was left over from yesterday's coffee into a mug and stuck it in the microwave. When he pulled it out, he wrinkled his nose. *How could anyone drink this stuff?* Hesitating, he finally dumped some milk and a few teaspoons of sugar into it before heading back up the stairs.

"Perfect." The boy smiled and cradled the mug, sitting cross-legged on the floor with a laptop balanced on his knees.

"You have a computer!" Liberty began to tremble. He'd been denied any form of technology since his capture, especially smartphones or computers.

"No, not really. I'd kill for one, but the state won't fund it. But this lets me do school work 'n stuff. It's a refreshable braille display but doesn't have Wi-Fi capabilities."

He shrugged, then brightened. "There is a cool laptop, though—entirely braille capable. Even pops the braille up on the screen or translates it out loud, whatever I want. I could even game on it!" His shoulders sagged. "But state won't fund it either. "Guess I'll just have to get rich and get one myself one day. Here, want to see?" Cole shifted the device and wrote something in braille because he knew…

…Liberty could read braille.

Truthfully, Liberty knew three languages besides braille: Spanish, French, and German. He was also moderately proficient in Arabic and could probably find the bathroom and order a beer if he was in China.

As Cole typed, what Liberty saw was a series of strategically place dots. What he *read*, however, was…

'*I am Vole.*'

The teen looked directly at Liberty now. Dark glasses hid how serious his eyes were as he said lightheartedly, "Cool, huh? At least it lets me write stuff, and read; it'll print stuff for me too—a braille printer—whenever the state gets around to delivering it. Anyway, it'll be pretty awesome cuz I can print off whatever shit I want, and no one but me can read it! Even porn!"

Liberty was stunned, his face frozen in utter surprise.

Cole, or Vole as it were, wrote something else on the display. *I knew you'd be able to read braille. Try to act normal. The whole place is bugged—video and audio. Why do you think they suddenly have smoke detectors in this lame-ass dive?* He nodded ever so slightly to the corner of the room.

Liberty turned his head, pretending to scratch Goo on the neck, and glanced up. There it was, in the corner of the room—a tiny hole that housed the miniature camera, small as a penny.

"You been here a month, you say?"

"Yep, took that long for the state to get my walking papers. I'm from Cali. Grew up in a blind school there, but I have an uncle out this way. I was too much for him, I guess, so they dumped me here." Vole tilted his head to one side. "It's not so bad, really. Bus picks me up and I get to be in public school for the first time, which is kinda cool. Roxy and her asshole boyfriend don't really know what to do with a blind kid though. They just leave me alone, mostly."

Liberty could hardly contain himself and metered his words out carefully. "I'll hang out with you. I love to read. I could read some stuff to you if you want. I have some comics."

Trembling, he thought he might have a full-blown freakout. Here, sitting right in front of him, hair dyed black and posing as a blind kid, sat probably the most notorious, espionage hacker ever known. Liberty struggled not to fawn like a little schoolgirl.

His mind whirled at the strategy of it all. How complicated it must have been for Vole to create an entire, virtual human being on paper, insert him into the social services system, and land him at Roxy's foster home. And he'd done it so fast! Not to mention hanging at *The Home* for a good month, living the ruse and waiting for Liberty to return.

"You know…" Vole nodded. "That'd be awesome. You could read, and I could write it down in braille. Then, whenever I feel like reading, I'd have a copy. Yeah, that'd be really cool!" He brightened even more. "I'm glad we met!" Reaching a hand into dead air, the blind boy waited for Liberty to grasp and shake it.

"Sweet!" Liberty hopped up and ran to the dresser, pulling out the lowest one. Beneath his worn shirts, neatly folded in faded piles, was his modest collection of comic books. He grabbed the stack and hurried back over to Vole, sitting beside him so that he could also see the braille screen.

"Justice League, Legion of Super Heroes, or Avengers?"

Liberty was more than excited to share his treasures with Vole.

"I have Teen Titans and X-Men Legacy too."

"X-Men Legacy, for sure, but only if it's a Jack Kirby edition."

"Oh, yeah!" he fished through his stack. "Number 267! The Avengers crash the party!" Secretly, Liberty picked that one because he thought it ironic, considering.

Vole grinned, "Perfect," and positioned his fingers over the braille keyboard. Liberty started to read, and as he did, the braille words formed on the screen, and so did a plan.

* * *

By midmorning, Liberty was nearly a third of the way through his comic book collection. Vole wrote diligently as he read, details of what was to come.

Outside, the security agents lolled lazily in their van, only half listening to the two boys lost in Geeksville.

* * *

That strategic day, when the MOAB bomb destroyed the military base in Hutchinson, no one saw the ship fly from the entry of the base. No one saw anything once the youth named Vole started dancing on everybody's screens. All they'd been privy to after that was the final explosion, the one that destroyed Hutchinson and the Lyons Salt Mine, burying everything beneath in melted rubble.

The chimney created by the tunnel to the surface had shot from it a mammoth, flaming Roman candle, followed by a dust cloud that rose to over twelve thousand feet.

The crater left at the base's opening was over three hundred feet wide and sixty feet deep. Even though the MOAB had detonated nearly two miles underground, the immense power of the nineteen thousand pounds of H6 had produced nearly forty-three million megajoules of energy. To put that more into perspective, it was the equivalent of eight hundred D-9 bulldozers, all going one hundred miles per hour, as they crash into a brick wall all at once.

Far underground, the intense heat had melted everything—stone, steel, and glass. The Ogallala aquifer had been reduced in significant areas to giant boiling pools that vented up through the Earth's crust in steaming, vaporous geysers. What might be left of the *Star*, if anything, would be unsalvageable, and it would take them years to get even close enough to look.

So…the military was unwilling to risk the possibility that the ship had indeed escaped and might return. For whatever reason, the aliens had first confiscated the child named Liberty. Scientists hypothesized maybe this was due to his extraordinary intelligence, and so it was reasonable to believe the aliens might choose to go after him again. And this time the military would be better prepared. That was why the boy was under surveillance and forbidden to leave the house, in anticipation of an alien return.

Stepping into the sunlight off the enclosed back porch, Liberty sat down on the wooden steps of *The Home*. Goo nosed him under the elbow, and the boy gazed into the damp, wet eyes of his friend.

Leaning against the steps were three hiking sticks, whittled down, worn on the ends, and carved with initials. He lifted the tallest one, saw David's initials—D C M—only the C looked more like a box missing one side. He ran his finger over them. The cuts were strong and deep, and he palmed where he thought David's hand must have rested when he walked with it. It was heavy— strong like David—and gave Liberty a warm feeling to be holding it.

Laying it aside, he picked up Alex's stick next. There they were, her initials. Next to them she had carved a little star on either side. They were crooked and unequal in size.

Stars must be hard to carve accurately.

He smiled bitterly. It was Alex who'd brought them back to the meadow after they'd first seen the beautiful, blue ship. No she had jumped to the stars, she and David. That's what Vole told him, that they had made it out. And now here Vole was at *The Home*, trying to help him find them.

In the distance, at the end of the curling dirt driveway and under the shade of a single, immense tree, a dark van with black windows was parked. A soldier stepped from it and walked toward Liberty, cradling his assault rifle casually in the crook of his arm. "Hey, Bert. Sorry, bud, but I gotta ask you to go back in the house. You know the rules."

Liberty didn't reply, only nodded and climbed the steps to go inside. Goo followed, tossing the equivalent of a doggy surly expression over his shoulder.

Cole reclined on the living room couch with his bare feet hanging over the armrest when Liberty walked in. "No go?"

"Nope."

"Yeah, that's a bummer. Hey, want me to go for ice cream or something? I know where Roxy keeps her cigarette stash."

Liberty's eyes brightened, and Sage leapt up from where she played with a one armed doll. "Can I go? Please, please, Pleeeze?"

Cole grabbed and stabbed nowhere near her with his cane. "You betcha, you little brat." He eased himself from the couch. "Alright, you little mongrel. Wanna' walk with me?"

"Yeah! Yeah!" she squealed and grabbed him by the crook of the arm like he was walking her up the aisle.

"You owe me for this." His face was serious, but the corner of his lip turned up.

What was expected in return remained unexplained, but Sage acted as though she'd won big. Julian and Charlie were both fast asleep on the rug in front of the T.V., so she would be the center of attention, for at least an hour.

"I'll watch them," Liberty said. "Just make sure you bring them one too."

"What flavor you want?" Cole asked.

"Doesn't matter, just get me something lactose free. You know..." He patted his tummy.

"Oh, right. The shits." This prompted a giggle from five-year-old Sage. Cole added. Minutes later, the two small ones, with the blind boy in tow, stepped from the back door steps. The guard approached them straight away.

"Where you headed, son?"

"I'm not your son, and since when's it a crime to take a brat out for rock climbing?"

The soldier held his hands up in an *I surrender* gesture. "Don't get all torqued. Just checking. You know it's protocol."

Cole paused. "What's so damn important about some little kid anyway? Why you gotta be all guarding him and stuff?"

"Classified, kid. Sorry."

Sage tugged at Cole's arm and the teen smiled, lifting his walking cane as though he would belt her a good one with it. She squealed and ran circles around him, poking him at intervals. When she stopped, she grabbed his hand and smiled brilliantly up at the officer. "He's taking me for milkshakes. Want us to bring you one?"

Cole tipped his head toward the officer. "It'll cost you."

At first it seemed as though the guard would say no, but then he fished out a ten-dollar bill, held it out to the boy, and said, "Sure. Bring two—chocolate and strawberry."

Cole just stood there, neglecting to reach for the bill. The soldier seemed to catch himself just as Sage snatched it and pressed it into the blind boy's hand. "Denomination?" the teen asked.

"Oh," the soldier checked himself a second time. "It's a ten."

"Don't expect change." He stuffed it into his jeans pocket.

About an hour later, Cole and Sage came walking back into the yard with half-melted milkshakes that were still amazingly delicious. They handed over the chocolate and strawberry ones, and the soldier said, "Gotta see your pack. You know the rules."

Cole just shrugged and unshouldered his backpack, holding it out, hooked on one finger, to absolutely no one.

The soldier snagged it, unzipped it, and shuffled through it, seeing only a billfold, some comic books, a half-pack of Roxy's cigarettes, and an open bag of Doritos. Unrolling the top of the bag, the man snagged a handful of chips before replacing the bag.

"Hey! I can smell that! Get outa' my chips!"

"Sorry, couldn't resist," The soldier *mmmphed* and took a slurp of his milkshake.

"M-kay, you can go." He waved the boy away, again forgetting that the teen was blind.

When Cole didn't move, Sage grabbed him by the arm.

"C'mon. Let's go find Bert."

* * *

It was very late when Vole's watch beep-beeped softly from beneath his pillow. He just lay there for a good long while, allowing his eyes to adjust to the darkness of the moonless night. As he listened, he could make out steady slow breathing and a dog's snore. Liberty was asleep.

Okay, he thought silently. *Here we go, one last time.*

This wasn't the first time Vole had wakened and wandered the house at night. He'd made it a habit for over a month to go and sit in the basement and smoke a cigarette every night, around two o'clock.

The soldiers had been staking out *The Home* even before Liberty was returned from the hospital, just in case. Every night they could faintly see the glow in the darkness as the 'loser' teen smoked.

One day, when one of them asked him about his late night wanderings, he'd said simply, "I'm a teenager. We rise from the dead at night, didn't you know? Besides, night, day—doesn't really look any different to me."

Tonight, however, he'd run the ruse for some time. Vole knew every possible type and size of cameras—plants, pens, sunglasses, USB sticks, and was certain there were none in the basement. The military probably didn't think it was necessary when they bugged the place. There was no escape from down there—the windows were way too narrow. Still, he must be very careful. Success or failure always came down to the details.

Slipping to the basement one last time, he pulled the old pillow, wrapped in a jacket, into the chair he sometimes sat in. Then he lit a cigarette. Smoking it to life, he finally clipped the cigarette to the bobble bird he'd bought on E-bay—the one that dipped its head as though drinking. From a distance, with the cigarette attached to the bird's beak, the glow of the ember would look like someone was smoking, if they didn't pay too much attention to the repetitiveness. So far they hadn't.

The bird sat perched on a tin platter so nothing could catch fire. Vole set it into motion.

"One last time, Tweety," he murmured and left the clammy basement for the even clammier tornado shelter. Lots of these old farmhouses had them, only this one hadn't been used for a while.

Tapping with his foot in the dark, he felt the trap door of the shelter—rough-hewn planks with a pull handle on them. Reaching down, he grasped the handle and eased the door open, slowly. He knew it would creak if he opened it too fast. It was scary, stepping down into the blackened, earthy pit, but he'd done it often enough that he had the routine down.

He hated the shelter, thought it smelled of spiders, so went immediately to work. "Okay," he whispered and started silently counting, *one one hundred, two one hundred.*

The cigarette lighter flickered to life for a second time, and he lit the candle, pushing it to the end of the only bench. Reaching for the first box of crushed Ping-Pong balls, he chuckled to himself about how long it'd taken to get five hundred crushed Ping-Pong balls sneaked into the house. The guards kept checking his backpack, and so he had to get increasingly inventive. He grinned. *I was beginning to think I'd have to stuff 'em up my ass.*

He got the last batch today—hid them under a thin layer of Doritos knowing they would feel and weigh about the same. It was a close call, though, when the guard kiped. Vole was a master in espionage, but he strongly preferred to do it in cyber-space. This face-to-face close call stuff was just not his thing.

Next to the four boxes of crushed Ping-Pong balls lay a heavy-duty roll of aluminum foil and some duct tape. He went to work, wrapping the crushed chips into a square packet of aluminum, about the same size and thickness of a dictionary and with one hundred fragmented balls within.

Triple wrapping the heavy aluminum around the packet, he duct taped it closed along the seam. Then, he taped two lighters—two just in case one glitched—onto one corner and marked it with black sharpie that read, "Light here."

That was all the time he could spare tonight and…all he needed. He was at seven minutes exactly when he blew out the candle and snuck from the tornado cellar one last time. Taking the cigarette from the bird's beak, he murmured, "Idiots," as he peered out the tiny basement window to the blackness beyond. Then, slipping his glasses on, he took one last, long drag of the cigarette before pinching it out. Under his arm was tucked the last strategic packet.

As Vole snuck out of the basement, he eased open the kindling box that sat at the top of the stairs, squeezed next to the back kitchen door. Then, he slipped the packet in. There were four hidden packets total—two in the kindling box by the back porch door and two tucked behind the winter boots in the mud closet by the front door. Both were fairly safe. Winter was still a long ways off.

At last, Vole stood upright as though just coming from the basement and walked over to the refrigerator, snagged a glass of milk, and went back to bed.

CHAPTER THIRTY-EIGHT

Δ

Today was Sunday. Liberty and Cole would have to go back to school on Monday. Vole was determined this wouldn't happen. In a mere six days since Liberty's return, he'd laid the plan out with him, and they'd completed the details. Finally it was time to put those details to work.

Late that afternoon, the blind boy lay on the couch downstairs, his usual spot, when he glanced Liberty's way and said, "I don't feel so good. I think the milk's gone bad or something. Gonna go upstairs and lie down." He grabbed his cane, gripped his belly and shuffled away, making his way to the stairs.

Behind him, Liberty called, "Can I get you anything?"

"Maybe a glass of water."

Liberty followed shortly with the water and set it on the floor next to Vole's bed. "It's on the floor, by the bedpost."

"Thanks," the teen said as he pushed himself up onto his elbow. "Wanna read some comics or something?" He fumbled around in his blankets for his braille translation pad and sat up, pulling it onto his lap.

"Yeah," Liberty grinned weakly. "That'd be great." His stomach was in knots, and he'd been nearly unable to eat, forcing down a stale Pop-Tart just to keep his blood sugar from going low. Today couldn't go by fast enough, in his opinion, and now, with it barely after three o'clock in the afternoon, he was sick with nervous anticipation.

Rifling through his collection of comics, Liberty went straight for his treasured favorite. If everything went as planned, his precious comics would no longer be his after today. He ran his fingers across the rag-tag cover of *The Amazing Spider Man*, Volume 1, #33. Within, Spidey struggles against intensely insurmountable odds to rescue his Aunt May.

The story always gave Liberty a feeling of victory, and he had picked it to bolster his own courage.

As he read, Vole wrote, delineating the final details of their plan. Conditions were perfect. He confirmed it was a go. The last thing he wrote was, *"We do this today. Got it? There's no going back. You don't belong here. You belong with your friends."*

It was such a stirring thing to say that Liberty stopped reading, choking back tears. He pulled it together and glanced up at Vole but the youth only yawned and quit writing, lying back on his bed. "Go on. I wanna hear what happens."

Liberty pulled it together and read on. Vole listened as the tale wove its way to the incredible ending. He murmured when it was done, "Why haven't I heard that one before?" Without saying anything else, he laid his glasses carefully on the floor, rolled over, and closed his eyes.

Liberty folded the comic and replaced it in the stack one last time— alphabetically by hero—neatly hidden in the bottom drawer. Then he changed into David's baseball jersey and also lay down. He watched the sunbeam drag slowly across the attic floor and up the ceiling wall.

Roxy and Hog left for the bar at their usual time and hollered for the boys to watch the kids. They waited until they heard Hog's motorcycle leave before clambering down to the living room to lounge with Sage, Charlie, and Julian.

Finally, the sun was sunk low enough that it hanged barely over the treetops in the distant western forest, just beyond the dried up cornfield. It was glaring in the late October sky, and the corn stalks cast ominous, fingerling shadows across the long, dirt expanse of the back yard.

The wind stirred up small plumes of dust as Liberty gazed beyond the cornfield at the woods—the same forest the three had played in on that fateful day when they'd come across Alex's 'birthday present'.

Liberty went to the kitchen, pulled out a vial of insulin and shot up one last time, palming the insulin and slipping it and a few syringes into his back jeans pocket, just in case.

Cole, the unofficial babysitter, lounged on the living-room couch. PBR was on T.V., and Little Yellow Jacket, a great but small bull, was about to slam another cowboy into the dirt in first-class style. Julian liked PBR and crowed his delight when the little bull tossed victory snot on the trampled cowboy before trotting, head held high, to the exit gate.

"I love Little Yellow Jacket!" Julian laughed over his shoulder at Cole.

"Yeah, those little bulls, they're just *crazy*," the blind boy smiled lazily.

Julian hopped up and darted for the bathroom. On the way back, he wandered into the kitchen and watched Liberty make a peanut butter and butter sandwich, his eyes widening with delight when Liberty offered him half.

"Julian, you like comics?"

"Yeah!" the smallest of the three little ones grasped his hands together in sweet anticipation, fairly squishing the half peanut butter sandwich. "Love 'em!" Truthfully, Julian had rarely ever seen a comic, and didn't have a single one to his name.

"Okay. Well, guess what?" Liberty knelt down and spoke softly. "You can have mine, *all of them*, but you can only read in the attic, so Roxy doesn't take them. Deal?"

"*Your* room?" Julian knew full well he wasn't allowed in the attic. None of the little ones were. "But we're not allowed in—"

"I know. But today is special. And after today, you can go up there whenever you want. But the only condition is you have to take Sage and Charlie with you, and you have to share the comics with them, even Steven. Okay?"

Julian nodded, grinning the biggest he had in a long time.

The beautiful face of the small boy tugged at Liberty's heart. He'd miss him and the others. His eyes softened. "Good. You go get Sage and Charlie now. The comics are in the bottom drawer, under my T-shirts. But you have to stay up there until dinner. Promise?"

The small one seemed confused by the strange rules, but he had no intention of passing on the comics *and* going into the attic—the *big* kids' room. He promised, pinky-swear, to stay up there until called down for dinner, and it wasn't long before Liberty heard excited voices and the scuff of small feet faintly overhead. He glanced at his Goofy wristwatch—the same one Alex had given him what seemed like so long ago.

Then…it began.

* * *

Liberty forced himself to walk casually as he could to the back kitchen door. "Goo, come," he muttered urgently as he eased from the kindling box the two cigarette lighters.

The little dog seemed disinclined to budge but finally pushed to his feet and teetered across the cool linoleum floor to Liberty's side when the human offered the remains of the sandwich.

"Walk, Goo? Walk?" Goo's face lit up and he came more to life. It'd been a long time since they'd gone for a walk.

In the living room, Vole sat up on the couch, and stretched lazily, giving a sneaky thumbs up as he nodded. Liberty went to work, gently retrieving the two aluminum packets from the kindling box before hiding them beneath his jacket before stepping onto the enclosed back porch.

Laying the packets by the inside back screen door, he stood up, grabbed his backpack from the hook by the door, and pretended to shuffle through it as though making sure it was ready for school in the morning. Just to be sure, he said, loud enough for the agents to hear over the hidden mic, "Do you have any extra number two's?"

"Who cares..." Vole called from the living room as he slipped from the couch.

Glancing once more at his watch, Liberty waited, watching the second hand sweep past Goofy's left hand before peering out the screen door. Two minutes. Nothing to do but wait for the signal. He reached for the packets, and just when he thought his gut would bust and he might pass, someone yelled from around the front of the house.

That was his signal. His hands shook terribly as he fumbled with the cigarette lighter. Finally, he held a small flame up to the two marked corners of the packets. It surprised him how easy they lit, and he pushed the back screen door open just enough to toss them just down the back steps.

Glancing right, he saw the first white plumes from Vole's packets as the thick smoke screen looped around the corner of the house and toward the cornfield. Within seconds, the curtain of white from the packets he'd lit filled the long back yard in a fat, white channel. It surprised Liberty how fast it grew and how much smoke there was.

"C'mon!" Vole yelled, bolting through the house, right past him as he snatched Goo up and leapt off the back porch. "Hold your breath!"

When they disappeared into the cover of smoke, Liberty grabbed his backpack and followed, leaping blind, straight into and through the billowing clouds of white smoke, holding his breath as he ran.

He wasn't even sure if he was going in a straight line but kept running fast as he could until he felt the cornhusks whip at his face. Skidding to a stop, opened his eyes, and exhaled as he spun about just in time to see the house practically hidden in a monstrous plume of white smoke, all of it…except for the attic.

"Goo? Goo, here!" Liberty called, glancing about.

The little dog burst from the smoke screen, followed by Vole. The teen, a flare in his hand, waved them on, and Liberty ran hard as he could for the woods. He looked back just in time to see his friend squatted down, lighting fire to the base of the first row of cornstalks. They went up like a tinderbox, and Vole leapt up, overcoming Liberty easily. He grabbed his hand and dragged him along as they dashed through the field toward the forest, Goo hot on their heels.

The guards were completely thrown off, never imagining the kids would take to the distant field. Instead, they thought briefly that the house must be on fire, and so wasted precious time searching the premises. By the time the Ping-Pong ball smoke bombs were spent and they realized it wasn't really a fire, the real fire raged in the nearby field.

The burning cornfield was swiftly becoming the second perfect cover screen. It sent up a black and gray wall of fire and smoke, drawing everyone's attention in short order. The breeze was heading toward the woods, away from the house—Vole and Liberty had counted on that—and it was dragging the fire quickly across the cornfield, *away* from house, towards…the woods.

Priority was evacuating the house and alerting the fire services. By then, Liberty and Vole were past the field, well into the forest, and heading for the cave.

Liberty ran faster than he ever had. Even so, it wasn't long before he heard the distant helicopters, crisscrossing the forest to find him. Liberty knew it was unlikely they would be picked up on infrared—the forest was still too warm from the day. Even so, they stayed beneath the thickest canopies of trees as they plunged on. Slowly, the daylight faded, and still they ran.

When Liberty was too breathless to run farther, they walked, only until his wheezing subsided. He was dizzy and weak when, well over two hours and two inhaler treatments later, they approached the cave in the near dark.

Standing at the foot of a small, hidden cliff, Vole squinted into the dimming light, trying to make out where Liberty said the cave was. He pulled from his pocked a very sophisticated watch and strapped it to his wrist. It was six fifty-two.

"You sure this will cover us? If not, we gotta press on."

"Uh-huh. It will," Liberty assured him.

Every other time they'd climbed to the cave, David was kind enough to haul Goo up for Liberty. The last time he'd climbed up, Sartek had carried the mutt up, and Goo knew the routine. He danced in place, one front foot to the other, anticipating the ride.

Liberty swallowed heavily. "I don't know, little buddy." He gazed back up the cliff, chewing his lip, weighing the benefits versus the consequences.

Finally, he unshouldered his backpack, unzipped it, and held it open. Goo crawled in, and Liberty wriggled onto his back to shoulder the straps. It was almost a bust, but at last he was able to flip over onto his belly and staggered as he struggled to his feet, Goo's head the only thing sticking out of the zipper. Vole just watched, a bemused expression on his face.

"Now I know what a turtle feels like." Liberty grunted and staggered.

His accomplice only shook his head. "Give it."

"No, really, I think I can—"

"C'mon. Don't be stupid. Give me the dog." Vole reached for the pack.

After trading backpacks, Vole said, "C'mon. We better get up there."

Following Liberty's lead, they started the climb. Goo was quite a bit thinner than he'd been in the past, and Vole climbed easily. Up, up they went. Liberty was methodical about it, reaching hand over hand, making certain he had a good hold with each step. It wouldn't do to come all this way to suffer a fall so close to the end.

"Three points at all times." He reminded himself of safe climbing technique, then hoped his strength would hold out.

After what seemed like an eternity, Liberty scaled the ledge to the cave. Rolling onto level ground, he unshouldered his pack and reached to give Vole a hand up.

Jumping from the other backpack, Goo gave the older boy a look of, *Well, that was the longest climb ever.*

Liberty was covered with sweat and filthy from the loose dirt that fell on him during the climb. Vole was even worse as he'd been climbing on Liberty's heels. He swept his tongue over his teeth and spat grit onto the ground.

"Not bad," he appraised the premises with one sweeping glance and rubbed his hands together. "What's say we camp?"

Only scant kindling surrounded the perimeter of a small fire pit. It didn't matter. Too risky to start one anyway. Vole dragged one of the half broken lawn chairs—the one that looked least likely to collapse—to where he had a clear view of the sky and took a seat.

"You don't think they'll come tonight?" Liberty wondered.

"Nope. I haven't been able to contact them for a few days, so they don't know for sure that we're here. It's safest for them if they check only at daybreak rather than linger."

He stabbed at the sky. "But they were here this morning, I'm guessing. Probably orbiting 'til tomorrow."

Liberty glanced at the sky, fading to black through the dense blanket of tree leaves. "It's gonna get cold. Forty-five or so. There's a few old blankets and a quilt." He indicated the stash toward the back of the cave.

"Seems reasonable." Vole slapped at a bug that circled around his ear. "Well, it's dark anyway. Let's get set up and eat, get some calories burning."

There was no way of knowing what would happen tonight. The forest would likely be lit up with the search, but the cave was secluded enough, for now. Either way, Liberty decided he would never go back to *The Home*, no matter the fallout.

"You think the kids are okay?" That's what he called Sage, Julian, and Charlie—the kids.

"Yep. Matter of fact, they're gonna be better than ever soon as they shut that shit-hole down." Vole didn't look up, only continued to pull stuff from his backpack. "Hey, food meister…c'mere."

Goo licked his lips and toddled over when Vole cracked open a can of Vienna sausages. The boy gave the better half to the dog before handing what was left to Liberty.

"Want some?" Liberty held a sausage up.

"Nope. Can't do it. Looks too much like a piglet penis. But this…" He pulled a half melted candy bar from his back pocket and bit off a big chunk, chewing thoughtfully. "Perfection."

Liberty sighed happily and gestured with a sausage. "You know, I'm so glad I met you. What you've done, it's…" He looked down, embarrassed.

"What do you mean, met me? We've known each other for years! You think I'm gonna let the feds crush my best old bro'?" Vole smiled broadly, bits of chocolate sticking between his teeth. Liberty stifled laughter.

After their modest dinner, they pulled the old quilt and a few armloads of dried grass the kids had hauled up as mattresses to the outer edge of the cave. Spreading the grass on the rock, they covered it with a blanket. Their bed was away from the ledge enough that they wouldn't roll off in their sleep, or be seen from directly overhead, but they strategically positioned it so they could see the stars, blinking one after another to life.

Night crept up from the forest's undergrowth, up the side of the cliff, eventually washing across the two boys and their dog. There was no moon, and as dusk gave way to blackness, the heavens splashed across the sky in magnificent form. Helicopters droned in the distance.

As the temperature fell, the boys pulled the quilt over themselves, Goo tucked in between. It was cold, even with the quilt, but in minutes, Vole breathing steadied into the deep, slow pattern of teenage sleep. Liberty shivered and pulled Goo closer to his chest. His mind refused to unwind, however, and it was several hours before his racing thoughts became disconnected enough for drowsiness to set in.

He'd left *The Home* this evening with insulin but was afraid to shoot up. If he went low and seized, it would be terrible for Vole. Consequently, by midnight, Liberty was mildly dehydrated, and his blood sugar was creeping above two hundred. And, when he did toss himself to sleep, he slept deeply.

The first thing Liberty heard, when 7:00 a.m. rolled around, was Goo, growling as though from very far away. The first sensation he experienced was thirst. That's how it always felt when his sugars were high. And it wasn't just a mouth thirst, it was a deep within his bones thirst, like his cells were shrinking he'd once described it to Alex and David.

Liberty stretched, taking a moment to squint and calculate his own whereabouts before sitting up with a start. He'd forgotten that he was in the cave, and it took a few seconds before he even recalled why he was there. Goo's deep throated growling vibrating softly against his leg, and the not so distant voices of men snapped him more awake.

He shook Vole by the shoulder, holding his hand over the teen's mouth as he struggled to wakefulness.

"Shh," Liberty whispered and pointed down, indicating nearly directly below the cliff edge.

He slipped his hand around Goo's snout when the dog growled again at the bloodhounds, circling below the cliff. They whined and bayed as though they anticipated a capture, and a voice on the ground called out, *"Here!* I think they went up here!"

Goo wriggled his snout free and barked, but not at the hounds. He danced in a circle, yipping at the overhead clouds. This was the first overcast morning in nearly a month, and the boys peered overhead, shielding their eyes from the glare.

Leaping to his feet, Liberty snatched up his dog. Vole hopped up next to him, staring now at the strange effect of vapidation on Liberty's hair.

"Holy shit! Look at your—"

Just as the soldier's hand reached for the edge of the cliff ledge, the two boys and a mixed mutt of questionable origin slipped into an oily shimmer and experienced, for the first time, the sensation of shifting. Half a second later, they disappeared from the face of the Earth just as the soldier scaled the cliff.

"Clear!" he called, "Looks like they were here…but they're gone now."

"They left their stuff, though!" The man kicked the quilt with his boot and picked up an empty backpack.

* * *

Everyone aboard the *Star* surrounded Liberty and Vole as they materialized on the deck of the ship. Vole hardly swayed and swept his black hair away from his eyes, appraising his surroundings appreciatively.

Alex muttered, "Well hel-*low*."

David shot her a surprised look.

Liberty was not nearly so composed. He lurched and almost fell, dropping Goo to the deck. He was dressed in a pair of Everlast ghetto shorts that were a size too big for him, white tube socks, discount bargain-bin tennis shoes, and David's sixth grade pitcher's T-shirt jersey. Grimy and thin, his hair was out of control, and his blood sugar was over three hundred.

Most notably, his eyes brimmed with tears from behind his oversized glasses, and he was grinning like he'd just won the lottery. Truthfully, he had.

He was finally…home.

CHAPTER THIRTY-NINE

Δ

The day the *Cerulean Star* plunged from the bowels of Hutchinson air base, just before the bomb exploded, the ship whooshed spectacularly from the mouth of the base in a silver flash. All five children, and E-I, let go a roaring scream as they launched into the atmosphere. And...*nobody* saw. The ship was simply gone, leaving only a load of speculation in her wake. What the military also did not see was how the vessel swung immediately into orbit and swooped, undetected and veiled, in an elliptical pattern around the Earth.

The planet looked so suddenly serene and peaceful beneath them as they cruised beyond the East coast, out over the Atlantic, and into a beautiful moonlit night. Immediately gone was any indication of the harrowing escape from just seconds before. The forward screens automatically compensated for the decreased light. It was as though it had not even happened.

Mesmerized and speechless, the kids simply stared.

Alex dropped with a sob to the deck, her knees at long last failing her.

Isara rested her hand on her shoulder. "Alex, what you did down there...."

"Our shields, will they hold?" Sartek crowded Blalok at the controls.

"We need to orbit sub-atmospheric for a bit. The shields regenerate with flight exposure to atmospheric helium, but with the damage we've sustained, it needs to be a gradual repair. We are stuck in orbit until then."

"You mean it will heal itself?" David asked.

"Yes. It will *heal itself,* if that's how you wish to interpret it." Blalok gave him a smug grin.

Below them, Hutchinson's underground air base and the salt mine had given a dramatic heave and were no more. The next time they would orbit over it, they'd see only a fading dust cloud.

Over the next month, E-I would go on to contact an amazing boy name Vole, and together they would orchestrate the mission that would help Liberty to escape, once and for all.

* * *

Liberty slid his hand over his abdomen. "Is it going to hurt?" He'd been exposed to enough procedures in his lifetime to realize that pain was sometimes necessary. Unexpected pain, however, was the worst, and he strongly preferred the truth.

"No," Isara said.

"How long will I be under?"

He sat on the side of a procedural bed in a small room that served as the treatment bay of the *Cerulean Star*. It was considered incredibly unlikely, when the ship had first been built, that something akin to surgery would ever be required.

Nevertheless, the designers were meticulous in the fabrication of all aspects of the *Star*, and so the treatment room was the equivalent of a sophisticated, miniature emergency room, complete with operating capability.

"It should only a few minutes. I make you sleep; E-I will robotically install the capsule." Isara indicated the freestanding robot.

"E-I controls it?" It was fairly apparent Alex was unconvinced this was a good idea, and she eyed the robot suspiciously.

"Yes," Blalok explained. "The robot will very precisely make an incision and insert the capsule. Closure will be with bio-laser, then Isara will heal what's left of the wound."

Liberty eyed the robot. It wasn't exactly what most humans would have envisioned. The device was tall, about six feet, bullet shaped, and perfectly smooth but with fine etchings all across the sleek, silvery surface of it. It was beautiful, in a way, and resembled something that should be on display in a modern art museum.

The etch marks were not artwork, however. They were communicating panels that shifted and withdrew into various sections of the robot, allowing articulating devices to extend from it when called upon. When this happened, it was fairly alarming—almost creepy.

There was also an eye, so to speak, about two inches in diameter, very much resembling a camera lens. This would project a three dimensional picture of the procedure, with precise imaging as though it were the real thing. Even more sophisticated was that the image could be visualized from *inside* the body.

"Why can't you just heal him, you know, cure him?" David gently paced the floor.

They were all aware of how Isara pulled Liberty back from a very dark place after the explosion in the salt mine and saw firsthand what she'd done the night he'd seized.

"It doesn't work like that. I can't *cure* illness. I can only stop the symptoms. And it isn't always perfect."

"I don't understand." Alex seemed puzzled. "You healed him when he had the seizure."

"I didn't heal his diabetes. I only took away the reaction—the side effects his illness caused."

"But the cut..." David wondered.

"Just a symptom. I can affect that."

"So, how do you get the graft in him?" Vole slid his fingers along the etched surface of the robot.

E-I had analyzed all Earth's research and databases regarding diabetes and, only then, had fabricated the device. It was incredibly sophisticated, about the size of a nine-volt battery, but smooth and oblong. He was now also intimately familiar with abdominal surgical procedure on humans.

"I will direct the surgical robotics to insert the capsule peritoneal, below the diaphragm, cradled by the medial margin of the liver. It will be attached to hepatic circulation."

There was a confused silence before David said flatly, "I vote no."

Blalok elaborated. "E-I will help the robot to surgically place the capsule in Liberty's abdomen. It is most protected and will function best from there. It's really quite safe."

"What does the capsule do?" Alex large eyes glanced randomly overhead as though E-I were a god not yet to be trusted. She lingered close to Vole as she'd fairly attached herself to him since he'd come aboard, which seemed to annoy David a great deal.

"The capsule is a genetically modified clone of Liberty's tissue sample," E-I replied. "After extracting his DNA, it has been inserted into host tissue. The result is a healthy pancreatic tissue module, capable of producing insulin spontaneously and in response to Liberty's blood sugar level.

"It will act as his pancreas should have, until it atrophies. Then it will simply need to be replaced."

"Uh…you get that we're kids, right?" Alex retorted.

Liberty ignored her. "But doesn't that require a donor egg?" His grasp of cloning and biogenetic engineering was well beyond everyone else present, except perhaps Blalok.

"Schlange moss," Blalok said simply.

"Excuse me?"

"Schlange moss. It is a sentient, biomorphotic plant entity that can incorporate itself into other matter, living and non-living. It's what brings E-I to life. It's in his circuits." Blalok lifted his chin as though everyone knew this.

"So this moss thingy, it's gonna work to make insulin so Bert won't need any more shots?" David was catching on and obviously excited at the possibility. It would mean no more ear sticks, finger sticks, low-blood sugars, or seizures.

"Yes, for now. It is simply a patch, but it will help mediate his diabetes, not unlike your earth's insulin pump, only more sophisticated," E-I confirmed.

"Yes!" David echoed with a fist pump in the air.

"Oh my God." Alex grabbed Liberty by both arms. "Bert, it's like a cure!"

"He will be, essentially, normoglycemic," E-I interjected, "However, as minor as the procedure is, it is not without risk. There is the potential for bleeding, infection, peritoneal rupture, organ laceration—"

"Too much information," Vole cut the computer short.

"Could I reject it?" Liberty interrupted E-I before he could continue. That was his biggest and only real fear of the procedure. He'd read vast amounts of material on pancreatic transplantation, and the risk of rejection remained the most dreaded one. Dealing with failure loomed heavy for him.

"Negative," Blalok explained. "The schlange moss has the unusual ability of infiltrating your genetic material. That is why it lives within the hardwiring of E-I's circuitry. It is literally part of it, growing and reproducing as part of that entirely new composition." Blalok indicated the tiny capsule held inside the robot in a sterile environment. "It already lives. All it needs now is the perfect host."

Grinning, Liberty could hardly contain his nervous excitement, and his eyes unexpectedly teared up.

"You scared?" Alex asked. "Cuz it's gonna be all right, you know."

"No, no…it's just that, I've never not been diabetic. I don't know what it would be like to be free of the symptoms. The possibility…" He swallowed thickly and his voice trailed off.

"Then, I suggest we get started," Blalok pointed to the viewing arena outside of the suite. "We can watch from out there."

They filed out, one at a time. The last to leave, Vole gave Liberty a fist bump. "Peace out."

Once everyone was gone, Isara smiled softly and patted the bed. "Lie down and get comfortable."

The robot simultaneously moved to the opposite side of the table. There was no mechanical whirring or buzzing as it slid along the floor, seeming almost to float into position. However, that was the only gentle feature of it once it came to life. One of its panels smoothly disappeared within the sleek body, and it extended, quite alarmingly, a metallic arm from the opening. Held within its pincer type grasp was a clear blue box.

"Okay, E-I! Be gentle." Alex's muffled voice could be heard from the exterior viewing room.

The tiny box shimmered as though made entirely of jelly, and suspended within it floated the bio-capsule made from schlange moss and Liberty's DNA. It flitted with tiny flashes of light, a characteristic of the moss itself.

A second arm extended from the robot, seven digits flexing as though preparing for a piano recital. Lying back on the bed, Liberty told himself that he really wanted this. He chose to look into Isara's eyes instead of at the frightful robotic arms that twitched as they snaked oddly about like some sort of arachnoid torture device.

"It's going to be all right." Isara smiled gently and rested one hand on his arm. "Just try to relax." She laid her other hand on his forehead.

Instantly, the mind connection was reestablished. Like a slide picture show, thousands of images flashed across his consciousness—images from the last few months. There was laughter, terror, sorrow, kindness—all of them so human, all so Bettuan. He relaxed, and the images faded.

Enveloped in a warm darkness, Liberty drifted away. It was somehow familiar and reminded him of a dusty mine tunnel, far, faraway. Yes, it was very familiar, for the last thing he was aware of was Isara's voice.

"Just sleep, Bert. I'll be with you, with you, with you...."

* * *

Isara's eyes were shut, and her chin sagged to her chest, but her hand remained on Liberty's forehead.

The human child's breathing slowed to eight breaths a minute.

Another silvery arm snaked from the robot, the communicating end of it exhibiting three human-like phalanges that glistened metallically and moved independently. It gently positioned these underneath Liberty's chin, lifting carefully to make certain the boy continued to breathe clearly.

The arm with seven digits twisted, wrapping entirely around the boy's throat, and a screen appeared on the surface of the robot, displaying the child's vital signs.

From the viewing room, everyone's eyes but Blalok's grew wider.

Two more arms extended from the robot. One was also very hand-like and flipped around, the wrist part of it spinning a full 360 degrees before bending to delicately lift Liberty's shirt, exposing the pale skin beneath his ribcage. The intricate fingers of the device clicked with unnerving metallic precision as the robot appeared to have Liberty firmly in a metallic web of snaking arms.

"Jesus," David muttered from outside the operating arena.

"It's like a friggin' metal medusa," Alex whispered. "Hey, good name for a band, huh?"

"Shh." David tried to put his hand over her mouth and she slapped it away.

The second operative arm was the most alarming of all. It was simply an extension with a razor thin tip and whipped about, spraying a wet substance across Liberty's skin. Then, without warning, it began slicing into the pale flesh beneath the boy's right ribs.

In the viewing room, Alex gasped. David squeezed her hand. "It's okay, he's okay. See? Just don't look." He, himself, glanced away for just a few seconds.

Alex held tight to his hand but could not draw her eyes away from Liberty.

The robotic arm cauterized tissue as it sliced so there was virtually no blood loss. Even so, to one not accustomed to robotic surgery, it must have appeared brutal. It was also alarmingly fast, appearing to nearly attack Liberty as it cut into his peritoneal cavity. When the robot retracted the wound, the smooth, reddish-brown surface of his liver glistened from beyond a three-inch hole.

From the eye of the robot now projected an image, the three dimensional depiction of Liberty's abdominal contents—the sleek, pink folds of intestines, the smooth pearlescence of the diaphragm, the ruddy red liver and biliary tree.

Sartek was the next to gasp. "Wait, are those *guts*?"

As the image rotated, it provided a perspective as though looking *out* of the wound, and the robotic arm and capsule appeared enormous as they advanced from a distance.

"Oh-kay, that's just freaky." Alex shifted nervously.

The arm holding the capsule positioned itself directly over the hole and advanced. The biomorphic capsule altered its shape, immediately accepting Liberty's body as its new host. The capsule, along with the blue square that held it, passed briefly out of sight as the silvery arm of the robot extended into Liberty's body another four inches.

"I might throw up," Vole murmured.

On the three-dimensional image, the liver was gently lifted, and the capsule, along with the blue square, simply adhered to the largest distal lobe.

"I'll be C-3-P-O's ass," Alex muttered.

The surgical arm suddenly withdrew, and the other arm—the one that was retracting the wound open—released and grasped the edges of the cut, clamping the wound neatly closed. The scalpel arm tip glowed white-yellow and smoke lifted in delicate plumes as it cauterized the incision.

Finally, and in less than three minutes from when it started, the robot retracted all arms at once, except the one gently lifting Liberty's chin. All that remained of the surgery was a neatly closed, red slice on the human's belly.

Isara laid a hand across the newly sealed wound of his abdomen, her flesh oddly contrasting to his, and hummed softly. Her voice echoed, oddly out of place in the starkness of the operating arena.

"What's happening?" David whispered urgently.

Sartek said, "Isara's repairing the wound."

Even as he spoke, the robot retracted its last arm and returned to the sleek bullet form of its resting state. Spinning about, it floated to the wall, paused, and disappeared.

Isara's eyes opened, and the others clambered from the observation room to their friend's bedside. "You all right?" Sartek lifted Isara's chin gently so that he could peer into her eyes.

"Yes, of course." She smiled.

Liberty's eyes fluttered, and he gazed sleepily at his friends with no immediate recollection of why they were all there.

"Did I seize? I...But..." His brow furrowed when he noticed his exposed belly. Pulling his shirt down, he struggled to sit up.

"Take it easy," Vole cautioned, grabbing his arm to help.

Liberty swung his feet gently "I had surgery, didn't I? It's so I don't have..." he paused, "It's my diabetes, isn't it?"

Alex exclaimed, "It's fixed, Bert! No more shots!"

EPILOGUE

Δ

The surgery was successful. For three consecutive days, Liberty was stable, without needing the shots and with no ill effects. Everything remained miraculously normal since the procedure, and he'd slept better last night than he ever slept before

Everyone surrounded Vole on the bridge. He was leaving, had chosen to return to Earth. Liberty was the most sorry to see him go; he'd grown very fond of the unorthodox youth with the brilliant soul.

"Are you sure? I think you'd love space. You'd have so much to contribute." That's not what he really meant. What he wanted to say was, "I'll miss you."

"Sorry," Vole said kindly, then became more serious. "There's some housecleaning I gotta do. Earth's not ready for me to leave yet. Besides, you'll need me here when you come back." He gazed down into the blue eyes of his best friend.

Liberty's hand trembled as he extended it to shake—the cool handshake Vole had taught him. Vole swept him into a big bear hug, then turned and kissed Alex on the lips.

Alex blushed, uncharacteristically speechless, and David shot her a *what the hell* look. Vole stepped onto the shift module and signed off with a sweeping, "Time to bounce, kids."

In the next instant, he was gone.

E-I would reestablish a connection, one last time, with the brilliant youth. Vole hacked into Kansas State's foster records and reported to Liberty that *The Home* was shut down.

Roxy faced charges of negligence regarding the disappearance of the boys named Liberty and Cole, and Hog had evidently moved on.

* * *

Paige Little sat behind her desk, furiously flipping through an impressive stack of papers, every so often signing one. Behind her, official placards littered the wall, and a beautifully engraved desk nameplate identified her as Senior Adoption Officer.

On the other side of the desk, a young, couple held hands, the woman chewing her lip and smoothing her dress at intervals. Behind them, Sage, Julian, and Charlie perched on an old church pew converted to office bench, hopeful expressions on their faces. Next to Julian's hip, beneath his hand, rested a modest stack of comics.

With a hearty smack, Paige stamped a final paper, glanced up, and smiled brilliantly, displaying nearly thirty years of exceptional oral hygiene. "Congratulations...you're parents!"

"Oh my God!" the young woman squealed as the couple huddled around their newly adopted children. Sage grinned and gave Paige a thumbs up over her mom's shoulder.

* * *

The next afternoon, the *Cerulean Star* swept in a graceful elliptical pattern around the Earth. A remarkable boy sat on the viewing deck in the dark, watching Hawaii disappear from beneath the ship as they arced slowly over the Pacific Ocean.

Liberty wasn't on a hover chair. He'd moved closer to the screen, sitting right on the deck floor with his knees pulled up under his chin, arms wrapped around his skinny legs. The visual before him was so real, as though he could step off into space if he wanted to.

The planet was exquisite, and he thought to himself how much he truly loved Earth; how much he loved humanity and all the potential it carried. Yes, it had its share of sorrow, cruelty, and lack of understanding. But this wasn't what he considered now. Liberty slid his hand over his abdomen.

How incredible to have met the Bettuan.

Goo, stretched out and pressed against his leg, appeared quite unimpressed by the view. His attention was captured elsewhere as he raised the edge of one lip, baring a single fang. He growled at the chakrat that skipped a short distance away in the shadows.

Cleo hissed and hopped sideways, stiff-legged and bristling all over so that the puffy furriness of her was significant, and fairly ridiculous. Her tiny claws click-clacked on the floor as she circled Goo, jaws open and smiling, tiny razor teeth glistening. It was an entertaining show and all of it an effort by her to be more menacing than she really was.

"It's okay, boy." Liberty said. The dog scowled, licked his lips, and regarded his master as though he'd endured just about enough of the chakrat stalking him as of late.

"You'll get used to her." Liberty patted Goo's butt.

The aft doors to the viewing deck slid open, and the chakrat took the opportunity to bolt dramatically from the room. She hissed, claws scrambling and slipping on the smooth floor as she scampered off.

Alex jumped aside and giggled at the retreating chakrat. Squinting to see Liberty in the darkened room, she walked up beside him and sat down, cross-legged, next to him.

"She's so cute! I want one so bad. Think Blalok will notice if I steal her? Maybe E-I can clone her for me," Alex bubbled with excitement. When Liberty remained silent, she leaned against him and murmured, "It's *sooo* pretty—so blue," meaning the Pacific Ocean at night.

He said nothing, and so they just sat for a bit, gazing out over the loveliness that was their home planet.

"Alex…" Liberty began. He wanted, no, *needed* to say something, but was having great difficulty finding the words. He scratched the lazy dog behind one ear, and Goo opened one eye as though to say, *Hey, it's finally gone; I'm trying to sleep here.*

The smile Liberty struggled with faded, and he just stared at the floor as the words thickened in the back of his throat.

"What? What is it?" Alex rocked gently against him with an encouraging nudge. She offered brightly, "I know—I get it. It's a lot different now, but it's gonna be okay. You'll see. We have such good friends now, and we have each other. We'll always have each other"

"You're right," he murmured. "Alex, please...never forget that."

He couldn't meet her gaze but rested one hand on her knee as he slid from his pants pocket an official looking envelope. It was folded over twice. Unfolding the envelope on his leg, he respectfully pressed the creases from it before gently handing it to her.

Alex swallowed and stared blankly at the envelope as Liberty laid it gently on the deck in front of her. Her eyes welled up, and she hesitated, finally picking it up. As she turned it over in her small hands, she noticed the return address from the President, the Secretary of Defense, and the Secretary of the Army—all three of them. She ran her finger over the presidential seal—an eagle doing the splits with an olive branch in one talon, a cluster of arrows in the other. She would, from that time on, hate that image.

"Alexandra Elizabeth Stutton," she murmured. She tried to force a smile, but failed miserably, and a tear ran down her cheek, dropping onto the soiled, white linen. She brushed it off and said, "I must be in big trouble for them to use my real name, huh?"

This was as much courage as Alex could muster, and the little girl who'd moved a semi-truck with a MOAB missile broke, sobbing outright as she allowed the envelope to fall from her hand to the smooth surface of the viewing deck. She wrapped her arms around Liberty, leaned her head onto his shoulder, and wept.

Reaching both arms around her, he hugged her for a good long while as she grieved the loss of her brother, James.

Alex never did open the envelope, never knew it was the Afghanistan war that had claimed him. Instead, she hid it in a secret place that only she knew of. She told Liberty she didn't ever want to open it, that in a way it made James still alive.

"Besides," she reasoned unrealistically, "it's probably a commendation or something like that anyway, and he'd only be annoyed if he thought I knew about it. Jimmy was always like that."

Back at *The Home*, Liberty had heard about how two soldiers in a black car had come while he was away in the army hospital. Roxy'd taken the letter and stuffed it into the utility drawer. Liberty discovered it the day after he'd gotten back, when he was fishing around for some string to fix Goo's collar.

That's when Sage told him about the strange visitors with the official looking letter.

They'd also given Roxy a flag. Hog had thrown it over a cigarette-burned loveseat in their bedroom.

* * *

When the Bettuan announced they wanted their new friends to remain with them on the ship, Alex leapt at the opportunity. And for Liberty, it was simply not a question. They were his family.

David, however, struggled with the decision. He was most connected with the idea of dirt under his feet. But in the end, the draw for the adventure of space, his truehearted loyalty to Liberty and Alex, and his growing friendships with Isara, Sartek, and Blalok, convinced him to stay aboard the *Star*. That, "...and this rockin' new super power I have!" He grinned widely, flexing his biceps at Alex.

After the incident at Hutchinson, Vole disappeared off the radar again. The military tracked his antics to Pittsburgh, but beyond that, he had erased his adventure with Liberty Lennox and the *Cerulean Star* completely.

In the wake of seizing the military compound's computer system and negotiating the dramatic release of the alien ship, Vole planted a new virus in the government's computer network. Appropriately called the Stupidity Virus, the consequence was every time a US Senator or representative sent an e-mail, they were greeted with a flashing screen that warned, "Take that bribe and you're *fired*!" along with a *wheet—wheet* alarm.

And that wasn't the end of it. All Pentagon badges, when scanned through security, were assigned new names. Among them, Lieutenant Colonel Taylor became Captain Shitnozzle. Furthermore, because the new names were linked to fingerprint and retina scans, each time they were re-modified, they reverted back to these new names.

That problem has yet to be fixed, and Captain Shitnozzle is as big an asshole as ever.

Exactly five weeks after Liberty was brought aboard the ship, the six children decided it was time to press on. They might eventually return to the lovely little planet called Earth but agreed with Sartek that a portal back to Bettua must yet be searched for.

They were alive, with all the potential in the universe, because of a boy named Liberty.

Bert taught Blalok chess, and the two play nearly every day.

That fateful day Liberty was pulled aboard the *Cerulean Star*, he had something else hidden in his pocket—the black queen of a long gone chess set. He'd never shown it to anyone…ever. Now it was the only original piece in his new set, the one E-I fashioned for him based on the queen, and Liberty always played black.

Blalok has only beaten him once and jumped up and down with a euphoric fist pump at his victory, a gesture he'd learned from David. The visual to this is beyond description, only, it appeared so much less convincing on Blalok that it sent the others into a fit of laughter.

* * *

Two months later, six misfit space travelers, aboard a very special starship, swept into a gentle orbit around a stunning ice moon to harvest water.

It was then that they saw for the first time…

…the *Rayze.*

THE END

BOOKS by SHARON CRAMER

THE WINTERGRAVE CHRONICLES

The EXECUTION
(Book One)

RISEN
(Book Two)

NIVEUS
(Book Three)

THE CERULEAN STAR

The Cerulean Star: LIBERTY

The Cerulean Star: SARTEK

JUST ANOTHER GIRL

About the Author

LIBERTY is the first of a six-book series, *The Cerulean Star*.

Sharon Cramer's first novel, *THE EXECUTION*, is also the first book of a series—*The Wintergrave Chronicles*—followed by *RISEN* and *NIVEUS*.

Sharon lived throughout the United States before coming to Washington State. Long settled in the Pacific Northwest, she says she will stay, "…because I love how beautiful it is, and the crazy weather patterns lend themselves to creative writing."

You can connect with the author at…

www.SharonCramerBooks.com

Made in the USA
Middletown, DE
29 November 2025

23527529R00208